Flameborn

The Path of Dragons, Book 1

Pedro Urvi

COMMUNITY:
Mail: pedrourvi@hotmail.com
Facebook: https://www.facebook.com/PedroUrviAuthor/
My Website: https://pedrourvi.com
Twitter: https://twitter.com/PedroUrvi

Translation by:
Christy Cox

Edited by:
Mallory Bingham

DEDICATION

To my good friend Guiller.

Thank you for all your support since day one.

Other Series by Pedro Urvi

THE SECRET OF THE GOLDEN GODS

This series takes place three thousand years before the Path of the Ranger Series.
Different protagonists, same world, one destiny.

THE ILENIAN ENIGMA

This series takes place after the Path of the Ranger Series. It has different protagonists. Lasgol joins the adventure in the second book of the series. He is a secondary character in this one, but he plays an important role, and he is alone…

READING ORDER

Chapter 1

Nahia looked up and saw, with horror, the enormous red dragon flying through the summer morning sky. She muffled a scream and watched it come down from its realm among the clouds to glide over her village in the distance. She was certain death was coming to get her.

The dragon roared loudly. The terrifying sound all Kraido races feared, echoed over the land and through the air. The leather bag with medicinal plants she had been collecting fell from her hands. The lord and master of the region was coming for human servants coming of age. Today was the Day of Servitude, a fateful day when she would be chosen to serve the all-powerful dragons.

She picked up the scattered dandelions and hastily put them in the bag. She had to get back home and say goodbye to Aoma, her beloved grandmother. She could not rid herself of this feeling of being sentenced to death, which tortured her as if the edge of a sword were lying on her nape. She had felt it ever since the scales had appeared on her skin five years before. And they were golden no less—the most rare. She was done for. Today, the dragons would see them at the ceremony and it would be her end.

She adjusted her hood to cover the top of her forehead and her temples, which was where the scales were visible. They only covered two fingers of skin from the edge of her blonde hair, but she felt as if they covered her whole face. They were the manifestation of a curse that ran in her blood and contaminated her soul.

She ran through the field of tall grass until she reached the oak forest and started into it. Through the tops of the trees, she saw two more dragons arriving. These were smaller, one blue and the other white. Today there would be dragons in the skies of every region, flying over all the villages and cities. Not to destroy the inhabitants, which they could do easily, but to show everyone that they were the lords and masters of this world, and the people who lived in it their slaves. They roared as if a winter storm were breaking and split up to continue terrorizing their defenseless subjects.

Nahia felt her heart beating wildly, seemingly wanting to jump out of her chest and escape the great winged monsters. Unfortunately, escaping their power was impossible. The dragons reigned over the eight races that populated the great divided world that was Kraido. Whoever tried to escape, disobey, or even simply look a dragon in the eye, died. No discussion, no delay; it was that simple, that cruel.

She picked up the pace and arrived at her grandmother's wooden cabin at the foot of Zurme, the great white mountain, from whose summit she could see the whole region.

"Aoma, they're already here!" she warned, running in.

Her grandmother stopped stirring the big cauldron she had on the fire. A thick smoke climbed up the stone chimney and a terrible aroma filled the room. She turned to Nahia and gazed at her with eyes filled with sadness in a face that had been very beautiful but was now creased by the over sixty springs she bore on her back.

"I know, little one. I heard them roar."

"I don't want to go. I don't want to leave you. I'll die, I know it," Nahia pleaded even though she knew it was useless. She could not help herself. No one could save her from the fate that awaited her.

"I don't want you to leave either, my dear child," her grandmother sighed deeply "This day was bound to come. We both knew it. Unfortunately, it was unavoidable. But don't you think this is the end. Your servitude hasn't been decided yet. You might be lucky. Keep your hopes up, hold on to them," Aoma said in an attempt to cheer up her granddaughter.

"I know I'll be chosen to serve above, in their realm. I'll die there."

"Don't say that. We must hold on and hope it's not that."

"I can still run away." Nahia looked around frantically, panic taking over her mind. She began to inhale and exhale, her breathing fast and short.

"My child, you have to calm down. You know that with your condition it's very dangerous."

"It might be better if my condition kills me. That way it won't give the dragons the satisfaction."

"Don't say that." Her grandmother came over to Nahia and put her hand on her granddaughter's forehead. "You're burning up. You must calm down, or else you'll have one of your fits."

"Then I won't be able to attend the ceremony."

Aoma shook her head.

"That's not the solution. You are of age, and it's the Day of

Servitude. If you're not there, the Drakonids will come for you. You'll be captured and die as an example to the others. It's already happened, many times," Aoma said in a serious tone and with a look of resignation on her face.

"I could hide in the high caves of the Zurme, they wouldn't find me there. They're large and deep, a labyrinth of rock I know and they don't."

"It's true they wouldn't find you for a while, but they would in the end. They'd force you to come out, to turn yourself in …" Aoma lowered her gaze.

Nahia understood. They'd come for her grandmother. If Nahia didn't turn up, they would kill her. She had heard stories of families that hid their children when they turned fifteen. They all ended badly. She left her bag on a chair, resigned.

"They are cowards without a heart."

"The Drakonids carry out the wishes of their dragon lords. They see it as an honor."

Nahia wrinkled her forehead, and her eyes burned with rage.

"They're the only race that serves them willingly and voluntarily. They're despicable."

"Because they were created in the image of their lords and masters."

"The fact that they have a dragon head and scales all over their body doesn't make them dragons. They walk on two legs, have two arms and can't fly, like the rest of races. They are not, nor will they ever be dragons, only their servants down here."

Remember that the Fatum can fly but are forbidden to do so."

"They cripple their wings so they can't fly. That's a terrible and despicable thing to do," Nahia had never seen one, but she had heard the older people tell what was done to them. She had not seen any other ethnicity either, since they were forbidden to leave their respective region.

Aoma nodded.

"Only dragons have a right to fly according to their law. It's forbidden for their servants."

"And death is the punishment," she said, contempt pouring out of her mouth.

"So it is, unfortunately."

"The punishment is always death. Dragons are heartless

10

monsters, the most terrible and horrendous there are." Nahia could not stop waving her arms she was so furious.

"They are also the most powerful, in this and other worlds."

"Are there really other worlds? Or is it only a story, invented to give hope to all the slaves in this one?"

"They exist. I believe so. The same way I believe in the Prophecy of Salvation."

Nahia shook her head.

"No human will ever free us from being slaves to the dragons. They're too powerful. Not even the eight races managed to do so when they joined together for the Great Insurrection, where Mother and Father... when they were... killed..."

"The dragons killed thousands and crushed all resistance, yes, among them your parents." Aoma's eyes dulled and a deep sadness filled them. She was unable to go on speaking, and she lowered her gaze.

Nahia tried to remember her parents. They had died when she was only four years old. A foggy, distant memory of two faces was all she was able to manage. She felt a great longing and sadness overcome her.

"Do I look like my mother? Or more like my father?"

Aoma raised her head to look at her and smiled gently.

"You have the golden hair and the delicate, beautiful face of your mother, Amara. The upturned nose I believe is mine," she said, her smile widening as she felt her own with her finger. "The intense, bright blue eyes are your father's, Jon. Your mother and I are brown eyed."

"And I have my mother's sharp mind and my father's determined character," Nahia finished. She had asked the same question hundreds of times and knew the answer by heart. Even so, it always soothed her to hear it. It filled her with a feeling of belonging that eased her heart, and the longing and sadness faded away.

"That's right," her grandmother said with a nod.

"How I wish it were all different... that we didn't live under the claws of those heartless monsters." Nahia raised her arms and paced the room. She could not stay still.

"Don't lose hope, my dear child. One day we'll stop being slaves. The prophecy will come true. And we are not the only ones with such a prophecy—the other races have it too. Each one is a little

11

different, but they all coincide in what's important. One day, a slave will rise against the all-powerful dragons and will defeat them, freeing the enslaved from their tyranny."

Nahia looked outside through the small dining room window.

"That's because they don't want to lose hope. It's nothing but a fairy tale for children, a dream that will never come true." She shook her head hard.

"Each race has suffered a lot. They're slaves, they lost a lot in the Insurrection and even before in the uprisings each race attempted on their own. The dragons have subjugated us with their tremendous physical power and their magic, but hope lives on in our hearts." Aoma sighed and went to the kitchen table.

"Do you think I could prevent... them from choosing me to go up... do you think they'll let me stay as your apprentice? You know... because of this," Nahia uncovered her head and pointed at the golden scales.

Aoma let out a long sigh.

"Those of dragon blood must serve their masters in their realm," she said, pointing at the ceiling with her finger. "That's the law of dragons."

"But you weren't chosen," Nahia said, opening her arms.

"My power is small and when I turned fifteen it hadn't yet manifested, as is your case. I passed the test on a day like today many, many years ago. They let me serve as healer of the village. In your case, my dear granddaughter, those scales mean your power is great. If they see them, the dragons will want you. Only those who aren't useful for the war are allowed to perform a profession. Those who are useful to serve in their armies are taken away. Especially those with dragon blood. It's always like that."

"Well, then I'm done for..." Nahia threw her head back and shook it. She had been fearing this for a long time. She had nightmares every night about what would happen to her.

"I'm very sorry, little one," Aoma stroked her face where the golden scales covered it.

"Perhaps they won't notice if I hide them with an ointment, wear a hood, and look down all the time..." Nahia said, trying to cheer herself up without much success.

"I wish it were so, but you must be ready in case you're selected. You must be strong. Don't break down, but survive. If you're not chosen to serve because of your blood, you might be chosen to serve in the regular army, like your parents. The dragon blood didn't manifest in them like in you."

"I'm neither strong or tall, and I have my condition…"

"True, that might save you. If they see you as weak and sickly they won't want you. They'll let you serve as my apprentice."

Nahia snorted.

"I have to stop them from seeing my scales and appear weak so they don't send me above or force me to join the army. That's what I have to do. Since I don't know how to fight or have the build of a warrior, I'll die fast if I don't stay here as a healer." Nahia tried to cheer herself and made fists of her hands to gather courage.

A new roar came from the sky and shook the cabin as if an earthquake were in progress. Nahia and Aoma went over to the windows. They saw a brown dragon flying over the area. This one was huge. Watching its power, Nahia once again had the feeling she was going to die before the day's end.

"I have a bad feeling, Grandma…"

"It's only natural. Today is a fateful day. It is for everyone your age. Survive any way you can, that's all that matters."

"I'll try…" Nahia's shoulders sank as if her arms weighed like solid iron.

"You'll survive. There's more in you than you know," Aoma said, holding her granddaughter's arms and squeezing them for courage.

Nahia took in a deep breath and then let it out. Then she hugged her grandmother. While she did, she realized Aoma had prepared a satchel for her with multiple bags of plants and components.

"Oh, Grandma, thank you." Nahia turned toward the table and put her arm around Aoma's waist lovingly, leaning her head on the shoulder of the woman who had raised her like her own daughter.

"It's to help you wherever you go."

"I see you've included the tonics for my condition, as well as the ointment for my scales."

"Of course. As soon as you begin to feel bad, take the tonic, don't wait."

"Yes, Grandma."

"Put on the ointment, hide them. Don't make it easy for those dragons."

"Not easy at all," Nahia replied, nodding. She went to the table and picked up the jar with the ointment she had been using to hide the scales. She went to the old mirror that hung on the wall and began to apply it all over her forehead. She remembered how at first she had thought it was a scratch from walking in the forest gathering mushrooms and plants and had not given it any importance. One morning she got up after having horrible nightmares all night, and when she had looked in that same, old mirror, she had discovered three golden sparks. When she looked closer, she saw them clearly: three golden scales. Dragon blood scales. She had fallen backwards from the start. The scales revealed the dragon blood in her veins. And it also meant she had Drakonian magic inside her. For all who had it, it was a curse. She had always suspected she had Drakonian magic within her, although she had always hidden it, pushing it down to the bottom of her being. Not because she feared or hated magic, but because those who had magic were of interest to the dragons, and that was the last thing she wanted. Unfortunately, now there was no way of hiding it, she could only cover them. She had tried to cut them away with a sharp knife one day in desperation, but her grandmother had stopped her. She would destroy her face, and it would be for nothing. They came out again, over and over.

"How does it look?" she asked her grandmother after applying the ointment all over her scales. It was easy to do so since she felt them as if they were over her skin.

"A little more here," Aoma said and touched under Nahia's right temple with her finger.

Nahia took some more ointment and applied it, spreading it to create a new layer. Her grandmother had managed a color very similar to her skin which would last all day without cracking and falling off. It had taken her a whole season to do, but Aoma had succeeded. Since then, Nahia never left home without putting on the ointment whenever she went to Heria, the village. When she was among people, she wondered whether there were more like her there at the same moment, hiding their scales just like she did. It could easily be the case. Drakonian magic ran strong through the veins of not only humans but all the races in Kraido.

"There you are, now you don't notice anything," Aoma nodded and turned Nahia's head one way and the other to make sure, as she always did.

"Oh Grandma, I'm going to miss these little rituals of ours so much."

"What I'm sure you're not going to miss, is preparing the tonics against the fevers."

"But they smell so bad and taste even worse," Nahia wrinkled her nose and made a face.

They both laughed and hugged.

"Be very careful. Resist. Survive. May Mother Nature protect you," Aoma told her, intoning as if it were a protection spell, and then she put a necklace around her grandchild's neck.

Nahia held the stone of the pendant and studied it. It was a flat white pebble, from the mountain.

"Have you enchanted it with your protection magic?"

"I'm a witch, am I not? It will help you."

"You're a healer and an expert on medicinal plants with a bit of magic, and I'm your apprentice. We're not witches."

"True, but don't tell me it doesn't sound better that way," her grandmother smiled.

"That I won't deny."

"We are witches in a way, by character and by the blood that runs through our veins," Aoma smiled.

Nahia laughed, and the good humor made her feel well for a moment.

All of a sudden, the calling horns rang. They imitated the roar of the dragons.

"Drakonids, they're calling for the ceremony," Aoma stopped smiling.

Nahia heaved a deep sigh.

"The time has come."

"Come, give your old grandmother a big farewell hug."

Nahia put her arms around her beloved grandmother's thin body and hugged her as if it were the last time she would see her.

They remained holding one another for a moment, sharing the love they felt for one another.

"Go, my dear child."

Nahia hastened to put some clothes in her satchel, and then she took everything her grandmother had prepared for her. When she was already at the door, she turned around.

"Thank you for everything, I'm not losing hope. I'll try to survive and come back someday."

"I'll be waiting here," Aoma smiled lovingly, opening her arms to encompass the whole house.

Nahia stepped out of the cabin. She had to face her destiny, the dragons, and not die. At least not today.

Chapter 2

Nahia arrived at the square in the small village of Heria where all those who had turned fifteen were required to report for the Ceremony of Servitude. Like every year, there was great expectation. Almost every inhabitant was present, as well as the farmers, cattle owners, shepherds, miners, and others who lived in the vicinity and belonged to the village. Very few would miss the event. Not because it was a festive one, not in the least; they did so because it was often a relative or neighbor or family friend who was due for the ceremony. They also attended to offer support to the year's chosen, so they would not believe they were abandoned to their fate.

She sighed when she saw the crowd. She thought of her grandmother. Aoma no longer attended, not since the death of her daughter and son-in-law. She would not be here today. They had already discussed it. It would be too painful for her old heart. To witness what was going to happen to her granddaughter, her only living relative, would break her heart in a thousand pieces. Aoma feared she would never recover and might yield to death, which was already lurking around her like a carrion bird. Nahia understood—she would rather her grandmother was not there. What was going to happen was inevitable. It made no sense to make her beloved grandmother suffer for a little emotional support in that tragic moment Nahia could not escape from. She would rather spare Aoma the pain; she had already suffered enough, and she owed her grandmother everything.

The crowd parted when they saw Nahia, and she went by with her head bowed until she reached the center. Once there, she saw that this year the unfortunate numbered a dozen. She knew them all by sight, although she had not treated them much. She was a loner and had accepted this fact a long time ago. It was mostly because of her condition, and also due to her horrendous scales. She had been sickly since childhood, and this had kept her bedridden for long periods every year. No-one knew what ailed her, why she suddenly and without warning became so ill. This had negatively affected her social life in the village. Her good grandmother had managed to develop a tonic that helped her after years of trials and studies. This tonic had allowed Nahia to lead a half-normal life, although it did not stop the seizures, but it allowed her not to remain prostrate in bed and her weak body had appreciated it.

She wrinkled her nose, remembering that the scales had appeared next. That too had kept her from socializing. Due to those two reasons, she had spent most of her life with her grandmother as her only friend and companion. She had focused on learning the art of healing through what the forests and mountains offered. Now she only visited the village when they needed some supplies or to help someone with a cure.

She was still an apprentice and was not allowed to practice healing without Aoma's supervision. Unfortunately, today she had no choice but to come, and it was not for anything good.

She watched those who were to participate in the ceremony with her as she approached. Most of them looked quite scared, with the exception of a couple who seemed confident that nothing was going to happen to them. They were fools if they really believed that. No one was safe when it came to dealing with the bloodthirsty dragons. As she approached the group, she had to admit that she would have liked to have had them as friends, although she understood why it had not been so. Who would want to befriend a weak and sickly girl who lived isolated in a cabin in the mountains and who, it was rumored, had an incurable, infectious illness? Kids her age had tried to befriend her when she was younger, but they had given up because of the long periods she had to spend in bed. They were also afraid of becoming infected with whatever it was that ailed her, which was such a strange illness that not even her own grandmother, who was an expert healer, could cure. She did not blame them. It was natural and understandable. Besides, when the scales appeared, it was she who had withdrawn from everyone to hide them.

Of those who were there, only Isa, the baker's daughter, and Max, the strong son of the cattle owner, had made a real effort to reach out to her. That was something Nahia was thankful for, although their friendship had not blossomed, but at least they had enjoyed something close to friendship, which showed they both had brave hearts. It saddened her to see them there; their fate would be decided shortly, and it might be a terrible one. She realized that with the exception of Isa, all the others were cattle owners, shepherds, or miners. She was not surprised—that was what most people were in the region. Dragons required enormous amounts of meat their servants had to provide for them. It was that or serving as the main dish themselves, which happened when there was a scarcity of meat because of cattle illness. The dragons did not seem to care whether the meat was beef, human, or any other species.

"If you're of age, get in the center with all the others!" a Drakonid suddenly shouted at her. He was wearing heavy armor the color of steel. He must have been the officer in command. He was standing in the north part of the square, and with him were two of his soldiers to escort him.

Standing around the square were a dozen more Drakonid soldiers. They all wore heavy armor and carried spears and shields and stood facing the people. At their backs, in the center of the square, were the dozen unfortunates whose life was at stake. The soldiers ensured the ceremony proceeded without any trouble. The despicable men were from a nearby garrison, and the fort controlled the region for their dragon lords. They made sure their masters' law was followed, and they were almost as ruthless as the dragons. The slightest disobedience, and the soldiers killed the offender on the spot. The twelve human regions were controlled the same way. The dragons did not even deign to come down for such deeds. They were superior beings and humans were not worthy of such an honor, merely slaves who had to serve or die. They delegated control over their slaves to their faithful Drakonid servants.

Nahia bowed her head and did as she was told without a word. She must not call attention to herself. While she went to stand with the others, she watched the Drakonids. Of all the other races, she had only seen them. They were the worst of all since they betrayed the rest to satisfy the dragons, and what was worse, they did so willingly. They really looked like a mixture between a dragon and a human. They each had the head of a dragon, only a lot smaller, closer to the size of a human's, perhaps slightly bigger with the crests they had on them and that came down their nape. Built somewhat stronger than humans, they believed themselves the strongest of all the races, but that was not true. The Tauruk-Kapro were somewhat bigger and stronger than they were. At least that was what Aoma had told her.

She breathed deeply and unobtrusively placed herself among the others, bowing her head as far as she could.

"I thought you were a year younger than us," Maika said. She was the daughter of shepherds who had recognized Nahia despite her attempt at going unnoticed.

"It's because I'm a weakling," Nahia replied without raising her head.

"That might help you today," Max said, smiling to cheer her up.

"Don't know, I wish," Nahia said in a dull tone with a shrug.

"The dragon lords always need meat. They'll let us go on with our trade," Lauri said hopefully. His family raised lambs.

"Miners too," added Ikatz, also hopeful. His whole family worked in mining. There was a large mine near the village. "The dragons need their minerals and precious gems." Dragons loved the stones for some reason that no one knew. After meat, they were what dragons most appreciated.

"I'm sure I'll be chosen for the army," said Max, pointing at his considerable muscles with both hands.

"Most likely, you're the biggest and strongest of all of us," said Samuel, another son of cattle owners.

"Perhaps they won't need any more soldiers this year," Isa tried to cheer him, looking at him with moist eyes.

Nahia felt bad for Max. The dragons always needed soldiers. They were always at war, or so it was rumored. Against who or where, no-one knew. Those who joined the Drakonian Army never came back to tell the tale. They died fighting or lived at the forts until they died fighting. It was that sad and desperate. It made Nahia think. The army rarely acted in Kraido, there had been no reason after the Great Insurrection. Therefore war must be somewhere else, on another world far from there. If it was so, and there were other worlds where dragons did not reign, there was hope. She put her hand over her heart and, closing her eyes, wished for it to be true.

"Let's hope that this year they need more meat than bloodshed," Iker, also a son of cattle owners, said.

"I doubt it. We won't be that lucky," Xavier replied. He was a tall and thin boy, son of a shepherd. "We'll be sent to the army and no one will ever hear from us again."

A silence of absolute discouragement fell on the group.

"Attention, roster!" the officer shouted.

Two Drakonids entered the square from the north and headed to where the officer was shouting orders. They were not soldiers, although they did wear armor, albeit lighter than what the soldiers were wearing. Nahia recognized them. One was a scribe, and a gray cloak around his shoulders identified him as such. He was carrying a large tome in his clawed hands. The other one was more dangerous: a warlock. He had dragon blood and some of their magic, and wore a silver cloak that identified him as such. In his clawed hands he carried a white pearl the size of two apples. They reached the officer with a firm step, looking at ease. They stood one on each side of the officer, who greeted them respectfully and nodded at each.

Her group began to show their nerves. Nahia had to make hard fists to try and control them. She had to stay calm—if she panicked everything would be over for her. She focused on thinking about the positive, that not everything was lost. She imagined a better future, a life full of joy, a world without dragons. She was trying to convince herself that there was hope. Unfortunately, she was not succeeding, and she was not the only one. Her companions were also very restless. Some were shaking, and she could hear the occasional muffled sob.

The villagers watching them started singing an old song about belonging to family, village, and community. They were trying to give the chosen courage so they would know they were not alone and that the whole village was with them.

The Drakonid warlock looked at the group, and when Nahia saw the reptilian eyes gazing in her direction she felt as if she had already been found out. She squeezed her fists even harder. They were not going to discover her scales—they were not. She was coming out of this as a healer. The villages needed healers or else illnesses decimated them, which hurt food production or the riches they obtained from the mines.

"I will now read the list," the Drakonian scribe said in the raspy sibilant voice characteristic of their race.

They all stiffened. Here came the moment of truth.

"Good luck, everyone," said Max.

"Xavier Lormas," the scribe called in a firm tone but without raising his voice.

"Come closer!" the officer ordered, and he did raise his voice. It appeared that he was unable to address them without doing so.

Xavier advanced, fearful, his hands shaking.

"Bow your head before me!"

The unfortunate boy did so.

"What are you here for today?" the warlock asked in a quiet tone.

"To serve my lords, the all-powerful dragons, as they see fit…" Xavier recited the way they were all supposed to.

The warlock closed his eyes and placed his right hand over the pearl he was holding in his left and began to mutter something under his breath. Nahia watched unobtrusively without lifting her head. She realized the warlock was muttering words of power, casting a spell and calling on his magic. He did not move but simply interacted with the pearl as he used his magic.

Then the pearl shone with a silver flash. The warlock reached toward Xavier with both arms as if he were showing the poor wretch to the pearl. Poor Xavier had his eyes closed, and his body trembled from the fear he felt. They were all aware that the power of the blood dragon was being used, and fear appeared on their anxious faces.

A silver ring formed a handspan above Xavier's head and remained floating there through magic. The warlock continued with his spell, muttering. The ring began to move, descending over Xavier. When it reached his head, it widened in size and surrounded his head without touching it. It continued down toward the shoulders, where it widened again so as not to touch them and continued sliding down. It went along the boy's whole body, widening or shrinking in size as required. The ring went down from his head to his knees and then feet.

Nahia watched without raising her head. She knew what the warlock was doing. He was examining Xavier. He wanted to find out whether this particular individual had dragon blood. He was using Drakonian Magic, which searched for itself in the body of the young boy. It was a fearful moment, since those with dragon blood were given to the dragons to serve them above in their domains. It was rumored that they became Warlocks like the one they were seeing. It was an unpleasant future.

The ring traveled back up Xavier's body, analyzing it. He was barely able to control his trembling. It floated over his head for a moment and then returned to the pearl, vanishing into it.

"He doesn't have the blood," the warlock said.

The scribe nodded and wrote something down in the tome.

"You are the third son of a shepherd. The older brother serves as a soldier, the second one as a shepherd..." the scribe went on. "By the grace of our all-powerful lords, you will serve your masters as a soldier."

Nahia cursed under her breath. They had them all registered in the census and they knew each family and their trade, as well as the age of every member. Not only that, they chose each villager's fate. One by one. The control the dragons exercised over them was absolute. A bitter rage climbed up her throat, and she had to make serious efforts to control herself.

"Open your eyes and go stand with the soldiers!" the officer ordered him, pointing at the two standing behind him.

With resignation, Xavier did as he was told. As he was leaving, he glanced at his family; he would never see them again. They saluted him with chanting and expressions of love while their eyes filled with tears.

"Let's continue," the scribe said.

One by one, he called them all. The chanting of the villagers continued as the number of chosen to serve in the army increased. Max was not lucky. As he had expected, it was his lot to serve in the army. Even Inma, who was a rather chubby, unfit farmer, was sent to serve in the army. When she saw this, Nahia knew this was a year of war. Against what nation of which world she had no clue, but that they were preparing for war was obvious. Ikatz was allowed to remain a miner, which was almost worse than being a soldier. Isa was fortunate though—she was allowed to follow her father's trade, the baker of the village.

Then the dreaded moment arrived.

"Nahia Aske," the scribe called.

It was time to face the test.

Chapter 3

Nahia let out a deep sigh and approached the officer. She went with her head down, looking at the ground. Before he told her to, she bowed her head even further She had the officer in front of her, the scribe to her left, and the warlock to her right. The chanting got louder and deeper. It was as if the residents knew Nahia needed help. More than usual.

"What are you here for today?" the warlock asked her, as he had done with all the others.

"To serve my lords, the all-powerful dragons, however they see fit," Nahia said in a firm tone, hiding all the rage that started in her stomach for having to go through all this and everything it meant. She did not know whether she had said the sentence the right way, but that was the meaning.

The warlock did not give her a second glance, which confirmed it. She listened to the spell that began to come out of his mouth. She had half-closed her eyes and clenched her fists hard. She wished with all her being not to be discovered. If she was not allowed to be a healer and had to join the army with the others, she would accept it. But to go to the realm of the dragons? No. Not that. Never. It could not happen.

The pearl in the warlock's hands flashed silver. Nahia clenched her jaw. Here was the moment of truth. The warlock placed the pearl above her head. The pearl shone and the silver ring took shape.

It was the moment: she had to try and fool them before they discovered she had the blood. If she did not try something, she would be found out. She was going to do something dangerous to herself—she might even die—but her fate was death in any case if she did not do anything. She concentrated and closed her eyes tightly. She awoke a flame inside her, one that lived in the middle of her chest. She had learned to do the opposite, to put it out, to not get sick. But today she was going to do just that. She had promised Aoma a long time ago that she would never do something like this, that she would not provoke a seizure. But there was no option, and Aoma would understand. This was not to study what the matter was with her and try to find a cure. She had to do it to try and escape from her current situation. It was a desperate moment, and it required a desperate action.

She started to raise her body temperature. This was something that happened to her sporadically, not intentionally, and that made her sick. On more than one occasion it had almost killed her. But this time, perhaps, it might save her. Her body temperature rose rapidly. She could feel her skin burning all over her body, and this burning was also occurring inside her. It felt like an intense fire in her guts, a fire that generated immense heat. On the other hand, her body did not outwardly manifest the change. She did not sweat, her skin did not change color, her hair was not altered. Nothing. But all of her was burning. Those who watched her would never know something was happening to her.

And so the great fire, as she called it, began. The heat was unbearable inside her and on her skin. Her heartbeat went up to a tremendous pace. She felt her pulse as if it were going to burst in her head. Her heart was beating wildly. She became dizzy and the nausea began. She lost her balance and fell to one side. She started trembling convulsively. Cramps whipped her legs and arms. She cried out in pain while she convulsed on the ground.

The warlock looked at her and stopped the spell. He withdrew the pearl.

"What's the matter with her?" the scribe asked.

"She's having some kind of seizure," the warlock deduced.

"It might be a ruse. It wouldn't surprise me, I've seen it all at this point. These humans try to escape their responsibility toward their masters and lords," the officer commented as he bent over to watch Nahia as she writhed on the ground.

"Is it?" the scribe asked.

The warlock bent down and held Nahia's wrist as she went on convulsing.

"Her pulse is very fast and she's burning up. She suffers from some condition, a very strange one."

"In that case, we don't want her in the army. She's already a weakling, and if she's sick on top of that she's no good for us. Besides, she might have something infectious," the officer said.

The warlock let go of Nahia's wrist and straightened up.

"I don't even know whether she'll survive."

"This certainly looks bad," the scribe said with a displeased wave.

"She's always been sickly, since she was a little child," Isa told them.

The three Drakonids turned to look at her and then focused on Nahia for another moment. The officer lost interest and barked a couple of orders to his soldiers to control the crowd better, since they were horrified by what they were witnessing.

"I'll write that down," the scribe said, noting in his tome all about Nahia and her illness.

The warlock, though, was still looking at her, interested.

Nahia knew from experience that trying to stop was impossible. Once one of her seizures began, nothing could be done. Neither she nor anyone else, healers included, could. That was why it was so dangerous. Because of that, and because it killed her inside. She was somehow killing herself. It was something as horrible as it was incomprehensible. She had been cursed from birth. She'd had to live with it, and she had. Today, perhaps, her curse might get her out of the ceremony. That's what she hoped for. The pain was so intense and the cramps so excruciating that she screamed as if she were being torn apart. She had to hold on and make her hand reach for her belt. The problem was that arm and hand were shaking uncontrollably. She could not make them respond to her mind.

She made a colossal effort, focusing on her hand, sending it the order to reach for her belt. Her hand began to move toward its destination, but her arm shook and moved it away. She concentrated even more and managed to make it obey. Once it reached her belt, she asked her hand to pick one of the five tonics she always carried there. She succeeded. Her hand closed around the first tonic. The pain was killing her. She convulsed and was on the point of losing it. But she did not give up and managed to put the tonic to her mouth. If she did not drink it, she could die. She managed to take the top off with her teeth and drank it while the convulsions and cramps went on torturing her.

She was used to suffering seizures and taking the tonic as fast as possible. At first she was not able to do it on her own and her grandmother gave it to her. With the passing years she had managed to do it by herself, although it was incredibly difficult. The effect of the tonic was quick though. Her body temperature began to drop, as if she had drunk ice and were putting out the fire inside her. As her temperature went down, the cramps and seizures ceased too. A moment later she was left lying, half dead from the terrible experience, but alive.

"Take her away, she's no use at all," the officer ordered.

Nahia could not be happier to hear that. She had done it. She had fooled them. She would not go to serve the dragons in their war. She would stay with her grandmother. If she was not so exhausted and sore that she could not even move, she would have stood up and run off.

"Wait a moment…" the warlock asked.

Nahia's heart skipped a beat, and then a crushing anxiety clenched it.

"Put her in position," the warlock asked the two soldiers.

They did as told and lifted Nahia from the ground until she was on her knees.

"Hold her up so she doesn't fall to the ground."

They held her up and kept her in place.

The warlock began to cast a spell using the white pearl in his hands. The silver ring formed above Nahia's head.

Nahia felt lost. She was going to be discovered, *No, please. No.* This could not happen. She closed her eyes and wished with all her heart not to be found out.

The ring began to slide down Nahia's head. When it reached her chest, it stopped.

Nahia did not see it, but somehow she felt it. She knew she had lost.

The warlock had a very interested look on his dragon face.

The ring started to shine more intensely without moving from where it had stopped. It suddenly gave off a silver light that went up to the sky where the ring projected itself.

The chanting stopped. The people were no longer singing. Something amazing was occurring. Something terrible for her. Her forehead began to burn. An instant later, her temples blazed. It was the scales. She bore the sharp pain and did not put her hands to her face. She held on so as not to reveal that it was the scales. What she could not see—because her eyes were closed—was that her golden scales were shining brightly. They were giving off a golden light that radiated from her face and hit the ground. She opened her eyes and saw the glow that gave her away. She put her chin on her chest, but she could not hide the light.

"She has the blood," the warlock pronounced as he analyzed Nahia with his narrowed reptilian eyes.

"She does? This weak and sick being?" the scribe asked the warlock in a blank tone.

"The blood of the masters runs strong through the veins of some in Kraido," the warlock replied, withdrawing the pearl. The ring was still around Nahia's chest and sent the intense projection toward the sky.

"She won't live, even if she does have the blood," the officer stated.

The warlock tilted his head. He watched her. Then he tilted it the other way and watched her again, studying her.

"Strange event," the scribe said as he wrote something down in his tome.

"Stand her up," the warlock said.

The soldiers lifted Nahia by her arms. She kept her head down and, half opening her eyes, saw that her scales were shining with a golden light.

"Uncover her head," the warlock ordered.

The soldiers took off her hood. Nahia felt a huge hole in her stomach, as if she had been stabbed through with a stake. She had been discovered. Everything ended here. She would not be able to go back to Aoma and be a healer. She would not go to the regular army either. She was going to be sent with those who had dragon blood. The worst fate of all. An intense anxiety began to take over her body and soul.

The warlock watched her with even more interest if possible.

"Turn your face up to me, human."

In the midst of a huge sigh, Nahia looked at the Drakonid warlock's eyes. She was shocked to see surprise in them, great surprise.

"She not only has dragon blood, this human is special. She's Flameborn."

Now it was Nahia who opened her eyes wide. What did that mean? Special? Flameborn? What did the warlock mean?

"Are you sure? That's … that's almost… impossible …" the scribe said, mumbling, which she found odd. Scribes were scholars, words were their thing.

"She has golden scales. She's tried to hide them, but you can clearly tell they're golden."

The scribe came over to check them.

"Stay still," he said, and with his clawed nail he scraped off Aoma's ointment from her forehead. The golden scales were revealed. They now shone even more brightly.

"You see now?" the warlock asked.

The scribe nodded.

"They're golden. But there has to be another explanation…"

"There isn't any. She has dragon blood and golden scales. She's what I'm telling you she is," the warlock said in a tone that brooked no argument.

"We have to report this to our lords at once." The scribe was now nervous, which made Nahia even more anxious.

The warlock looked up at the sky where the ring indicated. Nahia followed his gaze. When the ring reached the clouds, it projected on them.

"There's no need. They've already seen it," the warlock said and pointed east, in the clouds.

The enormous red dragon Nahia had seen that morning appeared, emerging from them. It roared loudly and headed straight to where they were.

"Oh no… it's coming for me…" Nahia muttered, watching the terrifying image descending from the sky.

"Exactly, human, it's coming for you," the warlock confirmed.

Nahia knew then that her foreboding feeling would come true. She was dead.

Chapter 4

The gigantic red dragon came down from the sky. It gave out a tremendous roar, announcing its arrival before it landed right in the middle of the village square. Everyone watching the ceremony ran away as fast as they could. They did not stop until they were outside the village through the back streets. The terror the enormous beast inspired in the hearts of the villagers made them flee, as if the incarnation of evil were falling on them from the sky. In the blink of an eye, only the poor wretches taking part in the ceremony and the Drakonid soldiers, who had withdrawn behind their officer, were left in the square.

The great winged monster landed in the middle of the square, raising a swirl of air, dirt, and dust in every direction. Its powerful legs, ending in fearful claws, settled into the ground as it drew its head high, showing off its teeth. The tip of its tail fell on the blacksmith's house and split the roof in two with a dull *crack*. The blacksmith threw himself out of a back window to avoid being crushed. The creature's size was so massive that the villagers had done well in fleeing, or else they would have been crushed to death.

"On your knees before your lord!" the officer ordered, shouting.

The soldiers who were holding Nahia dropped her on the ground and knelt. She tried to do so too but was unable. She was left lying on the ground. She looked around. Everyone left in the square had knelt: the dozen unfortunates and the Drakonids. They all bowed their heads, showing the respect they owed their lord and master. Out of the corner of her eye and with a clenched heart, Nahia watched the terrifying, colossal monster. It must have been about seventy-five feet long from the head to the tip of the tail, which it shook, causing the rest of the roof to crumble. Then it hit the side of the butcher's house, causing a fissure in it from top to bottom. It beat its wings, sending a powerful wind toward them. Nahia shut her eyes and tried to recover while the wind lashed against her like an unleashed whirlpool.

The great beast roared again powerfully, freezing the hearts of everyone present. It stopped beating its wings and gathered them at his flanks. From what she had seen, Nahia calculated they had to reach a span of sixty feet in total. She sighed anxiously. That reptilian, winged monster was so impressive that the human soul lost all hope in its presence. It was as if the human spirit knew that nothing could be done against such a mythological being. Nahia struggled to keep down her fear and despair.

"Our lord honors us with his presence," the scribe bowed as he knelt.

Bow your heads before Gorri-Buru-Koma of the Gondra Clan, lord of this human region, it announced, sending a mental message to everyone in the square. The message hit Nahia's mind so hard her head flattened on the ground as if the creature had stepped on it with one of its claws. She had never received a mental message from a dragon. She knew they communicated like that, without words. Aoma had told her that dragons considered verbal communication as something belonging to uncivilized beings without power, inferior beings. Now that she had felt a mental message for the first time, she could ascertain it was a very unpleasant experience. It was as if someone were pounding inside her head as she was being spoken to. This could only be achieved through power; it was not natural.

"The region and everyone who serves you in it," the Drakonid officer replied.

Indeed. Every being in this region owes me full loyalty. As lord of this region, it is my duty to my clan to rule over it with absolute firmness.

"The Drakonids serve their lord humbly in anything he requires," the scribe added.

Everyone here either serves me or dies, the dragon sent, and the mental message was so strong and threatening that the humans put their hands to their heads and some even fell sideways on the ground. Nahia withstood the mental blow, clenching her jaw hard. She felt it like a hammer to the back of her head, to her nape. The Drakonids bowed their heads but seemed to bear the blow better. Nahia thought they must either be used to it or their own race allowed them to assimilate that type of communication as well. *I have seen the indication that there is one of the blood in this village.*

"Yes, my lord. We have discovered a human with power," the warlock informed.

The human at your feet?

"That's so, my lord. There's something else…"

Rise and speak. You have permission from your lord and master.

The warlock stood up while the rest remained on their knees. He spoke facing the dragon but with his eyes on the ground.

"She is a Flameborn, my lord."

The dragon's fearful face showed a tiny grimace of surprise.

That is highly unlikely. Flameborns are an anomaly. They almost never occur.

"Yes, my lord. I am most likely mistaken. But the scales are a match... although I might have perceived them wrong."

Mistakes are not tolerated. For your own good, I hope you have not made one, because if you make me waste my time checking it and it turns out that what you are saying is not true, you will regret it.

"Always at my lord's service," the warlock bowed respectfully.

Human, come closer.

Nahia received the mental message and was stunned. The power of the message and the knowledge that the monster was addressing her made her dizzy. She raised her eyes slightly and saw it staring at her with its large reptilian, intense red eyes. It looked evil, predisposed to perversity. The scales covering its whole body were red, with several black veins that ran down its sides. Two thick, curved horns came out of its head. A wide crest went down its nape along its huge back to the tip of its tail with varying thickness according to the part of the body. The claws it leaned on were the size of broadswords, only more deadly looking. Nahia tried to get up, but the more she looked at it, the more paralyzed she was by fear.

What are you waiting for, human? A dragon does not repeat an order, it messaged, and this time there was an element of anger that hit her mind even harder. To make things worse, the dragon had opened its mouth to show its anger, revealing its maw. Nahia gawked at it with wide eyes. She tried to get up to obey but her knees shook and she could not.

Pitiful human. Incapable of following a simple order. You force me to check whether you are really Flameborn in a way I might have avoided. If you are not, you will suffer, although it will be a shorter, intense suffering. You will die instantly.

Nahia was petrified.

The warlock made urgent signs for the rest to move back.

The dragon opened its mouth.

It was the moment Nahia had been fearing, the one she had been foreseeing. She was going to die.

From the dragon's mouth came a great flame that headed straight at Nahia as she lay on the ground, defenseless and helpless. She saw the fire coming at her and shut her eyes. She felt a scorching heat that engulfed her, and at that final moment of her existence she felt a furious rage. That murderous monster was burning her with fire—it was a horrible way to die. And without reason or need, only because it felt like it. This was not fair, it was not right. It was evil. The fury she felt was unleashed, and she felt something awakening inside her in the middle of her chest. It was as if something had exploded inside her body, projecting outward. A large amount of energy seemed to emanate from her body. She thought it was the fire making her feel this novel experience before dying, consumed by the flames. She must be losing her mind from the suffering the fire was causing her. Her end was imminent, and she tried to scream in rage and pain.

To her great surprise, the pain did not come. She only felt rage. All of a sudden, she no longer felt the heat. She opened her eyes in surprise. What she saw left her speechless. The dragon was still sending its fiery breath at her. She was surrounded by intense flames and yet, incomprehensibly, she was not burning. She saw a golden glow above her eyes and she realized her scales were shining like the sun. But it was not only her scales—she herself was shining brightly. An intense golden glow emanated from her body. When the flames reached the glow, they stopped, unable to go further or reach her. What she was witnessing made no sense. Was she delirious with pain and not even know it? Was the pain so great that her mind showed her impossible things to protect her? Or had she already died and she was seeing herself burning without understanding?

The dragon stopped its fiery breath. It looked at her, tilting its head, its mouth twisted into a sort of grin. It looked amused.

Well, this is a surprise. One that will cause the clan to talk.

"Was my guess correct, my lord?" the warlock asked in a tone of great respect and some fear.

It was, and that saves you from having the test repeated on you. The human is immune to fire. She is Flameborn.

Nahia was looking at her arms and legs, searching for burns and unable to understand why she was not dead. She felt her face, her chest, her head, as she was still lying on the ground. Everything seemed to be all right. She felt no pain. Not even her blonde hair had been singed. She could not feel her legs, but they were not sore.

Do not search for wounds on your body, human. Fire cannot harm you, the dragon messaged.

"That… can't be…" muttered Nahia, who could not believe what had just happened.

Do not ever doubt my word. Or the word or wish of any dragon. If you do, you will die like the small, insignificant being you are. Fire cannot kill you, but my mind, my jaws, or my claws will kill you in a matter of moments.

The mental message reached her with such force that once again her head struck the ground. The intensity and anger the message carried were impossible for her mind to cope with.

"I won't…" she replied, trying to appease the dragon's anger. She had never dealt with one, but Aoma had warned her they were excessively egotistical monsters without the least empathy or pity. It was impossible to reason with them. It was their word or death, and they had no patience whatsoever. She was beginning to realize that was indeed the case.

Is there anyone else of the blood in this village?

"No, my lord. The rest are regular humans," the Drakonid scribe said.

Pity. Well, you cannot expect more of this place. Take this human to the city of Gorja. Have her prepared there for her Ascension. You, who are also of the blood will go with her and make sure there are no complications.

"Yes, my lord. Of course," the warlock said, nodding with a big bow of respect.

Anyone manifesting the blood must ascend and begin the Path of Dragons, Gorri-Buru-Koma messaged as if it were a dogma.

"The Path we follow, and by it we are guided. When the time comes, we die for it," the warlock recited, and with his right hand he made a strange gesture. He appeared to draw something in the air.

Human, be grateful. Fortune smiles on you. There are few of the blood, and being Flameborn besides is a rarity and a privilege. Your destiny is to serve us by using your power against the enemy, a destiny reserved for those who are special because our blood runs strong in your veins. It is time to learn the power striving to come out and that you do not know how to control. Be grateful you have been found, otherwise your magic would have driven you mad or killed you. You owe us your life, and your life we will have.

Nahia understood what that meant, but she refused to accept it. The dragon was dooming her to serve, to fight in its name, until she died in some meaningless fight. Not happy with this, she must thank them because the magic she had might harm her. She would happily have preferred not to have been discovered and risked manipulating her own magic herself. Surely with Aoma's help they would have managed to do so. Her grandmother had not gone mad or been killed by her own magic. It was true that in her case the power of magic was small. Perhaps that was why nothing had happened to Aoma. Or perhaps the dragon was tricking Nahia so she would feel grateful. She did not feel grateful. Not at all. She was cursed, and what was happening to her was a dreadful misfortune.

I have told you to be grateful. You do not want me to repeat it, do you, human?

Nahia's head was crushed against the ground once again from the power of the mental message. She felt the warning as if a freezing blade were drawn along her naked back.

"I am grateful for my good fortune," she replied hastily.

And the honor that serving me and fighting for me and the Gondra Clan means, Gorri-Buru-Koma sent her with a death warning.

"Yes, of course. It is a great honor," Nahia said fervently enough for the dragon to believe her words. The warning was of imminent death. This dragon was not fooling around. It had a bad temper. As she thought of this, she shivered. What if it could read her mind? Had it already read it? Her stomach began to turn—no, it could not, or she would already be dead. It would have torn her head off with its claw. Or squashed her alive, stepping on her with the tremendous weight of one of its legs.

You will learn your place and how to behave toward your dragon lords.

The message sounded like a clear threat. She had the clearest feeling she was going to learn the hard way and that if she got minimally distracted, she would pay with her life.

"Yes, my lord, I will learn," she hastened to say, imitating the tone the warlock used as he looked at her out of the corner of his eye.

I see you are intelligent. That is good. It will help you live a little longer. I will remember you, human, and those golden scales on your forehead.

Nahia did not know what to say. It would not be good if it remembered her. In fact, that was the opposite of what she had intended coming to the ceremony. She had wanted to go unnoticed and return to live with her grandmother and enjoy a simple, peaceful life. Everything had gone wrong, very wrong.

The dragon looked up to the sky. It spread its wings and beat them hard, taking a powerful leap and rising in the midst of a blizzard of dust and dirt. It flew to the north, seeking far-off clouds. Nahia was able to glimpse at least five other dragons in the distant sky, flying in different directions. Today they would be seen in every human region, but also in the lands belonging to the other races. Today she would not be the only unfortunate one discovered with power in their veins.

She heaved a sigh. Before the end of the day, many others would have the same feeling of misery and uneasiness she felt in her own stomach. That was what living in an enslaved world where dragons ruled at will felt like. Rage surged again in her belly. She would give anything to get rid of those monsters with evil hearts. Unfortunately, she knew that no one would come to free them. They had been left to their own devices in this world, and the only way for her was the Path of Dragons.

She remained on the ground, exhausted, her mind aching. She could not move and could not get rid of the dizziness. Once the dragon had left, the villagers began to reappear between the houses. They approached the square with sorry looks on their faces for the ones leaving who they would never see again.

"Good luck," Max wished Nahia when they were being separated. Those chosen to be soldiers were put on army carriages. They were being taken to Gudaein, a human military fort where they would be trained to fight and become soldiers against their will.

"Good luck," Nahia wished him without getting up. She knew she would probably never see them again. Perhaps in the middle of a war in which she would also take part. Those chosen to be in the armies were trained for a year and a half in the use of weapons and armor, then turned into soldiers ready for battle. From that moment on, they were sent to some war or remained at the forts until the next war. What they would never do was return to their villages. At least no one had returned so far. A retired soldier was a miracle.

She watched them leave guarded by the soldiers, and her heart shrunk. She was about to burst into tears but held firm; she did not want the Drakonids to see her like that. She wrinkled her nose and forehead. The dragons had no right. They were simple villagers, good people, innocent. They did not deserve to be dragged from their families like that. They did not deserve this. No one did.

The Drakonid officer finished arguing with the scribe and the warlock. They seemed to agree on something, because the three nodded. The officer turned on his heels and headed to where his horse was tethered at the entrance of the village with a steady step. Then he rode back to his soldiers. The scribe took his leave of the warlock and also went for his horse.

The good people of the village said goodbye to those leaving with chants and huddled around the three lucky ones who had not been chosen for the army. Nahia wondered what was going to happen to her next. The warlock gestured to her to stay put. She was glad. At least she could recover a little. Soon four soldiers came on horseback with a fifth one in a cart.

"Can you get up?" the warlock asked her.

Nahia thought about lying and saying she could not. She did not want to be taken. She wanted to stay there. She made do as if she could not, although the truth was did feel slightly better. Not much, but it was something.

"I don't think so…"

"It doesn't matter. You'll be taken to the cart. Soldiers, carry her and settle her down for the journey."

Nahia sighed. There was no escape.

They carried her gently between two soldiers and put her in the cart. It was a simple military one, used for the transport of soldiers and weapons. She made herself comfortable among some blankets. She was so tired and sore she could not even think.

"We're leaving," the warlock ordered.

Isa came out from among the people.

"Take good care of yourself, Nahia! Good luck!" she said.

"Thank you. Have the village look after my grandmother. She's alone now," Nahia pleaded from the cart, straining her neck.

"The village will look after her," she heard several people say in unison.

With that farewell and a feeling in her heart that she was never coming back, she left for a new life, to serve her dragon lords against her will. Everything had turned out wrong, but at least she was still alive. Her death premonition had not come true—not yet at least.

Chapter 5

Every bump in the road to the city of Gorja made Nahia's heart skip a beat and the anxiety she felt inside grow. She was heading to a more than uncertain future that no one came back from. She looked up and saw that the closer they got to their destination, the clearer she could see one of the dragon realms in the sky.

The warlock rode at the head of the group. She was in the cart behind him, with two soldiers driving it and the rest escorting them. The warlock only turned his head every now and then to make sure she was following but did not say a word to her. Drakonids were known to be gruff and sparing with words. Nahia had always avoided contact with them, but thanks to this forced journey she could now bear witness to it. They neither addressed her nor gave any sign of caring whether she lived or died. They looked at her with their unique dragon faces as if they were mad at her and focused on their orders. Nothing else.

Nahia spent most of the journey during the day looking up at the clouds. Not because her head was lost up there, but because in their midst she saw something unique and entirely unbelievable: a huge mass of land floating, suspended in midair among the clouds. This was a difficult vision for anyone to accept, even if they had seen it all their life. It was as if an enormous island had risen from the seas to the sky and then the winds had dragged it inland.

While she was watching it that afternoon, Nahia remembered the legend of Sekodrome Aoma had told her about so many times, and which was part of the foundation of human mythology. It told that thousands of years before, Sekodrome, the most powerful king of the dragons of his time, a despot, proud being, couldn't bear the idea of living at the same level as the other races that peopled Kraido. One day he decided to solve that situation. He first ordered all dragons to live on the highest peaks and not to set foot on the land the inferior races inhabited. The dragons did this for a time, but it was not enough for the overbearing king. He wanted himself and his people to be above the other beings of that world. He gathered the most powerful and wisest sages among the dragons to plan how to do it.

And they found a way. One day, using their great power, they made the island of Waten rise from the sea to the sky. Sekodrome made it his realm and ordered the dragons to live only on it.

The rattling of the cart made Nahia grab a hold, and she lost her train of thought for a moment. She recovered it when she glimpsed the mass of land in the sky. The fact that the dragons had been able to take an island out of the sea and make it rise up to the clouds was evidence of their amazing power. Now there were no less than five realms hovering in the sky, one for each of the powerful clans that ruled over Kraido and subjected the eight races in their lands. The one she was seeing now was the Kingdom of Gondra and the dragons of that clan which lived in it. From up there they ruled over the humans they considered their property. Gorri-Buru-Koma and the rest of the dragons she had seen that day came from there. She had only ever seen this realm in the clouds, since the others were far away over the lands of the other races. She grimaced; she had seen enough with this one, she had no desire to see any of the others.

A new bump in the road made her grab hold again. She went on watching the enormous chunk of land that hung suspended in the air by dragon magic with half-closed eyes. It was so large it could be seen from almost all the human regions. The underside had an oval, concave shape and an irregular, rough surface, while the top side was flat with what looked like mountains on it. Nahia had always had the impression that this realm looked like half of an unpolished sphere made of earth or clay. Or at least from the ground below that was what it looked like. She did not know whether the other dragon realms were the same, but she guessed they would be similar.

"Go to the right," the warlock ordered the group at the crossroads.

Nahia followed the road with her gaze for a while and then, becoming restless again, she could not help but look up at the sky once more. That vision in the clouds reminded all the races that their lords and masters watched them ceaselessly. Besides, and what was more maddening, they had no options against them since they could not even reach them up there. Her heart sank just thinking about it. How could they defeat the all-powerful dragons if they could not even reach their realms in the sky? There was no hope for the slave races. They would always be slaves. They would suffer the ruthless, oppressing yoke of the dragons.

She heaved a long sigh. She was trying to find some hope in the bottom of her heart despite it all. She did not want to admit the impossibility of being free one day. She tried to keep that hope in the bottom of her soul so they would not take it away. She secretly wished that somehow, someday, they would achieve freedom and might live happily ever after. She did not know how it might happen, and she realized that in the present circumstances it was impossible, but even so, her heart clung to a fragment of hope, and she refused to give it up. Perhaps someday the circumstances would change. Perhaps someday someone would change them.

The evening before arriving at their destination, they camped beside a stream. Nahia decided to elicit some information out of the warlock. She was not expecting to get any, but she decided to try all the same. Once the journey ended, she guessed she would have no other opportunity.

"What's going to happen to me?" she asked him straightforwardly while they ate some salted meat from their supplies beside a small campfire the Drakonids had built.

The soldiers looked a Nahia as if she had committed a crime by speaking.

The warlock raised his hand, and the soldiers nodded and went on with their tasks.

"Don't you know? You ought to," he replied without looking at her.

"There are many rumors among my people… differing stories… about what happens to those who are of the blood… none good…"

The warlock looked at her now and watched her for an instant with his yellow, reptilian eyes.

"I can assure you that what's going to happen to you is an honor."

"It is?" Nahia's tone of surprise was obvious and filled with disbelief.

"It is," the warlock nodded. "You are going to Ascend. Then you will become a warlock, like I am."

"In my case… will I be a witch?"

"That's right, since you're human. Besides, in your case, I have the feeling you will become a sorceress in the future."

"Is there a difference?" Nahia had no idea of what one thing or the other was in the world of dragons and magic.

The warlock nodded.

"Warlocks use weapons and magic." He patted the sword he carried at his waist and then the middle of his chest. He turned his hand with a slow movement until his palm was up and closed his eyes. He said some strange words and there was a blue flash on the palm of his hand. To Nahia's amazed gaze, it looked like water floating over the warlock's hand.

"Wow... magic..." Nahia muttered. She had never seen anyone use magic that way, so casually and with such perfect dominance. She noticed the scales of the warlock's neck glowed blue. Those scales were different from the rest covering his head, which were a darker, green color. They flashed and the others did not. He must have the same kind of scales she had on her forehead and temples.

"Those who have a lot of magic or power tend to fight with it instead of with weapons. Those are the warlocks," he explained and said something else Nahia did not understand. The water became ice, then he shaped it into a frozen stake, making it spin in his hand. When it was to his liking, he threw it as he would a knife, and it plunged deep into a nearby tree.

"Impressive... I think I understand. A warlock tends to fight more with a weapon than with magic, and a sorcerer would rather use magic than weapons."

"That's right. You're clever. That's good. You might survive longer than usual. In any case, both warlock and sorcerer must master the two: weapons and magic. That's the Path, and that we must follow. Your Talent will also be discovered, and a Mark will determine it."

"A Talent? What's that?" Nahia threw her head back. She had never heard of anything like that.

"A Talent is similar to a profession, only one of a martial type and of use in battles and war."

"A profession of war?"

"That's right. My Talent is that of a Warrior," he said and drew his sword. He held it in his hand and let the flames reflect on it. "I have learned to fight with the long sword, short sword, combat axe, spear, and other martial weapons. I am very good at it, especially with the sword. The Warrior talent is the most common, and therefore there are more of us."

"Oh, I see…"

"Don't worry about that now. You'll learn all that and a lot more in Drakoros, the Academy of Dragon Bloods, where you must go."

Nahia looked up to the starry sky and located the realm of Gondra, which shone like a bright star.

"Up there?"

"Yes, in one of our masters' realms."

"Am I going to Gondra?"

The warlock smiled.

"No, you're going to Drakoros. The Academy of Dragon Bloods isn't in any of the five realms of the clans."

"It's not? I thought it would be there…" Nahia pointed at the realm that was visible even at night, since it burned there with a thousand lights and twinkled silver like a star. It was most unusual.

The warlock shook his head.

"The five clans are always fighting to rule over Kraido. If one of these clans had the war academy for itself, it would have a great advantage over the other four. Therefore, and to avoid disputes among the clans that would end in war, another elevated realm was created, one that is neutral. That's where the academy is. None of the five clans has any right over this realm and the academy. That's where you will go, where all the chosen with dragon blood will go from all the corners of Kraido."

Nahia was trying to digest all that information and save it in her mind. It was hasty to draw conclusions so quickly, but she was beginning to get an idea of where she was headed to and the kind of teachings she would receive there. She did not like it at all. It was going to be something horrible. She did not want to learn how to fight and use weapons. She was going to be forced to kill in the name of the dragons.

"Has there been war among the clans before?" she asked as the information registered.

"There has been, indeed. Over a thousand years ago. Dark times, when our lord dragons were rival clans. They fought among themselves for the supremacy of their clan. But that is already in the past. Now the clans are at peace and the struggle for power is made without shedding the sacred blood of our lords."

Nahia found this knowledge most interesting. The dragon clans were rival clans. They fought among themselves for power. That might provide an opportunity, something to take advantage of. She internalized it and decided she must find out more, but she did not ask more questions so as not to raise suspicions.

"Do all those who are like us… end up in that school of war to then fight for the dragons? Isn't there another way to follow?" Nahia asked, hoping not to end up fighting, something that went against her nature. She was a healer apprentice, with a weak body. She could not even imagine fighting and killing.

"For our lords the all-powerful dragons," he corrected her. "Learn manners, or you'll die quickly. Our masters have no patience or mercy."

"Oh, yes, I'm sorry."

"Fighting and conquering are essential in the Path of Dragons. You'll soon learn that and will respect it. That's the only way."

There had to be another way. Nahia was never going to respect that, no matter how much they tried to make her. She said nothing though. She did not want to antagonize the warlock, who was giving her all this information that would surely come in handy.

"What's your name? I'm Nahia," she said, trying to be friendly.

The warlock looked at her tilting his head. His reptilian eyes in that mini-dragon's head were unsettling.

"You are a singular human. People of your race don't usually try to fraternize with mine."

"Perhaps because you don't usually bring good news or joy, like today for instance."

The warlock smiled, and Nahia found it very weird to see a smile on the face of a Drakonid.

"True," the warlock nodded. "My name is Asi-Dra-Koa."

"Pleased to make your acquaintance," Nahia said, trying not to let it sound ironic but as if she was making an effort to be friendly.

"Pleased? I doubt it."

"Well, within the terribleness of my situation."

Asi-Dra-Koa nodded and went on eating.

"I see you use the same kind of names as Dragons."

"We were created in their image. It's only natural that we try to emulate them in everything we do and are."

Nahia remained thoughtful. If this was so, if one day the dragons disappeared, the Drakonids would try to take their place, subjugating the other races and enslaving them like their masters had done. She did not need to get this out of him, she could see it in his reptilian eyes. They would follow the teachings of their masters and would believe they had the right to rule over everyone else by force. But they would be able to defeat the Drakonids if all the races joined. The dragons just needed to disappear first. That was going to be very difficult to achieve, if not downright impossible, but once again hope lit up in her heart.

"I understand. You must feel greatly honored." She had to make an effort for her voice to sound sincere. Her throat bothered her, and she drank from a waterskin beside her.

"It is a great honor. The rest of the races don't understand, which doesn't surprise me. Only we, who see ourselves reflected in our lords and masters, appreciate it."

The water had just been taken from the stream and Nahia enjoyed its coolness. The experience of being almost burnt and all the excitement lived through that day had left her dry and dehydrated. She drank as if she had not had a drop in two days.

"I needed that," she told the warlock when she noticed he was staring at her intensely.

"I know that now you see me and my people as captors, enemies, but you will soon change your mind and will see us for what we really are: your allies. We all serve our lord dragons. We all live and die for their greater glory."

That was not going to happen in a thousand moons. Nahia hid the denying look on her face but did not do so fast enough, and so Asi-Dra-Koa noticed.

"I hope that is so…" she said, pretending.

"It will be. There are many things you will change your mind on."

The two were silent and finished eating. A thousand ideas and questions came to Nahia's mind, most of them bad. She had to tell her head to stop thinking for an instant. The important thing was that she was alive. By a hair's breadth, since she was almost burnt to death, but she was alive. She had to focus on that and on not making a mistake and dying, which might very well happen.

"What did you mean by ascending?" she asked to carry on with the conversation and try to understand it.

The warlock opened his hands.

"In your situation, it has two meanings. There's the spiritual meaning, understanding that following the Path you will reach an elevated state," he said, moving his left hand. "And there's the physical one. You will ascend physically to the realm of the dragons," he said, moving his right hand.

"I'm not sure which one scares me more."

"Neither ought to."

"You mean there's no danger of me dying in either sense?"

"I didn't say that. Of course there's danger of you dying. That danger is constant and permanent in the service of the masters. Otherwise you can't advance along the Path. Motivation to survive creates propitious students and helps you reach all the achievements."

Nahia sighed. She was going to die either way. That was what he was telling her in a less direct way.

"I won't be able to avoid death."

"No one can, in the long run. We can only dodge it for a while. Then she finds us. We will die serving our dragon lords, and it will be a great honor."

Nahia did not think that dying was any kind of honor, least of all serving those merciless monsters that did not value any other life but their own. She decided, right there and then, that she was going to make it very difficult for them. If she had to die, she was not going to go easily. In fact, she would try to escape by any means so that her death would be as far in the future as possible.

That night, her rest was plagued by nightmares. She dreamed about wars in distant lands, fire and destruction, death and suffering, gigantic, monstrous dragons, and of herself fighting them to the death.

Chapter 6

In the evening of the following day, they arrived at Gorja. The city was surrounded by a crumbling wall that no one looked after anymore. It was a relic of a past where humans had tried to defend themselves from their enemies; at one time the other races of Kraido, then the dragons. They entered through the main street. Nahia looked at the buildings and workshops. Cities varied widely from villages, both in their distribution and in their purpose. The people living here were not dedicated to obtaining food or raw materials for the dragons. The function of cities was to provide everything else the dragons needed that had nothing to do with their nourishment. In them lived mostly craftspeople of different trades, especially those who worked precious metals and stones. The dragons valued them and considered both a treasure, and they always required large amounts that forced the enslaved races to produce and refine them. No one knew why it was so. The world of dragons was a mystery to their servants.

As they went down the main street, Nahia missed nothing and remembered everything she knew about cities. Each region had only one. This was so because of the dragons' decision, not the humans'. From what her grandmother had told her, in each region, six out of ten people worked on obtaining food, for the dragons first and then for themselves and other humans. Three worked in mines and quarries; they obtained precious metals like silver and gold, as well as precious gems like rubies and emeralds. One out of ten were the artisans who worked the materials and turned them into refined metals and jewels which the dragons, for some reason, considered invaluable. Nahia had met workers from the mine near her village. She had treated them for wounds because of cave-ins. From what they had told her, the dragons were after a very rare material, similar to silver but shinier, which they called Dragon Metal. They had told her it was supposed to have magical properties. Nahia did not know whether that was true. It sounded to her like mystical beliefs of the enslaved miners, without foundation.

When they arrived at a round fountain, Nahia saw other groups similar to hers also arriving. She was not the only human with dragon blood discovered in the twelve regions that year. She had not expected to be, and she was glad to see others like her. At the same time she felt sorry for them, since they would share their misfortune and fate. She did not know how many had suffered the same bad luck of being selected—she hoped not many. From a street to the east she saw a group of Drakonids approach, escorting a blond boy who looked as miserable as she did. From the streets of the west side of the city a girl with short brown hair appeared, also escorted.

When she saw them, Nahia felt like greeting them with a wave so they would know they were not alone, or perhaps so she would not feel so lonely by connecting with others like her. She was about to raise her hand but did not. She felt a little ridiculous, but she did cross gazes with them as they came closer. For some reason, Asi-Dra-Koa stopped his group and waited for the arrival of the other two retinues. The three humans with dragon blood pretended indifference but exchanged looks, trying to cheer one another.

Once the three groups met in the square where Asi-Dra-Koa was waiting, he started talking to the other two warlocks who led their retinues. The soldiers watched the three chosen who were to serve in the realm of the dragons while the warlocks commented on something in the language of the Drakonids. Nahia could not understand a word. Every race had its own language, but they had all learned the common language of Kraido thousands of years ago, that way they could all understand one another. When one race did not want to be understood, as was the case now, they switched to their mother tongue.

The girl with the short hair looked weathered by the sun and had freckles all over her nose. She must have worked in the fields. She was wiry, quite tall, and looked strong. The boy was also quite strong, and his face showed frustration and anger.

The few craftspeople who passed them by bowed their heads and went on with their tasks. They did not want to interfere or seem to be involved in whatever happened to the new arrivals. Nahia did not blame them. Drakonid soldiers were posted at different points of the city. The craftspeople were forbidden to do anything other than their purpose in serving the dragons. She felt sorry for them. There were not many soldiers in the villages except at specific moments like the Ceremony of Servitude, but in the city there were always soldiers.

"We keep going," Asi-Dra-Koa ordered once he finished speaking with the other warlocks.

They continued along the main street of the city and arrived at an enormous clear square. In it, Nahia saw about twenty humans surrounded by soldiers and several warlocks talking together a little further off. Those humans looked as unfortunate as the three of them were, coming from other regions and chosen in the ceremony. They must have arrived before them and had been waiting. She was not mistaken. They were being taken to join them. It saddened her to see so many. She had expected to see only about half a dozen in all. She counted them unobtrusively—with the three of them, they made twenty-five in all.

If meeting the unfortunates saddened her, what she saw beyond them left her frozen. In the middle of the main square, she saw what looked like an enormous white pearl made of granite. It was a sphere the size of a house, and it seemed to preside over the place. When she saw it, white, unblemished, and polished, Nahia knew this object had a purpose for the dragons. One they would soon discover and, most likely, regret.

"Go stand with the others," the warlocks ordered them as soon as they arrived.

Nahia jumped off the cart and directed a pleading glance at Asi-Dra-Koa in one last useless call for help. The warlock did not flinch and nodded at her to go with the rest of the chosen. He was not going to help her. He owed his allegiance to his masters and would carry out their orders. He did not care whether she died or not. Not him or any of the Drakonids there.

The chosen all stood together as they had been told. The group had looks that ranged from worry to fear, anguish, doom, and resignation. Only a few remained calm. There were at least four with wounds from having tried to escape or resist. From what she could tell at first glance, there were as many girls as boys. Was it coincidence, or was there a reason? It made her think. It might be happenstance, or it might mean dragon blood could run as easily through girls' veins as boys'. She guessed it must be that; it would be the most logical answer. Since she was not going to get an answer to that question, or the many others flooding her mind, she decided to stop thinking about it. Whatever the case, she was glad to see other girls like her. They could understand and help one another, or at least she hoped so. Or rather she wished so.

Another thing she noticed, and which greatly surprised her, was that all the chosen had scales on their faces. She was not the only one, which relaxed her. She had always felt like a freak, since there was no one like her in the village. She was sure there had to have been someone before, but no-one had ever told her about them. She noticed the others' scales. They were different colors from hers. They also covered different parts of the face, forming what looked like patterns, or at least so they looked to her. They were not uneven shapes, and they did not seem to appear randomly over the face either. No, they definitely formed shapes with a meaning, a pattern. The shades of blue, brown, red, and white predominated. They shone with metallic flashes when the sun's rays hit them. The shapes that appeared on each face varied, as if same pattern could not be repeated. She saw that some were covered down to the neck on different sides. She wondered if some of the chosen also had scales on their bodies. She did not so far, but she feared her scales would spread across her skin like an infectious illness. She saw two girls with black scales, one above the eyebrows and the other on her cheeks. They left her puzzled.

She watched all of them as unobtrusively as she could, although it was obvious they were all doing the same. Curiosity getting the better of them, they all stared at one another's scales. Nahia had been covering them ever since they had appeared, and she guessed that most of them would have done the same. Of the boys in the center, one caught her attention. He was tall and strong. His hair was as black as a moonless night and not very long. His light-blue eyes, almost gray, shone with intensity in a serious face which was handsome and angular. Nahia was surprised at that. His scales went down the left side of his face to the neck. It looked as if someone had drawn a winding river across his features, a silver one, since his scales were silver. That was strange. He was the only one with scales of that shade, just like she was the only one with golden scales. She found it an unusual coincidence.

The young man realized she was studying him and fixed her with his intense light blue eyes. Nahia wanted to look away, pretend, but she was unable to take her eyes off his. That boy was as unique as she

49

was. This was soon made apparent, because by the time she was able to look away she realized everyone else was staring at the two of them. The reason could only be because they were the only ones with gold and silver scales. All of a sudden, Nahia was aware of everyone's eyes on her and felt embarrassed. She blushed and bowed her head to avoid them. Particularly his gaze—he was still staring at her, unmoved by the scrutiny of the others.

Avoiding looking at the others, Nahia's eyes turned to the great pearl. She watched the great white sphere that looked like granite and saw that nothing seemed to come from it. It stood there, inert and stoic, like a toy a god might have forgotten. But she could feel its power. She had heard rumors about the pearls at the village. According to what they said, there was one in each of the races' nations. Eight in all. The one she was seeing was that of the humans. There were rumors that they emanated power and that their magic could be felt from a league away. She pondered on that for a moment. A league away from the city Nahia had not felt anything, and being so close now, she felt nothing either. Perhaps the rumors had no foundation.

A Drakonid warlock came out of one of the buildings beside the great pearl. He spoke with the other warlocks briefly, and when he finished, he adjusted his silver cloak and approached the chosen prisoners, who stiffened. Something was afoot.

"The time has come for you to leave. Your fate awaits you. Serve your dragon lords well," he told them in a dry tone.

Nahia realized that her life, as she had known it, ended here. She had no idea what awaited her, but she was sure she would have to fight and use her head in order to survive. Especially her head, since her body was not made for fighting.

"Kneel before your lords," he ordered them and pointed up at the sky.

Flying over the city, a brown dragon appeared. It was smaller than Gorri-Buru-Koma. They all knelt at once. The dragon made two passes over the group of chosen, who bowed their heads in fear. Then it landed on the great white pearl. It balanced on the spherical surface, beating its wings, then folded them along its sides.

Humans of dragon blood. Your fate is to serve us for our greater glory. You have been chosen because power runs through your veins. You will have the privilege and pride of going to Drakoros, the Academy of Dragon Bloods. There you will be trained in the use of magic and weapons to fight in the war to defend the interests of your lord dragons. Whoever survives the three years of training will serve with honor under our orders. You will become dragon warlocks to the greater glory of our lineage. You will do so by following the Path of Dragons. Those who die along the way will have not been worthy of following it, the dragon sent to them. They all received the message in their minds forcefully, as if an invisible force had struck them and left them half-stunned. It was not only an inexorable order, it was also a sentence. For some of them, it would be sentence of death.

"So it shall be. They will train and serve our dragon lords in battle," the warlocks replied, bowing stiffly.

The unfortunate ones who had just received the sentence were looking at one another with anguish and incomprehension on their faces. None attempted to stand, just in case. Nahia realized they were all as lost as she was, if not more. No-one there knew what awaited them. The dragon's message fell on them like a huge slab of stone, like being crushed by a tombstone. The comments "poor us" or "we're dead" began to be heard among the unfortunate youths, who were trying to make sense of the situation and at the same time control the fear and despair in their hearts.

I do not want to hear a single lament, least of all a sob. Only the weak without guts, weep when confronted with a complicated situation. Those with dragon blood smile at a challenge. They laugh at the enemy. They shed their blood without hesitation and give their lives for their lords with honor. The weak do not survive the Path of Dragons. That I can promise you. So take in the message and do it fast. Or else you will know my wrath, and the wrath of a dragon knows no bounds or mercy.

The message reached them hard with a clear threat. The moans and whimpers died instantly. Most bowed their heads, feeling stunned and overwhelmed, and avoided looking at the dragon on top of the sphere. Nahia glanced quickly out of the corner of her eye and had the impression of a god in the form of a huge reptilian predator bird that watched them. Not to help, but to end the life of whoever did not behave as expected.

The dragon roared, making them all cringe. It was as if it wanted to make sure they all understood what was going on. Then it shut its brown, reptilian eyes. Even with its eyes closed, the dragon was terrifying with its pure mythological and beastly presence.

Nahia felt a chill, but not of fear or cold. She felt something different, although she did not know what it was. The hair on her nape stood on end and her skin crawled. It was a strange experience. She looked at her companions, and it seemed that several were also feeling chilly and some were staring at the goose bumps on their arms. Whatever it was must come from the dragon. It had to be power. It could not be anything else, since there was no breeze and the weather was balmy. Was the dragon using its magic? Before she could decide whether that was the case or not, the great pearl flashed with a silver glow that blinded them all, making them shut their eyes. She had no more doubts—the dragon was using its power. She did not know the reason behind the power, but that the great pearl was shining in response to the dragon she was sure of. It made her very uneasy.

The moment was here. Nerves made her stomach sink. She opened her eyes carefully and looked. She saw that above the pearl, a great silver sphere was forming. It was five times the size of the dragon, which remained still. The sphere was translucent, intangible. She watched as it gained consistency. A second silver flash emitted from the pearl, and again she had to shut her eyes. When she opened them again, she saw a second sphere inside the first one growing and taking shape. A third sphere appeared after a new flash.

All the hair on her body stood on end as she felt the enormous magical energy the pearl and the spheres above it gave off. The three began to melt into one that finally finished forming and took on a physical shape. It was colossal, at least three times the size of the pearl it was standing on. This colossal sphere seemed to be filled with liquid silver, and she could see how it undulated. It appeared as if someone had tossed a pebble into a silver lake, only this one was vertical and spherical.

Enter the portal. They received the order from the brown dragon. It was an imperious order: there was no place for a refusal.

Portal? What did the dragon mean by portal? How were they to enter it? Nahia was puzzled, and she was not the only one. The unfortunate chosen were looking at one another, not knowing what to do. The dark-haired boy with blue eyes stood up and marched forward decisively as if he were not afraid. He glanced at her, and Nahia understood he wanted her to follow him. She watched where he was going and saw that the soldiers had set up a wooden ladder on one side of the pearl. The boy with the silver scales began to climb easily. He was not only strong, he was also nimble and, it appeared, very determined. Nahia followed him. She was not strong or determined, but she was nimble, one of the few advantages of having a slight frame. She started up. She did not do it as gracefully as he had, of course, but she was not clumsy either, and she reached the top without any trouble.

She looked down and saw the rest following. The dark-haired boy was beside the dragon. He did not seem to fear it, but he was not challenging it either. He was standing beside the great winged reptilian, kneeling with his hands behind his back and his head bowed. Nahia walked to his side and placed herself like him.

This is the way I like it. All on your knees, humans. Wait for the rest. You must all cross at the same time, the dragon ordered.

They both waited.

The others began to reach the top and place themselves around them.

"My name is Nahia," she whispered at him with her head down as the others began to arrive.

"I am Logan. We'd better keep silent," he warned her, and with his eyes he indicated the dragon.

Nahia understood. Better not to risk it and make that creature angry. If it was already large and ferocious looking, kneeling there beside it made it seem even more gigantic and monstrous to her. She felt like an ant it might squash at any moment. The dragon shook its tail, and Nahia's heart nearly stopped beating. She really thought it was going to squash her, and her days would be over then and there.

She let out a breath, and after a moment she raised her gaze unobtrusively toward the dragon for a brief instant. She had the impression that the creature was interacting with the great silver sphere, which emitted another silver flash.

One by one, all the chosen climbed onto the pearl and knelt behind them. Once they were all on top of the Pearl, the dragon beat its enormous wings and with a leap took off. It rose about two hundred paces and started flying over the portal in circles. The soldiers took the ladder away.

Now you will stand up and cross the portal. Walk toward it and enter. Whoever hesitates, even for an instant, will pay with their life. The dragon's mental message carried with it a strong feeling of indisputable order mixed with a threat which they all received as if they were being pushed abruptly.

Nahia stood up. She looked at the dragon in the sky and then at the sphere with the silver liquid. She sighed and took a step forward. Logan followed her. She took two more steps and entered the portal.

Darkness swallowed her.

Chapter 7

She woke up with a pounding head and terrible stomachache. She was lying on a cold, hard rocky floor. Nahia half-opened her eyes. The light struck them with a searing brightness. She felt dizzy. For a moment she thought she was suffering the red forest fevers. Her head felt all fuzzy, and she felt so dazed she could barely think. Her stomach felt upside down. She managed to open her eyes completely and saw that she had vomited to one side. She raised her head and managed to look around, holding her stomach with one hand while she leaned on the other to sit up. She saw the rest of the group of chosen scattered around her. Half were still passed out, and the other half were trying to recover. Logan was already on his feet and helping a blond boy get up.

Nahia's head began to ease on her, and with an effort that seemed titanic, she got up. She nearly lost her balance and almost fell again, but somehow she managed to stay upright. She looked ahead to try and focus and see where they were. What she saw made her take a step back. Fifteen paces away, a blue dragon with shining silver-streaked scales watched them. It was still, erect, showing off its powerful look. It had to be about sixty feet long, and its eyes shone with a gleam which Nahia interpreted as very unfriendly. A white mist rose behind the dragon, and there was no way to see what was beyond.

In an unconscious attempt to escape from that being, Nahia looked behind her and saw the great white pearl a few paces away. It was identical to the one they had come through, but this one was not above an open portal. The mist that surrounded it did not let them see what was behind the object of power. In the midst of her confusion and daze, she wondered if that was actually the same pearl and they were still in the same place.

She focused, and through the mist she glimpsed some stone structures that rose right and left. She did not recognize them. No, that place was not the city of Gorja. They were no longer there, so this was not the same pearl. She made sure her satchel was on her back with her things and several vials in her belt in case her condition flared up again. Everything was in place. This eased her a little, although not much.

Wake up, weak humans! The order reached them as a mental message from the dragon, accompanied by a feeling of anger.

Nahia's head swayed, and she became dizzy. She nearly vomited again but managed not to and stay on her feet. Both actions seemed to her true feats, given how badly she felt. Around her, the moans and gagging were more than ostensible.

On your feet! Everyone! You are a disgrace! the blue dragon sent, and its message reached them, along with contempt and rage.

Nahia withstood the force of the mental message by clenching her jaw and shutting her eyes hard. Then she helped a red-haired girl beside her to get up, since she was even dizzier than herself. The dragon's mental messages made this situation worse, making them all dizzy. Why did it message them when they were all feeling so poorly? It was most likely doing it on purpose. Those still on the ground slowly got to their feet, some by themselves, others with the help of whoever was closest to them. There remained three who seemed unable to get up. Maybe they did not want to get up and face the new world they had awoken to and the guardian waiting for them.

The blue dragon approached the group with heavy steps. Its presence emanated power, both physical and magical. It stopped in front of them and swept the group with its reptilian blue eyes. They shone, with hatred and rage most likely. Nahia did not like that look at all. She felt that something bad was going to happen. Perhaps it was simply the fear she felt at being before an imposing dragon that might be clouding her judgment. Or maybe that was the look of a ruthless and monstrous being. Her bet was on the latter.

First rule of the Path of Dragons that you must learn. Dragons do not repeat orders, it sent, and with its tail it delivered a terrible blow to the two boys who had not managed to get up. They were both thrown off and landed on the hard ground several paces away. They were struck hard. Nahia feared they might have broken some bones. They stayed lying there.

On your feet I said! the blue dragon ordered furiously.

"Poor things…" she heard a girl with chestnut hair say beside her.

Nahia started to move to help them.

No one will help them. The Path must be traveled alone. Only the weak and unworthy require help, the dragon sent them.

The message reached Nahia so hard she threw her head backward and was unable to go on.

One of the boys managed to get up and stumbled from one side to another, holding his left arm, which had been badly hit. Luckily, the pain he felt had forced him up. The other boy tried a couple of times but could not stand. His face was etched with pain. He remained on all fours, looking up at the dragon. He began to weep, looking defeated. He tried a third time, screamed in pain, and stayed as he was. He did not try to stand again.

You are not worthy of walking the Dragon Path, it messaged, and then it opened its mouth. A freezing steam issued from it, followed by a powerful stream of water and freezing breath. It hit the poor boy straight on. Nahia thought the boy would be thrown back, given the power of the stream, but something odd and terrible happened at the same time. The powerful breath froze the unfortunate chosen right where he was. The power of the freezing breath instantly froze the boy to death.

Nahia covered her mouth with her hands to muffle a scream. The dragon had killed the boy in cold blood. The scene horrified her. Dragons were truly monstrous and ruthless. She watched the face of the dead boy. He did not seem to have realized what had happened. His frozen look was one of incomprehension, not of suffering. At least he would not have felt any pain. It was little consolation, but it was something at least.

The first casualty of this year's harvest of chosen ones. I trust the rest of you have learned the lesson. I will not repeat it, it messaged, and this time the feeling that came with it was one of entertainment. The dragon was laughing at its own joke.

Nahia found it despicable. She narrowed her eyes and glared at the blue monster. One day they would pay for all the deaths they had caused. One day they would be punished for killing and torturing innocent people and treating them like they were nothing. One day, humans would get rid of the dragons. That hope began to take shape in her heart. Come what may, whatever fate awaited her, she would hold on to the hope of a world free of dragons.

My name is Sarre-Urdin-Olto, Guardian of the Gate. It is my duty to watch the entrance and exit of this place. I receive and see off whoever comes and goes using the portal. To you I am your lord, and you will respect me not only as your lord, but also as Guardian of this Gate. Remember this always. I will not tolerate either lack of courtesy or mistakes. Lower your gazes, immediately!

The message carried such hostility that they all felt their minds shaken. They bowed their heads at once. No one dared defy the dragon. They were all very aware that if they did, it meant death. No human could confront a dragon and come out victorious. Many had tried along the centuries of slavery, and they had all failed. Dragons were not only gigantic beings with powerful jaws and fearsome claws, but they were covered by impenetrable scales. Steel could neither slice or make holes in them. And if that was not enough, their elemental and mental magic were extremely powerful. Nahia knew full well that whoever defied a dragon died. Her parents had done it and paid the price. There was no other possible result. She sighed deeply and drowned the pain that remembering them caused in her heart and soul.

You never look either me or any other dragon in the eye. You must always keep your head bowed and your eyes on the ground. You are not worthy of being in our presence. We are superior beings and your masters. And you will treat us as such. You will never speak without being asked, and you will always obey without hesitation. Whoever does not comply with these simple rules will die.

Nahia swallowed. She had already expected this place to be terrible, and she was beginning to have proof of it. She heard sobs behind her. She turned slowly without raising her gaze so as not to meet the dragon's. A girl was weeping. She had brown scales on her forehead that came down to the beginning of her nose. She had long, straight brown hair, and her moist green eyes showed anguish. The dragon was not going to like that. Unobtrusively, Nahia stepped back to stand beside her. She grabbed her hand.

"Take it easy and don't cry. We have to survive," she whispered, trying to imbue some cheer in her and calm her down.

"I'm… trying…" she replied through the sobs she was trying to hold back.

"My name's Nahia. Stay strong," she whispered and squeezed her hand to give her strength.

"Ana …" she replied and wiped her tears off with her sleeve.

Another girl, the brunette with short hair who had arrived in Gorja at the same time as Nahia, approached them unobtrusively.

"My name is Maika. No weeping, or that one will turn us into a piece of ice," she whispered, leaning forward.

Ana stopped sobbing and glanced at Nahia thankfully for comforting her.

Nahia looked at her out of the corner of her eye without raising her head and winked at her.

"That's it. Stay strong."

Now that you've been received and I have done my duty of welcoming you, form five rows. Stand straight, as if you had some honor, and look ahead. Not at me, of course, the dragon messaged.

Looking at one another, they organized themselves according to where they were and formed five rows. The looks on all their faces showed tension and fear. Any mistake might earn them death under the reptilian gaze of the winged monster. Nahia was on the second row, with Ana and Maika beside her. They were a little to the left of the dragon. Once they managed to form the rows, they all stood still and firm with their gaze straight ahead, as it had told them.

Nahia was trying to see where they were, but a dense white mist surrounded them and she could only see the pearl and some parts that looked like rock structures she could not define. The ground they were on was stone and had some strange symbols carved around the pearl, forming a large circle that surrounded it. They were incomprehensible, dragon language. Perhaps they were runes carved with their magic. Aoma had told her it was possible to imbue stone with magic by creating runes. It was an ancient practice, usually to protect a house or precious belongings. Thinking about it made Nahia nervous. She wanted to see what this place was like, but she could not. The fog blocked her view and created a damp environment, cold and glum, which did not help the situation they were in at all.

They waited in formation. Suddenly, from within the fog a new dragon came down to land in front of them. It had appeared out of the blue, giving them the scare of their lives. More than one chosen let out a scream, and several had stepped back in fear. The dragon was red and a little bigger than the blue one, about sixty feet long. Nahia was beginning to realize there were dragons of all different colors and sizes. There had to be a reason, although for now she did not know it and almost preferred not to.

Attention. This is Sergeant Major Irakas-Gorri-Gaizt of the distinguished Drakoros, the Academy of the Dragon Bloods, Sarre-Urdin-Olto introduced.

They all remained silent and still with their gazes on the ground as the blue dragon had told them to.

This year's harvest of humans? the red dragon asked the blue one.

Yes. They have just woken up. They don't look like much. I find them weak. Not apt, in my opinion. If you want, I can reject them and get rid of them.

The red dragon looked at them with narrowed ruby eyes.

I see. We'll have to make do with these wilted fruits this year, although you are right, they are pitiful.

Nahia did not understand how she could be listening to the mental conversation of the two dragons. Unless, that was, they were messaging on purpose to intimidate them. Yes, that had to be it, most certainly. The monsters.

The red dragon studied them again.

You are in the Realm of Cael-Utrum. This is the sixth dragon realm. It is neutral, not ruled by any of the five clans. Here is where the military academy, Drakoros, is located. That is where you are going. I know you do not understand everything I am telling you, but remember it. It is important, the dragon messaged, along with great authority and firmness.

Nahia sighed. That confirmed her fears. She had wished by some chance of fate that they would not end up here. That was not the case. She would have to get used to the idea that she was going to spend the next three years of her life here. She had no other choice. Well, that was if she did not die before then, which was a distinct possibility, as they had just had proof of. She did not wish to be there and least of all to die. A shiver went down her back, and she realized this was her fate now: this place and death.

I guess they are the last to wake up, of all of them? Irakas-Gorri-Gaizt asked Sarre-Urdin-Olto.

They are. Humans are always the last to arrive and recover, Sarre-Urdin-Olto replied, and they all felt the tone of disdain clearly.

I guessed so. Let us not waste time. We are already late. I will take over this group, Guardian of the Gate.

The two dragons saluted one another, bowing their heads.

Irakas-Gorri-Gaizt turned to them while Sarre-Urdin-Olto vanished in the fog.

As is tradition, all who arrive at this distinguished place to join the martial academy will do 'The Climb'. This is a petty acclimatization exercise. It will do you good. You will learn certain things, and I will save myself the trouble of having to explain them, the dragon announced, and its red eyes glowed.

This did not sound at all good to Nahia. What was this climb, and what did the dragon intend with it? She glanced at her fellow chosen. They were all thinking the same thing.

Follow me, humans. Do so without leaving formation and keep the same pace. Show me you are not the most inept of all the races like so many assume. The message did not carry irony but a tiny hope. The dragon meant this.

They followed the red dragon, which moved quite nimbly for its great size. It took them a few moments to adjust the steps they had to take for one of the dragon's as it moved its enormous body on its four strong legs that ended in tremendous claws.

They went through the thick fog, and Nahia felt it soaking her face, hair, and hands, which were uncovered. It made her shiver with cold. They followed the dragon, whose long tail swung from one side to the other. They walked without breaking formation, all keeping their heads down, and by the looks on their faces, with even lower spirits. Nahia had the impression they were like chicks following the wrong mother. At any moment it would turn around, open its mouth, and devour them all with its huge mouth.

Irakas-Gorri-Gaizt led them toward a stone tower. The mist surrounded it but, as they got closer they were able to see that it was square, tall, and military looking. It had to be about sixty feet high. The dragon stopped in front of it. It opened its mouth, and without warning it sent a tremendous flame which swept the base of the tower. The fog vanished upon contact with the fire and they were able to see more of the structure. Then it sent another great flame toward the top of the tower to clean the mist.

They could now see the structure better. Nahia realized that the tower was odd. It was about fifteen feet wide in every direction. It had no windows, and at the top they could see a platform wider than the tower itself, as if it were a flat roof. Placed right and left were two long ramps that went up from the ground about fifteen feet and then ended on the sides of the tower.

Time to start 'The Climb.' Do not disappoint me, humans.

Nahia felt in her stomach that something bad was about to happen, something that would end in death.

Chapter 8

Form two groups, orderly and quickly, Irakas-Gorri-Gaizt commanded them.

The order was simple. But for a group of frightened and inexperienced kids it was not so easy. It created confusion mixed with uncertainty. Some went to one side while the rest went the opposite way. So far so good, but when they saw that the others were not following, they turned back and got mixed up in the middle. Nahia realized this was not going well at all. If they did not fix it at once, the dragon was going to make them pay in blood.

Logan grabbed a couple by the arm with each hand. He told them to stand on either side of an invisible dividing line he drew with his right foot. Once they heeded him, he grabbed two more and repeated it. He went on doing so and pushing whoever got distracted to the corresponding place. He was trying to organize the reigning chaos before the dragon punished them for not carrying out its order as specified. Nahia stood on the side with Logan. She took Ana with her, and Maika joined them.

They finished getting in line. But there were not two equal groups. There were more people in Logan's group than in the other. Since he was organizing them, some had taken him for the leader and more people had joined his half than the other, even after Logan had specifically told them where to stand. They had not paid attention. It was only natural, but not good at that moment.

You have not carried out the order, and one that was quite simple. The message reached them neutrally without anger, simply disappointment.

The dragon's tail moved, and before anyone could react it hit the first five people in Logan's group, who were thrown away and rolled along the rocky ground. Ana grabbed Nahia's hand hard and muffled a scream. Nahia had seen the tail pass right in front of her eyes. It had not struck her by two fingers. Her heart skipped a beat and then galloped so hard she thought it would leap out of her mouth. Maika's eyes were as open as they could go.

The red dragon watched the five unfortunates as they tried to get back on their feet, all sore.

Carry out the order or die, it messaged, but they did not receive it as a threat, just as something that had to be that way, an inexorable truth.

Four of the people struck down managed to stand and ran to join the other group. The last one could not walk from the blow. He started to crawl as best he could, trying to get to where the other four were.

The dragon watched him with dull eyes, like someone who saw something so disappointing he considered it lost. Then it gave off some sort of dull roar.

How pitiful, human. You do not deserve to live. But today I feel generous. I was going to burn you, but I will let you continue your inane existence a little longer.

The poor unfortunate reached the others, who helped him stand and stay on his feet.

The group with that unfortunate in its ranks, go to the ramp on the right of the tower. Quickly, Irakas-Gorri-Gaizt ordered, and the mental message was accompanied by a feeling of urgency.

The group ran to the ramp. Once they got to it, they stopped and stood staring at the great tower rising before them undaunted. Nahia watched them. They were as lost as she was. She felt sorry, just like she did for herself and the horrible situation they were all in so unwillingly.

The rest, go to the left ramp.

Nahia heaved a long sigh. It was her group. Logan and the other chosen began to run, she followed readily, pulling Ana with her. Maika came immediately after. When they reached the foot of the great ramp, she found that the slope was very steep. The two ramps seemed to hold up the sides of the tower. She reconsidered. No, they were not to hold it up, they must be to climb the sides.

At my order, you will go up the ramp and then you will continue climbing to the top of the tower. Whoever does not succeed will not be worthy of walking the Path. You know what happens to those who fail. So, I recommend you make an effort. A great one, or you will never make one again.

"Oh no …." Ana started to sob again.

Nahia looked at her and saw her lovely delicate face shadow over. She felt pity. Ana seemed fragile of spirit. She felt fate was laughing at them: a fragile one in spirit and one in body. How were they going to survive here?

"Don't worry, we'll make it," she promised, although she didn't have much hope they would; in fact, she doubted it very much. She looked at the ramp and then at the vertical rock wall of the tower and the world fell on her. How were they going to climb up there? It was impossible, especially for someone like her, with a weak constitution and barely any physical strength. She looked at Ana, who was not strong either, and then at Maika. She, at least, looked much more prepared in the physical aspect. She might succeed.

Go up. Now, Irakas-Gorri-Gaizt ordered, and the feeling that came with the message was of unquestionable authority.

Both groups, on both sides of the tower, started up the ramps. Very soon they realized the surface was extremely smooth and slippery. It looked wet, as if it had been rained on, although the rest of the area was dry. The most daring ran up at top speed, but they slipped and fell sliding backward and causing the ones behind them to fall. In a moment, the climb became a nightmare. Those who managed to reach halfway up the ramp began to slip and fall backward, taking several others who were behind with them. There were shouts, bumps, protests, and even some sobs.

It is sad to see how, indeed, humans are the most incompetent of the eight races. This simple exercise makes it evident, Irakas-Gorri-Gaizt messaged to them, along with a feeling of great disappointment.

Nahia was trying to go up the ramp following Maika, who was doing much better than her. She looked around and realized that almost everyone was doing better than her. Even Ana overtook her on the right. She felt ashamed and tried not to lose hope. She found herself struggling to stay on her feet, so she dropped down onto the ramp. That was the only thing she could think if. A girl slid past her without control. Nahia tried to grab her, but she did not manage to get a hold of her arm. The poor girl ended up at the foot of the ramp with a big blow. She looked at the dragon out of the corner of her eye and thought it was looking down at her. Nahia felt panic running freely through her body. She got up as if a snake had bitten her and began to climb again.

Shortly after, she had to throw herself on the ground again. Things were bad for all of them. Only Logan and a few others had managed to get past halfway up the ramp. Since she had to go up, Nahia started crawling up the ramp like a snake. To her surprise, she began to overtake several who were trying to climb half crouched and were making every effort not to slide, without much success. They slowed themselves down with their hands while their feet slid down. At moments they managed to stop and climb much faster than her, but soon their feet slipped again and the difficulties returned.

One of the large boys in the lead beside Logan slipped and started coming down backward. He was slipping while he tried to keep his balance by waving his arms. He was trying not to fall and at the same time stop his retreat, but he did not manage to. He took a blond boy with him and a red-haired girl who were unable to move away, and they all ended up in a tangle at the foot of the ramp.

Nahia continued her ascent pressed against the ramp and realized that, although slower, at least she didn't slip. Her clothes and the weight of her body seemed to exert enough friction to keep her from sliding. This puzzled her. She felt the surface of the ramp and looked at it closely. It was not wet from rain, they had applied some substance to it, a slippery liquid.

"Throw yourselves on the ground," she told Ana and Maika who were ahead of her and holding onto one another. At times it worked, but not completely.

Ana looked at her and nodded repeatedly while struggling not to fall down. She let go of Maika desperately and threw herself on the floor of the ramp. Maika started to slide sideways and seeing herself lost threw herself on the ground too. They both broke their slide down the ramp a moment later. They were almost at Nahia's level.

"We have to snake up," Nahia told them, gesturing so they would understand amid the reigning chaos on the ramp.

Maika seemed to get her meaning, because she began to go up like a snake. Ana started doing the same. After a moment, half a dozen of them were going up that way.

"Everyone on the ground, against the ramp!" Nahia shouted at them.

The two girls with black scales were a little further up, but when they heard her they took her advice. They flattened themselves on the ramp and began to snake upward. Seeing them, other boys imitated them and threw themselves on the floor.

"Crawl up!" Nahia shouted to the others who had not paid attention to her. One of them rolled down without heeding her. Logan dropped flat on the floor and with him, others who were in the lead.

The whole group was writhing like water snakes going up the slippery ramp. The last who had fallen soon reached Nahia, who although she was making progress, went slower than the rest. She raised her gaze and saw Logan and another blond boy had reached the end of the ramp.

"Let's help them," Logan told the blond boy as he pointed at the ones starting to arrive.

The boy nodded.

They both prepared to lend a hand to those arriving. Little by little, they all reached the end of the ramp.

"Come on, Nahia, we're waiting for you here," Maika said, looking at her with her brown eyes as she waved for her to keep going.

Ana reached the top and held on to the wall. Her face showed great fear.

"This is a nightmare..." she commented.

Nahia realized she was the last. She felt terribly ashamed of herself, but she did not give up and went on crawling. She already knew she was a lot weaker than the others, even poor Ana. This did not come as a surprise. Any cattle breeder or shepherd, not to speak of miners, had a much more developed physique than hers. What could she do? She would have to manage somehow. She thought of Aoma. Her grandmother would tell her to keep going and to never give up. The situation might be difficult, desperate, insufferable even, but defeat only came if one gave up.

She continued snaking upward; she had to follow her grandmother's wise teachings. Nahia could not fail her.

"Never give up, always fight and keep going," she muttered under her breath. If she failed, it would not be for lack of trying with her whole being. She clenched her jaw and moved one arm in front of the other, pushing with her feet and dragging her body up the ramp.

"Give me your hand," she heard Logan say.

Nahia raised her gaze and realized she had done it. She was at the top of the ramp. She took Logan's hand. Her own hand was lost in his firm grip. With one heave, Logan lifted her to the ledge at the end of the ramp as if she were as light as a rag doll, as if she weighed nothing. This boy was really strong.

"Hold on here," he told her and put his hand on a projection in the wall of the tower.

Nahia managed to stay on her feet, leaning against the wall. It seemed a real achievement to have reached the top. There was only one small problem. Now the worst began—they had to climb the vertical rock wall of the tower.

"Come on, we have to get going, the dragon is watching us," Maika warned them, and she began to climb up the wall. Nahia watched how she did it. She was putting her hands and toes on uneven projections in the vertical wall.

Ana wiped her nose with her blouse sleeve and followed Maika.

"This is terrible...." she said, and her green eyes moistened and dulled.

It seemed the wall was not smooth on purpose. Nahia narrowed her eyes and studied the tower wall. It had been built by placing blocks of rock that stood out at some points throughout the wall. She guessed they were support points for climbing. They were quite separate and scattered. It was not going to be easy, but at least it was not an impossible task as she had believed at first when she saw the wall stretching up so high and vertical. They had a chance.

She looked at her own hands and feet. She was going to need them, a lot. And her legs and arms. This worried her. She had very little strength in them and still less endurance for long tasks. Climbing that tower was going to take her an eternity. Her body was not going to hold up. She noticed her comrades as they climbed as best as they could, holding on to every projection, ledge, and hole with all their being. They were staking their lives, and they were all very much aware. She saw how the girls seemed to be doing okay; they were more nimble and less heavy than the boys, who were having trouble.

"Will you be able to climb?" Logan asked, still at the top of the ramp.

"I don't know... to the top? I doubt it," she shook her head. She remembered how in her short life she had tried many times to climb trees and some wall or another. The result had always been the same. She ended up on the ground with a good blow and her bottom sore. Her hands, arms, and legs were not strong enough to hold up even her weak body, which was quite light. Hope began to wane, and her spirit left her. The more she thought about it, the more the climb seemed impossible for her.

Remember that the weak ones will not survive. Stopping to help them is only obvious proof of a lack of character and leadership. No one must help the weaklings. Only a being without character stops to help another with a weak body or spirit, Irakas-Gorri-Gaizt's message reached them.

"That's for us," Logan told her as he quickly checked the dragon out of the corner of his eye.

"Yeah, you keep going. Go with the others. Don't help me, or it's capable of incinerating you."

"What he's saying isn't right. I don't agree. My parents taught me to help whoever needed it."

Nahia nodded.

"And it's the right thing to do, but we're no longer with our loved ones. Now we're in one of the dragon realms. We must follow their rules and orders, or else we'll die. Go, I beg you, keep climbing."

Logan sighed.

"Hold on hard and follow me. I'll tell you where to put your weight."

"Thank you, I'm following. You go up."

Chapter 9

While Nahia grabbed the first ledge to climb, the other group on the other side of the tower was already climbing. Nahia wondered how they were doing. Probably better than she was. She would rather not know: she already had enough trouble.

Logan began to climb nimbly with amazing speed and ease, as if he had spent his life climbing towers. She followed him and at once realized she had great trouble securing herself flat against the wall and not falling backward. How were the others doing it? It was not easy. She not only had to find support points, but she also had to hold on tight and maintain her balance to avoid falling down. And the satchel on her back did not help. The only thing she could think of was that all the others had spent a lot of time climbing trees, walls, and roofs in their villages. Otherwise she could not understand it.

"Come on, you can do it!" Maika cheered her, already halfway up the tower. Ana was slightly behind, but she seemed to be climbing quite well.

"Yeah…" was all Nahia could say in return as she panted from the effort, and she had only climbed fifteen feet.

"You just follow me, it's easier than it looks. Flatten yourself against the wall at all times," Logan tried to cheer and advise her.

Nahia held on to a jutting stone with both hands and put her toes where she remembered Logan had done. Her memory was good, at least that was something, and she took comfort in the thought. She started to feel sore, not only her fingers and toes but also her legs and arms which hurt more and more. She looked down and saw she had climbed pretty high, at least for what she thought she was capable, and took courage from the fact. Luckily she did not have a fear of heights, and that comforted her too. She was not that flawed after all. Just a little physically weak.

She kept climbing up, trying to mimic every one of Logan's movements as precisely as she could. Suddenly she felt very hot, and she freaked out. Was her condition striking now? Here, at this moment? If it was that, she was dead. She would fall to the ground from that height and would break her back and head. She felt anguish clenching her throat. She had trouble breathing and felt the heat in her chest.

"No, not now," she muttered, trying to control herself. She took a deep breath through her nose and let out a long exhale. She repeated the breathing exercise and then for a third time and felt a little better. She was no longer so hot, and this eased her a little. Had it been the beginning of one of her seizures? She stayed flattened against the wall, holding on with enough strength to not fall backward and without holding too hard in order to save her energy. No, it had not been one of her seizures. The heat she had felt came from her effort. She was sweating down her forehead and arms. It was because of the climb, not her condition. Her body was protesting, and she understood the reason very well.

My patience is running out. You are the most regrettable group of humans I have received in ten years! Climb! Reach the upper platform!

The mental message hit Nahia's mind hard, and she had to grab on with everything she had so as not to lose her balance.

There was a desperate scream and a boy who was ahead of Logan fell backward.

"No!" Logan cried as he tried to grab him.

He could not and the boy fell against the ramp with a dull sound, almost hollow, before he bounced and ended on the floor at the base of the tower. There were cries of horror and muffled screams.

One less weakling who will not travel the Path of Dragons. We have already lost two, and you have not even finished a simple exercise of initiation. It seems to me that very few of you, if any, will survive the whole Path. I had hoped this year we would have a better harvest, but I can see it is not going to be so. You are not worthy. Climb! Go!

Horrified by what had just happened and fearing the dragon's wrath, they all continued climbing. Those who were higher up managed to reach the platform, and they lay there, looking down. They tried to cheer and help the ones arriving.

Nahia had passed the middle of the height of the tower, and she thought she had achieved the greatest of landmarks. Unfortunately, her achievement was worthless. She had to reach the top, or the dragon would finish her. The problem was, tired as she was and with her whole-body aching, she was not going to be able to make it.

"Keep going, don't give up. You can do it," Logan told her as he held on with one hand and waved at her with the other so she would keep climbing.

Nahia was grateful for the encouragement. It helped her not feel so bad for not being able to climb like the others. She felt so frail, so worthless... a burden.

"Keep going, Logan, don't wait for me."

The young man looked at her blankly for a moment. Then he shook his head.

"Humans help one another. At least in my region. I'll wait for you, just keep climbing."

That showed Logan's good heart and she was very grateful for it, but it made her feel terrible. She did not have the necessary energy; she was going to be a burden on all of them. This test was just the beginning: how was she going to survive when things got worse? And what was even worse, she would be putting in danger anyone noble, like Logan, who wanted to help her.

Maika had stopped three thirds up the tower and was waiting for her.

"If I made it this far, you can too," she told her and waved her hand for courage.

Ana was moaning as she climbed, but with each moan she managed to make some way. It was a weird technique, but it seemed to work.

Nahia fought against despair. She breathed deeply through the nose three times, letting the air go out in long breaths, and she managed to feel slightly better. She raised her gaze and saw Logan and Maika waiting for her. If she did not go on, the dragon was going to lose all its patience and would incinerate them both, and it would be her fault. She had to keep going. She thought of her grandmother. Nahia had to make it, for her.

"Coming..." was all she could say as she placed her right toes on the jutting stone where she remembered Logan had set his. She started to get closer to him. The light eyes of the dark-haired young man watched her with concern. No doubt he could see that her arms trembled with every effort.

"Shake them," Logan told her, and he shook his right arm. One in which she could see strong muscles she did not have. Hers seemed to lack anything besides nerves.

She shook her right arm as Logan was indicating while she held tight with her left and mostly her toes. She was surprised that her feet were holding out. She did not know why it was so, but it was a salvation. Her hands were killing her, but her feet seemed comfortable stepping on those projections on the rock wall and bearing her weight. It seemed amazing, to say the least, but she did not give it more attention because she did not want to jinx it so that they suddenly gave out. If her toes gave out, she would be killed.

After shaking her arms, she shook her legs.

"Much better," she told Logan and went on climbing. She knew that would only help for a short while, but she decided to take advantage of it. The least breath might mean the difference between living or dying on that never-ending tower.

It was not long before she had to stop again to shake out her arms and legs. This time the rested feeling lasted less time, but she again used the advantage to climb a little more.

She continued with that strategy and gained height. Logan and Maika were watching her and cheering. Ana reached the end and they helped her get onto the platform where she let out a final moan.

Maika was next in reaching the summit.

"I'm already here. Now it's your turn," she said, cheering Nahia, waving her arms so she would climb faster.

Logan also reached the end, but he did not get up onto the platform. He stayed just below, waiting for her.

"Here's my hand," he told her and reached down for her.

Nahia saw the extended hand and sighed. She seemed to be so close that her hopes rose. She thought of reaching out for it, and at that moment she seemed to be a world away. She wanted to reach his hand and take it, for Logan to hold her and help her reach the platform, but her body could go no further. She was exhausted. Her hands were cramped and hurt so much. Her arms and legs were not even responding, they seemed lifeless. She was only staying on the wall by her toes, which in some inexplicable way, were still firm, as if they had not climbed that enormous tower almost to its end.

She looked down and the height was tremendous. She could not explain how she had been capable of climbing so far without falling and killing herself. It had to be because of the fear she had of the dragon as it watched her from below, and Logan's help. Never in her life would she have imagined she would be able to do something like this, so demanding for her physique. She was very close to getting there. The problem was that her body could give nothing more.

The exercise is over. Whoever is not on the platform will not see a new dawn, Irakas-Gorri-Gaizt's message reached them all.

Several of those who were up stepped back toward the center of the platform, as if to prevent the dragon from thinking they had not made it.

After a moment, they all withdrew from the edges, including those on the other side who had already climbed all the way. Only Maika remained lying on the corner with her arms stretched down. Logan did not move either, in spite of the dragon's deadly threat.

Nahia knew the dragon would not forgive her. She was going to die, in a horrendous way. Something lit up inside her, a mixture of fire and rage. Her inner fire she already knew, and it was not good. No good at all. Rage sometimes came out unwillingly, as if a small volcano exploded inside her. This time both combined. She felt her arms and legs begin to burn. The fire was followed by a burst of energy which recharged her limbs with strength and vitality. Her hands stopped being cramped, all other cramps vanished, and she felt strong.

She looked at the dragon that was spreading its wings. It was coming for her. To kill her. Her prediction was going to be fulfilled on her first day of being here. She was not going to survive even a day. Her body reacted and, propelled by fear, she began to climb toward Logan at top speed. She was going even faster than what the young man himself had. How that could be she did not understand, and she did not have time to reason it. She concentrated on climbing where she had seen Logan go. She had to escape from certain death. Her body knew and was propelling her.

Logan saw that Nahia was reaching him. With a look of surprise, he withdrew the hand Nahia no longer needed and climbed onto the platform with great ease. He stood beside Maika, looking down. Nahia was coming up now as if she were an expert climber, something she was not by far, mimicking Logan's every move. She felt a strong gust of wind reaching her back. It was the dragon, flying toward her. She did not want to look—if she did it might distract her and she would fall or cramp and the dragon would shred her to pieces. She clenched her jaw and kept going as fast as her flaming body would allow. She reached Logan and Maika. The arms of both reached down to grab her and pull her up, lifting her onto the platform.

Nahia put her feet on the firm surface and her legs gave out. The fire that had propelled her to the top had gone out inside her. She collapsed. Ana grabbed her so she would not fall backward, and she remained on the floor, unable to get up. Her arms did not hold her either.

"I did it..." she mumbled, exhausted, and lay on the rock's cold surface.

Chapter 10

The dragon rose above the tower, brushing the point where Nahia had managed to climb up onto the platform. It looked at them as it beat its great wings. It had not killed her by a heartbeat. Nahia let out a long deep sigh of relief. She was up. Alive. She could not believe it. She had been sure the dragon was going to kill her. She had been spared but did not know how. If she were not exhausted, she would have leapt and cried in joy. Unfortunately, she could do neither. Simply moving her head became a colossal effort, she was so tired.

"I told you you'd make it." Maika sat down beside her, crossing her legs and smiling shyly.

"It nearly hit you with its claws," Ana said as she made signs with her hand that Nahia had escaped a horrific fate.

Logan remained standing while he gazed at her in a reserved manner.

"I'm glad you made it," he said at last.

"Thanks… for your help… I wouldn't have done it if you hadn't guided me along the wall."

"It was nothing. The least I could do. I wasn't going to leave you to your fate."

"Thank you too, girls…"

"You're welcome," Ana said, making light of it with a wave of her hand.

"Before, on the ramp, you helped us. A favor for a favor," Maika said, convinced.

"That one… didn't like that you helped me…" said Nahia, watching Irakas-Gorri-Gaizt fly in circles above them.

"Doesn't it look like a huge vulture flying over carrion?" Maika asked, wrinkling her nose and frowning.

"We're people, not carrion," replied Logan in a dry tone, also watching the dragon.

"Not for dragons. For them we're only slaves or food," Ana said in a bitter tone.

"Or soldiers to die for them," said a boy with freckles and curly hair the color of a pumpkin who had heard them. He was angry.

Nahia looked around, barely moving. Most of the group were lying on the ground or sitting, scattered along the flat stone roof of the tower. They were resting and recovering from the tough experience. The area where they sat was large, a lot larger than Nahia would have imagined while she was climbing. A couple of dragons would fit there. She noticed she was having a hard time breathing. She was forced to take fast and short breaths, and when she did her lungs stung. It was a small torture she wished would soon go away. A light breeze lulled them, and Nahia was grateful for it. It made her feel better. She stayed there lying on the ground, trying to recover her breath and rest her battered body. The cold up there ended up soothing her body somewhat, and she appreciated it.

"Look where we are, it's awesome…" a thin girl with curly brown hair said. She was standing near the edge, pointing right behind them to the south.

"It's horrible," said another girl, this time a blonde who shaded her eyes with her hands.

Maika and Ana rose and Logan turned to look. Nahia made an effort and got onto her side to try and see, but she could only see the edge of the platform they were on.

"Awesome and terrible at the same time," Maika said anxiously, looking upset.

"There's no escaping this place…" Ana realized with a sigh.

Logan said nothing, but his face was troubled.

"What is it?" Nahia asked, already guessing it was nothing good.

"We'd better help you see it. You can't appreciate it from there," Logan made a sign for Maika to help him. Between the two, they picked up Nahia by the arms and lifted her until she could see.

"Oh… wow…" Nahia mumbled. From up there she could see the ground below them at the back of the tower. It traced an irregular round shape and ended in a cliff. But it was not a regular cliff, not by far. There were no ground rocks, no sea, and no lake. What they could see was something that could not be, something that made no sense. They saw clouds, a white padded mass that extended not only around the cliff, but outward covering everything—the tower and the ground around it, which ended in a precipice that looked on the sky. "We are… in the air … above…" Nahia realized.

"It's one of the dragon realms in the sky, yes …" Logan confirmed with a nod.

"This is madness … those are clouds, and they are lower than we are," Maika stared with wide eyes.

"And there, in the distance, through the clouds, there's blue…" Ana could barely believe what they were seeing, and her face showed it.

"It must be the sky. It's… unbelievable," Maika shook her head, unable to believe her eyes.

"Then this place must be one of the islands in the sky, one of those floating among the clouds. That's what is said where I grew up," Logan reasoned.

"Yeah… the Drakonid warlock who took me to Gorja told me we'd be brought up here," Nahia nodded. "I didn't want to believe him …well, rather I'd hoped it wasn't true, but I can see he was telling the truth."

"Amazing. How do the dragons manage to keep them from falling out of the sky?" Maika wondered out loud, scratching her head.

"Powerful magic," Ana replied, looking terrified.

"Then the fog that surrounded us below and didn't let us see, isn't fog really, they're actually clouds," Nahia guessed.

Logan nodded.

"It looks that way," Maika agreed.

"There's no escaping from here. Whoever tries to escape will fall from the sky to die on the land we were born on." Ana heaved a deep sigh.

Nahia felt faint.

"Let me lie down, please, I don't feel well."

Maika and Logan helped her down gently.

"Rest, it'll be good for you," Maika said, stroking her forehead and smiling.

"Thank you…." Nahia wanted to, but everything she had been through and finding out they were on one of the islands in the sky was too much.

"It's horrible …" Ana kept saying. She was weeping now. Maika went over to her and hugged her.

"Everything will be all right. We're alive," she told her to cheer her up.

Little by little, they all realized where they were and what Ana had deduced. There was no escape. If falling from the tower meant death, falling from that place was falling a thousand times more and dying a thousand times worse. Their faces shadowed and their spirits dulled. While they were all trying to digest this terrifying realization, Nahia focused on recovering. There was nothing she could do about the situation right then. The smartest thing to do was rest and try to survive. The fact that they were up there did not mean that they were dead. Not yet. She had to recover to go on living. The cold breeze returned and with it she felt better, relieved.

Maika followed the edge of the cliff with her eyes.

"Look there," she said, pointing to her left.

"It looks like we're not the only unfortunates forced to climb a tower," Ana said, looking toward where Maika was pointing.

Logan also turned to look. His close-mouthed face showed some surprise.

Nahia made an effort on the ground to get onto her side and look in that direction. She was able to glimpse another tower, almost identical to the one they were on. A dragon was flying over it just like Irakas-Gorri-Gaizt was doing. On the top of the tower was another group of people, although they looked quite strange. To Nahia they seemed stronger than they were, and she was puzzled by one thing: they had horns on their head. Indeed, some had horns like a bull's. Others like a ram's. It was that, or she had lost her mind from the effort.

"Who are they?" Ana asked.

"I'd say they are Tauruk-Kapro," Maika said, watching them with her head to one side. "From what I know, they have those kinds of horns and they are big. I can't see their faces from here, but they look like large bulls and rams on two legs... so they have to be of the Tauruk-Kapro race..."

Logan, who was also watching them, nodded.

"I've never seen one, but from what I've been told, they fit the description."

"They are most... intimidating," Nahia was staring at them, and she was getting a feeling of danger.

"They're said to be very strong. They're also supposed to have bad tempers," Maika explained. "Although they might be malicious rumors."

"They do look strong," Logan calculated.

"They might be good and only look rough," Ana said wishfully with a shrug.

"Yeah, like the dragons," Nahia replied.

"Oops, I think you're right there," Ana said, changing her mind.

"If they're on that tower, it means they're going through the same thing as us," Logan guessed. "I think we'll meet them soon."

"You think so?" Maika was surprised.

"I don't know for sure, they might keep us separate. Who knows what the dragons have planned."

"Certainly us humans don't," Nahia replied, beginning to feel somewhat better.

"To our right there's another tower… with a different race on it …" Maika found as she continued exploring their surroundings.

Nahia and Logan turned to look to the right. They glimpsed what looked like human beings like them, only they seemed to have folded wings on their backs.

"Those are Fatum, without a doubt," Logan said.

"They have to be, I agree. They're the only ones who have wings out of all the races," Ana agreed.

Nahia shifted on the ground until she managed to get in a position that allowed her to see better without standing up. She had to look between the legs of several of her companions who were also watching the tower in the east. From what she was able to glimpse, that tower was very similar to their own and to the one the Tauruk-Kapro had climbed. She noticed that the Fatum looked very much like humans. It was said that of all the races in Kraido, they were the ones most like the humans, and so they looked to Nahia. The two main differences were that they had wings on their back similar to those of a butterfly or dragonfly and that they had pointier ears than humans. She could not see their ears from afar, but she glimpsed the wings. She found them most singular and interesting. They were like flying humans, only they were not allowed to fly. The dragon flying over their tower would annihilate them if they dared to try, which they could not do anyway since their wings were clipped. Or so it was said.

"They look like cousins of ours," Maika commented in a cheerful tone.

"If it weren't for their wings, they could pass for humans," Logan agreed.

"Don't they look thinner than us? Or is it me ..." Ana asked.

"Good observation. Yes, they look thinner and not as tall as us," Maika had shaded her eyes to see better.

"I guess that a race with wings, who once upon a time must have been able to use them, would have to be light," Logan said as he studied them.

Nahia was watching the Fatum on their tower, and that led her to the reason why the dragons might have placed several of those towers. Did they have one for each race? Maybe. But what for? Why not use one in turns if this was an initiation exercise? It might have another function. The world of dragons was a mystery to Nahia. She would have to discover it. Well, that was if she survived long enough, something she doubted after what she'd seen.

"This is all quite strange ..." she commented, thoughtfully.

"Do you mean the other races?" Logan turned to her.

"Yeah, but it's not only that. I mean the towers, their location, and this island in the air. Tell me, what do you see below in front of us?"

"The great white pearl is in the center down there," Maika said, pointing.

"What do you see around it?" Nahia was feeling better, but her strength was very limited and she decided to save it just in case. She did not stand up.

Maika and Logan studied the surroundings of the pearl from the height they were at, getting close to the edge. Then they went back to Nahia.

"There are six towers around the pearl, counting ours," Logan counted. "And they're located at the same distance from one another. They make a full circle around the pearl."

"And a different race has climbed each tower," said Maika, who rubbed her chin in thought.

"There's more. We are in a round area surrounded by abysses," Logan said.

"Like another island?" Nahia was surprised.

"Almost, there's a bridge that joins where we are with what looks like a larger stretch of land."

"Yeah, to the north," Maika nodded.

"And we're to the south, right?" Nahia was not sure.

Logan looked toward the sun.

"It's hard to tell from up here, but I'd say yes, we're south."

"Then this is like an arrival port," Nahia reasoned.

"If you think of the clouds as the sea and the portal as a ship, yeah, it is a port," Maika smiled.

Logan made a sign that it did make sense.

"Hmmm … it appears that each tower has another one in front, on the other side of the sphere," Ana pointed out.

"Yeah, and in front of ours is the worst of the races," Maika said.

"The Drakonids?" Nahia asked.

"Exactly. I can't see them very well because of the distance, but they are Drakonids. Dragon heads and scales, that I can see."

Logan nodded and crossed his arms.

"They're on the tower directly in front of us, and a dragon is flying over them."

"Although they're faithful servants of their masters, it looks like they get the same treatment as the other races," Ana said.

"I'll have to see that to believe it," Nahia said, guessing they would receive preferential treatment from the dragons.

"On the other side of the pearl and to the left is a tower with a most interesting race," Maika commented.

Nahia was already looking there. Curiosity got the better of her. It was one thing to hear about the races in her village and a very different one to see them there. It was like mythology becoming real. She had rolled over and managed a better angle of vision between the legs of a tall brown boy. What she saw on that tower made her jaw drop. Those did not look human, or cousins in any form. They were lions, tigers, and panthers, but they were standing on two feet. For a moment she thought that the position she was in was playing tricks on her. It could not be that they stood erect like humans.

"That is indeed strange and interesting. The feline race," Logan commented as he watched them. "I always thought they couldn't be real."

"They're the Felidae, and from what it looks like, they're pretty real," Maika commented, straining her neck to see better.

"I can't believe they walk upright like us. They look like real tigers and lions," Ana said, holding her face with her hands.

"They're a part-feline, part-humanoid race," Logan commented. "They're said to be truly fierce."

"That I believe," Maika said as she watched them with narrowed eyes.

"I'm not sure I want to meet a walking lion or tiger..." Ana commented. "It might bite off my head."

"Let's hope not," Nahia said, understanding Ana's fear.

"They're a slave race, like us. They won't be that different..." Maika said.

Logan did not say anything one way or the other. He simply studied them from a distance.

"Well, in my opinion we still have the most singular race of all left," Maika said, pointing at the tower to the right on the other side of the pearl.

Nahia crawled on the ground, seeking a way to see the race on the tower. She pushed away the feet of a girl who had stood in front of her to look.

"The Scarlatum," said Logan, already watching them.

Nahia finally managed to see them on their tower. The first thing that surprised her was that their skin was different shades of a deep purple-red. The second thing was their horns, curved and pointy. Their physiognomy was similar to that of humans. She found them strange and striking.

"In my village they say you must never trust one of them," said Maika.

"Why not?" Nahia did not know much about this race. From what her grandmother had told her, they were smart and attractive. Everything the Tauruk-Kapro were not.

"They're very good at captivating and deception," Ana said, "Or so they say."

"Perhaps it's only a bad reputation. It's better not to make hasty conclusions," Logan said, calling for prudence.

"Fables and myths have a base in reality. You should heed them," Maika said.

Logan bowed his head and said nothing more.

"Now that I think about it... we're missing two, aren't we?" Nahia asked. "Do you see two other towers?"

Maika and Logan scanned the surroundings.

"No, only six towers," Maika confirmed.

"With six races," Logan added.

"And the other two?"

Maika scratched her head thoughtfully.

"From what I've heard, the dragons don't use the Tergnomus and Exarbor for war."

"They don't? Why's that?" Nahia asked blankly. "Why use the rest of us and not those two races?"

"The Tergnomus are very small. The dragons despise them for their small size. They're not good fighters. They use them mainly for mining, which they're good at," Logan explained.

"They also despise the Exarbor for their slow movement," said Ana. "They're a mix between a tree and a human being. They live very long, but they're slow and barely have any agility. They're not good for war and catch fire too easily."

Nahia bowed her head.

"It makes sense. Well, from the point of view of a dragon, I mean."

"A horrible point of view," said Ana.

Nahia and Maika nodded. They all agreed on that.

The time has come to get off the tower. Everyone, get ready, they received Irakas-Gorri-Gaizt's message, which took them by surprise. Several lost their balance and fell on the ground of the terrace. Luckily, none went over the edge.

"Oh no..." Nahia felt her stomach clenching. She did not have any strength to climb down.

The red dragon began to circle down from the sky, and without warning it headed to the center of the tower where they all were.

"Move back!" Logan warned, seeing that the dragon was going to land on top of them.

"Run!" cried Maika, pointing at the descending dragon.

Chapter 11

Nahia began to crawl along the roof platform as she had done up the ramp to escape the clawed legs of the enormous dragon. Her arms were very tired. Her legs responded slightly better, so she used them to push herself forward. Around her they were all running and screaming, seeing the winged monster fall upon them.

"To the corners! Stay in the corners!" Logan was shouting as he personally withdrew, together with Ana and Maika.

Nahia reached the edge and stopped. She looked below and saw the clouds covering the lower part of the tower. If she moved forward any more she would fall over and that would be her end.

They all ran to the corners and sides of the terrace roof while the dragon landed in the middle, raising a whirlwind of wind with its awesome wings. So that these did not reach them and push them off the roof, most threw themselves on the floor. They held on as best they could so as not to be dragged off. Whoever did not hold on ran a serious risk of being carried away by the strength of the gust of wind the dragon's wings caused.

That's the way I like it, insignificant humans. Prostrate yourselves. I see you are learning how to behave toward your masters. Learn the lesson well, Irakas-Gorri-Gaizt messaged to them as it folded its wings.

No one moved. They all remained flat on the ground along the four edges of the terrace. Nahia noticed that, on the next tower, the dragon that controlled the Fatum had also landed in the middle of the terrace roof. She guessed the six dragons were doing the same. She managed to see the Tauruk-Kapro tower, and it was the same case as hers. The Fatum and the Tauruk-Kapro were on the ground like them. Seeing the dragons standing on the towers, she realized that those pillars were actually watchtowers for the dragons. From up there, they watched and controlled the entrance to their domains in that realm in the air.

All of a sudden, they heard a rocky crack and under Irakas-Gorri-Gaizt a rectangle opened in the middle of the terrace. The size of the square was nine feet by nine, and it was directly under the huge body of the dragon, which stood on its four powerful legs. It was still looking down at the white pearl below, in the center of the place they had arrived that was shaped like a circle.

Crawl to the opening and go down it. Everyone, down. Now, Irakas-Gorri-Gaizt ordered.

Aware that if it had to repeat the order someone was going to die, the group started to crawl toward the opening. Nahia stayed behind, hoping to be the last one. The longer she had to recover, the more chances she would have to survive what came next. Ana and Maika stayed with her, looking worried. Logan went forward, but when he saw that they were not following he stopped to wait for them.

The first ones to arrive under the dragon moved forward with uncertain looks and fearful movements. They reached the opening.

"There are several ropes going down," the first one commented to those beside him. The message traveled back, passing from one to another in whispers until it reached Nahia, who was immobile where she was.

"Will you be able to go down a rope?" Maika asked her.

"I don't know, but I'm sure it's better that climbing up a rock wall."

"Or going down one…" Ana added, looking disgusted.

"Yeah. I'm sure I wouldn't have managed…." Just thinking about it gave her gooseflesh.

The first ones started down the ropes.

Fast and daring. The slow and cowards will not walk the Path.

The threat had immediate impact, and the group hastened to go down. Those who reached the opening quickly determined who was going down next. Nahia had no choice but to start crawling toward the descent. Logan went before her, and Ana and Maika went with her. They arrived under the dragon's body. No sooner had they entered its shadow when Nahia saw how terribly large and powerful those evil-hearted creatures were. Crawling under its body, she felt like a worm under a powerful eagle. Suddenly, all her hope dwindled—there was no possible way for a human to defeat such a beast. Dreaming of it was simply crazy.

They reached the opening; they were the last four. Logan looked inside and felt one of the ropes.

"Tear a couple of strips off your shirt and protect your hands with them. That rope will burn them," he told them and showed them how.

Ana, Maika, and Nahia imitated him. They tore their shirts, and with two strips they protected the palms of their hands as best they could, wrapping them in the pieces of cloth.

"I'll go first. Do what I do," Logan told them and started down, holding onto one of the ropes.

He began to descend. Ana looked at Nahia, and with a look of fear she grabbed the same rope as Logan and started down.

"Hold tight," Nahia told her, fearing she might fall.

Ana nodded. Then she looked at Logan. He held on with one hand while with the other he indicated how to pass the rope between his legs so as to break the fall with them wrapped around it. Maika and Nahia did not miss a thing. Maika went down next, doing what Logan had shown them.

Nahia looked down. She could see the three going down slowly. She was about to start and then stopped; she did not feel at all sure she could do it.

Time is up, human. Must you always be the last one? Are you testing my patience? I assure you, I do not have any, the dragon's message reached her threateningly.

Her head hurt as if someone had stuck a red-hot iron rod in it. That was not a message for everyone. The dragon had sent it to her alone. How she was so sure she did not know, but she was certain. She had to hurry. She grabbed the rope Logan was going down along with one hand, then with the other, and she started down. The pull she felt in her arms was followed by a sharp pain that almost made her let go of her hold and fall. But she withstood the suffering by clenching her jaw, and she held firm. She put the rope between her legs the way Logan had told them and looked down. She could see Maika, even Ana, but she could no longer see Logan. It was too dark inside the tower. The light only came in through the upper opening and the dragon's body covered it, preventing the sun rays from entering.

She started down the rope. She had the feeling of having done this when she was younger, although she did not remember when or where. This feeling gave her some optimism, which vanished as soon as the darkness swallowed her and her arms began to hurt too much.

"You have to hold on ..." she muttered under her breath, clenching her jaw.

She could not see them, but she knew that Maika, Ana, and

Logan were going down below her, not far. So, with this certainty in her head, she went on down. She felt the thick, rough rope scraping her hands and legs. Thank goodness Logan had shared the idea of protecting their palms, or else by now she would have them all raw. To her surprise her legs were holding up pretty well, perhaps because she had to use her thighs, which she had not used much on the way up. Perhaps it was because she was so light.

She went on down. Suddenly, in the midst of the reigning darkness, a scream was heard, followed by a dull blow. Someone had fallen. It could not have been Maika, Ana, or Logan, because the scream had sounded much lower. Nahia wished that whoever it was had not been killed.

The descent became difficult. Her arms hurt terribly, and the protection around her hands had ended up disintegrating. She felt the rope scraping her, taking off skin and even bits of flesh. Despite everything, she refused to give up. She went on down. Soon the pain in her arms and hands became insufferable. Even so, she continued going down. She did not give up. Giving up meant death, and she was not going to die. She had to avoid death, as she had decided. She would not give the dragons the satisfaction of failing and dying. No, she would fight to her last breath.

She tried not to yield with all her being, to stay on the rope. But her body betrayed her. Her strength ended. She had nothing left, and was absolutely empty from the effort she had made. Her hands and arms gave, and then her legs.

She fell. It was her end. She would crash against the rocky ground at the base of the tower.

She screamed, cursing the dragons for killing her.

A sea of arms stopped her fall.

She never touched the ground.

"Are you all right?" Maika asked as they set her on the ground.

"Yeah... you stopped my fall...." Nahia could see nothing; everything was very dark.

"We knew where you were coming down," Ana told her.

"Thank you... thank you all..."

"We humans have to help each other and survive," Logan said.

"Yeah, we have to help one another and survive," Maika said firmly.

"Let's all work together to survive," said Ana.

There were other voices Nahia did not recognize that joined those of her friends who had just saved her life.

They heard a new crack and the sound of a wall scraping on another as it slid to one side. An opening like a door appeared in front of them. The light came in, and with it, part of the cloudy mist.

Come out of the tower. Stand in line in front of it. The introductory exercise has finished, Irakas-Gorri-Gaizt's message reached them, along with a feeling of great disappointment.

They came out in front of the tower, thankful for the light and warmth of the sun, although it was chilly. They formed up like they had before, but the wounded were held between two comrades. Maika and Ana were holding up Nahia. The boy who had fallen was brought out between two other boys and were holding him in line. He had not been killed, but seeing the way he could not lean on his right foot, Nahia guessed his ankle or leg was broken. Another boy was also brought out between two others. Nahia looked at Ana questioningly.

"It's the boy who hurt his arm at the beginning. He also fell during the descent, a little before you. But we stopped his fall like we did with you, avoiding a greater evil," she explained.

Nahia nodded. She was so tired she could not even speak. Her hands hurt terribly and her arms seemed not to work at all. They had just arrived at this place, and the experience was already an absolute nightmare. She could not believe what bad luck they had, not just her but all those with her. She was beginning to see that surviving here was going to be very complicated. More so for her—she was one of the weakest, if not *the* weakest in the group, at least physically. She thanked her stars for having Ana, Maika, and Logan helping her.

As the place grew clearer, they could see in front of the tower to their left, the Tauruk-Kapro, who were waiting behind a white dragon the size of Irakas-Gorri-Gaizt. Nahia watched them with interest. They were bigger and stronger than they had seemed on the tower. They all wore simple leather clothes that hung over their chests and came down to their waists to continue as short skirts. Their faces were a mixture between the face of a bull and that of a human. The truth was they looked more beast-like than human. She hoped they were not beasts and that appearances were deceiving.

Part of the Tauruk-Kapro were watching them, and another part watched the Fatum. Nahia looked at the winged race they could also see much better now, who stood in front of their tower to the right. A blue dragon was in front of them. If the Tauruk-Kapro looked bigger and more beastly, the Fatum looked the opposite. They seemed smaller and more fragile than humans. The contrast was significant. Perhaps it was only a weird optical effect and her sight was tricking her. Really, in the pitiful state she was, seeing badly or even double seemed to her most natural. They were dressed like the humans, although much more elegantly, with breeches and shirts made of materials better than the leather, wool, and linen the humans used, but the patterns were more refined.

Prepare to move forward at my order. We are going to cross the Bridge of the Sky. From there we will access the Square of Neutrality. And from there we will head to Drakoros, your new home, Irakas-Gorri-Gaizt announced.

The first to get moving were the Felidae, who were following a brown dragon. Nahia was able to see that they really were like great cats, only they walked upright on two legs, like humans, although they did not resemble humans to any degree. They were big and powerful, especially the tigers and lions. They were certainly larger and looked more ferocious than humans. She was impressed. Another thing that surprised her about them was that they were dressed in leather garments made according to their bodies. She found it very strange to see them walk upright, in formation, behind the dragon. Nahia could not decipher their expressions and gazes since they looked so fierce. She wondered whether they were as upset and lost as her group was. Maybe they were. She had the impression that the Felidae were a race to respect. They walked toward the bridge they could see to the north.

They were followed by the Drakonids, led by a black dragon. Nahia was surprised to see one that color. It looked most intimidating, like the picture of evil—of death, even. Its scales did not shine; they did not reflect the light but seemed to devour it when it touched their surface. She felt a shiver. The Drakonids did not surprise her, she knew them. They were the only race allowed to leave their territory and enter others. They did so by serving the dragons as soldiers, scribes, or warlocks. They marched proudly after their lords, wearing colorful tunics with a pattern of scales.

If the Drakonids did not surprise her, the Scarlatum did, very much. They were a most singular race. Their skin of various shades of purple-red and their pointy horns, besides their ruby eyes, gave them a look that was impossible not to stare at. As for their bodies, they were similar to humans' and very well proportioned. They were attractive, which drew her attention. They wore tight clothes which accented their curvy bodies, but although they were easy to look at, there was something about them that made Nahia not trust them. She watched them for a moment, and they gave her the clear impression they weren't trustworthy. It was a big assumption, and she might be completely wrong, but that was her first impression of the race.

The Tauruk-Kapro and the white dragon that led them were the next to head to the bridge.

Attention. We march, Irakas-Gorri-Gaizt ordered, and it began to move toward the bridge. At once, they all followed the dragon, trying to maintain a rhythm that resembled something martial. But between the people who had to be carried by two others and the anguish of the rest, they could not manage a steady pace. They all kept looking at the back of the red dragon in case it decided to turn around and incinerate them all for being such a pathetic group.

Nahia could not even think, she was so tired. She only wished to cross the bridge and stay alive, and that her premonition of death would not come true.

Chapter 12

They arrived at the bridge. It was wide and went up before sloping back down. They could not see the other end from where they stood. Irakas-Gorri-Gaizt walked with large steps, and the group tried to follow as best they could. The bridge was so wide that six dragons could walk abreast.

"I can try to walk…" Nahia told Maika and Logan. She was ashamed they had to practically carry her. She was a burden, and she regretted the fact that they had to help her because of her own physical weakness.

"No way. You can't even stand," Maika refused.

Logan did not say a word, but he shook his head.

"You're also tired… you shouldn't have to carry me…"

"What do you mean? You're lighter than a feather," Maika told her. "I don't even feel your weight at all."

Nahia knew it was not altogether true, but she was grateful to Maika for making light of it.

"I'll take over whenever you say," Ana volunteered.

Maika and Logan nodded, but they continued carrying Nahia, who barely set her feet on the rocky ground of the bridge.

They reached the highest point of it, which formed a great arch, and Nahia understood why it was called the Bridge of the Sky.

"We're crossing the void," Maika commented.

"The sky," added Ana.

Logan looked right and left. Everywhere they looked they saw clouds and blue sky. He nodded repeatedly; he seemed impressed.

"This bridge joins the arrival port with what must be the realm," Ana said, looking back toward the pearl and then ahead once more.

Nahia did the same and saw the Fatum following them, led by the blue dragon. She realized that the bridge was surrounded by clouds— not in the distance in the sky, but beside them at the same level. They were white as snow. They surrounded the bridge and passed below. She had the odd feeling of crossing an infinite sea of white clouds. It was strange and looked like something out of a dream. They were crossing an ocean of sky over a bridge. However, their situation transformed that dream into a nightmare. She looked down to make sure it was solid rock and the bridge was something solid as well. The whole place seemed to float among the clouds, which was crazy.

She let out a sigh, trying to digest everything she saw. The sky above them was clear in parts and was of a shade of blue she had never seen before. The breeze was cool, and she was beginning to feel cold. When she realized where she was, she understood the reason for her short, rapid breathing and that low temperature. Nothing was wrong with her, it was the height they were at. The higher up in the mountains, the harder it was to breathe and the colder the air was. Being among the clouds was causing the breathing trouble she was having. She would have to be careful because she might faint; that happened at great heights. One more thing to worry about, as if she did not already have enough.

They finished crossing the bridge, and when they reached the other end, they found a wall and a large arch-like opening with no gate. They passed under it and entered a great square. It was walled on all four sides, and they saw three other entrances apart from the one they had come through. The wall was about ninety feet tall and the square was huge, about a couple thousand feet in every direction. The floor was stone. Thousands of rock squares formed it, but that was not the astonishing thing; what left them all agape was the fact that in each rocky tile there were precious gems inserted in them which shone in the sunlight. The whole square gave off infinite crystalline flashes at different intervals, as if following a song sung by the sun rays.

"That square is... unreal..." commented Ana as she swept it with her gaze.

"Are they diamonds?" Maika asked. "They can't be, can they?"

Logan looked at the floor and frowned.

"Dragons love jewels, they might be."

"But there's thousands... hundreds of thousands!" Ana said.

Nahia had the same doubt but said nothing to save the little strength she had left. She felt so bad she even had trouble speaking,

"It's possible they're diamonds and other precious gems and they use them as decoration," ventured Logan.

"By all heavens, what a waste!" cried Maika.

"Shhhh, whisper, don't let the dragon hear you!" Ana warned.

They said no more. Whispers and cries came from the other sides. They were not the only ones blinded by the floor of that square. Not only that, but the other races were also murmuring and crying at such a show of decadence.

They went forward, stunned, and saw three massive concentric circles carved in silver on the floor of the square's center. They surrounded a large fountain, beautifully shaped. All of a sudden, as if it knew they were approaching, the fountain ejected a stream of water that rose over forty-five feet in the air. Several in the group startled and lost the group's rhythm, affecting the advance and the formation. They had to adjust at once and get back in their places, and Irakas-Gorri-Gaizt glared at them in anger. They all feared for their lives.

The fountain really looked like a geyser. Nahia wondered whether the water would be cold or hot. It had to be boiling, considering it had been built by dragons, or at least by one of the slave races, for the enjoyment of the dragons. Nahia could not imagine the dragons carving fountains or building towers and walls. No, that had been built by the slave races for sure. Either that, or the dragons had some kind of magic that allowed them to do it, but for some reason that idea did not fit. Dragons had fiery breath and mental magic, but she doubted they had any kind of building skills.

They moved on, following Irakas-Gorri-Gaizt and the rest of the groups that marched ahead. Nahia saw that in each of the four cardinal directions there was an arch. They had come through the south and were heading north, crossing the immense square. The arches were so big that several dragons could walk underneath.

This is the Square of Neutrality. To the south is the Bridge of the Sky we have left behind. To the north is the gate to Drakoros, the Academy of Dragon Bloods where we are going. Move on and keep up the pace and formation. Whoever lags behind and discredits me will die. The threat struck their minds like a whip, making them all pick up the pace and do their best to not break formation.

They crossed the square. To Nahia, it seemed like an eternity it was so huge. She was beginning to understand that in the realm of dragons everything had colossal proportions. She did not find it strange—they built things according to their size, that of titanic beings, not that of their tiny slaves. Seeing the other two arches, east and west, she wondered where they might lead to. Irakas-Gorri-Gaizt had not mentioned them, so they must not be interesting, or perhaps they were forbidden to cross and only the dragons were allowed to pass. Whatever it was, it intrigued her. What other things were there in this neutral realm in the sky apart from the Arrival Gate, the Bridge of the Sky, this Square of Neutrality, and Drakoros, the martial academy?

Curiosity assaulted her with every step they took forward. She almost wanted to go to one of the two side arches and take a glance on the other side. An acute pain went up her side as punishment, and she decided it was not the time or a good idea. The image of a dragon biting off her head because she had poked it out past the arch came to mind and took away her wish to snoop. Perhaps one day she would find out, but it was not going to be now. Well, that was if she survived her first day up here, something she seriously doubted.

They finally arrived at the end of the square and Ana took over for Maika. Logan did not want to be relieved. He shook his head firmly. Nahia could not thank Ana, Maika, and Logan enough for their help. She tried, and the words stuck in her throat with emotion. She wanted to tell them she was better, that she could walk by herself, but it was not true. She was not well, and for now she could not manage on her own. She hoped she would recover, but she did not know if she would feel better before exhausting the comrades who were carrying her. She felt bad again for being a burden on them. It was not her fault and she knew it—she had been born with this physical weakness and had not asked to be here. She was being forced. Even so, at that moment, knowing that did not comfort her either.

They passed under the north arch, following the long, irregular parade they seemed to form. The humans had trouble maintaining the rhythm and pace, although they were not the only ones. The other races seemed to struggle too. Nahia guessed that with the exception of the Drakonids, who surely rehearsed military formations and parades before being chosen, the rest of the races would also be in trouble. Besides, they carried several wounded among them.

After leaving the great arch behind, they arrived at what looked like an immense, well kept garden. A wide stone path over a hundred paces wide crossed it, and that was what they were walking on. On both sides they could see some wonderful gardens. There were roses, lavender, azaleas, poppies, jasmine, carnations, lilies, and a number of different flowers and plants that were really beautiful, even orchids. Their inebriating scents reached them and Nahia looked everywhere, enchanted. She could not believe that dragons appreciated the beauty of delicate flowers and kept such gardens worthy of true kings.

"This is amazing," Maika commented.

"More than that, considering where we are," Ana added who, although not as strong as Maika, was holding up pretty well.

Logan looked around, filled his lungs with the pungent perfume of the flowers, and nodded.

"Shocking."

Nahia looked east and then west and noticed that behind the gardens rose forests of leafy trees. Narrower stone paths, that would fit a couple of dragons, went from the main path they were on and got lost in the forests after crossing the gardens every few hundreds of paces.

"Do you think someone might escape and hide in those forests?" Maika asked in a tone that sounded wishful.

"That's very risky. I wouldn't dare...." Ana shook her head.

"You wouldn't get anywhere. A dragon would catch you..." Logan said in a tone that meant it was a bad idea.

"I guess you're right... it's just that they're right there... makes you want to run off."

"Flat distances trick your eyes. I think those forests are quite far away," Ana said, trying to discourage her.

Nahia noticed that indeed it was all a flat expanse. There were no mountains. It was as if a god had cut off a top layer of soil for leagues around and then built roads, squares, gardens, and forests on that flat layer.

"I bet someone has tried already. If I feel like doing it, others..." Maika commented and then stopped. As if he had heard, a Fatum behind them started to run along one of the side paths in the gardens. He ran like the wind through the flowers and plants, heading west.

"Oh dear!" Ana threw her head back when she realized.

"Pretend not to notice, let him have a chance," Logan said.

"Don't look," said Maika to whoever was beside her and had already noticed.

Nahia saw ahead of them a Tauruk-Kapro running through the gardens to the east.

"Another one is trying..." Ana murmured and shut up at once.

The cries of surprise and support for the escape attempt were quickly muffled so the dragons would not realize and the fugitives might have a chance. For a moment they all watched unobtrusively, in silence, hoping the runners would make it, wishing they would not be seen in their intrepid attempt to escape.

Suddenly, the blue dragon that led the Fatum spread its wings and took off.

"Oh no…" Ana muttered under her breath.

"Don't let it catch him…" Maika wished.

The Fatum was running at great speed. He seemed agile and fast and was very close to the west forests. Nahia hoped he would reach them and manage to get into those trees with one last effort and disappear in their thick vegetation. She silently cheered the young Fatum—maybe he could spread his wings and glide the distance left to the trees.

The blue dragon came down from the sky toward the Fatum. It opened its mouth, and from it came a powerful jet of icy water. It reached the Fatum when he was just about to reach the trees. He was frozen on the spot in a running stance. He did not manage to escape, and he did not manage to save his life. He died frozen. The blue dragon rose in the air and roared triumphantly.

Nahia looked to the other side where the Tauruk-Kapro was running as fast as he could. Being a lot bigger and heavier than the Fatum, he was not running as fast. He was having more trouble crossing the gardens to reach the trees in the east. Up in the sky she saw the white dragon that led the group in front of them. It was already flying to hunt him down. Nahia knew he was not going to make it. Even so, she closed her eyes and wished him success, that somehow he would be able to cover the distance he had left before reaching the forests without the dragon killing him. She opened her eyes, fearing for the unfortunate. She saw the dragon coming down onto the Tauruk-Kapro and sending a terrible stream of thunder and lightning, as if out of the worst of storms, from its open mouth at him. The lightning bolts reached the fugitive and smote him where he was, killing him instantly. He fell to the floor, convulsing, already dead.

"How awful…" Ana said, starting to weep.

"Let me take over," Maika told her, and they exchanged positions. Ana was very affected and her scarce strength left her.

Nahia saw Maika holding her up, and she thanked her with a glance.

"We'll come out of this one," Maika said.

Nahia wanted to believe her, but after what they had just seen, she highly doubted it.

We call this place the Gardens of Useless Hope. I am sure you understand the reason. I also hope you have understood the underlying message of this place. There is no possibility of escape, no hope to get away. It is useless to even consider. If you have not understood the message, I encourage you to run off through the gardens and try to reach the forests. I will be delighted to teach you the lesson with fire, Irakas-Gorri-Gaizt messaged along with a feeling of *I dare you to and you will pay with your life.* No one dared to try. It was crazy to even think about it.

The groups renewed their march once the two dragons returned to their leadership positions. Crossing those marvelous gardens now had a less poetic and more drastic meaning. They were like a mirage in the desert for someone who had no water. They brought hope to the soul where there was none for the body. Whoever tried to cross them would die.

Ana and Maika changed places again once they reached the end of the gardens. Logan simply shook his head when they asked them if he wanted to be relieved. Nahia felt great admiration for him. Not only did he not complain for having to carry her the whole way, but he did not want anyone else to take his place. Besides, he did it from his heart without complaining or asking for any recognition. Nahia thought he was an amazing young man.

When the gardens ended and they went on along the wide stone path, they saw some high walls over ninety feet high. Behind them they glimpsed several buildings made of stone, rectangular, solid, tall, regal, and over a hundred and fifty feet tall. Nahia knew they were military buildings, since they looked like an enormous castle with several fortresses on its sides. Behind them they could glimpse high mountains in the distance against the sky. She found this striking. At last they could see some mountains although the huge, majestic walled military complex was in front of them.

Attention. We are before the distinguished Drakoros, the Academy of the Dragon Bloods. See how magnificent it is and show respect, Irakas-Gorri-Gaizt messaged to them, along with a feeling of great pride.

Nahia received the message, and it felt as if a waterfall had descended upon her. She realized at that moment that dragons could not only transmit harsh, evil messages but also positive ones. In fact, she felt much better, even if it was only for a moment. They stopped at the gates of the walls. The first group seemed to be asking for permission to access the great military complex.

Nahia stared at the immense castle in the center; the tremendously high, colossal walls that surrounded the place; the twenty-odd lookout towers along the wall with dragons posted in them, and she knew that once they went inside, there was no escaping it. It was not that she had thought there was a way after what she had seen in the gardens, but the academy looked like a majestic, colossal fortress with no way out for them.

"It's the most incredible thing I've ever seen in my life," Maika said.

"It's so grand it takes your breath away," Ana stared in shock.

Even Logan seemed surprised and was staring at everything with eyes popping. He said nothing and only shook his head as if the scene before him was impossible.

Nahia looked, trying to assimilate how gigantic and splendid the castle-fortress and buildings that surrounded it behind the walls was. Her mind was having serious trouble understanding how it was possible for something so enormous and regal to exist. She was speechless.

The entrance gates to the academy were over ninety feet tall and another thirty wide. As they passed through them, Nahia was able to see that on the two panels of the solid-silver door, there were several large carved runes, and a seal within each with the image of a dragon in profile showing its jaws and claws threateningly. She had no idea what the runes or the depictions of the dragons meant, but she had the feeling this was a place of war, of aggression.

"I'm beginning to be very frightened ..." Ana admitted to her.

"Don't worry, you're not the only one," Maika tried to comfort her.

Nahia looked around and noticed that the rest of the group was also scared and wanted to run away from there. No one dared, however, because they knew what waited for them if they did.

They went into the huge military precinct and walked from the south gate toward the castle that rose in the middle. As they approached it, they began to notice certain details that left them speechless. The whole main front of the castle and the adjacent buildings were covered with precious stones. Silver carvings in the runic style bordered windows and cornices. The doors to all the buildings, more than a dozen as far as they could see, were large and had silver engravings. The doors themselves were pure gold.

But, what most surprised Nahia was not that, but how immeasurably large all the buildings were, as well as the courtyard they were in, the walls around them, the lookout towers, everything—it was gigantic, dragon sized.

The groups stopped in front of the castle.

Welcome to Drakoros. Here, your destiny will be forged. Those who are strong of body, mind, and magic will survive and enjoy a glorious fate. The weak ones in any of the three major attributes will fail and die on the Path of Dragons. Yours is the fate, ours the Path.

With that lapidary message, Irakas-Gorri-Gaizt welcomed them to the military academy. Nahia was positive few of them would survive. She wanted to think she would, but looking at herself as she leaned on her comrades, she knew that if someone had little chance of surviving here, it was her.

Chapter 13

The parade with the six groups of chosen ones of that year, led by the dragons, entered the great parade ground in front of the majestic castle. As they arrived in front of the colossal building, the dragons stood three on each side of the great gold doors. Irakas-Gorri-Gaizt stood on the left, following the order they had arrived in. It stopped and turned around, facing its group. It seemed to want to make sure its hatchlings were all there.

Stay in line where you are and keep absolutely silent. I want you all to stand like stone statues. Whoever dishonors me here will die on the spot, it messaged and stood with its head high and erect, its back to the colossal castle.

They followed the order quickly, seeking to remain as stoic as possible. Nahia indicated to Maika and Logan to let her stand on her own and not hold her up. She did not want to risk the dragon incinerating them. Luckily, some vitality had returned to her body and she was able to stand on her own two feet and remain motionless. Maika and Logan studied her out of the corner of their eyes in case she needed help. Nahia indicated she was all right with a look, since she did not want to risk nodding and having it considered as movement.

They saw the rest of the groups standing the same way. The other dragons must have given the same order. The six groups stood in line, three on each side of the doors, leaving ten paces of separation between them. Nahia looked and saw the Tauruk-Kapro on their left and the Fatum on their right. On the other side of the doors, the Felidae, then the Drakonids, and finally the Scarlatum further away were forming their line.

They all waited in silence. Nahia looked around and noticed that all the groups had a similar number of members. If her eyes were not tricking her, there were about two dozen in each group, after the casualties they had suffered at their arrival. There was not a race that had a significantly larger or smaller number. She found this curious. Was it coincidence, or was there a reason for it? She had no way to know. She did not even know whether the populations of the different races were similar or if there was much difference between the various peoples. She realized she knew very little about Kraido and its peoples. She knew even less about the dragons and their realms among the clouds. All this had seemed so distant when she was in her cabin with her beloved Aoma. She had never attached any importance to it, since it did not really matter in her quiet life. Now she was in the midst of this nightmare, and everything that had not interested her because she felt safe and away from everything was beginning to be important. Very important, she feared.

The doors of the solemn, radiant castle opened without the slightest noise, as if they had no weight and did not scrape the rock of the building or the floor. A gigantic dragon came out from within. It was red with lavender streaks that went down its crested back. Its shocking size, much bigger than Irakas-Gorri-Gaizt at nearly a hundred and fifty feet long, was intimidating, not only because of how huge it was but for its head with long horns that curved back and ruby eyes that seemed to burn. With it came another dragon, white, also with lavender streaks on the sides. It was slightly smaller but also larger than Irakas-Gorri-Gaizt, about a hundred and thirty-five feet long. They were both magnificent and terrifying at the same time.

The red dragon stopped in front of the castle without coming into the courtyard where they were all standing in line and gave a powerful roar. It was sharp and short, as if to draw attention to itself. As if it were going to announce something. The white dragon stopped beside it and also roared once. It appeared to call for attention to the red dragon.

Welcome to Drakoros, the Academy of the Dragon Bloods. I am Colonel Lehen-Gorri-Gogor, executive leader of this institution of martial training. My opinion is law, life, and death here. Beside me is Commander Bigaen-Zuri-Indar, second in command of this illustrious, famed school with a long military tradition, the red dragon messaged, with a strong feeling of authority which made everyone cringe.

The white dragon gave a tremendous sharp, short roar, introducing itself.

The colonel looked at all of them with its intense fiery gaze and rose its head to address them again.

I am a thousand-year-old dragon. You do not yet understand what that means, but you will. I am tough, inflexible, and I live by the purest discipline. I am also fair, although your inferior minds will probably not comprehend this.

Discipline rules here. You will follow every order a dragon gives you, whatever their rank, without the least hesitation. Whoever breaks this simple rule will die. Without exception. Whoever is disciplined, does everything they're told at once, might survive. The training you will be given in this academy is martial, and you will learn to serve your purpose in the dragon armies.

Nahia looked at Ana and Maika. In their eyes she saw that, just like her, they feared the worst. Those two dragons were terrible, and the message of the academy's leader was not exactly comforting. Ana's eyes were moist. The only one who looked whole was Logan, who was frowning.

You are confused, anxious, and afflicted. This is natural, since you have just been taken away from your quiet, peaceful, and insignificant lives to serve in this illustrious and glorious place. This academy is where you study the Path of Dragons, and it is called the art of war and conquest. You must understand that it is a great honor to be given the opportunity to train here. There are few of our blood, the chosen from among the inferior races who have the privilege of serving us by training in this school. The sooner you understand this and accept it, the better it will be for you. It will allow you to survive in this place. Those who refuse or have difficulties accepting this honor, this destiny of glory opening in your insipid lives, will perish. This I can promise you. This is a place of glory but also of death, since they are both always linked. There is no glory without death, and so the Path says.

The dragon's message reached them all, not as a threat, but as if a glorious future in war and at the service of the dragons and dying for them were a real honor they had been granted. Nahia realized that the red dragon used the power of its mind to make its message sink in deeper, almost as if what it said was an unbreakable truth. But she knew it was not so. They had been brought here to fight, kill, and die for the dragons. That was neither an honor nor glorious. She would never accept that message. And if that meant her chances were minimal and that she was going to die in that place, she accepted it. She would fight so it would not be the case, but she was not going to be persuaded.

You have completed The Climb, our little welcome ritual. It appears that some have perished and others have been injured. That does not please me. It shows weakness, and if there is something a dragon hates, it is weakness. Luckily for you, chosen of the dragon blood, we will turn your weakness into strength in this martial academy. Or else you will die in the attempt. That is now in your hands.

When she received the message and the feeling of warning, Nahia's body stiffened in spite of the aches and exhaustion she was feeling. She did not want to appear weak, not in the least, or her existence would be abruptly shortened.

After the introductions, the first thing we will do is form the squads. Squad Captains, explain what it means, the Colonel messaged.

Irakas-Gorri-Gaizt raised its head, straightened, and sent them the mental message. *A squad is the smallest military unit. In the dragons' army, a squad is made up of three pairs, or in other words a total of six members. You will train as a squad during your entire stay at the academy. Once you finish your training, you will fight as a squad in the battle fields.*

Nahia immediately looked at Ana, Maika and Logan. They looked back at her. Nahia nodded at them, indicating the four of them. Ana gave her a hopeful look. Maika nodded slightly and smiled. Logan also nodded briefly, although he remained serious. They were not the only ones who sought to form groups. The looks and gestures were clear. Nahia calculated that there were three squads there and a couple of additional people who would be left hanging. She wished with all her being not to be one of the people left out and that she could be with Ana, Maika, and Logan.

Nahia noticed that the other races were going through the same feelings they were. The dragons that led the other groups, which Nahia guessed were captains too, were sending them the same message.

The Commander gave a tremendous, deep roar, announcing it was going to speak.

It is likely some of you have already made some friends during your journey here. You are surely thinking you will be part of a squad with your new friends. That is the mentality of weak, inferior beings. Captains, explain how the squads are formed in the dragons' army.

Irakas-Gorri-Gaizt raised its head once again.

The squads are made up of a member of each race, and the choice of the members is random.

"No!" Nahia could not help herself.

Ana opened her eyes very wide and looked shocked.

"Of each race?" Maika was looking at the other groups with a blank look on her face.

Logan was biting his lower lip.

A murmur of protest and unrest followed the announcement.

And it came from all six groups.

Silence, everyone. Who said you could speak, you filthy beings? Irakas-Gorri-Gaizt messaged, along with a feeling of fury that struck their minds like a hot iron bar.

Nahia felt like she was drowning. This could not be happening. They could not separate her from her friends. It was not only ruthless, it would also mean her death. She would not survive without them by her side. She looked at them with anguish in her eyes, and the three were as upset as she was.

This time, the Commander spoke.

Let us begin with the forming of the squads. The first one on the right of each line, take a step forward, the white dragon ordered with a direct order and a feeling that it could be no other way.

To ensure there was no confusion, Irakas-Gorri-Gaizt sent a mental message to the boy who had to step forward. It was evident because his head was thrown back and he stepped forward at once. In the other groups of the other races, the same situation was repeated.

Very well. You six will form the first squad. Stand behind the groups in a three by two formation. Do not speak and do not move, the commander ordered.

The six did as they were told while all the rest watched them out of the corner of their eyes without looking up. Once they were formed in two lines of threes, everyone was able to appreciate how different the races were from one another. The Tauruk-Kapro was taller and stronger than the others. The Felidae was next, then it was the Drakonid. The Human and the Scarlatum were similar in height and strength, and the Fatum was the one with the least physical strength.

Good, let us continue. The next one in line on the left, step forward.

Again, Irakas-Gorri-Gaizt left no doubt and sent the message to the redheaded boy who had to take the step. And so he did after a moment of bewilderment. He soon stood beside the other five from the other races to form the squad.

The process went on, and those called took a step forward to withdraw and stand in their squad. Logan's turn came. He was on Nahia's right. He received Irakas-Gorri-Gaizt's mental message, but his head barely moved. He looked toward Nahia, Maika, and Ana.

"We have to survive," he whispered to them and went to form in his squad.

When she saw him leave, Nahia felt her heart drop down a black, bottomless well. A great sadness and a void in her stomach assaulted her. Logan would no longer be with her. She suddenly felt defenseless. Without his help, how was she going to survive?

"Don't worry, you'll make it," Maika whispered as if she were reading her thoughts.

And then it was her turn.

One step forward, human, Irakas-Gorri-Gaizt messaged to her.

Nahia withstood the mental message pretty well and stepped forward. She did not want to look at the other groups to see who she would be with. She was going to find out in a moment anyway, so she decided not to worry.

Stand in line, two lines of three, Irakas-Gorri-Gaizt sent her.

Before she moved, Nahia let out a deep sigh. She gathered her courage and went to stand with her squad, fearing the worst. She walked to the place where she had to stand slowly, letting the others go first. She was in no hurry to integrate her new squad. She wanted to be with Ana, Maika, and Logan, not with the five unknown members of strange races.

She saw that the Tauruk-Kapro had stood in the middle of the first line. He was very big and strong, as Nahia saw when she passed beside him, since he was a head and part of the chest taller than her. He looked most fearsome with those bull horns and beastly face. She did not look at him too closely, just in case. The Drakonid stood on his right. This one was like all the Drakonids she had already seen and did not call her attention much. On the left stood the Felidae. This one did surprise her greatly. It was a white tiger, almost albino, and beautiful. Nahia had the feeling it was a boy.

She went around them and saw that behind, on one side, stood the Fatum, and this one was undoubtedly a girl, a very pretty one. Her hair was brown, smooth, and long, and she had it tied in a queue. Nahia could not help staring at her wings, which she had folded at her back. At the other end of the line of three stood the Scarlatum, and there was no doubt either that it was a girl, because she was not only beautiful but very attractive. Nahia stood between the two without a word. She stared at the broad back of the Tauruk-Kapro who was in front of her and did not let her see anything of what went on ahead.

The squad assignation continued until they all had their own. The last one was left with only four members since the numbers of that year did not square up. Nahia wondered what would happen to them. She soon had her answer.

It looks like this year we have a squad short of two members. This is something that sets the squad at a disadvantage, so they will be assigned two second-year members who have spent part of the last year in the infirmary, the Commander told them.

Nahia did not want to know why those second-year people had spent almost a whole year in the infirmary. Falling from a tower and breaking a bunch of bones came to her mind. On the other hand, they had not been killed and that was strange, dragons being as ruthless and merciless as they were. There had to be a reason. She would try to find out, more than anything else because it gave her some hope that not all paths led to death in this place, although the infirmary was not exactly where she wanted to end up.

Commander Lehen-Gorri-Gogor spoke again.

Once assigned to the squads, it is time you understand how this illustrious martial academy works. This is a place for military training. You are here to learn the art of war and become Dragon Warlocks. You will train in the use of dragon magic and weapons, and I am warning you now that it will not be easy. There are casualties every year, it is inevitable. This training requires maximum concentration and effort. Those who do not make the required effort or are unsuitable will not survive the training. You will train for the next three years. At the end of each year, there will be a graduation ceremony. Those who obtain their stripes in their disciplines and the privilege to graduate will pass a final test. This will be a real test in the battlefield, in enemy territory. Those who complete the test and survive will graduate. Those who do not, like the rest who perish along the Path during the year, will be nothing more than ashes in the wind, he messaged to them, along with a feeling of warning mixed with danger.

Nahia shook her head, her spirits down. She had to train in killing others, which was the last thing she had ever wanted to do in life, and survive the training, she already clearly knew might finish her off easily and at any moment. Besides, if by any chance she managed to get to the end of the year, she would be sent to enemy territory. It was crazy. How was she going to survive in a war zone? Why were they going to be sent into enemy territory as unfortunate newbies? It was one thing to endure tough training, and a very different thing to be sent to death headlong. She felt lost. Even if she survived the course, which seemed impossible to her, how was she going to survive a real war mission? She decided not to think about it anymore, because the more she did the worse and more discouraged she felt.

Commander Bigaen-Zuri-Indar, finish the presentation, the Colonel ordered.

The white dragon roared and stood straight.

You have much to assimilate. Think about it and prepare yourselves for a glorious future at the service of your dragon lords. That, or death. Yours is the choice, the only one you will always have. Your training will begin at dawn. Be ready.

The brief message of the commander dragon left Nahia with an upset stomach. Assimilate all that? Prepare themselves? It seemed to her like a cruel joke. She was going to die and her premonition would come true. Yes, that was what would happen, and she would not be able to stop it.

Colonel Lehen-Gorri-Gogor turned around and headed inside the great castle.

Commander Bigaen-Zuri-Indar remained and addressed them all.

The barracks are the three large square buildings beside the eastern wall, to your left. The building belonging to the first-years is the furthest away. The other two are for the second- and third-years. Perhaps one day you will be able to use them, who knows. For now, go and take a space in the one designated for you. Each squad, choose a room. There are plenty. This year there are not so many of you. Training will begin at first light. Be ready. Remember: only the strong and quick minded survive in Drakoros. Go now.

The message reached them like a direct order, and they were practically forced to physically follow it. The squads began to move, and Nahia's did too. The Drakonid in hers stepped forward, and the rest followed him. They crossed the parade ground to reach the first-year barracks. It was also colossal in size, three stories high and very spacious. The door was curved and dragon-sized, which allowed them to all go in at once.

Once inside, they found a large foyer and stairs right and left to go up to the other levels. Nahia noticed that for a simple barracks for newbies they were also extravagantly decorated inside. The walls had runes in silver shades and the windows also had silver decorations.

Several squads went upstairs, some right and some left, but the

Drakonid in her squad, who was leading Nahia's group, decided otherwise. He went straight along the ample corridor where two large dragons easily fit abreast. The ceilings were very high, over forty-five feet tall. Nahia felt once again like a dwarf in a world of giants. The Drakonid went for the first door on the right. He opened it, but there was already a squad inside. He turned around and went for the door in front. This room was empty.

"This is ours," he said in the common language of Kraido, and he went in.

The rest followed him while the other squads scattered throughout the colossal barracks.

"We have managed to get the room closest to the door. We'll be the first," the Drakonid said proudly.

Nahia sighed deeply. Everything was going badly. She took comfort thinking that at least there were no dragons here.

Chapter 14

Nahia was right behind the Tauruk-Kapro at the entrance to the room, and she could barely see anything, his back was so broad. The ceilings were very high, that she could see, and she moved to one side to see what the room was like. She saw six bunk beds, large and robust, on one side and a large closet on the other. A dozen windows let the last rays of daylight in.

"It's very big," the Fatum commented in a thin voice.

"Large for you who are like tadpoles. For me it's the right size," the Drakonid said, who seemed to bark rather than speak. Since his voice was a little sibilant, the combination was very odd. He went over to the first bed to see if it would hold his weight and dropped backward with arms spread. It held.

"It's a big enough size," the Tauruk-Kapro said as he sat slowly on the next bed also to try it. "I find it comfortable, I like it," he said in a nice, quiet tone, almost sweet.

Nahia was shocked that the Tauruk-Kapro acted and spoke so quietly and gently. From what she knew, they were very wild, brutish creatures, prone to destroying things. She found this very curious.

"I find this room most cold and uninhabitable," the Scarlatum said as she went over to the immense closet and began to check it to see what she found.

The Felidae moved nimbly to the end of the room and opened the back door.

"There's a bathroom. They've even hung a curtain, and there's a round wooden tub."

Nahia still could not believe the albino tiger walked upright on two legs, not to mention that he could speak. He left her stunned.

The Drakonid jumped up suddenly and went to see it, moving with heavy steps.

"I don't fit in that tub," he protested when he went in to look at it, and he waved his arms, upset.

"You fit in standing," the Felidae said with soft, raspy voice.

"How neat. I won't be able to take a bath," the Drakonid protested again and shook his head.

"You Drakonids like to bathe?" the Scarlatum asked him.

"Of course we like to bathe. Why wouldn't we? Or are you insinuating we are dirty?" the Drakonid asked the beautiful, crimson-skinned female glaring from the bathroom door.

"I'm not insinuating anything. I thought you were more comfortable on dry land, being reptiles and all that," the Scarlatum explained, unruffled, and looked at the Drakonid, who did not seem to intimidate her.

Nahia was watching the barracks from the door in silence. It was no doubt enormous. It had lots of space, although few comforts. The size did not surprise her—it was clear that everything in this world of dragons was huge and made for their size. It felt unreal to be there in that enormous room made of stone with five strangers who were not only from other countries but belonged to other races. Seeing them so close, she realized that they were really very different for one another. Some had skin, others fur, others scales, and even wings. It was strange, and it was causing her some anxiety. How were they going to understand each other and get along, being so different? It seemed difficult to her. Besides, one of them was a Drakonid. The Tauruk-Kapro was not too trustworthy either because of his bestiality, and the Scarlatum were famous precisely for being untrustworthy. Only the Fatum and the Felidae transmitted good feelings.

"I think the best we can do right now is introduce ourselves, don't you think?" the Fatum suggested in her thin voice from the middle of the barrack.

They all turned toward her. Nahia studied her. Besides having her smooth, black hair tied in a ponytail, her face was fine and delicate. Nahia had to admit she was also very beautiful, even more than the Scarlatum. She had eyes of very light blue which shone in the light. Nahia noted some very curious scales on her forehead, crystalline like small diamonds. She found them most singular. Would they be special like her own golden ones? She would have to ask the Fatum, but perhaps now was not the best time. The pattern they formed on her face seemed to take the shape of a bird, seen from above with the beak toward the nose and the open wings across her forehead and temples.

"Yes, we should get to know one another," the Felidae agreed, who apart from having a raspy voice spoke very low, almost at a whisper.

"It's impolite and inappropriate to be social without having been introduced," the Scarlatum said and smiled, showing an enchanting smile. Nahia noticed that she spoke in a sweet, enticing tone, especially the latter. She found this significant.

"I am Ivo of the Tauruk-Kapro. Pleased to meet you all. I am glad we have a pleasant group," he said, standing up and opening his arms as if he wanted to hug them all.

The Drakonid looked at him with surprise.

"You don't behave like a Tauruk," he said reproachfully.

"I don't? And how should I behave?" Ivo asked him with a look of surprise on his beastly face.

"Like this, all calm and such? Certainly not."

Ivo shrugged.

"If you say so… it must be."

The Drakonid was puzzled again by the Tauruk's behavior, and he showed it with a look of total puzzlement on his mini-dragon face. Nahia watched him; he was tall and strong. Compared with other Drakonid soldiers and officers she had seen, he was definitely bigger and stronger. He had two dragon horns that came out of his head and went backward toward his nape. The tone of his scales was a dark black-green, very characteristic of his race. What caught her attention were the discordant scales on his face. They were white and came down the right half of his face in a sort of lightning bolt. It made quite a contrast with his other scales, which were so dark.

"I am Aiden-Zuri-Suge, but you can call me Aiden for short. I know that you other races aren't used to Drakonid compound names."

"You know because your race is the only one allowed to visit the other nations," the Fatum replied in an acid tone.

"It's one of the advantages of being the favorites of our dragon lords I guess."

"You must be the favorites for something, don't you think?" the Scarlatum said with sweet irony in her tone.

"If you're insinuating it's for something dishonest, I promise that's not my case," he replied, and his tone was threatening.

The Scarlatum looked at the Drakonid with narrowed eyes, as if trying to read whether there was truth or falsehood in his words and ignoring the threat. She smiled enchantingly and said nothing more.

"I hope it's so," the Felidae tiger intervened. "My name is Taika."

Nahia studied him. His tiger appearance was lethal, but the voice he had was not aggressive, but thoughtful like that of a fox, intelligent. Nahia thought that in any case, with two claw blows he could kill anyone. His body, covered with white fur, was crossed with black streaks. He was not entirely albino. The scales on his face were black. Two lines came down diagonally on his cheeks bordering his mouth where his maw could be seen when he spoke.

"Pretty name, I like it," the Scarlatum said, smiling. "Mine is Lily."

"Very pretty too," the tiger replied, nodding.

"I'm Daphne, pleased to meet you," the Fatum said with a small curtsy.

"A delightful girl with manners. I like her," Lily said with a broad smile, returning the curtsy.

"And there's only the Human left, quiet and skinny," Aiden said.

"Don't mess with her. We're all the way we are, and we'll all suffer the same ill fate here," Daphne told him.

"Well said," Lily joined her.

"Ill fate? For having been chosen to serve our lords in war?" Aiden looked surprised.

"Not everyone wants to fight in a war and kill," commented Daphne.

"How can you say that? It's a great honor. More so with the blood of dragons running in our veins. It's our duty," Aiden replied and looked at all of them, one by one, seeking agreement. No one gave it.

Nahia could not hold back.

"It might be the duty of a Drakonid. It isn't that of a Human, that I can swear to. The dragons enslave and kill us. Being here is a terrible thing, and if you don't see it that way it's because your race has been indoctrinated with very wrong ideas."

"Well, our skinny, quiet Human here has strong beliefs after all. What do you think of that, Aiden?" Lily asked in a playful tone.

"I think she's wrong. It doesn't surprise me either. Humans have always been the most conflictive of the races."

"Maybe it's because we don't like being enslaved and killed," Nahia retorted.

"She also has a sharp tongue," Daphne joined the comments.

"Perhaps we'd better not argue. After all, we've just met," Taika said in an attempt to calm things down.

"She's the one arguing. I'm right. There's nothing else to say," Aiden said, crossing his arms.

Nahia was about to retort and saw Taika giving her a look asking her not to escalate things. She heaved a sigh, letting the air out in a long breath.

"I'm Nahia, and I hope we manage to live together and get along," she said without much conviction.

"We ought to. After all, we're here for the same reason, and we must all reach the same goal," Taika said.

"What's that goal?" asked Ivo.

"Our goal must be to finish the first year and graduate," Taika elaborated. "To stay alive, I mean, which is what matters most."

"I'll drink to that!" Lily said, raising an imaginary glass.

"We'll make it. I'm optimistic," Daphne said, imitating the gesture and pretending to toast with Lily.

"It's a good goal. Yes, graduate and not die in the attempt. I hope we manage," Ivo said.

"Follow my leadership and we'll do it without a doubt," Aiden said confidently, raising his fist.

"Your leadership?" Taika asked, raising a bushy white eyebrow.

"Yes, of course. The Tauruk doesn't seem to have leadership skills, which makes me the best option. I'm the strongest and most adept at fighting."

"Modest and subtle you are certainly not," Lily replied, raising her fine, well-defined eyebrows.

"If anyone is to be leader of this group, that's going to be me," said Taika.

"You aren't stronger than I am," Aiden said confidently.

"Why do you think that?"

"Because you aren't a male lion who might, perhaps, be stronger than me."

"You want to find out?" Taika opened his mouth and showed him his fangs.

"Let's all calm down, there's no need to kill one another," intervened Daphne, stepping in between Aiden and Taika.

"The Fatum is right. The dragons will do that," Lily added as she watched the situation develop with amusement.

"We shouldn't argue, and least of all fight among ourselves," Ivo said.

Aiden looked at him with his reptilian eyes wide open.

"You definitely aren't a real Tauruk-Kapro," he said, shaking his head.

"I am a different Tauruk. A lover of peace and quiet," Ivo corrected him in a gentle tone.

"That's a contradiction, at least as far as the reputation your people have," Lily told him.

Ivo shrugged his enormous shoulders.

"I'm different, I accept it. I like it."

"Is anyone else different?" Lily asked.

"I… well …. I am too… but now is not the time…" Nahia admitted.

"Yes, you look different. Those golden scales are unique," Taika said.

"Yeah… I think it's because of that. Aren't Daphne's scales also different?" Nahia asked, hoping to no longer be the center of attention.

The others looked at Daphne who, finding herself under scrutiny, blushed.

"I don't think they're so…"

"The Fatum is right. I've seen those scales before, among my people," said Lily.

"So have I," Taika said. They're less common than the red, blue, brown, and white, or my black ones, but they happen."

"The uncommon ones are the golden," Aiden stated, pointing at Nahia.

"Well, then we have two different and a half among us," Lily counted.

"That's one way to look at it," Taika commented.

"And the silver ones? Are they rare?" Nahia asked, thinking of the ones Logan had.

Lily and Taika shrugged.

"I've never seen them," said Daphne.

"They're rare, like the golden ones," Aiden confirmed.

"In any case, we shouldn't make too many conclusions for now," Taika commented. "I'm sure we'll soon find out the meaning of the scales we each have."

"As long as we don't die finding out, I'm okay," Lily commented.

"I'm with you on that," Daphne agreed.

"Good thoughts, they'll bring us good auras," Ivo commented.

Aiden threw his head back and then shook it several times while he muttered under his breath.

Nahia watched Ivo. He was enormous, the strongest and tallest of them all. His face looked beastly, a mix between the face of a bull and a human. At first Nahia had been afraid, both of his physical appearance and his face with those bull horns that stood out to the sides and ended in points. They looked fatal. But now that she gave him a closer look she saw that his eyes, although black, were not beastly. They were eyes with a soul. Or a least so they seemed to her. Brown scales covered his forehead. Strangely enough, they seemed to her to be in the shape of a tree, with the trunk starting at Ivo's nose and the foliage forming a circle on his forehead. It could also be that her imagination was running a bit wild and the shape was nothing of the sort.

"Are you all right, golden girl?" Lily asked her, coming closer and putting her arm through Nahia's.

"Yeah... well... I'm exhausted."

"Choose a bed then and rest. We don't know what's awaiting us tomorrow, but I guess they'll have prepared a first day of training to remember," she smiled.

"Yeah, I fear that too."

"What bed do you prefer?"

Nahia looked at the one Aiden had picked, which was the first one, and decided to pick the one farthest, at the back.

"That one," she told Lily, pointing.

Lily looked at the bed, then at Aiden and laughed.

"I don't blame you."

"In any case, we should divide the barrack," Daphne suggested.

"Divide? What for?" Aiden asked.

"For privacy, decorum?" Daphne said. "Boys on one side and girls on the other."

"Oh...." the Drakonid made a surprised face. "I hadn't even thought of that."

"It would be for the best, yes," said Taika.

"There's a folded screen at the bottom of the closet. It must be for that," Lily told them.

"Wonderful," Daphne brought it out and opened it. It was indeed for that. It stretched from the wall to the closet.

"Each on our own side," Lily said with a chuckle.

Daphne picked the first bed on the girls' side, Lily the second, and Nahia the last one.

Aiden and Ivo stretched out on theirs, one beside the other. Taika picked the last one on the boys' side.

"It's big and pretty uncomfortable," Lily commented from her bed.

Nahia looked at her. The Scarlatum was a real beauty—her crimson face was beautiful, her ruby eyes captivating, her body curvy and well proportioned. Even the two small, red-and-black horns that pointed upward suited her, giving her a mischievous air. Nahia felt envious. The Scarlatum was a hundred times prettier and more attractive than her. Besides, she was surely able to climb towers and slide down ropes without any trouble. Her scales were blue and they went down both sides of her neck, forming what looked like two rivers. They really suited her.

"Do you like them?" Lily asked her, noticing Nahia was staring at her scales, and she turned her neck so Nahia could see them better.

"Forgive me… I didn't mean to be rude."

"Don't worry, it doesn't bother me in the least that you admire my scales. Or the rest of me," she added, and she moved her hand along her body from head to feet.

Lily's self-confidence shocked Nahia. *She* did not have the same confidence at all.

"They're very pretty."

"And the rest?" she asked naughtily.

"Well… that too," Nahia nodded.

Lily laughed.

"Thank you, I know."

"Where do you get that self-confidence from?"

Lily tilted her head and looked at Nahia in amusement.

"If you don't believe in yourself, who's going to do it?"

"Yeah… that's a good thought…"

"Besides, my confidence is well founded, don't worry."

"I wish mine were too."

"You're adorable. You and I are going to be good friends, you'll see. I'll help you with your self-confidence."

"Thank you, that will be very good for me," Nahia smiled. The truth was, she needed friends if she wanted to survive here. If they were from her own squad, all the better, she thought.

"Rest, Nahia, you need it. You look terrible," Daphne told her from her bed where she had been listening.

Nahia nodded and lay down. She was so tired that it hurt to think. It had been a horrible day. The problem was that there would be more days like this one, many more. At least she was alive, and that was what mattered most. Now she had to focus on surviving tomorrow, at least. She thought about Taika's words: the goal was to finish the first year and graduate in order to stay alive, which was the important thing. He was right. That was her goal, and she would fight to reach it.

Chapter 15

A tremendous roar woke up Nahia, almost making her fall off her bed.

"What? What is it?" she asked, startled and still dazed. She was not fully awake and her eyes were half-closed.

"The masters are calling," Aiden said from the door.

Nahia looked toward the Drakonid, although she could not see him with the folding screen that divided the two sides of the room.

"What's all this racket? I need my beauty sleep," Lily protested on the bed beside her as she stretched out.

"I believe it's the call to stand in line," Daphne informed them as she got up. "A bit abrupt, dragon style."

On the other side of the screen, Taika had his head inside the large closet.

"It's funny, the closet is huge, but there are only blankets and some washcloths. I thought they'd give us some sort of clothes."

Ivo got up and stretched out to his full length with a grunt that echoed through the rock walls of the barrack.

"Better. I like my own clothes. If they gave me others, I bet they'd be too small and uncomfortable."

"Sure, since you only wear that funny skirt and a rustic leather garment on that bull chest of yours, I guess that any other clothing would feel uncomfortable," Daphne said as she looked at him, poking her head out from behind the screen while she put on her fancy vest of fine silk with silver embroidery.

"Clothes are superfluous. They hide the soul," Ivo said.

"I agree with you on that," Taika said. He had slept in his clothes. "In my tribe, clothes are only used for decency, and they have to be resistant and allow mobility."

"You're just envious of the exquisite materials and designs we Fatum have to create our beautiful garments. I understand it, and I don't judge you for it," Daphne said, raising her chin proudly while she finished getting dressed. The Fatum had carefully folded her clothes before going to sleep, as if they were a treasure.

Nahia tried to rise and felt a thousand aches all over her body.

She grunted and lay down again on her bed, bearing the pain.

"It's still night outside," Lily moaned as she looked toward the widows through which light was barely making its appearance.

"It would appear that training begins with first light," Taika guessed and shrugged.

"As it should be. We must be ready to fight for the masters from dawn to sunset," Aiden said as if it were a mantra.

"What tree did this one fall on his head from?" Lily said to Nahia, making a sign that he was out of his mind.

Nahia forgot a little of her pain with the joke. She tried to stand up again and endured the various aches every part of her body was sending to her brain. She looked at her hands; they were cramped. She had better not need to use them that morning. She had slept in her clothes. She had been so tired the night before she had not even managed to undress, so she only had to stand up to be ready.

Lily went to the bathroom and made herself pretty before coming out.

"One has to be pretty and ready to face every day," she said from inside.

Aiden put his half-dragon claw to his face and shook his head.

Taika, on the other hand, smiled.

"Image is essential," Daphne joined Lily. "I'm glad at least one person among those present appreciates it."

Nahia looked down at her healer clothes, which were simple, worn out, and somewhat dirty after the last few experiences she had been through. She had a change in her satchel but decided to save it for when it was really needed. For now, she would go on with what she was wearing, even if it was neither elegant nor clean.

A second roar, this one more threatening, reached them.

"You'd better hurry up…" Taika advised them.

"We have to line up in front of our masters, hurry up!" urged Aiden.

"Let's go before the Drakonid has a fit," Daphne commented with a face that clearly said she could not believe it would happen.

They left the room in bed order with Aiden signaling them to hurry.

They found the wide lower corridor of the barrack with various people running along it. Several squads were coming out just like them. Nahia crossed paths with Logan as he passed her with his squad.

"Logan!" she called, waving at him.

Logan heard her and turned his head. Their eyes met.

"Nahia, are you all right?" he asked, stopping.

"Yes, don't worry. You?"

"Fine, yeah," he nodded, looking her up and down as if he wanted to make sure she was still in one piece.

"Have you seen Ana or Maika?" Nahia asked him.

"No, only you."

For a moment, their eyes locked.

"Come on, Nahia, don't lag behind!" Aiden called from up ahead as he noticed she had stopped.

Logan looked at his own squad, who were calling him as well. He turned to Nahia.

"We'd better go."

"Yeah, or we'll be in trouble,"

"Be very careful here," he warned her, and his eyes showed concern.

"I will, don't worry," she repeated and tried to sound self assured, although she did not manage completely.

He nodded and turned to follow his squad at a run.

Nahia sighed and followed hers. As she was joining them, Lily fell into pace beside her.

"What a handsome guy with dark hair and light eyes," she said with a wink and a smile.

"Yeah... well...." Nahia did not know what to say, so she continued running.

Once they arrived at the colossal parade ground, they saw everyone running to form their squads. There was a moment of chaos, not only in her squad but in every one of them. They stopped when they saw the six dragon captains from the previous day. They were standing in the north area of the square with their backs to the great castle, as they had stood the day before. What puzzled the squads was that they had not received any order from them.

"Quick, stand in line, we're the last ones. What a terrible discredit being so late," Aiden said, and on his Drakonid face they could see how upset he was.

"Arriving a little before or a little after doesn't change anything in life. Let's be calm," said Ivo.

Aiden did not like the comment at all. He glared at the Tauruk.

"I like to be the last to arrive, it makes sure they look at us," Lily said nonchalantly, not at all in a hurry.

"I'm not sure that's good here. I don't think the dragons will like it if you keep them waiting," Taika warned her.

Nahia fully agreed with the Felidae. She hurried, not wishing to incur the wrath of any of those six dragons.

"Let's go where we were yesterday, I think that's what they're expecting us to do," Taika suggested as he watched the dragons and the other squads with his large cat-like eyes.

"Not knowing how to act before our dragon masters is unacceptable." Aiden raised his hands to the sky.

"If no one tells you what to do, it's not unacceptable not to know," Daphne replied with distaste in her voice.

"Not knowing isn't an excuse to our masters," Aiden retorted in a warning tone.

"We'd better stand as Taika suggested and not argue. It doesn't lead anywhere," Ivo intervened with a serene face.

They stood in the same place and formation they had the day before. Nahia noticed that practically everyone had done the same. Those who had not were soon told by the other squads to do so. In a few moments, they were all in line and awaiting orders.

A dragon came down from the sky and stood in front of the six that waited. It was white with lavender streaks and about a hundred and thirty-five feet long. They all recognized Commander Bigaen-Zuri-Indar, second in command of the military academy.

Attention, everyone. First order of the day. Assignment of squads to squadrons and these to their leader, the commander messaged to everyone, and the message reached them so forcefully they felt as if they had been hit in the head with a hammer.

Nahia looked at Lily beside her. She made a face of pain. Daphne shut her eyes to bear it.

"Do you know what that means?" Nahia asked in a whisper to her fellow squads.

"Military things, I guess," Lily whispered, making a face that meant she had no clue.

"I think they're going to group us up, and I guess we'll be

assigned to one of those six dragons," Taika said.

"Oh sure, that makes sense," Nahia agreed. She hoped she might get lucky end up in the same squadron as Ana, Maika, and Logan. That would be wonderful. She searched for them with her eyes. She strained her neck, turning in every direction to see if she could find them. She managed to see Logan, which cheered her some, and Maika a little further down, but she could not see Ana. There were too many people to be able to locate her. Nahia hoped she would not be under the red dragon. She had already seen how ruthless it had been during The Climb, and although she guessed the other dragons would be similar, she wanted to believe that perhaps there would be one that had some heart and decency, if that was even possible.

This year, based on the number of squads we have, each squadron will have three squads. It is a pity, because the ideal number is four, but this harvest has not been at all fruitful, and we will have to make do with what we have.

The message reached them forcefully again, like another mental blow, and they had to bear with it.

Nahia recovered and could not hold back.

"Fruitful? But we've lost people coming here because of them."

"So did we," Lily said.

"All of us," Daphne confirmed.

"Casualties are inevitable in the army," Aiden told them.

"We hadn't even arrived here yet, we weren't in any army," Nahia told him angrily.

"Our lords know how to prepare us best. The Path will be tough and long," Aiden replied with his eyes fixed on the Colonel.

Nahia glared at him.

"We'd better stay silent, it's dangerous to be heard," Taika advised them in his raspy, gentle tone.

Nahia made an effort to calm down. Daphne looked at her and indicated with a gesture that she agreed with her.

As is traditional in this academy, the selection of squads will be random. This is more fair and balanced for the leading captains. I will start by creating the choosing sphere. I do not want to see or hear any reactions. You will stand in line where you are. If we must lose one more squad, so be it, the Colonel messaged and shut its eyes.

Nahia received the message and an overpowering feeling that she must not move. She noticed that the feeling affected her body, because she tried to move her right foot slightly forward and could not. That dragon affected the mind with the messages and feelings it sent. This troubled Nahia very much. The dragons had great power over the slave races, and what was worse, they could not defend themselves.

In front of the Colonel, a translucent sphere about nine feet in diameter began to take shape, suspended in midair. When they saw it, they realized the colonel was using power to create it, and those present struggled to hold back their nerves. Nahia heard several muffled cries that did not make it out of some mouths and others who tried to step back but could not, their bodies frozen in place.

The sphere finished forming. It was white and perfect and gave off a white glow. Nahia thought it was beautiful, although she realized it would be used for something that would not be good for them. It was hovering about fifteen feet off the ground in front of the colonel and between the six dragons.

Let the random selection begin. Captains, go ahead, the Colonel messaged.

Nahia watched, shifting between scared and curious. What were they going to do with that gigantic sphere? All of a sudden, the six dragons stood up straight. Nahia guessed they were going to use their magic, and she was not mistaken. The six creatures opened their mouths and directed their elemental breaths at the crystalline sphere. The brown dragon sent its earth breath, the blue one water, the white one air, the red one fire, the black one a dark breath like night, and the crystalline dragon a bright white light.

Very well, let the selection begin, the Colonel ordered, and at his command the sphere began to spin on itself while the six dragons continued sending their elemental breath at it.

Fear began to climb from Nahia's stomach to her chest. This was beginning to look very bad. The sphere was spinning faster at every turn as if out of control, but it did not stir from the spot where it was suspended in midair.

Suddenly, three brown beams issued from the sphere and headed to three squads. Once it reached them, they split into another six beams that hit each member of the squad in the chest. They were all marked with a brown circle on their chests.

Nahia's eyes were about to pop out of their sockets, and her fellow squad members were the same. Three blue beams followed the brown ones and chose three other squads. They split into six beams and marked all the members with a blue circle. No one cried or moved because they could not, but the experience caused intense fear. Nahia realized that the beams the sphere emitted, although they were formed from the elemental deadly breath of one of the dragons, did not harm those chosen. The white beam followed the blue and chose three other squads, whose members were marked with white circles on the chest.

Everyone was so astonished with what they were witnessing that they did not even realize which dragon they were being assigned to. But that was not Nahia's case, who knew at once the moment she saw the red beam reach her squad. It split into six beams while Nahia cursed their bad luck. Everyone in her squad was marked with a large red circle in the middle of their chests.

Nahia looked down at the red circle and felt her heart sink. The last thing she wanted was to be assigned to the red dragon, and she had been. They belonged to the Red Squadron of Irakas-Gorri-Gaizt. She could not believe her bad luck. She looked at the other two squads that had been marked red. They were further away, and she strained her neck to see which humans were in them, hoping that her friends would be joining them. She glimpsed a dark-haired boy and her heart skipped a beat, thinking it was Logan. She looked more closely and saw with sadness that it was not Logan but another boy with similar hair. She sought the other human and despair fell on her. He was a blond boy. None of her friends were in her squadron. Her heart sank down into the ground—not the one she was standing on but much lower, where the slave races lived.

The selection went on, and Nahia saw that Logan was assigned to the White Dragon. Maika was chosen for the Brown Dragon's Squadron, and Ana for the Blue one. Nahia could not believe it. It was as if the forces of nature were against her. They had all been assigned separately. It would have almost been easier if some had coincided in the same group. For some reason, they were doomed, as if a curse had fallen on them. This way, their chances of surviving were even slimmer. She was sure the one who was cursed was her.

The sphere stopped spinning and the six dragons extinguished their elemental breaths. A moment later it began to fade away until it vanished entirely, as if it had never been there.

We already have the squads assigned to each leader. Your captain and leader of the squadron corresponds to the color you have been marked with, the

Colonel messaged to them, along with a feeling that whoever did not understand this was less intelligent than a maggot. *From this moment on, you will follow each and every order of your squadron leader. You will live and die by their orders, which you will follow without hesitation.* Now *Captains, the squadrons are yours,* the Colonel messaged together with the feeling that it was an imperative order, and spreading its wings, it took a giant leap and soared in the sky.

While the great white dragon flew up, Nahia's spirit dropped down to the abyss.

"What bad luck…" she muttered under her breath.

"This in particular, or our whole wonderful situation?" Daphne said.

"This and everything," Nahia shook her head with a look of resignation.

"I'm sure we'll get good news next, you'll see," Daphne gave her a look of pure irony.

Taika turned around.

"Remember the goal: survive the course and graduate. We just need to keep our spirits up," he encouraged them.

"Glory awaits us. We'll be the pride of our masters and lords," Aiden said, bursting with satisfaction.

"We're truly lost with this one. He's going to run us straight to the enemy, leading the charge," Daphne said.

"Of course. We'll lead the Red Squadron and be the pride of our leader," Aiden promised confidently.

Daphne rolled her eyes and Lily shook her head.

"It might be better if we relax and take things calmly. There's no need to go and charge or die right away," Ivo said quietly with a serene expression on his half-bull, half-beast face.

Nahia watched the two other squads that made up the squadron with them.

"Do you know the people of your race in the other squads belonging to our squadron?" she asked Lily.

The Scarlatum looked at them and shook her head.

"I don't know them, my country is big."

"You?" Nahia whispered to the others.

They all looked at the members of the other squads.

"No, I don't know them," said Taika.

"I don't either, but it doesn't surprise me. My country is massive and the Tauruk-Kapro tend to live separately," Ivo said.

"We are rather tribal and we live in packs, but they're not from mine," said Taika.

"Most of us live between forest villages and tree houses, they're not from mine," Daphne shook her head.

"I don't need to know them. They're Drakonids. They'll be proud, loyal, and brave."

"It couldn't be any other way, of course," Daphne added with sarcasm.

The red squads will form my squadron in front of me, Irakas-Gorri-Gaizt ordered, and it took flight to land at the upper left side of the square.

"Let's go quickly to our leader," Aiden told them.

"Yes, we'd better go," Taika agreed.

They ran to stand in line in front of their leader, and with them the two other red squads. The same thing was going on with the other five squadrons. Each dragon had chosen one area of the square to stand in and gather its squadron.

Nahia ran with her heart broken and a fixed idea in her mind that she repeated over and over: *survive the course and graduate.*

Chapter 16

As they ran across the parade ground, they saw the other squads also running to line up in front of their dragon leaders. There was a commotion, and they had to be careful not to bump into one another or trip and fall.

"It chose the farthest spot in the square," Lily complained as they approached the red dragon.

"Are you surprised?" Daphne asked her, making a face.

The Scarlatum made a sign that it was not shocking at all.

They hastened to get to Irakas-Gorri-Gaizt. They stood in front of the dragon on three squares marked on the floor. The design on the floor surprised them all—it had been done with precious stones. They had to be rubies by their red flashes when the sun hit them. Nahia and her squad had no doubt that those squares were for them because the floor shone red. They lined up in front of their leader, one squadron beside the other. The first on the left was Nahia's. Aiden had run to claim that spot and the rest had followed. They had no choice, since they did not want to give the dragon any reason to get mad at them.

This is the place where you will always line up for me throughout this first year of training. In order to mark it and so that you recognize the banner of your squadron, I will place the banner before you. Stay still and quiet, the dragon messaged, and they all received the message loud and clear in their heads.

Nahia was beginning to bear the messages that had no negative feeling attached much better. They did not impact her so much, and she interpreted this as her mind adapting and getting used to that type of direct communication.

All of a sudden, between them and the red dragon, a column of fire shot out of the floor. It was over fifteen feet tall and three feet wide and it looked like a column ending in a burning crown. They all took a couple of steps back, startled.

Stay in line! Do not leave your square! This is the banner of our squadron. Whenever you see it, you will go to it.

They all returned to their initial positions, although their fear of the tall column of intense fire persisted.

Now take a look at the banners of the other squadrons, Irakas-Gorri-Gaizt ordered.

Nahia looked right and saw the blue dragon raising a banner of water and ice. This was also fifteen feet tall and of a bluish-white. The outside was frozen, while in the inside they could see a jet of water that first went up and then down. She continued looking and saw the brown banner made of earth. This one had a hard stone crust and inside they could see thousands of small rocks going up and down at great speed. The white banner impressed her a lot, since it was made of wind and lightning. The lightning bolts went up and down the fifteen-foot length without slipping out and hitting the members of its squadron. They were contained in strong currents of air that enveloped them. She could not see the rest of the banners; she would have to look at them some other day. All the banners seemed alive, which surprised her.

She crossed gazes with Lily and Daphne, and they both looked impressed by the dragons' show of magic. They said nothing to not risk making their leader angry, but she could tell they wanted to comment on it just as much as she did. Aiden, for his part, had a look on his face of pure delight with what they were witnessing. Taika watched and analyzed with his cat-like eyes, always alert. Ivo didn't seem to even be present. His beastly face was calm and his odd eyes seemed lost, as if he were meditating about what they had just seen. They certainly were a most singular group.

The great red dragon looked at its three squads with the red eyes of a great predatory reptile.

You now belong to the Red Squadron. The other squadrons will take the color of their leader and you will refer to them by color. This squadron is made up of the three squads that have been chosen, and it will be this way for the rest of the year. Each squad will have a name by which I will address it. I will give you that name now. The blonde human girl's squad will be the Igneous Squad. The dark-haired human boy's will be the Ardent Squad. The blond human boy's will be the Searing Squad. That is how you will refer to yourselves.

The message reached them, along with a feeling of belonging. The members of the three squads looked at one another and then at the other groups. Nahia found the names significant. The dragon was red and had elemental fire breath, so she guessed the names of the squads also had to do with that natural element.

Now that you belong to a squad and a squadron, it is time you learn how to behave properly. I will explain the basic rules that drive this martial academy. Memorize them and do not make mistakes. When you are before a dragon in the academy, you will first kneel, showing your respect. Do this by dropping on both knees, sitting on your heels, and leaning your body forward. Do it. Now!

They all knelt. Looking at one another, they understood the pose. They sat on their heels and then bowed forward on their knees. Nahia had no difficulty, the same as Daphne and Lily. Ivo and Aiden, on the other hand, could not bend all the way. They were not at all flexible. Taika was though, as much or more than the girls, which Nahia found shocking since he was such a large tiger. His innate feline skills must provide him with extra agility.

Stand up! Line up as a squad!

They all obeyed at once and stood as they always did.

It is time to establish the Formation Order. The way you are doing it is incorrect. The first line will be formed by Human, Fatum, and Scarlatum, and the second line by Drakonid, Tauruk-Kapro, and Felidae. You will do this every time. Do not forget the order, or you will lose your head. I will bite it off if you make such a big mistake regarding such a simple thing.

The three squadrons lined up in front of their leader as indicated. Irakas-Gorri-Gaizt examined each of them from head to toe, as if it wanted to memorize who they were.

What you see in the center of the square is a sun dial. It serves to indicate and measure time. I know you are not used to the notion of time or to measuring it, or respecting the hours. But up here, in this academy, it is very important. Who among you can read it? if you can, step forward.

Nahia had no idea. She did not know what a sun dial was. She looked at Daphne and Lily, and by their puzzled looks assumed they did not either.

The Drakonid from each squad took one step forward.

Lily and Daphne made a funny face, as if to say "how weird that they know."

You three will explain to your squads how the sun dial works. As of today, you will all line up on the first hour of every day. Whoever is late will be punished. There will be no excuses or pity. After lining up, you will proceed to break your fast in the common dining hall. At second hour, you will begin your training. Every day of the week, a different subject will be taught during the whole day. Training will last seven daylight hours. The last four of every day you will devote to strengthening the areas you are weak at. For some it will be the physical part, for others the magical, and for the clumsiest, both. I recommend you use those hours well, or you will not survive the Path. You will spend the night hours in the barracks. In your room in the barracks. It is prohibited to wander around the buildings. It is prohibited to leave the barracks room at night. It is prohibited to talk to other students except in the dining room at your table, in the library for studies or in the gym to practice and exercise. It is prohibited to arrive late to classes. Whoever discredits me before the trainers will pay. Now, go to the sun dial and learn to read it. Break formation!

They broke the line and Aiden signaled them to follow him. He led them to the sun dial, which was in the center of the great parade ground. It was round, over thirty feet wide. A tall needle projected a shadow on it.

"It's easy to understand," Aiden started to explain. "The day is divided into twelve parts. They're the lines you see drawn on the floor. The shadow of the needle marks the time of day."

"Interesting system, advanced," Taika commented as he looked at the dial, reasoning how it worked.

"I don't see the need to measure time. We go by the position of the sun in the sky, as always, and everything is a lot more natural," Ivo said.

"I agree with our little beastie," Lily said, nodding.

"The traditional system is good, but this one is more sophisticated. I'm not sure I like the idea of having to check this device every time I want to know what time of day it is," Daphne commented, wrinkling her nose.

"We don't measure time," Nahia said, scratching her temple.

"This system is exact, yours aren't," said Aiden. "That's why the masters taught us."

"And what happens at night, genius?" Daphne asked him.

"The dial only marks the daylight hours. There are also twelve night hours, but they aren't represented since the dial works with the sun marking the hour with that needle you see," Aiden replied.

"To sum it up, it doesn't work at night," Daphne said with irony in her tone.

"If the dragons measure time like that, we'll have to pay attention to the movement of the sun and the hours," Taika said.

"We have no choice..." Lily complained, and she looked unhappy with having to measure time and adapt to whatever it marked.

"I'm dying to see what training we'll have today," Aiden

commented, very excited.

"Yeah, we're all dying to know," Daphne ironized.

Lily laughed infectiously.

Attention, squadron, Irakas-Gorri-Gaizt messaged them, along with a feeling that it was an order and orders were indisputable. The great dragon spread its wings, beat them hard, and with a great leap it took off. It rose above the square and, passing between the great towers of the wall, left the academy, flying over the south gate they had entered through the day before.

"Do you know what's happening now?" Nahia asked Taika.

"No, I don't, but I guess the dragon will come back shortly and give us our orders."

The Felidae was not mistaken. Irakas-Gorri-Gaizt returned and landed at the top left side of the square, beside the living banner that was still burning where the dragon had planted it.

My squadron will line up in front of me, it messaged.

"Let's hurry up," Aiden urged them.

They arrived and lined up as their leader had instructed.

Now you will march to administration. It is the square building with bars on the windows that is in the middle of the west wall. There, everything pupils need, from clothes to weapons, traditional and magical, is kept. The first thing you will be assigned is the academy dress. Go and get the clothes you will wear from now on. Once dressed, you will go to the dining hall located in the south wall. It is the low, long building. You will break your fast and join me here when you hear my call. You do not have much time, so I advise you hurry, or else there will be no breakfast. Break formation! Go!

Nahia felt the order hit her mind, but she withstood it well. She saw Daphne and Lily throw their heads back. She had the impression the dragons' mental messages affected them more. She felt a little better, although she knew this kind of comfort was fleeting. She had to find a way to protect her mind better from those dragons' mental attacks. One more thing to add to the long list of things she had to perfect in order to survive there.

"Come on, quickly," Aiden urged them. He once again wanted to be the first, even if it was getting to administration. He picked up his pace.

"Take it easy, not all of us have your wish to stand out," Daphne told him reluctantly, not walking as quickly.

"You should be. We have to triumph in everything, for our leader and master," he told them and waved them on.

"We have to cross the whole parade ground, there's time," said Ivo, who was not picking up pace, although his great strides were like two of Nahia's.

Nahia started after Ivo, trying to keep up with his double stride. They soon saw they were not the only squadron heading to administration.

Taika noticed.

"There's going to be a long line at that building."

"Really? Well I don't want to miss breakfast," Ivo said, and he started taking longer and faster strides.

"Wow, it appears there is something that makes our Tauruk-Kapro move fast," Lily commented and smiled.

"I've already told you, we must be first at everything, always," Aidan said reproachfully, and he began to run.

"This one's going to drive us up the wall," Daphne said, shaking her head.

They went to administration at a run, following Aiden. Nahia glanced at the other squads to try and catch a glimpse of her friends. She saw Maika but her friend was too far away and Maika did not see her. Nahia did not see Logan and Ana at all.

By the time they arrived at administration, there were already two squads ahead of them and they had to wait in line.

"Third? This is not acceptable," Aiden said, upset.

"As if they were giving medals for speed," Daphne retorted.

"It's as if they did. We must stand out in everything. Didn't they teach you anything in your lands?"

"You're pretty crazy," Daphne told him, and she waved her hands above her head, which Nahia interpreted as the way to say lunatic in the world of the Fatum.

"Third. Good, we won't miss breakfast." Ivo said, rubbing his broad, muscular abdomen.

They had to wait, and Nahia took the time to take another look at her squad companions. For a Human like her they were most shocking; she would have to get used to them. It did not look like she had a choice. These five were not who she wanted to live with and create bonds with, but she clearly saw she would have no other option. She sighed deeply and resigned herself to her fate.

Chapter 17

They waited for the other two squads before them to finish, and then finally it was their turn. They went into the building, which was a large warehouse of solid rock. They walked up to a long counter. Nahia was surprised to see there was no one assisting them, and after a moment she was even more surprised. It was not that there were no assistants, they just did not see them because they were so small. Nahia and the others had to lean over the counter to see them.

"Those are… Tergnomus…" she muttered, surprised, looking at them as if she had stumbled upon some mythological, magical beings. They were short and diminutive, half as tall as a human, with the exception of their feet and hands, which were big in comparison. They had a sharp face and long nose that looked like a long beak. The ears were also very long and pointed and they folded backward among ruffled curly hair in green shades. Their eyes were dark and their skin was a color between white and brown with a little green in the mixture. Nahia found them fascinating.

"Wow, this is a real surprise," Taika commented, tilting his head to one side as he watched them. "How curious."

"These are the ones giving out the uniforms?" Daphne was also surprised, and by the look on her face it did not add up that they should be in charge of supplies.

"I did not expect them to have Tergnomus here. Our dragon lords don't appreciate them," commented Aiden.

"Perhaps they don't appreciate them for their war skills, but as servant laborers they seem to," Taika said.

"They're charming and so tiny, I could take them home with me," said Lily, smiling at them.

"I don't think that's a good idea. They're said to have bad tempers," Aiden said.

"You mean like you," Daphne said, raising an eyebrow.

"I don't have bad temper. Why do you say I have bad temper? You don't know me," Aiden barked defensively.

"Maybe it's because you speak like a lion with a splinter in his foot, always in a hurry to go somewhere," Lily said.

Aiden raised his head and shook it, looking stunned.

"What's actually happening here is that you're envious of a Drakonid who's sure of himself and of what has to be done here. That's what's happening."

"Yeah, that's it, no doubt. And have you forgotten to add that you are also irresistible?" Daphne added with a voice full of sarcasm and wide eyes.

"I said next!" the Tergnomus yelled angrily.

"We're the Igneous Squad of the Red Squadron," Aiden said quickly and confidently, proud of himself.

"I am Hiputz, the supply manager. Everything you need has to go through me. I will get it for you as long as it's approved."

"Pleased to meet you, Hiputz," Lily smiled beguilingly and winked at him.

"Your charms won't get you extra materials, Scarlatum. No matter how pretty and irresistible you are."

"Oh, no...? What a pity," Lily said and threw him a kiss.

The Tergnomus seemed to blush, although his rough skin made it hard to tell.

"Red Squadron, huh?" Hiputz climbed onto a box and studied each of them from head to toe.

"Yes we are. Why do you ask?" Taika inquired in a suspicious tone and stared at the Tergnomus.

"Nothing. It's just that it irks me to waste such good materials every year," he commented as he turned to climb down from the box.

"Waste?" Taika frowned, and his feline gaze sharpened.

"Don't you know what squadron you're in?" Hiputz said, although they could no longer see him since he had disappeared between large wooden boxes in what looked like an endless, sprawling store. There were thousands of huge boxes, and they could only see a part of the warehouse.

"We are in the Red Squadron and proud of it," Aiden confirmed.

The Tergnomus said nothing. He vanished for a while and left them there, waiting. Nahia and Lily exchanged puzzled glances.

At last, Hiputz reappeared, followed by three other Tergnomus. They were carrying six green backpacks.

"You're in the most famous squadron of this military academy," Hiputz told them.

"I knew it! We'll be heroes!" Aiden could not be happier and raised his fist in a sign of victory.

"Yeah? Curious." Taika suspected something, because he was looking at the manager with narrowed eyes.

"It's also the one with the most casualties, always. There are years when none of its squads make it out alive," Hiputz told them as naturally as if he were saying "good morning" and giving them a piece of trivial gossip.

"The one with the most casualties?" Daphne raised both eyebrows and straightened so much she looked on the brink of flying away, if only she could.

"That sounds awful. I'm too beautiful and charming to die so soon," Lily commented, shaking her finger.

"I'd simply rather not die," said Nahia, who had not liked the news. Was nothing going to come out well for her? Was she not going to have a tiny bit of luck? Everything was going awry and getting worse with every step she took.

"We have to take bad news in stride. Perhaps we should sit down and consider the future awaiting us," Ivo suggested.

"The very short future, it seems," Daphne said in a huff.

"Is there any special reason why this squadron is so prone to casualties?" Taika asked Hiputz.

"Its leader, Irakas-Gorri-Gaizt, likes risky missions. It presents its squadron to the most complicated and dangerous ones, or so I've been told. But what do I know, I'm only a Tergnomus of supplies," said Hiputz with a shrug.

"Tergnomus supply manager," the second Tergnomus pointed out.

"Who has a lot of information," added the third.

"Because we hear and see everything," said the fourth.

"Yes, I know what I am. I have a good memory. And I've told you time and again not to talk, you big mouths," Hiputz scolded, turning to them angrily. Then he switched to the Tergnomus language and started to yell at them. The Tergnomus yelled back at him, and in a moment there was chaos.

"Look at the Tergnomus. They definitely do have tempers," Taika commented, looking upset.

"I don't find them charming anymore, and I'd be crazy to take one home with me. Look at how they're shouting, and those faces unhinged with rage? How awful," Lily made a horrified face.

"Arguing and becoming enraged is foolish. They should relax and enjoy being alive and appreciating this wonderful day," Ivo said optimistically.

The Tergnomus ignored him and went on shouting at the top of their voices, now waving their hands about. Things got ugly when one of the Tergnomus tried to hit Hiputz with the backpack. He missed, but only barely. The Tergnomus manager defended himself and hit the other with his own from the top of the box and the Tergnomus fell backward. The other two started hitting one another with the backpacks while shouting at the top of their voices.

"Stop this argument and help us!" Aiden shouted at them.

The Drakonid's words had no effect whatsoever.

"I told you to tend to us!" he shouted angrily.

They continued to ignore him and continued arguing and hitting each other on the head with the backpacks.

"Hey! Pay attention to us!" Aiden cried so loudly they almost had to cover their ears. Then he started banging the counter with his fists.

"I don't think they'll heed you that way," Daphne told him.

Aiden went on banging the counter, faster and harder. After a moment, he was furiously banging. He banged and banged and banged.

"Aiden, take it easy, you're going to hurt yourself," Taika told him as he tried to hold his arm. The Drakonid continued smashing the counter with all his strength over and over again. He did not seem to hear or see anything.

"Stop it now, Aiden, you're going to injure yourself," Daphne told him.

The Tergnomus realized what was happening and stopped arguing to stare at the Drakonid who was banging on the counter with his fists.

"Help me," Taika called as he held him by one arm.

Nahia and Lily grabbed his other arm. Even so, the Drakonid continued banging his fists with a lost gaze.

"He's having some kind of seizure," Daphne diagnosed as she passed her hand in front of his face and saw that Aiden did not react.

"Can you think of a way to get him out of it?" Taika asked as he was forced to use all his strength to control Aiden's arm.

"I guess he'll either come out of it or exhaust himself," Daphne shrugged.

"Or maybe not," Nahia said as with Lily's help they tried to hold his other arm, which was a struggle.

Ivo walked up to him and without a word made a fist and gave Aiden a sharp blow on the nape. The Drakonid collapsed on the floor and fainted. Because they were holding him by the arms, he did not strike the floor.

"Ivo!" Taika protested with a look of absolute surprise on his face.

"What do you think you're doing?" Lily gasped, staring at Ivo in disbelief.

"Solving the problem," Ivo said nonchalantly and stepped back again.

"The beast here's not wrong, you know," Daphne said with a smile.

"That's no way of solving it," Taika complained as he knelt to check on Aiden. Nahia did the same.

Lily turned to Ivo.

"Weren't you all for peace, serenity, quiet, harmony, and all that?" she asked him, raising her eyebrows.

"I am indeed. But if I have to solve a problem, I solve it."

"Tauruk style, I see," said Lily.

Ivo said nothing and shrugged.

"I'm liking this Tauruk more and more," Daphne said with a smile and patted him on the back.

A moment later, they were leaving the administration building. Taika and Ivo were carrying Aiden and the rest were carrying the backpacks. They went to their room in the barracks and left Aiden resting on his bed.

"Let's put these clothes on," Taika said.

Daphne nodded in agreement.

"I hope they're not too ugly, all military and that," Lily said wistfully.

They took out the clothes from their backpacks. There were leather boots, breeches, a long-sleeved tunic that came to their waist, and a cloak of a material similar to linen. They were all black and covered with large red scales which shone with silver flashes when the light hit them.

"Hiputz has given us one of every size. He has a good eye, that Tergnomus," said Daphne, taking the one her size and beginning to dress.

"The red over the black looks very attractive and goes well with my skin, I'm going to look great," Lily smiled, not at all displeased with the garments.

"They are striking and colorful," Taika commented, and the way he said it made it obvious he did not think that was a good thing.

"Look, the cloaks have a picture of a dragon engraved in silver in the middle of the back, and under it the number 1," Lily said, showing them.

"It's so we don't forget we're first-years who belong to the dragons," Daphne commented ironically.

"Even the boots are covered in scales," Nahia commented, "Curious, isn't it?"

Taika was scraping a scale from his cloak with the strong nails of one claw.

"These are dragon scales, you can't scratch them. They'll protect us. Steel won't penetrate them."

"You think so?" Daphne started to check those on her breeches.

My clothes fit perfectly, that's amazing," Ivo said in a happy tone as he adjusted his cloak.

"I'll need all the armor they can give us," Nahia admitted.

"Well, if it's armor, its super light. These clothes barely weigh anything at all," Daphne said, holding the cloak in her arms and calculating how much it weighed.

"That suits me too," Nahia nodded as she put on the cloak and realized it was indeed light, although the black material was thick and the scales ought to weigh the outfit down but for some reason did not.

"It's armor, light and resistant," Taika decided after conducting several tests on his cloak, tunic, and breeches. I don't know what the material might be, but the scales are dragon's, without a doubt."

"Do you think they came from our leader?" Nahia asked.

Taika shook his head.

"They'll be from some red dragon that died in some battle."

"That makes more sense. Our leader needs its scales," said Daphne, "I don't think it would get rid of them."

"Perhaps dragons sometimes shed their scales," ventured Nahia.

"That's an interesting idea, yes, that could be," Taika said and was thoughtful.

"Anything's possible with dragons, especially bad things," Daphne said.

"Does anyone know if this is true?" Nahia asked.

The others looked at her and shook their heads,

"Perhaps the little dragon knows," Daphne said, pointing her finger at Aiden. "But, our peace-lover with bull horns has knocked him out."

Ivo made an apologetic gesture.

"Once he wakes up, he can tell us. We have time, and patience is a virtue."

"Yeah, one you sometimes forget about," Daphne replied, making a funny face.

"What I'm not forgetting is that both soul and body need feeding. Right now, it's the latter. Let's go and have breakfast."

"What about him?" Nahia said, looking at Aiden on his bed.

"We'll wake him up afterwards," Daphne suggested, "He might not take it well if we do so now."

"I totally agree," Ivo said, going out the door without waiting for anyone.

Nahia, Lily, and Taika looked at one another and nodded. Better to let him rest and avoid his anger, which would be capital once he woke up. More than anything, they did not want to miss breakfast. They were all very hungry—even Nahia, who was not used to eating much, but at that moment she felt like eating a whole grilled cow.

Chapter 18

They headed to the dining hall, and as they did they noticed they were not the only ones. People were coming out of the second- and third-year barracks and formed their squads as they crossed the square on their way to breakfast. Nahia watched them unobtrusively. The second-years were closer, and she saw they looked quite older than them. They were only one year older, but they appeared to be a least three years their seniors.

A second-year squad passed in front of them, and Nahia saw a larger dragon embroidered in silver and the number 2 on the back of their cloaks. A moment later, a third-year squad went by them at a faster pace, almost at a trot, and Nahia's jaw dropped. If the second-years looked three years older than them, the third-years looked at least five. Not only that, but their faces and gazes were those of someone who had lived through difficult situations that had marked their souls.

"Interesting, huh?" Lily said beside her.

"Rather terrifying, I'd say."

"Why's that? They're handsome and older."

"Don't you think they look too old? As if horrific things happened to them that forced them to grow up faster than normal?"

"That's because that's exactly what happened to them," Daphne said with a nod as she came up behind them.

"Nahia is right," Taika turned to them. "They seem to have grown up fast, very fast. And it's all the races."

"Life's experiences mark us and change us, forcing us to grow up," said Ivo as he went on toward the dining hall, led by his appetite.

Once they arrived at the enormous building, Nahia encountered a new surprise. On both sides of the huge door, through which a thousand-year-old dragon might pass, she came upon two beings she had never seen before. They looked humanoid, but their bodies were covered with bark and short, leafy branches sprouted from their arms, legs, and even heads. Their faces were not as marked by the bark and looked almost human. They had brown eyes like their supposed hair, which tangled with the branches and leaves and looked like lianas.

"Those are Exarbor," Taika said.

"Yes, they have to be, they look like a cross between a human and a tree," Daphne added.

"A great race. They take their time and enjoy their life," Ivo said as he greeted both, bowing his head with his large horns. Every time he swung his head, everyone moved back.

"Careful with that rack, you're going to take our eyes out," Daphne protested.

"Keep a prudent distance and nothing bad will happen to you. Besides, well-bred people give breathing space to others," Ivo replied in his usual quiet tone.

The two Exarbor returned the greeting, also bowing. In doing so, the group quickly understood the reason for their reputation. It took them three times longer than Ivo, who had been pretty slow himself.

"The first-years... must... register," the one on the right said, and his slow voice sounded like green wood snapping.

"We're the Igneous Squad of the Red Squadron," Taika said.

The Exarbor had a ledger in his hand, and he wrote something down with the other. Nahia noticed that he used his own sap, that came out of his index finger, to write.

"The three tables... of the Red Squadron... are at the back on the left. You can't miss them... they're painted red. Your table has the name ... of your squad engraved on it."

"How well organized," Taika said, positively impressed.

"We like... organization... and efficiency."

"But swiftness not so much, huh?" Daphne burst out.

The Exarbor looked at her for a long moment.

"Ho... ho... ho..." he laughed heartily, albeit slowly, leaving them all very surprised.

"Wow, he has a sense of humor," Lily smiled. "You should moisten your face a little more, perhaps with dew. It would improve your facial look."

"Thanks... I'll remember..."

Nahia looked at Lily to see whether she was being serious or joking. The Scarlatum winked at her.

"They're not very smart," she whispered in her ear. "There's no way to revive that face."

"Come in… please… a line is forming…"

Nahia looked behind her and saw several first-years squads waiting.

"Come, let's eat," said Ivo, and he entered the dining hall with long strides.

They followed him, and no more than two steps inside they stopped short and stared at the place. Like everything else there, it was an unthinkable size—rectangular shaped, longer than it was wide, with a lofty ceiling. The walls were rock, and colorful, precious stones were encrusted around the large windows on the front and sides in various colors: brown, red, green, blue, white, black, silver, and gold. The light of day poured into the room through the large panes.

"A whole army could fit in here," Taika said, looking around.

"It's wonderful, I love that there's all this space," Ivo said, opening his arms.

"It's filling up quickly. It seems everyone is also famished," commented Daphne.

Nahia noticed that on the two opposite sides of the building there were long counters where people went to ask for their food. Half the people went to one counter and the other half visited the other side.

"It's curious, the third-years sit at the first tables, by the door," Taika commented.

"Yeah, the second-years are in the middle, and us newbies are at the back," said Daphne, who was watching the people sitting at their tables.

"I guess it's because they've earned the privilege," said Lily.

"As long as I'm fed, I don't mind where I have to sit, even if I had to sit on the floor with my legs crossed and meditate while I wait," Ivo commented.

"You meditate too?" Daphne said, opening her eyes wide.

"Of course, don't you?"

"Errr… no. I think it's a waste of time, and I don't understand how a Tauruk, which is supposed to be the most beastly race of Kraido, meditates. It's… totally illogical."

"Not all the Tauruk are the same, and meditating would help you with that temper and acidity of yours."

Daphne smiled obliquely.

"I love my temper and acidity. I don't want to change them."

"And here I was thinking all the Fatum were sweet and nice," Ivo said and glared at her.

"It seems that not all the Fatum and not all the Tauruk are the same, our squad is living proof of that," Taika said.

"We'd better go sit down. I don't know whether you've noticed, but there are two dragons in the middle of the hall, looking around," commented Taika.

"I've noticed," said Nahia. "They're both blue and not so big. About thirty feet long."

"They're young, they must have been punished with surveillance and control tasks," Lily guessed.

"That could be the case," Taika said as he motioned them to go toward the far end table.

They reached the first-years' Red Squadron section. They recognized the tables at once and sat down at theirs. They watched the place, sitting at their table and saying nothing for the moment, observing everything around them and internalizing it all. They were once again in a new sub-world that was part of the Drakoros Academy. It was not the flashiest place but it did not give them a feeling of overt danger, except for the two dragons in the middle that seemed to control everything by moving their heads from side to side every now and then.

"Have you noticed that the third-year tables are half empty?" Taika commented.

"Maybe they're no longer part of the academy," said Lily.

"Rather no longer part of the world of the living, if you get my meaning," said Daphne, and she winked at them repeatedly.

"We understand, unobtrusiveness and subtlety aren't exactly your forte."

Daphne smiled.

"I'll have to work on improving them."

Lily waved her hand to indicate she would have to work on them a lot.

"If it is truly the case that they have parted, may Mother Nature gather them in her womb and create new life out of death," Ivo recited and joined his huge beastly hands in prayer. Nahia noticed that the Tauruk's hands were like those of a human but about three times bigger and thicker. His hands and horns were even more disproportionate than his huge body, although his hoof-shaped feet were what most surprised her. Not because they were big, but because they were hooves and he stood on them.

"The second-years have one third of their tables empty..." Taika commented, who never missed any detail. His feline attributes made him alert to everything, both to what surrounded him and to what might be lurking in the vicinity.

"Perhaps they are out on an excursion," Daphne said in a cheerful tone with a comical wave.

"Yeah, sure. The dragons look like the kind to organize festive activities every now and then," Lily retorted.

"I'm going to get some food. We'd better leave the bad omens for after lunch." Ivo got up and nonchalantly went over to the counter closest to him.

"I'm going too, I'm famished," Lily said and went after Ivo.

"I hope they have good food, although I doubt it," Daphne said, getting up and following them. Odd, I would have thought they would get their food first, then go sit down. I know that is how I would do it at any rate.

Nahia watched the place and the people in it for a moment. For the first time since they had set foot in the dragons' realm, she heard conversations between people. She was surprised. The second- and third-years were talking among themselves as they sat at their tables, and they were doing so naturally. They looked at ease in spite of the dragons in the middle of the hall. They did not look worried about them, as if they knew that as long as they were at their tables, they could talk in peace. That was not the case for the first-years, who were sitting at their tables, not knowing how to behave or act and looking at the rest with troubled eyes.

The other two squads of the Red Squadron arrived and sat at their tables. They were as lost as all the others. They looked around and then at Nahia, who looked down, a little ashamed to find that everyone was looking at her. They were actually wondering where the rest of her squad was. Once they saw them at the long counter, they decided to go themselves. Nahia found it strange not to exchange greetings or talk among them, but she did not know them at all, not even the humans, and the rest least of all. In fact, she did not remember having seen the two human boys in the other squads, and she felt bad for not having noticed. Then she remembered how awful she had felt during The Climb and did not blame herself anymore. She had been through enough with surviving.

"See how tasty this food looks," said Ivo, coming back with a wooden tray and a huge plate of what looked like a roast.

"It does, and it smells very good," Nahia nodded. "I see they don't beat around the bush with portions."

"No, and that surprised me. I asked for a double serving and they gave it to me. It's because we, the Tauruk—well, and the Kapro too—eat a lot, like double the other races."

"Wow, I didn't know that, but from the looks of you I'm not surprised."

"I'll let you know if this is good," he said and took a big bite out of the roast in the purest beast style: holding it with his hands and using his teeth as a tearing weapon.

Nahia hid a shocked look.

Taika arrived with another good serving of roast, but smaller than Ivo's, and sat down beside the Tauruk.

"What's it like?" he asked him.

"Delicious, I'll have to go for more."

"Wonderful," Taika nodded and began to eat. He ate with his claws and jaws, tiger style, which also surprised Nahia, although not as much.

Daphne came with a smaller serving of roast and some vegetables.

"They have vegetables?" Nahia asked.

"Yeah, but these two went straight for the meat," Lily told her, also arriving with some roast and vegetables.

"What's your relative like, Ivo? Don't you have any qualms about eating him?" Daphne asked him.

Nahia could not believe Daphne had made such a joke. It was totally inappropriate.

Ivo looked at her with his beastly face.

"This is no relative of mine, and that was very rude and uncalled for. You should reconsider and think about why you feel the need to say things like that. I'm sure it would do you much good."

Ivo's calm and meditated reply left Daphne without a retort.

"The truth is, that for how pretty you are and your delicate appearance, you have a foul mouth, girl," Lily told her, who to Nahia's surprise used her fork and knife for the roast and vegetables. The Scarlatum had similar hands to a human. Only her nails were much longer and flexible, like a raptor bird.

"I guess it's out of contradiction," Daphne shrugged.

"Delicious indeed," Taika commented, getting back to his roast, "it's a shame there's only one course, but I guess it's so everyone gets fed."

As Nahia got up to go for her serving, she noticed Daphne was also using a knife and fork and did so delicately. She had manners, even if her character was something else. The Fatum's hands were very similar to a human's, almost identical.

Nahia went over to the counter and saw that the food was being served by about twenty Tergnomus, all dressed in white robes and white berets. She stared at them in surprise. One of them saw her and came over quickly.

"Today we have old cow roast with grilled vegetables, garlic, and onion. One course. Need any cutlery?"

"Huh? Yes, cutlery, yes."

"Single serving of both?"

"Yes, please."

"Right away," the Tergnomus told her as he went behind a wall and came back a moment later with the two plates on a tray almost as big as he was. He climbed the platform behind the counter and offered the tray to Nahia.

"Thank you."

"There's no need to thank me, it's my job and duty," the Tergnomus replied and turned to see to another person.

"This place is picturesque..." Nahia commented under her breath.

"Isn't it?" a familiar voice said.

Nahia raised her head from her tray and saw Maika.

"Maika! I'm so glad to see you!"

"Same here!" Maika grabbed Nahia by the arms and rubbed them in a friendly manner, careful not to make her drop the tray.

"What a pity we're not in the same squadron," Nahia said sadly.

"It is. We're all scattered. The system they use here is for that exact reason, so that we're not together."

"I realized that."

"Are you all right?"

"Yeah, I'm doing pretty well. My body is still aching, but I'm happy to be alive."

"I told you that you'd make it," Maika said, smiling.

"I wish I had your physique, then my chances would drastically increase."

"I'm sure you have other qualities I don't that will help you here."

"I'm not so sure."

You are only allowed to talk at the tables, they both received suddenly. The mental message caught them unawares. Maika's head lashed forward and Nahia's was thrown back. She grabbed the tray hard for balance and managed not to knock the plates over.

They both looked at the blue dragons in the middle of the hall. One of them was looking at them.

"We'd better leave it at that," Maika said.

"Yeah, we'd better. Take care and survive."

"You too," Maika nodded and went to order at the counter.

Nahia went back to her table and sat down.

"A friend of yours?" Lily asked as she looked at Maika.

"Yes, well… we met when we arrived."

"I see. Those are bonding experiences, like The Climb," Lily said, smiling.

"That's right."

"Wonderful. I'm going for another serving," said Ivo, standing.

"Don't speak to anyone. It's forbidden to talk outside the tables. One of those dragons just messaged it to me," Nahia informed them.

"New rules, what do you know?" said Daphne.

"It was too good to be true," Lily added.

Ivo went in search of his extra serving. As he was walking over to the counter, he passed Aiden, who had put on the clothes they had left for him in their room. Ivo ignored him and went to order.

"What happened?" Aiden asked when he reached the table.

"Don't you remember? How funny…" Daphne said with a mischievous smile.

"I remember we were in the administration building…"

"And then?" Taika asked him, watching the Drakonid with narrowed eyes.

"Then… I don't know what happened."

"Do you remember banging on the counter?" Nahia asked, interested. It was odd that he did not remember what had happened. Odd, and it might even be serious. Perhaps the strong blow was the cause that might explain it. But it had been in the nape, not the head… no, it was not the blow. Something else was wrong with

148

Aiden, something unique.

"Yes... I believe so."

"Nothing else?" Taika asked him.

"Well... no... until I woke up in my bed. Did you carry me there?"

"Yes, it was us," Taika confirmed.

"Because you'd fainted," Daphne informed him with a sly grin.

"Fainted? Me? That's impossible."

"I'm afraid so," Daphne assured him.

At that moment, Ivo came back with another serving of roast meat.

"We were telling Aiden that he fainted in the administration building," Daphne told him with a wink.

"Oh yes, fainted. Perhaps from the excitement of the moment," Ivo ventured and sat down to eat.

"It's the strangest thing. How embarrassing. I hope no dragon lords saw me."

"Don't worry. No one saw you," Taika assured him.

"Go get something to eat, it'll do you good," Nahia suggested.

Aiden sighed.

"Yes, perhaps it was the lack of food. I'll go get my strength back. This can't happen to me again. How unfortunate."

Aiden left, and the others watched him.

"Shouldn't we tell him the truth?" Nahia asked.

"To that 'head first', 'I'll do anything for my masters' dragon head? Of course not. Now we have something to take the wind out of his sails," Daphne said.

"But he has a right to know..."

"We'll avoid a fight this way," said Taika. "If we tell him Ivo hit him, there will be a fight. He won't let it stand, Drakonids are very proud."

"It was for his own good," Nahia said.

It was," Ivo nodded and went on eating.

"But he won't see it that way. He's a Drakonid," Taika made a gesture with his claws.

"Then maybe we should tell him and see what happens," Daphne chuckled.

"You're terrible," Lily chided.

"We won't tell him, and we'll avoid a fight that might end badly,"

Taika said. "Everyone agreed?"

Nahia nodded, then the rest followed suit. Daphne was the last one.

"All right, we won't tell him. What a bunch of party-poopers you are," the Fatum complained.

Aiden came back with a double serving of roast and sat down to eat. The others commented about the dining hall, the Exarbor, the Tergnomus, and the dragons in the middle of the hall. Just when Aiden was finishing eating, a terrible roar reached them.

"That's the call for us to go to class," Taika said.

Then they heard more roars, one after the other.

Nahia snorted. She had no idea what to expect from the classes, but she guessed they would be difficult and painful—possibly even deadly.

Chapter 19

They left the dining hall and went to the parade ground. They stopped to look around, since many people were coming out at a run and there was quite a bit of a chaos.

"It seems like they're calling everyone," Nahia commented, trying to find her way.

"Let's head toward the flame banner," said Taika, pointing at the upper left quadrant of the immense square where Irakas-Gorri-Gaizt was waiting. The great flame the dragon had created was still standing and burning.

"I wonder why our dragon has chosen that particular spot of the square," Lily commented.

"Because it's the farthest from the castle." Daphne replied.

"The masters' decisions are unquestionable, especially those of our captain and leader," Aiden chided them in a serious tone.

"You should take life a little more calmly," Ivo advised him.

"I don't need advice on how to behave, I know perfectly well how to."

"Yeah, sure, that's why you have seizures and then don't remember most of what happened," Daphne said sarcastically.

Aiden glared at her with hate. Nahia then noticed the likeness between Drakonids and dragons. She found them a little too similar.

"Let's have peace," she said so the conversation would not escalate and end up in a scuffle.

"Let's go before our leader gets impatient," Taika suggested.

Aiden ran off as if he were being chased by a pack of hungry monsters. The others followed him. They arrived with the other two groups belonging to the Red Squadron.

Line up in front of your leader and pay attention, Irakas-Gorri-Gaizt messaged, and they received the message like a painful sting. It was followed by a feeling of displeasure.

They all formed in the order and positions required. They stood still and directed their undivided attention to the leader of the Red Squadron.

Before you leave for your training, here is a concept you must understand and assimilate. Your squad is everything. You will train, eat, sleep, bleed, die, or live with your squad. From this moment on, your squad is your life. I hope I have made myself clear.

No one said anything, but the message came with the feeling that it was an unalterable truth everyone needed to internalize as such.

The time to begin the training has come. There is magical and martial training, and they are equally important. You must master each of them equally. Failure in training is not tolerated. Whoever is incapable of assimilating the teachings will die. Remember this.

The message did not surprise Nahia at all. She had been expecting it. The dragons did not allow a simple mistake, and they would never tolerate failure. The punishment was always the same: death. The moments of relaxation they had enjoyed in the barracks and the dining hall were only a mirage of tranquility. They were once again in danger of death. The worse thing was that it was clear this would be throughout all the year. They would be taking classes while doing their best to not fail and die. This was going to be pure agony, and Nahia would have to survive it, along with all her comrades.

You will now head to the Square of the Path located behind the castle. It is round and the color of silver. In the middle of the square there is a fountain, and around it you will find some Exarbor. They will tell you what training you have today and where you have to go. Do not go through the castle—you are not worthy of setting foot on its floor. It is forbidden to you. Go around it. You can only enter the castle with a leader, and only when said leader says so.

Nahia had no intention of going into the castle where she had seen the Colonel and Commander. They would surely be there, apart from other officers. Best not to even think of going anywhere near it.

Attend your training and do not fail. Remember that being here in this academy and training is a privilege and an honor you are being granted. Killing you is only a waste of time for everyone.

After the fateful message, the three squads began to head out toward the castle. Nahia's group went first as once again Aiden left first at a lightning pace, as if he would receive a prize for first place. A moment later he was setting a breakneck pace the others were trying to keep up with, although marching was obviously something they did not do very well.

"Can't you go any slower? There's no need for such a rush," Daphne told him.

"Yes, there is. We've received an order, and we must carry it out at once," Aiden replied with indignation.

"If we fall over we won't look good either," Lily intervened.

"We have to be the first, before all the other squads," Aiden insisted.

Nahia looked back, trying not to miss a step, and saw that the other squads were following them, competing to reach them. The Drakonids in the other squads urged them on the same way Aiden did with them. He was not the only one who had been indoctrinated to be perfectly obedient to the dragons and their orders.

They crossed the immense square, passing by two of the watchtowers located on the tall west wall. On top of both there was a dragon on watch duty. Nahia wondered for what end. There was no one who might come up here: they were on a floating island among the clouds. No one could attack them up here. Then she thought that perhaps those dragons were not watching to prevent an attack by the slave races, but because of the possibility of an attack by other dragons. This idea appealed to her. The clans vied for power. This realm was neutral, perhaps that was the reason. Or perhaps they were simply watching them in case other dragons tried anything.

They traveled past the side of the castle in a hurry. It was not as elegant as the front façade, and it was very long. The building's enormous size intensified the race to reach the Square of the Path. The Ardent Squad was at their heels, and the Searing Squad was pressing to overtake them. Aiden was all too aware of this and led them at a near sprint.

They went around the castle, following the west side of the great building, and arrived at the back. It left them speechless. A new world had opened before them. There was a large silver square with a fountain in the middle, and behind it was a dozen colossal buildings. They had no idea what they were for, but they were as massive as the whole back of the castle, which was gigantic.

Nahia looked everywhere, trying to grasp all of it, but it was so large and majestic that it was impossible. What did come to her mind was who might have built all those enormous, grand buildings. And it was not only the buildings themselves, but also the great wall that surrounded them and appeared to have no end, as well as the lookout towers which also continued all the way north beside the walls.

Aiden looked back and saw that the other squads were on top of them.

"Quickly, they're going to overtake us," he urged his comrades, waving them on.

"My goodness, you're a pain in the neck…" Daphne complained, panting.

"As if they were giving delicious dishes of food as a reward," commented Ivo, who with his long strides did not have much trouble following the Drakonid.

Lily was shaking her head.

Aiden headed straight to the round silver-colored square, which had runes and symbols engraved throughout. A fountain with a tall geyser in the middle threw water over forty-five feet in the air.

They reached the fountain and saw six Exarbor surrounding it with their backs to the water. Each one wore a breastplate in a different color. Aiden went to the first one to be faster. The Exarbor looked at him and wagged a long, leafy finger negatively.

"What? What do you mean no?" Aiden huffed, annoyed.

"They have different colored breastplates, I think we have to speak to the Exarbor wearing our color," said Taika, who was watching the whirl of people forming as the rest of the squads arrived.

"Yeah, I think you're right," Daphne said, and she moved away to see the six Exarbor standing around the fountain.

"Where's the red one?" Lily asked, looking down at her own red cloak.

"There, on the other side," Daphne cried.

"Let's go to him then," Aiden said as he ran, passing the two other groups in the Red Squadron that were reaching the same conclusion.

Nahia followed her comrades as they chased after Aiden. This world was so strange, and she felt utterly lost. But seeing all the other squads going from one end to the other around the fountain, seeking their Exarbor, she realized they were all as lost as she was and she felt a little better. Not much, but somewhat.

"Igneous Squad of the Red Squadron," Aiden reported, speaking rapidly to beat the Drakonid of the Ardent Squad who was arriving.

The Exarbor with the red breastplate began to consult an enormous tome he had in his hand-like branches.

"Quick, we don't want to be late," Aiden urged him.

"Don't be rude, let him do his job in peace," Daphne scolded him.

"Besides, no matter how much you press them, I doubt the poor little thinking trees can go any faster than they're already doing," Lily said.

Aiden glared at both of them.

"Red Squadron... first day of the week... Basic Dragon Magic... Arcane Arts Building... Red Classroom."

They were all puzzled at the Exarbor's words.

"Basic Dragon Magic?" Daphne asked, raising an eyebrow.

"Arcane Arts Building?" Aiden was looking to the north where the buildings were, trying to locate it.

"Which building is it out of the ones we can see?" Taika asked.

The Exarbor did not flinch at all the rushed questions, and with his innate calm he explained.

"It's the building... with a silver façade... and a white sphere... on top of the flat roof. There's no... mistaking it."

"There, in the middle of that square," Lily pointed her finger which ended in a sharp, red-nailed claw.

They all looked and identified the building at once.

"It has to be that one, indeed," Aiden said, ready to run over.

"All the groups in the Red Squadron have to go there?" the Drakonid of the Ardent Squad, who was listening behind Aiden, asked.

"Yes, all... the squads train together... all the squads of a squadron always have... the same classroom," the Exarbor explained.

"Oh, all right," the Drakonid nodded and signaled to his squad, which was listening a few steps back. They turned around and ran to the building.

"Blazes! They're overtaking us! Everyone, run!" Aiden said, racing after them.

"This dragon head is insufferable," Daphne shook her head.

"She's right, you know," Lily agreed, also shaking her head.

Aiden tried to arrive first, alone, but the other two squads, who were right behind him, overtook him and he was left alone at the door, waiting for his squad and cursing in his Drakonian language. Nahia was glad she did not understand what he was saying, because she was sure they were not nice things.

As they went in third, Ivo caught up with Aiden.

"The one who runs more does not arrive first, but whoever

thinks more. And whoever thinks more doesn't see the need for such haste."

Aiden looked at him with wide eyes, unable to believe what the Tauruk had said.

"Bathe in the knowledge he's bestowed on you," Daphne chuckled as she passed by his side.

"Our Ivo is very wise," Lily commented, passing Aiden with a broad smile on her seductive face.

Taika and Nahia looked at one another, smiled, and went in without a word.

Aiden continued to rant and rave in his own language under his breath.

Chapter 20

The Arcane Arts Building was almost as majestic as the great castle. The whole front façade was silver, with huge gold runes and symbols in the dragon language. From how intricate the runes and symbols were, Nahia thought they were not in the dragon's language but rather in the language of their magic. But, as both were unintelligible to her, all she could do was admire them and shrug.

They entered the grand building, which was round and three stories high. Every story formed a circle above the one below. Nahia assumed there was one for each year. In the center she found a sprawling garden, well-tended, with trees of gold and silver, around another of those huge fountains that spouted water forty-five feet high. Nahia wondered whether those trees were real or only for decoration. She did not know any kind of tree with leaves like those. The roof of the grand building had a wide terrace, and on it was an enormous white sphere. It looked similar to the white pearl they had used to access this realm. She wondered whether this one would also have power.

Finding the Red Classroom was not hard, since the doors leading to the classes were marked with the year and the color of the squadron they belonged to. The first-years were on the ground floor, and the Red Classroom was the third one on the left as you entered the building.

Inside the classroom, which was sizeable, they found a silver dragon waiting at the far end. With it was an Exarbor who seemed to be about a thousand years old. His leaves were charred and spent, his branches dry and expired. By the entrance, following the rounded shape of the building, were long benches at three different heights.

"Sit down… everyone… on the benches…" the Exarbor beside the dragon said.

The three squads sat down in the order they had come in with Nahia and her comrades on the third tier.

Welcome, pupils. This is a place of learning and personal development. It is not a hostile environment. You have nothing to fear here. My task is to teach you, not punish or kill you. There are others for that, it messaged, along with a feeling of calmness.

Nahia was surprised when she received it. It was the first time she had received a pleasant mental message from a dragon. She wondered whether it was sincere or if it was nothing but a trick to make them trust it and then fail more easily. She would have to wait and see to solve this riddle. Something else that surprised her was that this dragon was undoubtedly female. It was somehow difficult to say why, but it was prettier and more refined than the other dragons they had seen so far. The message had also come in a feminine tone, silkier, very different from the others she had received.

I will introduce myself. I am Mag-Zilar-Ond, and I will be your instructor of Basic Dragon Magic during all this first year. My work will consist of teaching you to use the magic within you, and later on to use it efficiently and quickly, which is most important, as you will discover. This, my class, only deals with this discipline, but there are more magical ones you will study. I will not rob you of the surprise and suspense, so I will not tell you what they are. Only that you will learn a lot and eventually become dragon magi of great power. That is if you survive this first year and then the next two. But let us go step by step. Before you become great warlocks and witches who have mastered the magic of dragons, you must awaken it and learn to use it. This is Mabor-Exarbor. You may consider him my assistant.

"A pleasure… to meet the new batch… of this year's pupils… of the Red Squadron," he greeted them and bowed very slowly.

Nahia was watching the silver dragon unobtrusively, and she thought the creature was quite old. Its reptilian eyes looked tired and its size and scales were even bigger than those of Irakas-Gorri-Gaizt, so it had to be older than the captain. This class was the initial class on dragon magic and any instructor could probably teach it, especially considering they did not know anything about magic. She found it odd that it should be taught by an elder who must have great knowledge.

The first day of learning in this class of dragon magic is one that none of you will ever forget. I do not say this to frighten you, that is not my intention, although some of you might panic. I say it because the first thing we are going to do is awaken your inner power, your magic, and that is something very special. Mabor, let us begin with the ritual. These are three complete squads, and it will take time.

Mabor walked very slowly to the center of the hall, where there was a pedestal with a large tome open on it.

Nahia became nervous at once and looked at Lily, whose eyes

were wide.

"This is getting scary," Daphne whispered in a low voice.

Aiden motioned for her to be quiet.

"It's on the other side of this huge hall, it can't hear us,' Daphne retorted, sure that the dragon was too far away.

"I don't think it'll hear us from there if we speak very low," nodded Taika, who was calculating the distance with closed eyes.

"Unless dragons have very sharp ears," commented Lily.

"Well, that's all we need. As if they weren't already overpowered creatures!" Daphne protested.

"Dragons have normal hearing and vision. They aren't exceptional," Ivo said.

"How do you know that?" Aiden asked, surprised, and the look on his face showed that he knew this too, so it had to be true.

"Not only Drakonids know about their lords," Ivo said nonchalantly.

"Have any of you had your power awakened?" asked Daphne.

"You mean if our magic has ever manifested? Not mine," Lily shook her head.

Nahia also shook her head. Taika did the same.

"I've tried to awaken it, but I haven't been able to," Aiden admitted.

"I have preferred to be at peace," Ivo said.

"So no one, not a whiff," Daphne confirmed.

The Exarbor wrote something down in the tome.

"I am ready, my lady," he said to the dragoness.

Very well, let us begin with the ritual. You will not feel too much pain, but some is inevitable. As with everything in the world of magic, there is always a price to pay, in this case a little suffering. It will not kill you, do not worry. You will bear it. The fear, anguish, and nerves, that is all on you. Whoever masters them will find it easier to pass this small and somewhat painful rite. Whoever does not master them, well, they will suffer—not from my doing, but from your own. Everyone's mind is powerful and may facilitate or complicate an experience to unexpected extremes. In that, I can do nothing.

"Everyone, take it easy. Let us face this test with serenity and without fear. Everything will turn out well," Ivo said calmly.

"Sure, because nature will protect us," Daphne snapped in disbelief.

"Exactly," Ivo gestured.

Daphne rolled her eyes.

Lily took Nahia's hand and made a cheering gesture. Nahia appreciated it and smiled at her.

Let the first pupil come forward, Mag-Zilar-Ond messaged.

Mabor-Exarbor pointed his hand-like branch at the first student on the left in the bottom tier group.

It was a Drakonid, and he got up quickly. With a determined step, he went forward. When he was at Mabor's level, the Exarbor asked him his name. The Drakonid told him, and the Exarbor wrote it down in the tome.

Come over to me, the silver dragoness messaged.

The Drakonid showed no fear or doubt as he walked until he was in front of the dragoness as it sat on its hind legs and leaned on its fore ones with a raised head. The Drakonid knelt as he was supposed to do in front of a dragon.

Rise. For this ritual I need you standing,

The Drakonid stood up.

Open your arms and close your eyes. You will feel something inside you coming to life. Do not resist, let it awaken.

The Drakonid nodded and opened his arms.

Mag-Zilar-Ond opened its mouth, and from it came a silver beam that hit the Drakonid in the middle of his chest. The dragoness kept the beam steady, as if it wanted to pierce him through. The Drakonid kept his arms open, and he now had his head thrown back. He began to emit a grunt, as if it hurt. The dragoness continued projecting the beam for a long while. The Drakonid grunted louder now, as if it hurt more. In spite of this, the dragoness continued with the ritual, the beam uninterrupted. After another long while, the grunt became one of pure suffering. He was now in real pain.

Nahia feared for the worst. She had no idea what that silver beam might be or what it was doing to that poor wretch, but it was clear he was in great pain.

"Hold up, like a true Drakonid," Aiden encouraged him under his breath.

"That looks bad," Daphne said.

"Yeah, we're going to suffer, and I don't suffer well. Apart from the fact that it's terrible for my complexion," said Lily.

"We can cope with that," Taika said, and he raised his fist in a cheering gesture.

Do not resist your inner power. Let it awaken, Mag-Zilar-Ond messaged to the Drakonid and extended it so they all might understand what was happening.

The Drakonid let out a sort of grunt-roar. After what seemed like an eternity, a silver flash came out of his chest.

That is it. Very well. The power has awakened in you. Mag-Zilar-Ond stopped the beam and the Drakonid fell to his knees in front of the dragoness and lowered his arms. For a moment he remained there, still, overwhelmed by the experience.

Rise and go back to your place. Now you have power.

The Drakonid got up with difficulty and stumbled back to his place. His face showed suffering. They could all see a silver light coming out of his chest, as if he had a silver star encrusted in him.

Let us continue. Let the next one come forward. This ritual must proceed until you have all passed through it.

Nahia realized the ritual was going to be long and painful. Only with the first one Mag-Zilar-Ond had taken a long time. She was not mistaken; the ritual took the whole day. One by one, they all went through it, and they all suffered. When it was Nahia's turn, she got up and walked over with determination. Aiden, Taika, and Ivo had already been through it, and although she could see in their faces that they had suffered, the three had born the ritual and now had that silver star shining in the middle of their chest. She did not want to be less than her comrades. If they had passed the ritual, she would too. It did not matter that it hurt.

She opened her arms and shut her eyes in front of Mag-Zilar-Ond. The beam hit her in the chest and at once she began to feel a pang of pain in her chest, which increased gradually as time went by. Nahia did not feel anything awakening inside her. Only this sharp pain that kept growing. What she did notice was that the silver beam penetrated inside her and acted on something. It was not her flesh or any of her organs, it was something different. It was as if the dragon was radiating power to a small egg with silver scales inside her chest. This picture appeared in her mind, which felt very odd. Why was she seeing an egg with silver scales in the middle of her chest? It had to be the pain she was enduring that made her see things. But no, it was not, the pain was not so intense, and she had her eyes closed. This was no hallucination. It was her mind trying to rationalize what was going on.

Mag-Zilar-Ond continued sending power to her body through the silver beam and Nahia felt the pain sharpening. Her suffering was increasing. She clenched her jaw and focused on the silver egg she saw inside her chest. She guessed that if it was an egg, it would need to break for its magic to awaken. It was as if the dragoness were incubating that egg through the silver beam. Nahia decided to try and help the process and make the pain subside. She focused and wished with all her heart that the egg would break and that whatever was inside would be born. She wished for it strongly as the pain increased. Since nothing happened, she wished it even more in the midst of her pain. She did not know whether it would have any effect, perhaps not. Probably not. But that did not stop her from trying. And it happened. The top of the egg broke in a thousand pieces, and from inside a small dragon came out, the size of the palm of her hand. It was very bright; it gave off a blinding light and radiated power.

Perfect. Very well. The power has awakened in you, Mag-Zilar-Ond stopped the beam.

Nahia opened her eyes. She looked down at her chest and saw it was shining with a light that came from within, from the dragon that had just woken up. She did not know what it meant or the effect it would have on her, but she was glad the pain had finally stopped. The consequences of this process she would find out tomorrow, but right then she felt exhausted and could barely stand. She went back to her place as best she could.

Next were Daphne and Lily. They both bore the process and took a little longer than Nahia, so their agony was greater. But they succeeded, and when the three of them sat together, they held hands to cheer and comfort one another.

They had to wait for everyone else to pass the ritual, which was additional torture, since they were exhausted and sore from the experience. Once they had all gone through the test, the dragoness messaged them.

I am very pleased with this squad. You have all managed to awake the power within you. This does not always happen. There are those who are incapable of awakening it and have to be... expelled. It is a pity, but it happens every year. You have been lucky in that sense. Now go and rest and recover. Do it with the certainty that magic, the power of the dragon, resides in you, the message reached them, along with a feeling of achievement.

The positive feeling surprised them, but no one said anything.

They all headed back to the barracks, exhausted and sore. They passed by the castle on their way back, and this time Aiden was not running. Nahia decided to ask her comrades, since she felt different.

"Does anyone feel, oh, I don't know, different after this?"

"Well, we do have a shining silver star sort of encrusted in our chests, so I'd say a little different, yes," Daphne replied, looking down at the glow that shone through her clothes.

"I'm exhausted. I have no idea what they did to me in that ritual, but I'm sooo tired," Lily said, yawning.

"My inner peace has been disturbed by today's experience. I need to meditate and concentrate in order to calm my being," Ivo said.

"I think we're all feeling physical exhaustion," Aiden commented, stretching.

"If that star leaves a mark, that dragoness instructor is going to get what for," Lily said angrily.

"I think Nahia means whether we feel different inside, don't you?" Taika said and turned to her.

"Yeah, that's it. Has this changed you internally in any way? It's just that I... feel as if a bright dragon had awakened inside me..."

"That's what we should all feel," Aiden told her.

"A dragon?" Daphne asked blankly.

"Yeah, that's what I felt, like a dragon hatched from a silver egg within me," Nahia explained.

"I was only able to feel a strong light within me," Taika said.

"And do we all have to see that dragon?" Lily asked, raising an eyebrow.

"That's how it should be," Aiden confirmed.

"Have you seen it?" Lily asked in a challenging tone.

"If anyone sees it, I bet he does. He lives in a fantasy where dragons are wonderful, of course he would see one inside him," said Daphne.

"Of course I feel it and noticed it, as it should be," Aiden said.

Lily and Daphne made faces that meant it did not surprise them in the least.

"We must think that we will all manifest it and feel it at some pint. It'll be part of our being, a new and wonderful experience," said Ivo with a mystic tone in his deep voice.

"Yeah, like the one we've just been through, painful and not transcendental in the least," Daphne refuted.

"If I have a bright dragon inside me, it'd better not spoil my skin," Lily said.

"Let's focus on the positives. We should all manifest the power and feel it. We will," Taika assured them. "Let's go and rest now."

The group arrived at the barracks, and as soon as they went in they all got into their beds. They were so exhausted they fell asleep at once. Nahia had strange dreams where a bright dragon came out of her body to take shape in front of her, radiant and powerful, but instead of being her enemy, this one was her defender and friend. She slept and rested like she had not done in days.

Chapter 21

The first light of the morning came in through the barracks' windows. Even before the morning roar woke them up, Aiden did by jumping out of bed with a shout.

"Wake up! The day begins!"

Ivo gave a grunt that sounded like "don't bother me" and turned over in his bed to go on sleeping.

"Dawn is almost upon us," Taika murmured as he opened one feline eye to check the morning light.

"Just a little more time," Daphne pleaded, covering her head with the sheet.

Nahia was still so tired she said nothing. She did not move either. She stayed still, trying to recover a little more of her exhausted strength.

"I need a little more beauty sleep," said Lily.

Aiden got dressed at top speed, and once ready to run out, he went through the room to see whether his comrades were getting up. Only Taika had risen and was finishing getting dressed.

"Wake up! We have to go and line up!" Aiden shouted.

Ivo grunted again and opened one eye.

"Waking up must be peaceful, like sleep. These morning shouts aren't good for the soul."

"So? Get up! Our leader is waiting!" Aiden's shouts were incredulous—he obviously could not believe his eyes.

Nahia half rose onto her side and felt very sore and tired again. She needed at least another week of rest and long relaxing hours of sleeping in order to recover. She knew she was not going to have that luxury, so she tried to clear her head.

Daphne got up with her fingers in her ears.

"It's bad enough to have to get up at first light, you don't need to scream as if the barracks were on fire."

"But you're not moving!" Aiden argued, waving his hands, beside himself.

Lily got up, stretching her arms and yawning.

"All this racket affects my beauty sleep. If I get bags under my eyes because of you, I'll tear off those white scales of yours and make a necklace with them," she threatened Aiden.

"You're the worst squad anyone could have!" Aiden yelled and waved his arms furiously.

"You'd better get ready before he has another seizure," Taika said. He was dressed and ready to go.

Ivo began to get dressed quite parsimoniously. His movements were big and slow, at least so early in the morning.

"I'm ready," he said with his cloak half on.

The girls took a while longer: Nahia, because everything hurt and every movement invited a complaint, Daphne because she decided to change her hairdo and wear it loose, and Lily because, well, it was Lily, and getting ready always took her an eternity.

"You three don't wear boots, we do," she said as an excuse.

Taika smiled.

"Now that you mention it, Aiden and I have claws instead of feet and Ivo has hooves. What do you have?"

Lily made an exaggeratedly insulted face.

"Please, you never ask a lady what her feet are like. How rude, I can't believe it."

"What a drama queen. She has feet like Nahia's and my own, but her nails are like red eagle claws. Big boots fit her well for some reason," Daphne explained, sounding annoyed.

"Daphne, what a sour person you are when you first wake up, really… you should never tell a young lady's secrets, least of all to a boy," Lily scolded her.

"Have you noticed we aren't glowing like yesterday?" Nahia asked, looking down at her own chest.

"True, we're not shining anymore. How curious," Daphne commented.

"I prefer it this way, it was making me nervous," Lily admitted.

"I hope it doesn't mean anything bad," Nahia said wistfully.

"I'm sure it's normal," Taika said in an attempt to comfort them.

"If none of us are shining, it must be the natural state we should be in. The odd thing would be if some of us glowed and some didn't," Ivo said, scratching his head.

"We're the last ones, this is an embarrassment!" Aiden shouted at them. He had half his body out of the door and was watching the other squads going out into the corridor.

166

"We're… coming… you dope…" Daphne said.

"I believe the skin around my pretty red ears is wrinkling with so much shouting," Lily said, massaging her ears.

Nahia took a couple of steps, and seeing that her body held up decently, although muscles she did not know she had hurt, she decided to take it as a victory. The others seemed to have recovered from the first day quickly. That was not the case with her. She decided she would make it through the second day however she could. It was wishful thinking, but she came out of the barracks with that idea in her head. Survive another day.

They did not have to think where to go or what to do. As they came out, they heard calling roars. At once, they looked at the fiery banner of their squadron. They saw their leader was beside the great flame, waiting.

"Come on, our leader is waiting!" Aiden cried and ran off.

"Someone should tell our little rock-headed dragon to calm down a little," Daphne commented as she followed him, although she was not running. "You don't necessarily get better prizes by running more."

"I agree with you. Such haste messes up my hair," Lily said as she fixed it on one side of her head.

Nahia noticed the long, wavy, jet-black hair of the Scarlatum. It was beautiful.

"What beautiful hair you have," she told her.

"Only my hair? All of me is a work of art," she replied, half joking, half serious, and laughed with her seductive laughter.

Daphne shook her head.

"Go on, feed her ego, as if she didn't do it all by herself."

Lily waved her hand for her to let it be and laughed again. Nahia envied not only her hair but her spirit. Of all of them, the Scarlatum seemed to have the greatest self-esteem and the best sense of humor. The shocking thing was that Daphne was the prettiest, but her surly, grumpy temper seemed to eclipse her radiant, physical beauty.

All of a sudden, Nahia realized she was not cold, although the air on her face was chilly. She looked down at her scaly clothes and felt the inside of the cloak, the thick black material. She did not know what kind of material it was, but it kept out the cold completely, which made her wonder. As she approached the banner, she also realized she was having less trouble breathing. They had already talked about this and Taika had assured them it was because of the height they were at, as Nahia had suspected. If it was easier to breathe, it must be because they were acclimating to the height. This thought comforted her. The longer they spent up here among the clouds, the better they would acclimatize and the less difficult it would be to breathe.

They crossed the great parade ground, and as they approached their banner, they were joined by the other two squads. Nahia noticed that, like in hers, the ones leading them were Drakonids. She wondered what they had been taught since infancy in their land for it to be like that. Nothing good, she was sure.

Line up, squadron, Irakas-Gorri-Gaizt messaged to them, together with a feeling that it was an unquestionable order.

The three red squads lined up in the established order and remained firm and with their heads bowed in front of their leader.

You will now go to break your fast and then to training. This is a routine you will follow without exception at the first hour. From now on, there will be no more calls. You will go by the sun dial. Do not arrive here late or to training every morning, or the punishment will be exemplary. Now, break ranks and go!

Breakfast was quick, and they did not talk much. They were all intent on being prompt. Someone had to watch the sun dial. Taika suggested doing so in turns, but Aiden refused. He would take over that task because he did not trust the others. He made this clear enough and earned himself several acid comments from Daphne.

They arrived at the Square of the Path and went in search of the Exarbor with the red breastplate. Today they were not the first to arrive either, which annoyed Aiden. The Searing Squadron was already marching to the north buildings.

"Igneous Squad of the Red Squadron," Aiden reported.

"We could follow the Searing Squadron," Lily commented, seeing them march. "We'll have the same assignment.

"That is correct... Red Squadron... second day of the week... Basic Martial Training... Weapons Building... Red Classroom."

"What building is that?" Aiden asked almost before the Exarbor had finished, in an impatient tone for the Exarbor's slowness.

"The fortress building to the north... behind that of magic... you will recognize it because on the façade... are drawn...a knife, a spear, a sword... and a silver shield."

"I don't think it'll be difficult to find," Lily smiled.

"Come on, let's not be late!" Aiden urged, already running.

"This one's going to get to war before it even starts," Daphne commented, putting her hand to her forehead.

They arrived at the building, and there was no doubt it was the Weapons Building. It looked like a great fortress, long and without walls around it. The building was long and expanded to the sides, to then form a square with an open space within, where about thirty squadrons or more could line up.

On the front and central part, which looked like the main building, the knife, sword, spear, and shield were drawn in silver, and very large. They could be seen from afar. Nahia wondered why the building only depicted those weapons and not, for instance, a bow.

"Hurry up, they're already going in!" Aiden urged them, seeing that other squads were also entering the building,

"Can he not see that those squads are second- and third-years?" Daphne commented, annoyed.

"How do you know they're second- and third-years?" asked Ivo, who was watching them go in.

"They look a lot more mature and weathered than us," said Lily, looking at them with narrowed eyes.

"That too, but their cloaks are different," Daphne said.

"Different how?" Ivo asked, apparently unable to see the difference.

"They have a different dragon on their back, and underneath it the number 2 and the number 3. If you look closely, you can see it," said Taika.

"Oh… true…"

Nahia had already noticed. What she did not know was what it meant to have different dragons to theirs. What she did find curious was that they all wore the same colors as the first-years. She guessed that the squadrons were maintained when they passed the first course. Realizing this brought her spirits down a little, since it meant they would surely have the same leader. They would be the Red Squadron for the whole three years and would serve Irakas-Gorri-Gaizt. That was a lot to swallow and digest.

They went into the large building and saw that the squads were heading to different halls. They started to look for theirs. It was not difficult to find, since the first-year classrooms were located closer to the entrance. They only had to find the one assigned to their squadron. A red rune above the wooden double door arch made it clear it was their classroom. The door was open, so they went in. The other two squads were already inside.

They found that the classroom consisted of an empty space, wide, without furniture. At the far end, a male black dragon of considerable size was waiting. In front of it stood a Felidae lion, a Scarlatum, and a Drakonid. They were all males and older than them. They were wearing armor different from theirs, heavier and more solid, although also with scales. They had gold and silver detailing which shone in the light, and at their waists the three carried long swords. They looked like real warriors. The lion had white scales on one cheek, the Scarlatum had brown ones above his nose and eyebrows, and the Drakonid had red scales running diagonally down the left side of his face.

They all stood in line in front of the dragon and its warriors. They knelt, sitting on their heels, and bowed forward to show respect, as they knew they must.

Welcome, Red Squadron, to Basic Martial Training. I am Mai-Beltz-Gaiz, and I will be your teacher. A Dragon Warlock must be capable of mastering both magic and weapons. I will teach you the initial part of the Path of Weapons, which you must follow and master.

With me are three expert warriors who will act as trainers. Experience has shown that in the art of weapons, the inferior races learn better if they can emulate a master of a similar race. It is for this reason that these three are here. We dragons do not need auxiliary weaponry, we have enough with our claws and jaws. That is not your case. In yours, weapons are of great advantage, although some of the races have claws and jaws they can use. Trainers, speak.

The three trainers stepped forward.

"Everyone, stand up!" the lion ordered.

"Line up as a squad!" ordered the Scarlatum.

"Keep your head down before your lord and master in weapons, Mai-Beltz-Gaiz," the Drakonid ordered.

They all stood up at once and lined up straight but with bowed heads.

"I am sure you are all thinking about what weapon you will use and how to wield it. You look at the swords the trainers are carrying at their waist and figure that you too will carry one. That is totally erroneous. In order to use a weapon properly, you first have to prepare the body and learn to fight without one. That is what you will learn in this class."

The Felidae lion stood in front of Nahia's squad and her comrades, the Scarlatum in front of the Ardent Squad, and the Drakonid in front of the Searing Squad.

We will begin the lesson with a simple exercise. Each one of you will try to knock down the master with your hands and physical strength.

Nahia looked at Lily and Daphne with fear in her eyes. She was never going to be able to knock down a lion as strong and weathered as him. Not in a thousand years. Lily looked at her and made a face; she was not going to be able either. Daphne said nothing but she let out a massive sigh. It sounded like her two comrades.

"Come on," the Felidae lion told Nahia.

Nahia cursed the bad luck that had placed her at the front of her squad. If she was always going to be first, she was going to suffer a lot. She was not going to be able to see what the others did and learn something before the humiliation that would inevitably come every time.

She stepped forward and looked at the lion in front of her. He was strong and fierce-looking. Just the thought made her knees knock.

"Put your arms on my shoulders," he ordered.

Nahia did as he said.

The Felidae lion placed one leg backward.

"Now put one leg forward, a little flexed."

She was beginning to see what the lion intended. Nahia did as he told her.

"Now, push with all your strength. Move me from my position."

Naha let a sigh escape her. She took a deep breath through her nose and pushed with all her little strength. Nothing happened. The lion had to weigh at least three times her own weight. It was impossible for her to move him. Besides, he was also in some kind of defensive stance which prevented her.

"Keep pushing, make an effort," the instructor told her in a harsh tone.

Nahia clenched her jaw and tried to move him with all her being.

While she tried, the other two humans, two strong boys, were trying to move their instructors with the same lack of luck as Nahia.

"Stronger," the instructor ordered, and Nahia knew she was running out of strength. She made one last effort and gave her everything. The lion did not budge an inch from where he was standing.

Nahia gasped, out of strength.

"Very well. Now it's my turn. Imitate my pose."

Nahia looked into the lion's feline eyes, expecting him to be joking. The hard, determined gaze indicated he was not. She did not dare protest or say anything. She did what the instructor asked.

Without another word, the instructor gave Nahia a dull push with the palm of his claws. Nahia flew toward one of the walls. She barely missed it because the instructor had calculated his strength so she would not. Nahia was left sitting on her sore bottom.

A moment later, the two human boys were flying backward like her with the same result.

There were murmurs of protest.

Silence. Pay attention. You are weak of body and mind. This test only proves it. Make a bigger effort. The weak will not survive, the black dragon messaged, and they all grew silent at once.

"Next," the Felidae lion called.

Daphne sighed and went to do the exercise while Nahia got up, feeling sore, and returned to her place in the line.

The Fatum tried with all her being and part of her will, which she had in abundance. She managed nothing. She ended up in the same place Nahia had fallen, with her bottom sore. She did so clearly displeased.

Lily was stronger than Nahia and Daphne, but she could not make the lion budge at all. He threw her backward, the same as her comrades, and she ended up in the same place.

Then it was the boys' turn. Aiden was first, convinced he was going to succeed in the test. He pushed with all he had in the hopes that his physical power might move the instructor. He really tried, with all his muscles and spirit, in the certainty that he was one of the chosen by his masters, someone strong and powerful, more than the other races. He did not succeed. Not only that, the lion sent him flying like the girls and he ended up in the same place as them. Nahia noticed that this instructor was not only strong, but that he

172

controlled his physical strength with precision.

Ivo was next. His comrades wished him luck under their breath. If anyone might beat their instructor, it was Ivo. On the other hand, Ivo was not the typical Tauruk-Kapro, so the squad was not sure what to expect from him. That he was the strongest, there was no doubt. That he could defeat the instructor was another story, because Ivo never used his brute strength, unlike his fellow Tauruk.

To begin with, he got in position with much more delay than the other two Tauruk-Kapro because he had walked at a much slower pace. In fact, he appeared to be meditating on the test, which was pretty puzzling. They were all hoping Ivo would at least affect the instructor; he was at least a head taller and broader of shoulder.

The instructor met Ivo's gaze and Nahia realized there was no doubt in them. That Felidae lion had not the least doubt that the great Ivo would not make him budge. This made her lose heart. If Ivo could not, there was no hope for any of them. And as if she had had a premonition, that was what happened. Ivo tried with all his bestiality, and he did bring it out. He did not hold back—he behaved like the other two Tauruk-Kapro in the other squads, one of them a Kapro with large ram horns called Cordelius. The other was a female Tauruk not as big as Ivo but with a much worse temper known as Valka.

The three tested their instructors. They pushed with the strength of beings born to run over anyone with their enormous and powerful bodies. But, and to everyone's surprise except Nahia's, who had guessed it already, they did not manage to move their instructors from where they stood. Not only that, what was worse, they made total fools of themselves when the three instructors threw them flying back to the same spot where they had sent the others as if they weighed nothing, as if it were no effort for them.

Nahia sighed deeply while she watched Ivo get up, sore and a tad humiliated by the defeat, although he was hiding it. It was Taika's turn, and he looked at them with eyes that knew what was going to happen and that it was inevitable. And so it was. If Ivo had not succeeded, being the strongest of them all, Taika would not either. He ended up like all the rest, and after getting up nimbly, he returned to the lineup.

I hope you have learned the lesson. Brute force does not conquer all. You will work until you are able to move your instructors. And not only that, but until you are able to throw them backward as they did with you today, because it is possible, and whoever wants to move forward on the Path must do it. The instructors will now teach you a basic defensive stance and a series of exercises and movements to improve your balance, agility, and body strength. My advice is that you apply yourselves and work hard. Because what you have proven here today is regrettable.

Nahia looked at her comrades, and they returned glances that meant they were not sure what to expect. The instructor showed them the defensive stance he was using and then several combinations of feet and arm movements for the rest of the day until the instructors considered the class finished.

As Nahia was withdrawing to the dining hall with her squad, she was thinking about falling in her bed exhausted. She realized that every muscle in her arms, legs, and abdomen hurt from the effort. The worst was that they had only done moves and nothing more. The fact that her body hurt so much seemed to her a symptom that things would only get much worse and the pain would only skyrocket.

Chapter 22

The following day, the Red Squadron reported for the class on basic magic.

Welcome, Red Squadron. Sit down and pay attention. Today will be another interesting day for you, Mag-Zilar-Ond the silver dragoness messaged them in greeting.

They sat down and listened, shifting between feeling nervous and expectant about what would happen in class. The first thing Nahia noticed was that Mabor-Exarbor was in the center by the pedestal with the open tome and that there was a large chest at his feet. She wondered what might be inside and what it could be for. Just having these questions wandering through her head made her nervous.

We have already awakened the power that lives within you. We have made the dragon of power break out of its egg and manifest. But this is only the first step. I want to know, who among you felt the dragon be born? Whoever did, stand up.

Aiden and the other two Drakonids stood up.

You were expecting to feel it, since you have knowledge of the process. Anyone else?

Nahia hesitated. She did not want to draw attention to herself, it might be a trick question. She did not trust the dragoness. On the other hand, if she did not tell the truth and somehow the silver dragoness found out, it would not forgive the lie. She decided not to take the risk: she preferred not to lie. She rose slowly.

A Human? Well, this is surprising, Mag-Zilar-Ond messaged, along with a feeling of surprise which reached Nahia very clearly.

"What is… your name… Human?" Mabor asked her.

"Nahia…" she replied with some fear.

Mabor wrote something down in his great tome.

"It is… registered," he said.

If that was good or bad there was no way to know, but the fact that her name was registered did not please Nahia at all.

Now, those who felt it but did not see it clearly in their mind, sit down, Mag-Zilar-Ond ordered.

To Nahia's enormous surprise, Aiden and the other two

Drakonids sat down. Only she remained standing. She realized that everyone else was staring at her.

Very interesting. And tell me, Human. Did you see the egg and how it broke too?

Nahia could not believe the dragoness was speaking to her directly. It had asked her a direct question. But they could not speak to a dragon, so she nodded and remained with her head bowed.

That is even more interesting. Very few have that skill. I see you have golden scales. Are you a Flameborn? Have they done the test?

Nahia was getting more and more nervous. She nodded twice quickly, wishing the questioning would end.

Write that down, Mabor. It has been a long time since we have had a Flameborn in the academy. A true anomaly, and from the symptoms she is beginning to present, it is one of the significant anomalies. We will have to watch her and study her.

"Absolutely," Mabor nodded and began to write in his tome.

Those notes seemed to Nahia as if she were being sentenced to death, and from how nervous and anxious she was, she began to feel sick. She felt an extreme heat that began to consume her body. She tried to swallow but had trouble doing so. Her breathing began to be difficult as well. She recognized the symptoms: she was beginning to have one of her seizures. She reached for her belt under her cloak.

Sit down, Human. You are a rarity, something singular. I hope you will be able to understand what it means and the difficulties and opportunities linked to that. I will not lie to you. Your Path will be a little more complicated than that of your comrades, but the opportunities you will have will also be greater. That is if you do not perish, of course.

Nahia sat down like lightning and, bending over, she uncorked the tonic she already had in her hand. She pretended to cough to hide the motion and took it in one gulp in the blink of an eye.

Very well, those of you who did not feel the dragon awaken within you, it is because you are not aligned with your magic. It is strange to you, alien. That must change. In order to walk the Path of Dragons, it is necessary to know the dragon you carry inside you. Whoever does not will not succeed, and I do not need to remind you what happens to those who do not walk the Path.

The message filled everyone who had not managed to feel the awakening of the dragon within themselves with anxiety. Daphne and Lily looked at one another with troubled faces. Taika put his hand on Ivo's back, who had a twisted look, something unusual for him.

Nahia was recovering from the attack she had begun to suffer and which the tonic had prevented and had not had time to think through everything going on.

Mabor, the spheres for the pupils, said Mag-Zilar-Ond.

"Yes, my lady," the Exarbor said, and with his usual slowness he stood in front of the chest and opened it carefully. He put his hand in and took out a crystal-white sphere and showed it to the squads.

What Mabor is showing you is a Learning Pearl. It is an object which from now on you will carry with you always, and which you must not lose. Whoever does will be punished. No excuses, no mercy.

Nahia found that lapidary sentence the dragons were so fond of, "no excuses, no mercy," terrible. Every time she heard it, her skin crept because she knew it would cost someone's life, perhaps her own.

"Come... pick your... pearl," Mabor told them.

One by one, in squad order, they stepped forward to pick their pearl. First the Igneous Squad, because Aiden rose first at the speed of lightning, then the Ardent Squad and finally the Searing Squad.

Nahia had the pearl in her hands and was watching it carefully while the delivery finished. She was trying to see whether it was magic, if it gave off any power. She did not feel like it was, at least she was not able to pick up any magic emanating from the object. Her comrades were all acting in a similar way, manipulating the pearl and trying to see whether it had magic. All except Ivo, who put it down beside him in his seat and was not even looking at it. He did not seem interested.

The Learning Pearl is your best friend and will be throughout the year. The first thing I want you to do is form a bond with it. This bond will allow you to interact with its power, and in turn, the pearl will be able to help you manage your internal dragon, the source of your magical power.

This explanation left Nahia very interested. It seemed that the dragon she had seen being born within her was not only real but was the source of her magical power. If the pearl helped her communicate with that magic within her, perhaps she would have a chance. She looked at her comrades. Daphne was looking at the pearl with a frown, as if annoyed because it was not responding, while Lily was stroking it and playing with her fingers as if it were a precious jewel.

"Everyone, stand up..." Mabor told them.

They all got up from their seats at once.

Place the pearl in front of you, holding it with both hands and level with your face, Mag-Zilar-Ond's message reached them, together with a feeling of importance.

Nahia stretched her arms with the pearl in her hands and lifted them to the level of her face. Once everyone had done this and Mabor had corrected the posture of a couple of them, they all remained still, expectant.

Mag-Zilar-Ond closed its eyes. A bright sphere formed in front of the dragoness and stayed hovering in midair. It gave off a silver glow at unsteady intervals. From the sphere there began to issue some silver-colored threads of energy that seemed to dance as they expanded. They headed to the pearls the pupils were holding. The threads of energy which formed in rising and descending arcs reached the pearls. There was a thread for each pearl. They linked the sphere of energy to the learning pearls. They stayed linked and the arcs seemed to mimic sea waves without breaking or detaching from both objects. These threads seemed to have a life of their own. The pearls began to react to the energy they were receiving from the sphere and emitted silver flashes.

Hold the pearls firmly. No matter what happens, no one must drop their pearl or they will pay, they received the order from Mag-Zilar-Ond as the dragoness opened its eyes.

Suddenly, a thread of energy pulsed out from the pearls and hit each person in the forehead, as if it were trying to connect the pearl with their minds. Nahia was taken aback, but she did not let go of the pearl. Neither did her comrades. However, the blond human in the Ardent Squad got frightened and dropped it. The sphere hit the floor but did not break. It rolled forward.

"I will pick it up..." said Mabor as he went for the pearl with slow steps. He picked it up and gave it back to the boy who had dropped it.

"Name?" he asked him.

"Brendan..." he replied with fear in his voice.

"You... are registered..." Mabor told him, and they all sensed that was something bad, very bad.

Close your eyes and concentrate on the pearl. Open your minds to it. Let it in. A bond must form between you and it, a mental, magical one.

Nahia felt that the pearl, in some way she did not understand, wanted to interact with her. She allowed it. She closed her eyes and opened her mind. *Enter*, she thought and gave it access. In so doing, something strange happened. The pearl sent a charge of energy through the fluctuating thread that linked them. The energy entered Nahia's mind, and suddenly she was able to see the bright dragon in the middle of her chest. It flashed. The pearl sent more energy, and this time she was able to see it with absolute clarity.

What was happening was very singular. Nahia understood that the pearl was showing her the source of her power. Now she saw it clearly. All of a sudden, another thread of fluctuating energy issued from the pearl to the center of her chest where the bright dragon was. A moment later, the pearl sent two simultaneous discharges of energy, one to her mind and the other to her chest. At that moment, Nahia knew that the pearl had bonded with her, through her mind and magic. She felt the energy discharges like two sharp pricks.

Some of you will feel that the bond forms quickly, in about three discharges if you have already felt the dragon within you. Others will need quite a few more. The least apt will require many discharges of power to be able to appreciate the dragon and complete the link. The learning pearl will help you. You must withstand the pricks of pain. Whoever does not will be catalogued as magically weak, and that is something you really do not want, believe me, Mag-Zilar-Ond messaged in warning.

Nahia's pearl broke the two threads of energy that joined them, making them vanish, and gave off an intense silver flash.

Very well, golden Human. You surprise me again. You have bonded with one single discharge. You may open your eyes and lower your arms, Mag-Zilar-Ond's message reached her, and Nahia knew the dragoness was speaking to her alone.

She did as the teacher told her. She opened her eyes and looked at her comrades. They all still had their eyes shut.

Keep going like that until you identify the dragon within you and the link is completed. Whoever gives up will have a brief stay in this academy, so I repeat the importance of achieving this, Mag-Zilar-Ond messaged, this time to all of them and with the threat of failure.

Nahia waited, watching her comrades. She hoped they succeeded. She realized she feared for them. What if someone did not make it? He or she might die. Time passed, and Nahia could see discharges taking place, the bodies of her comrades showing pain when they received them. No one opened their eyes. She began to worry in earnest. They could not fail and die—that would be terrible. Acid anxiety began to climb from her stomach to her throat. She realized she cared for her comrades. No matter that the squad was a group forced together and that they had practically nothing in common except for the fact that they were all slaves, she felt a terrible fear of losing them.

The binding process finished, and Nahia was more anxious every moment. All of a sudden, Daphne's pearl flashed silver. Nahia looked and saw that the threads were vanishing. She had succeeded! Nahia was ecstatic. Daphne opened her eyes and grunted in pain.

"Ouch…"

"You did it," Nahia whispered, very happy.

"It was… a piece of cake…" she grunted again, and the pain she had sustained was visible on her face.

"Thank goodness you succeeded," Nahia whispered. She was very relieved.

"The others?" Daphne asked, lowering her voice and noticing that Mabor was looking at her.

Nahia shook her head.

"None, not even in the other two squads," she whispered back.

A few more moments passed, and the two Fatum of the other two squads succeeded.

"It looks like it's beginning to sink in," Daphne said,

"You saw and felt the dragon, right?" Nahia asked her.

"You don't say! Mine is a fighter."

Nahia had to smile.

"Being you, it could be no other way,"

Lily followed, and Nahia had to hold herself back from hugging her.

"Has it left a mark on my forehead?" she asked, concerned.

"Not at all. You are as beautiful and irresistible as always," Nahia smiled.

"I bet your dragon is a flirt," Daphne told her.

"Of course," Lily smiled, but she put her hand to her chest in pain. "Blasted pricks, they hurt like crazy."

"Don't worry, it'll pass momentarily," Nahia reassured her.

The Scarlatum of the other two squads succeeded, and a moment later the two human boys did too.

"Let's see if these three make it," Lily said, looking at Taika, Ivo, and Aiden.

"These three are clumsy and thickheaded, they're going to find it hard, you'll see," Daphne said.

She was not mistaken. They had to wait a good while until Taika managed at last.

"An interesting experience," he commented with a look of pain in his face.

Another long while went by, and Aiden managed at last.

"I'm one of the last ones, what a disappointment," was all he said.

"He's an endless source of joy," Lily said, and the girls giggled.

Finally, when they were beginning to lose hope, Ivo succeeded.

"Trying to reach the heart of a tree is not a task for one day," he said and put both hands to the center of his chest.

A moment later, Mag-Zilar-Ond considered the exercise well done.

I am glad to see that everyone has succeeded. I do not like to have to get rid of pupils so soon. You are sore and tired. It is a good moment for you to go to the Library of Dragon Magic.

Nahia looked at her comrades. She had not known there was any library here, least of all one of magic. By the looks of surprise on her comrades' faces, they had not known either.

"The Library... is the building behind this one... before the Weapons Building," Mabor told them.

At the Library you will ask for the tome of Basic Dragon Magic. *It is an extensive tome you must study and memorize. Everything it explains about dragon magic and its use is essential. You must know it. The classes, from now on, will be divided between time with me and studying in the library. Magic requires a lot of study. Those who do not like to read and study will have a very complicated Path, I can assure you.*

Ivo snorted. He did not seem happy. Aiden said nothing, but his look was full of certainty, as was usual for him. Nahia suspected that studying was not his forte. For her, reading tomes came very easily because her grandmother had many in her home and she had read since she was very little, especially on botany and medicinal plants, as well as homemade remedies and all kinds of illnesses.

Go now and start studying, I want you to have memorized the four first chapters by the next class.

They all stood up and went out. It was time to find out what the Library of Dragon Magic was like.

Chapter 23

They went to the building at the back, and as soon as they saw it they felt it was something special. It had the shape of a great white sphere with silver nuances that shone in the sunlight. It did not even look like a building but more like a grand monument, a larger replica of the pearl they had come through to reach this realm in the sky. Perhaps that was why they had noticed it. They had to search for the entrance because they could not find it at first. It turned out that the door was open but they had missed it. Since it was a spherical building and the entrance hall was the same color as the outside, the door was practically invisible and it looked as if it had none, only a wall. It appeared to have been done on purpose.

"The optical effect is amazing," said Nahia in front of the door, reaching out with her hand toward the inside and moving it in and out to make sure it actually was an opening and not a wall.

"Well thought and elaborated on," Taika agreed, watching the sphere with narrowed eyes.

"I see myself reflected on the sphere, although it distorts my divinely curved body," Lily commented, posing in front of the bright wall.

"We don't have time for that, we have to go in and study," Aiden told them, and without waiting for anyone he went into the building.

"There he goes, ruining the optical illusion, how very stone headed of him," Daphne said in disbelief.

"This spherical shape and that silver color don't seem very reassuring to me," Ivo commented.

"Well, it might be because it's a lot like the portal that brought us here," Daphne relied.

"That's true," Taika agreed. "It might have something to do with that. I don't know whether you've noticed, but in the world of dragons, spheres seem to be pretty important."

"I hadn't noticed, but I believe you," Lily said.

"I had noticed," said Nahia.

"That's because you are 'singular,'" Daphne said and mimicked sending her a mental message.

Lily laughed.

"I don't want to be singular… the dragoness said things would be more difficult for me…" said Nahia, with low spirits. "As if they were easy now."

"Let's not get ahead of ourselves," Taika told them. "So far we know you are very attuned to magic. That's an advantage, something positive."

"That's right. It's not something negative, don't worry," Lily told her, and she put her arm around Nahia's shoulders. "Besides, now you're the celebrity of the Red Squadron."

"That's for sure," Daphne nodded.

"I'd rather not be."

"We'd better go in before we draw the attention of some dragon," Taika told them, looking toward one of the lookout towers where a white dragon was on watch duty.

"Yeah, that'll be most prudent," Ivo joined him, following Taika's gaze to the dragon.

They went into the Library of Dragon Magic and Nahia froze. The place was incredible. It had six round stories with glass railings which looked onto a round courtyard. In the middle was a grand silver column with what looked like an enormous book with gold covers. Around the monument there were counters, and at them about twenty Exarbor seemed very busy, apparently consulting large open tomes.

"Wow, I wasn't expecting this," said Lily, wide-eyed, looking at the amazing place.

"You can see tables, and large shelves with books. I did not know dragons read, or appreciated books," Daphne commented with a frown.

"There's a lot we don't know about dragons," said Ivo.

"In fact, we know very little about their world," Taika pointed out.

Aiden came toward them.

"I've already asked. We have to go to the second floor. There, they'll give us the books and we can get a table on that level to study at. We can't go to the other levels."

"Why not?" Daphne asked blankly.

"Because," Aiden snapped.

"So you don't know," Daphne replied.

"You don't ask when told what you have or don't have to do," Aiden retorted, jabbing his clawed finger at her.

Daphne made a face and ignored him.

"That huge golden book wouldn't be..." Lily began to say.

"It's *The Path of Dragons*," Aiden confirmed. "Can you believe it's right there? It's amazing!" he said, very excited.

"Did the Exarbor tell you that?" Ivo asked.

"Yes, it's a wonder."

"It's certainly dragon sized," Lily nodded.

"Couldn't you read it?" Daphne asked him with irony.

Aiden stood very straight.

"It's written in the ancient dragon language. But there are copies in the unified language of Kraido on all the levels. We can consult them. It's wonderful!" Aiden was overjoyed.

"Yeah, super wonderful!" Lily said jokingly.

"Remind me not to leave without reading it, because with my memory I'll surely forget," Daphne said sarcastically.

"Let's go to the second level for our study tomes," Taika suggested. "That way we'll get a better view of this special place."

They went up some spiral stairs to the second level. Against the spherical surface of the wall were shelves filled with books. In front of the shelves were several study desks and some square columns that appeared to hold up the upper level. On the columns, they saw what looked like framed writing. They looked at the closest one.

"'There is nothing more despicable than weakness,'" Lily read.

"What do you know, that's one we didn't know," Daphne said ironically.

"This one we do. 'The Dragon warlock will master magic and weapons equally,'" Ivo read on the other side of the column where there was another piece of writing framed.

"They're extracts from *The Path of Dragons*," Taika guessed.

"That's neat, this way I won't have to read it," Daphne said cheerfully.

"Of course you'll read it! We must all read it!" Aiden was beside himself.

"Shhh!" the warning of an Exarbor came from a table not far away who had a finger over his bark lips.

Aiden held back, and shaking his head went over to the Exarbor.

"We need the tome of *Basic Dragon Magic*."

184

"Squad…. and Squadron…?"

"We are the Igneous Squad of the Red Squadron."

"Very well… follow me…"

The group followed the Exarbor, who walked as slowly as he talked.

"It's forbidden… to make noise."

"Understood," Aiden nodded.

"And bring… food…"

"All right."

"And… take books out…"

"We can't take books out to study?" Lily asked blankly.

The Exarbor stopped and turned.

"You study… only here…"

"Oh, well, I'd rather study in the barracks…"

"No… only here…" he replied, wagging his finger, which looked like a twig with one leaf.

"We will comply with all the rules, of course," Aiden promised.

"Of course," Daphne repeated, imitating Aiden's tone and making a face.

Aiden glared at her with hatred.

The Exarbor turned around very slowly and went on. After a moment, they arrived at a large set of shelves.

"Here are the tomes… remember what I said…"

"We'll remember. We won't cause any trouble," Aiden promised.

The Exarbor bowed slightly as greeting and left them.

"Here," Aiden said as he gave each one a copy of the tome.

"What now?" Daphne asked.

"Now we study," Lily said cheerfully in a sing-song voice.

"Let's find a table," Taika said, looking at the closest ones. There were people from other squads studying.

Suddenly, Nahia saw someone she recognized and a great joy filled her heart.

"Maika!" she waved at her.

"Nahia!" she said the moment she saw her. The girl was sitting at one of the tables with a tome.

Nahia ran to her side and hugged her tightly.

"I'm so happy to see you!"

"Same here!" Maika laughed.

"Shhhhhhh… don't make noise…" an Exarbor scolded them as

he was putting a tome back in its place close by.

The two looked at him and nodded.

"Sit down with me and we'll pretend we're studying," Maika said.

"All right," Nahia took a chair and sat down beside her at the table.

"Tell me, how's everything? How are you managing?" Maika asked her.

"I'm still alive, which is saying a lot," Nahia replied with a half smile.

"Very true. Me too."

"I had no doubt you would adapt and survive. You're tough," Nahia said, putting her hand on the other girl's arm.

"So far I'm managing, but you never know in this place…"

"What's your squad like?"

"Rock Squad of the Brown Squadron. We're tough," Maika smiled.

"Do you get along well with your comrades?"

"Well, let's just say it's not ideal, but we manage. Our Drakonid is unbearable with her excessive loyalty to the dragons. I can't stand her."

"Yeah, she's like ours then."

"The Kapro we have is a tremendous brute. He runs over everything at the smallest offense."

"Our Tauruk is a little peculiar…"

"He's not a beast?"

"Not really… he's quite peaceful…"

"That's weird."

"Yeah, so I've been told."

"What about the Felidae? I have a lioness who's quite noble, although fierce."

"We have a tiger, very smart. He's always thinking and reasoning."

"My Fatum is a charming, handsome boy. He's the one I get along better with."

"My Fatum is a girl and beautiful. But her character is a little bitter, although I like her."

"And the Scarlatum?"

"Oh, mine is a charmer, I like her. We get along very well."

"Mine is a boy. Vain and very handsome. Not so trustworthy,"

Maika winked at her.

"What a description we've given of the groups, if they should hear us…" Nahia shook her hand and looked around, hoping none of her comrades had heard her. Luckily, they were far away at another table.

"You don't say!"

"What do you know about Ana and Logan?" Nahia asked, interested in their well-being.

"I was able to speak to Logan for a moment. You know he's very reserved. He barely told me anything. He said he was okay and not to worry about him but about myself."

"Yeah, that's very Logan-like," Nahia nodded, remembering what he was like and how he behaved.

"Ana's having a hard time."

"Is she?"

Maika nodded.

"I've seen her a couple of times… she's not doing well at all. A girl in her squadron, a Fatum, died. She didn't tell me what had happened, but it seems to have affected her a lot."

"Oh, that's terrible. This place…" Nahia shook her head.

"You know she doesn't have a strong spirit, and I have the feeling this whole experience is overwhelming her."

"Yeah… but she must be able to deal physically. Better than I am at least."

"Perhaps. But if she lacks spirit, her body isn't going to take her very far," Maika said, and in her eyes Nahia saw she was worried.

"Let's see if I get a chance to see her and cheer her up," said Nahia wishfully.

"Yeah, it's not as if we can do much more."

"Let's try to help her. We have to," Nahia said determinedly and squeezed Maika's arm.

"Good, we'll do that," Maika nodded and smiled.

"If you see Logan, you tell him too. And if I see him I will. Let's see if the three of us can't cheer her up."

"You have a good heart," Maika said, hugging her.

"Like yours," Nahia replied, grateful for the hug and the human contact.

"Mine is colder," Maika laughed.

For a long while, the two chatted in whispers to avoid being scolded by the Exarbor of the Library of Dragon Magic, enjoying each other's company. Nahia was delighted to having spoken to Maika at last and had a chance to share experiences and feelings. Life in the academy was tough, strict, and dangerous. Having a friend to talk to about all that was a luxury, and it was like a balm for her soul and her head. And yet, when they said goodbye to go to dinner, Nahia was sad, thinking about poor Ana and wondering whether she would be all right. She would have to pay more attention and see if she caught a glimpse of her and could speak to her.

Chapter 24

Talking at the table during dinner, Nahia wanted to discuss with her comrades how they felt after what they had been through in magic class. She found it hard to find the right moment, since they were all hungry and that took priority. Once they all had brought their serving at the table and had started to enjoy it, she gathered enough courage to ask.

"How do you all feel?"

"Very well. This stew of meat with carrots and bay leaf is delicious. These Tergnomus cooks here are phenomenal," Ivo replied, putting spoonful after spoonful into his mouth as if someone were trying to steal his plate.

"She doesn't mean that, you big ox," Daphne said.

"Tauruk," Ivo corrected her. "I have no ox in me, not even the horns."

"The forehead and what's behind it are likely from an ox," Daphne replied with a mocking smile.

"You're not going to ruin this magnificent dinner, no matter how hard you try," Ivo said, leaving the spoon on the plate and putting his hands together. Palm with palm, he began to meditate.

Aiden shook his head.

"I'm not happy at all. I don't know whether you know, but there are squad competitions later on, and I don't think this group is going to do well in them."

"There are?" Lily asked blankly.

"Yes, at mid-year we'll be evaluated individually and as a squad. They call it the Squad Competition. To prove our worth, we'll have to face other squads," Aiden explained.

"Is there anything you don't know about this world we've found ourselves in?" Lily asked him.

"I bet he knows everything, he's been preparing for this his whole life," Daphne said.

"I don't know everything. And yes, I have been preparing, as you should have done. Preparation leads to victory. That's why I believe we have very few possibilities when the evaluation comes and we have to face the other squads."

"That's what you're saying," Daphne made a face of total disagreement.

"I'm not just saying it, it's the truth. You're not ready. Besides, we have a Tauruk who meditates, a very weak Human, a Fatum who doesn't excel in anything except taunting people, and a Scarlatum who's only interested in being irresistible."

"Wow, what a good opinion you have of us," Nahia said, surprised by the brutal honesty of the Drakonid.

"I'm just telling the truth, and you know it."

"You haven't mentioned me," Taika said.

"That's because you are indeed worthy for the squad. You have a good head and fast reflexes."

"So, according to you we are not worthy of your squad," Daphne said.

"This is a pathetic squad. Not even in my worst nightmares did I think I would be so unlucky."

"Ask to be switched. There are squads that have lost members," Nahia told him.

"You don't ask for a change of squad. It's cowardly. I must make do with what I have."

"Well at least we, the pathetic ones, are nice, not like you, who have the grace, manners, and sympathy of a piece of coal," said Lily.

"The Drakonids don't value those things, so I don't care if I have none of those traits. What we do value is strength and honor. That I have. You don't," he stated and went on eating.

Nahia, Daphne, and Lily threw their heads back. He had insulted them, and he did not care. Ivo did not lose his calm and continued meditating, pretending he had not heard. Or maybe he had not.

"The Drakonids, you in particular, are unbearable and detestable," Daphne told him.

"And ugly, to say the least," added Lily.

Aiden shrugged.

"That doesn't change a thing. We're still a pitiful squad."

"I think it would be better if we didn't argue," Taika recommended. "The situation is complicated enough as it is. Better not to make it worse with petty quarrels."

"I only wanted to know what you thought of what happened today during magic training," Nahia said and spread her arms, "not this."

"It was a painful experience but quite interesting," commented Taika.

"Interesting? I only found it painful," said Lily.

"I'm with Lily on that. It isn't necessary to stick burning needles in our minds to make us see a dragon," Daphne said, wrinkling her nose.

"Don't exaggerate. It wasn't so hard," sad Aiden.

"Sure, if a dragon tore your leg off you'd say the poor thing was hungry and had to be fed. I bet you'd offer the other leg," Lily said.

Daphne laughed out loud.

"So true."

Aiden shook his head.

"I felt the dragon the first day, and today I saw it. From now on I'll be able to use my magic. That's a great step forward and what really matters. The pain I suffered to reach it is irrelevant."

"This loser is hopeless," Daphne shook her head.

Taika narrowed his eyes.

"When I succeeded, I realized our girls had already done it, all of them. Congratulations."

"Because girls are the best," Daphne said confidently.

"And the prettiest and most intelligent," Lily added.

Taika smiled.

"I meant I was the fourth to succeed. Aiden the fifth and Ivo the last."

"Ivo nearly killed me with anxiety with all the time it took him," Lily said.

"Good things in life always take time, they make you wait," intoned Ivo.

"Huh, you're not longer meditating," Daphne realized.

"No, I must feed myself, that's most important now," he said and went on eating his stew.

"Human, Fatum, Scarlatum, Felidae, Drakonid, and Tauruk-Kapro was the order of our group," Taika said. "Was it the same in the other two squads?"

"No, it wasn't the same in the other squads," said Nahia.

They all looked at Nahia.

"She was the very first," Daphne explained.

"Out of everyone?" Aiden asked, clearly shocked.

"Well... yeah..." Nahia admitted.

"When I succeeded, only Nahia had finished."

"Then you were second?" Taika asked her.

"I think so, or tied with the Fatum of the Ardent Squad."

"Interesting. Tell us who finished after that, and in what order," Taika asked.

"From what I saw and with the exception of Nahia, who was first, it was the Fatum, Scarlatum, and the other two Humans, then the Felidae, Drakonids, and Tauruk-Kapro last," Daphne explained.

"That's very interesting and significant," Taika said, stroking his long tiger whiskers, "it fits in with my people's beliefs about which races are most akin to magic."

"My people are the most magical, in all senses," Daphne said.

"Followed closely by mine," Lily winked at her.

"Humans come next, although our Nahia is a special case," Taika commented.

"And then come you three, who have very little magic," Daphne said, smiling and pointing a finger at Taika, then at Aiden and finally at Ivo.

Aiden was upset, and he stopped eating.

"Remember that any Dragon Warlock must master weapons *and* magic. Your races might be more powerful magically, but I can assure you that my race and their races," he said with a wave at Taika and Ivo, "are superior to yours when it comes to weapons."

"There he goes getting all competitive again, the freak," Lily said.

"It's not a competition between the races," Taika said, trying to make peace and raising his hands. "Some races are better at some things and others at other things."

"Well said. That's how we achieve balance in nature. Some stand out in some aspects and some in others."

"And in Nahia's case?" Lily said, putting her arm through Nahia's.

"I believe Nahia is an anomaly, someone special," Taika said in a reflective tone and watched her with his feline eyes filled with interest.

"Yeah, because the other Humans took longer than Lily," said Daphne.

"Don't talk about her like that, poor thing," Lily stroked her arm.

"I know I'm weird, I've known for a long time. It doesn't bother me," Nahia said with a shrug.

"In any case, we're reaching conclusions based on our own squadron," said Taika. "We don't know if the order was similar in the other squadrons."

"Our tiger-fox is right, as usual," Daphne agreed with a nod.

"Fox?" asked Taika.

"Because you're clever. You're always pondering things in your head," Lily explained with a giggle.

Daphne joined in the giggling.

Taika threw his tiger head back.

"I hadn't realized... I guess I am what I am..."

"We could try to find out what happened in the other squadrons," Nahia suggested, looking around the tables and searching for Logan. She saw him sitting with his squadron. She felt like going over there and asking him, but then she saw the two blue dragons and thought again. That was not a good idea. She searched and saw Maika at her table, as well as Ana. At dinner time, they were all here. If she could communicate with them somehow... but it was forbidden to speak to other squads or leave their respective tables.

"Good idea," Lily agreed.

"I like it," Daphne joined them.

"No, that's too dangerous. We risk major punishment," Taika warned them.

"They don't need to find out," Daphne put her index finger on her lips.

"If you try something like that, you'll be found out," Aiden said.

"We only have to make sure the Drakonids don't find out," Daphne said with an accusing look.

"For such a small thing, Fatum, your tongue runs too loose," Aiden warned her, and this time he sounded very serious, like a death threat.

"Let there be peace," said Taika, "and I insist that it's too risky and not worth it."

"It is worth it if we manage to establish relations with the other squads," said Nahia.

"Why would you want to do that?" Taika asked.

Aiden was staring at Nahia with great interest.

"Because there might come a day when it's convenient to be organized," Nahia said.

Aiden's dragon eyes opened wide.

"I hope you're not suggesting any folly like the ones in the past, which have ended up with thousands of dead."

"She's not suggesting anything," Lily told Aiden. "Don't misinterpret her words."

"And don't you dare go snitching to your masters," Daphne said, giving him a long, hard glare.

"I'm not going to inform our masters, because there's nothing to inform. But if there were, be sure I would tell them."

"You're a heartless snitch," Daphne accused him.

"I am faithful to my principles and masters."

"Your masters enslave us, torture us, and kill us. How can you be so blind?" Nahia said.

"Blind is he who believes his truth is better than that of others," Aiden got up and left.

"Let him go. He is what he is. He's not going to change," Ivo told them.

"Well, we're going to have a problem," Daphne said.

"Why do you think there's a Drakonid in the group?" Lily asked.

"To inform the dragons, that's their function," Daphne stated.

Lily nodded.

"That's how they control what goes on at squad level," Nahia guessed.

"We can't be entirely sure..." Taika said, raising his hands.

"You're not going to tell me you trust a Drakonid?" Daphne asked him.

"By that rule I could only trust a Felidae, one of my own."

"The tiger isn't wrong. We'll have to trust ourselves and those closest to us," Ivo commented.

"In any case, we shouldn't take risks, that's not our goal," Taika said.

"Don't you want something other than simply surviving the year?" Nahia asked him.

"What I want is to stay alive. Taking risks isn't a good tactic. Besides, what would be the point?"

Nahia thought about how to word her idea.

"Being free of the dragons one day."

They all looked at her.

"That's been attempted before, and it was a great failure," Taika

194

told her.

"I know, my parents died in the Great Insurrection."

"And you *still* have that idea in your head?"

"Dreaming is free," Nahia replied.

"Not here. Here, it'll cost you your life," Taika warned her with a look in his feline eyes that encouraged caution.

"Many of us lost loved ones in the Great Insurrection," said Lily.

"True. All the races did," Daphne joined her.

"Yes. We lost so many. We were the ones who charged against the dragons," said Ivo.

There was a tense silence.

"Taika, you are intelligent, noble. Why are you so against trying to change the situation we're living in?" Daphne asked him, raising an eyebrow.

"I follow my survival instincts. Everything I observe and learn I use to that end."

"You could aim for higher goals," Lily told him.

"I don't want them. Among my people, the lions are the leaders. We, the tigers, are warriors. I am a warrior concerned with staying alive in this hostile jungle, surrounded by predators much stronger than us."

"You sell yourself short," Daphne said. "There's a lot more in you."

"I'm no leader, I'm not interested in that. Leaders end up sacrificed—I've seen it and I've lived through it." Pain appeared in his eyes for a brief moment and then vanished.

"I'm no leader either. But I do believe we should try and understand this world to one day bring it down," Nahia said.

"That is a very high aspiration for someone who barely survives," Ivo warned. He said it with his usual calm tone, but it made an impact on all of them.

"Sometimes you deliver truths like mountains, without warning, and they are crushing," Daphne told him.

Ivo shrugged.

"Truths must be told naturally, when they must be heard. Not before or after. This was one of those moments."

Nahia nodded.

"He's not wrong, you know."

"We'd better leave these matters for now, the other squads are looking at us," Lily warned them as she smiled unobtrusively.

"Forgive me, I got a little carried away," Nahia apologized.

"Don't apologize for feeling, and least of all for feeling the right thing," Daphne told her.

Nahia nodded and thanked the Fatum for her support.

The rest of the dinner went on in silence, each one drawn into their own thoughts.

Chapter 25

Days and weeks went by fast at the academy. Once they had gotten used to the early hours of the day, breakfast, classes, dinners, and the sun dial that marked them, everything flowed like the strong breeze that welcomed them on many days, and drove away the clouds that used to get stuck in that island realm. Discipline, which made them fear their squadron leader, and fear of making a mistake or misdemeanor, pushed them to get everything done without delay, favoring the feeling that time flew by. In the evenings they were so tired from their classes and the tension they lived in at all times, that they dropped down exhausted and slept like logs.

Nahia did her best to not lag behind with the classes, or at least she tried not to make it noticeable. Magic lessons were not going too bad. Besides, she applied herself to the study of the tomes at the Library of Dragon Magic. She had to admit that she liked that place. What the tomes of magic explained and taught made sense to her, and she was beginning to understand how she had to interact and make use of the dragon of power she had inside her. Now she knew that to call on its magic, the dragon had to pass its power onto her so she could use it.

On the other hand, the Basic Martial Training classes were a real torture. No matter how much she tried, she found it extremely hard to follow the exercises and instructions. She always ended up worn out. Not only because of how tough the classes were, which were given without any mercy or courtesy, but also because she did not have the physical endurance of the rest. She could not keep up with the exercises demanded during a long day of training. By midday, Nahia was without strength, and exhaustion began to take over her body.

That day, the three squads of the Red Squadron were lined up and listening to the great black dragon Mai-Belt-Gaiz as he gave an explanation. In front of the dragon were the trainers who helped in the class: the Felidae lion, the Scarlatum, and the Drakonid. They wore their heavy, solid armor. Under their strict gaze, the squads had been working on the movements of offense and defense using only their bodies, without weapons. At first Nahia did not see the sense in performing offensive and defensive movements in the air, hitting and blocking with their arms and legs while also maintaining perfect balance. To her it was more like training for some kind of martial dance. The instructors showed them how to make the movements, and the students did their best to mimic their teachers.

A Dragon Warlock must be able to defend him or herself and kill without weapons. Unarmed combat is the base on which you will build your weapon mastery. It is what the Path marks, and we follow the Path, Mai-Beltz-Gaiz messaged to them as a reminder. The dragon did this every class, so they all knew it by heart.

The problem for Nahia was that they did the same exercises the whole day. To make it even more difficult for her, the last few days they had been forced to practice the offensive and defensive movements in pairs. Nahia had already practiced with Daphne, Lily, and Taika. Today it was Ivo's turn, and she was afraid. If the great beast did not control himself, he would tear her head off with one kick or break her sternum with a dull fist blow.

Ivo winked at her, letting her know he would be careful. It was something they had already talked about at the dorm when they chatted in the evening about the classes before they dropped off, exhausted. They did the exercises and Ivo, who was the slowest but at the same time the most powerful with the blows, did them equally slow but a lot less powerfully so as not to hurt Nahia, for which she was immensely grateful.

Once they finished with the round of exercises, Mai-Beltz-Gaiz addressed its pupils.

You have done all the combinations of exercises with enough competence. I see significant improvement. That pleases me.

The message reached them with a feeling of achievement. It surprised Nahia that the black dragon would send them a positive message. It was not the dragon's style. If anything characterized it, it was its iron hand and surly temper.

But you still have not reached the degree of dominion in this technique I expect of you. Therefore, in order to help you improve faster, you will change partners and do the exercises with someone from another squad. This way the exercise will be more competitive and the technical improvement faster.

Nahia looked at Ivo, horrified. Until then they had always practiced with the members of their own squad and they had all behaved, even Aiden, who had not been cruel with Daphne or Lily. This complicated everything.

Instructors, select the pairs.

The three instructors began to pair the members of different squads, and suddenly Nahia found that she had to do the exercise with a Felidae black panther, a female called Lara from the Ardent Squad. Nahia sighed and her stomach took a turn. Lara looked lethal. She was a feline of considerable size and had a fierce, unfriendly gaze. Nahia took comfort in the thought that at least she had not been paired with the Tauruk-Kapro of that squad called Cordelius, who was a huge ram with terrible-looking spiral horns.

"I'm Nahia," she introduced herself in a whisper while they got into position in front of one another. She reached out her hand to her rival in the hopes that she would not use all her strength.

"Lara," the panther greeted her with a brief nod without taking Nahia's hand.

"I'm not very strong..." Nahia told her, hoping the panther would not strike with all her might.

"I see that," was her reply, and by the look in her feline eyes, Nahia understood that the panther had no intention of going easy on her.

Once they were paired up, the instructors gave the order to start the exercises. It was a combination of ten attacks with punches and kicks which one of them did and ten defenses the other had to do. Nahia had to attack first. She threw a right punch forward, advancing her left foot and keeping her body flexed and balanced. She did it with the power and speed she used with her squad. The panther blocked her attack with her forearm with great speed and strength. Nahia had to hold back a cry of pain when she was blocked. In general, whoever was defending was only trying not to be hit and did not use to much force. That panther had blocked her forcefully and fast. Nahia looked at her and knew she was not overdoing it; in fact, it was more likely the panther had restrained her strength when she blocked the attack.

Nahia concentrated and continued performing the attacks as she was supposed to do. The three instructors moved between the pairs, watching them and making improvements and corrections. Lara blocked or deflected all the attacks with her fist and leg without any problem. She was fast and had incredible reflexes. Worst of all was that each block or deflection left Nahia in terrible pain and bruised.

Then it was Lara's turn to attack, and Nahia knew she was in serious trouble. The panther was going to attack with great speed, and Nahia was not going to be able to defend herself from all the attacks. She was not fast enough to deflect them. But she had no choice. The three instructors were walking around, watching the pupils closely. The black dragon did not miss a detail either. She would have to bear the pain and suffer. Lara began attacking. Nahia was able to block the first punch to her torso and deflect the second one to her face. The side kick to her stomach she was unable to fully deflect though, and Lara's heel hit her in the waist. Nahia bent double with pain and fell to her knees.

The Scarlatum instructor came over.

"Get up, Human. You must deflect that kick like this," he said and showed her the movement, which he did with astonishing strength and speed.

Nahia nodded and stood up. The blow had hurt a lot.

"Continue," the instructor told them.

Lara attacked again. Nahia managed to more or less avoid, although not entirely, the first two attacks, but not the third, a direct punch to her sternum. Nahia fell backward and was left breathless.

"That block was too slow and not strong enough," the Scarlatum instructor scolded her.

Nahia took a moment to recover. They went on with the exercises, and when it came to the spinning reverse kick, the blow Nahia most feared, she crouched with the speed of a gazelle. Lara's heel brushed her head but did not hit her. Nahia was so happy that her opponent had not hit her that she had no time to avoid the last attack: a sweep with the other leg. Both her legs were hit, bending forward as she fell backward. She took a blow on her back and hit her head hard. She was left on the floor with her head spinning.

"You didn't jump in time to avoid the sweep. Very bad," the instructor reproached her.

Nahia took a moment to get up. By the time she had, she had been assigned her next opponent. When she saw who it was she knew it was going to be even worse than her confrontation with Lara. She stood up and muffled a couple of moans of pain. Her next partner was already waiting in position. It was no less than Lita, the Drakonid of the Searing Squad.

"Ready?" Lita asked, looking at her with those reptile eyes set in a female dragon face. Her body, although feminine, was big and strong, almost as large as Aiden's. Just from looking at her, Nahia knew this was going to hurt, a lot.

"I'm not very strong and I'm not very good at this..." she admitted, trying to appeal to her good heart.

The Drakonid looked at her with disgust.

"You're weak, you shouldn't be here."

As she had guessed, the Drakonid had no heart.

"You don't need to punish me too much... you'll defeat me easily enough."

"Of course I need to. We must always do our absolute best and show our masters what we are capable of."

Nahia sighed deeply. She was dead. This little dragon was going to make her suffer with each punch.

The instructors gave the order to begin the exercises. Once again, Nahia had to attack first. If Lara had defended herself well, Lita did so as if she was the one attacking as the Drakonid hit her with every block or deflection. Nahia felt the blows on her arms and legs. Lita crushed her mercilessly, seizing advantage of every attack to punish her. When Nahia's turn to attack had ended, Nahia was so sore she could barely think.

Now it was Lita's turn to attack and Nahia's to defend herself. The large Drakonid was going to crush her, she could see it in her opponent's dark eyes. The instructors gave the signal and Lita advanced her left foot, delivering a dull blow to Nahia's sternum. She knew what blow it was, she only had to block it. She tried with her left forearm. It was like hitting a board. She deflected the Drakonid's arm, but not completely. The punch hit Nahia in the left shoulder. She felt the pain of the block, as well as the impact of the fist.

The exercise went on, and with every one of Lita's attacks Nahia suffered double punishment, trying to defend herself and failing to do so. Her body hurt so badly that when the leg attacks began, she nearly ran off. But she knew that was not an option—she had to stay and endure the suffering. To flee was to die. She did not manage to stop the next kick to the head and received the blow in the right hand which she was using to protect her face. She crashed to the floor like a felled tree and stayed there, somewhat dizzy.

The instructor came over and bent beside her.

"Very weak defense. That hand has to bear that kick. Get up."

Nahia nodded as best she could and stood up, still a little dazed. She thought that Lita would immediately continue the exercise and destroy her, but to her surprise the Drakonid waited a moment, looking her in the eye without attacking.

"There's no honor in defeating the defeated," she whispered. "Tell me when you can go on."

That surprised her. The Drakonids had a pretty strange sense of honor. She took three deep breaths, letting the air out in long breaths until the dizziness passed. When she recovered from the dizziness, all the pain throughout her body returned at once. The worst thing was that more was coming. She prepared to receive it.

"Come on," she told Lita.

The Drakonid attacked with a kick straight to the face. Nahia blocked upward and the claw passed above her. She had freed herself by very little, and had been able to bear the pain of blocking. It was not that bad. She prepared for the next attack when she felt something she knew and feared: not something external but something internal. A flame lit up inside her, one that lived in the center of her chest. She thought that perhaps it was the dragon of bright power, but at once she knew it was not. Her body temperature began to rise rapidly and her eyes opened wide. She was having one of her seizures.

Lita noticed and looked at her with puzzled eyes, but she could not stop, and she executed the next kick to Nahia's ribs. The deflection had to be with both forearms, and Nahia managed to execute and deflect the kick, although again with terrible pain upon contact with Lita's kick. But that was not what worried her. Her temperature continued to skyrocket, and she felt her skin burning all along her body. She felt the flame generating inside her and making her burn as if a fire were consuming her from the inside out. But her body did not manifest it, and for Lita nothing was happening to Nahia.

"Wait…" Nahia said, raising her hand so she would stop.

Lita looked at her. She stopped the kick she was about to deliver. Nahia was already nothing but a roaring bonfire. The heat was unbearable inside her and on her skin. Her pulse accelerated so much that her heartbeats seemed to be ready to burst her veins. Her heart was beating like a herd of wild horses. She was terribly dizzy and tried to keep her balance, but she could not and collapsed to the floor. She fell forward and Lita had to step back to avoid her. On the floor, she began to shake compulsively. Terrible cramps ran down her arms and legs. She cried out in pain, unable to stop convulsing. This seizure was one of the bad ones.

Chapter 26

The Scarlatum instructor came over and bent down to watch what was going on but did not touch Nahia.

"She's suffering some kind of seizure, my lord," he informed Mai-Beltz-Gaiz.

A seizure? That is not acceptable, the great black dragon messaged, wavering between surprise and frustration.

The rest of the pupils stopped the exercises to see what was happening. Nahia on the floor, convulsing. She had managed to reach her belt with her right hand even though she was unable to stop the terrible tremors. She managed to grab one of the tonics she carried in it. Now she had to get it to her mouth, and that felt impossible because her right arm would not stop shaking. She was unable to control it, and the cramps wracked her with terrible pain. But she had no other option, she was already beginning to choke, and if her heart did not burst first from how fast it was beating, she would die from suffocation. The pain from the cramps was torturing her, but she refused to give up—she did not want to die.

Her squad mates came over to help her.

Let no one touch her. A warrior recovers by herself. No one must help her. That is not the way of the Path.

The five stopped one step away from Nahia. They wanted to help her, but they could not ignore a direct order from a dragon. That was instant death.

Nahia fought to put the tonic in her mouth. She was beginning to asphyxiate. She barely had any time left. This attack was one of the bad ones. It would kill her if she did not drink the tonic. She fought to control her right arm, and gradually she drove her hand to her mouth. She almost had it. She tried to take out the wooden stopper with her teeth, but her hand was shaking and she did not make it to her mouth.

Everyone was staring at her. Lily and Daphne had their hands out, trying to reach her, but now the three instructors were between them and Nahia. They would not let anyone help her, as their dragon master had ordered.

With one last effort, Nahia put the container to her mouth and this time succeeded in biting off the stopper. Now she only needed to make one move she had well rehearsed, one pull back and another forward to get the stopper out and take the uncovered container to her mouth. She got ready and executed it with her trembling hand. She did it. The open container was at her mouth, and as her hands shook, the contents fell into her mouth and from there down her throat. She swallowed it all.

A moment later, her lungs filled with air. She was no longer suffocating. She took in a ragged breath and coughed. Her body temperature began to drop, and she stopped trembling and shaking. She remained lying on her back, staring at the ceiling. She had done it. She was alive—by a hair's breadth, but alive.

Weakness, as you well know, is unacceptable in this academy. Being weak is a true dishonor, Mai-Beltz-Gaiz messaged them, very annoyed.

The message hit Nahia's head, pushing it to one side. The feeling that came with the message was one of disappointment mixed with rage. Nahia was truly scared. She opened her eyes wide, and the fear she felt showed in them. She had just saved herself but, was this dragon going to kill her for being weak? Dragons could not stand weakness. They had made that very clear from day one. It could kill her right there and then. From what they knew, it had already happened in other squads. The dragon was going to kill her for sure. Fear overwhelmed her, but there was nothing she could do. Her body was exhausted. No matter how much she wanted to defend herself or escape, she could do nothing. Her body was not responding.

Only the strong of body, magic, and spirit walk the Path of Dragons. Those who are not must leave it. This is a clear example, it messaged, and the message reached everyone with a feeling of disapproval.

Her squad comrades realized Nahia was in serious danger of being killed for disappointing the dragon and not living up to its expectations. They looked at her on the floor. Daphne and Lily went around the instructors and lined up beside Nahia. A moment later, Taika did so too. Ivo seemed to hesitate, but he went to stand in his place. Aiden did not seem to have any intention of moving. He saw how the other squads were watching what was going on, then he moved and stood in his place. They lined up in front of the dragon with Nahia in her place, only on the floor. Nahia felt tremendously grateful. It was an amazing gesture, since they were risking their lives for her.

Your squad protects you and that does you credit, and it also implies there is some value or leadership in you. Even so, you deserve punishment. But it will not be me who gives it to you. I will let your squadron leader decide. After all, it is your leader you dishonor. At the end of the class, you will go to your banner and wait on your knees for your leader to decide what to do with you.

That sounded to Nahia like a death sentence or something even worse. If she was killed it would be quick: everything would be over in the blink of an eye. Punishment would be even worse, for sure. They would make her suffer. In any case, she could not let herself be carried away by such negative thoughts. She was not going to die, and that was what mattered—she did not want to die. She wanted to live and make those heartless monsters pay for all the evil and suffering they caused. The rage in her stomach made her feel a little better. Not much, but slightly. She had to stay alive and fight, even in the worst of circumstances.

Continue the training, instructors, the black dragon ordered.

"In positions, two by two," the three said, addressing their squad.

Instructor, let the weak one's squad know what happens when one of its members fails.

"Yes, my lord," the Scarlatum instructor bowed before the great dragon.

Since Nahia could not get up, it was Taika who had to do the exercises with the instructor. In a moment, they understood what the dragon had meant. The Scarlatum began the exercise and started fighting with extreme fierceness and strength. The next moment, he was giving a beating to Taika, exerting all his strength. Taika defended himself as best as he could, but the instructor was an expert master. The tiger received blow after blow, defending himself as well as he was able, and he did so without complaining a single time. He took the beating with muffled grunts of pain and went on with the exercise.

From where she was on the floor, Nahia could see how brutal the instructor was being and knew it was because of her, and she felt awful. Then they swapped partners and it was Lily's turn. The unfortunate Scarlatum ended up on the floor with another beating. Daphne grunted and complained with every blow she got and tried to return them all with the same intensity, but her blows were either deflected, avoided, or blocked by the master fighter. The Fatum ended up like Lily, very sore and on the floor. Nahia wanted to weep with rage and frustration. She felt powerless. They were being hurt because of her.

Ivo and Aiden bore the punishment better, especially Ivo, who did not seem to suffer at all, although the blows he received were tremendous. Aiden tried to defend himself to the best of his ability, and he did pretty well, but in the end the instructor overwhelmed his defenses and gave him a good beating. Instead of taking it badly or cursing or complaining, he took it as if the instructor were granting him an honor by working him so hard. He saluted him with respect when they finished.

Once the class was over and they were going out, Nahia apologized to her comrades.

"I'm so sorry, it's my condition… it happens … sometimes… I can't control it," she said with moist eyes.

"Don't apologize, it's not your fault. Those despicable dragons are to blame," Daphne said. She had a tremendous shiner on her right eye and she was holding her ribs in pain.

"Yeah, Mai-Beltz-Gaiz did this to us, not you," Lily said. She was limping and cradling one inert arm with the other.

"I will not stay quiet while you besmirch the names of our lords. What happened is our fault and no one else's," Aiden said, looking at Nahia.

"It's my fault, not yours," Nahia corrected him.

"We must take it as another lesson in this world," Taika said. "There will be situations where one of us will fail and we will be forced to pay the price."

"I won't fail," Aiden said confidently.

"I hope you do," Daphne said spitefully.

"You won't see that," he promised.

"Taller trees have fallen. There's nothing sure in life," Ivo told Aiden.

"Honestly, I'm really very sorry," Nahia did not know how else to apologize.

"You'd better go and receive your punishment," Taika advised her. "Don't make our squad leader wait, that'll be worse."

"You're right. I'm going."

"Good luck," Daphne wished her.

"I hope it's not too bad," Lily said.

"What are you going to do?" Nahia asked them before she left.

"I believe it's the right time to use that pretty building next to administration for the first time," said Daphne.

"Oh, the infirmary," Nahia realized.

"Yeah, it's about time," Lily said. "We'll tell you what it's like."

Nahia nodded and left them. With her spirits low, she headed to her banner as Mai-Beltz-Gaiz had instructed her. When she got there, she knelt and waited. She saw her comrades heading to the hospital. She hoped they would give the two girls something for their bruises, and once again she felt like a burden and failure.

For a long while, Nahia waited while in her mind, self-pity and rage were fighting a ferocious battle. She knew she should not pity herself, but she could not help it after what had happened. Luckily, rage won over self-pity, and although this academy in the sky was a horrible place, Nahia was determined to overcome whatever they threw at her.

Irakas-Gorri-Gaizt came down from the sky, beating its enormous red wings. It landed beside the flaming banner. It was huge and powerful, and its eyes seemed to burn. It roared, showing its terrible jaws. Nahia felt like an ant in front of such a monstrous creature.

You have dishonored me, Human, it messaged along with a feeling of restrained fury.

Nahia felt it as if she was being hit on the head with a blacksmith's hammer. Her face flattened to the ground and she grunted in pain.

You are of the Igneous Squad, part of the Red Squadron. The squadron I lead. My squadron. What has happened cannot happen in my squadron.

Nahia felt every word, every sentence as if something inside her head had exploded, causing her unbearable pain. She put her hands to her head. This was not like the first message. It wasn't a feeling it was sending which caused her pain when she received it. This was something else.

When you fail in the training, you dishonor me. When you show yourself as a weakling, you disrespect me. That is unacceptable. I cannot tolerate it.

The intense pain returned with every word. There was no feeling associated to the pain, it was only pain. Excruciating and direct. In the midst of her suffering, Nahia realized the dragon was hurting her on purpose. It was attacking her mind.

I should kill you, but since this is your first offense, I will not this time. But you deserve a punishment, and you will have it. Starting tomorrow, and for one month, after classes you will clean out the dungeons. It is an eye-opening experience. You will go straight away, without having dinner, and you will work until the cleaning shift ends. You will not miss or arrive late to any class in the mornings. If you do, I will have no mercy.

The words, each one of them, caused a pain so excruciating that Nahia could not bear the last one, and she fainted.

A while later, Ivo carried Nahia over his shoulder, taking her away. The rest of the squad was with him, all of them with different bandages and traces of ointment on their faces and limbs.

"How did you know she would need us?" Daphne asked Taika.

"I didn't, but I thought she might."

"You're a most intuitive tiger," Lily congratulated him and patted him on the back.

"Most rational," Aiden corrected her.

"Infirmary or barracks?" Daphne asked, watching Nahia's face, still unconscious.

"Let's take her to the infirmary first, just in case," said Lily.

"All right," Ivo headed to the infirmary with the squad beside him.

That evening, they missed dinner and all slept with aches. Luckily, none had any broken bones, only a few cracked ribs and dark bruises on their faces, arms, and legs. Nahia's whole body was bruised and she had a monumental headache. Luckily, she was so exhausted that sleep defeated pain and she dropped off like a log. Her last sentence before falling asleep was, "Thank you… squad…"

Chapter 27

Nahia reported at the door to the dungeons after training to serve her punishment. She was nervous. The building gave her the willies, not only because it was a prison which she guessed was full of prison cells but because it was a dark building with a twisted air about it. She studied it for a moment. It was a black fortress surrounded by high walls with four round towers with a spiral around them ending in a pointed tip. The main building was also round with a spiral that went all around it from the base to the tall tip. It was located at the end of the academy, by the north wall. Just getting there had taken her a good while.

She glimpsed a dragon watching at each of the four towers that formed the walls around the fortress. They were not very big, so she guessed they must be young. The colors of the watch dragons were the most common: red, blue, white, and brown, the colors of the main elements. She thought it clever to have a dragon of each element in case whoever tried to escape was immune to one of the elements, like she was to fire. The red dragon would not be able to burn her if she tried to escape, but the others would destroy her with their elemental breaths in the blink of an eye. She did not know why she had thought such a thing. She did not want to be a prisoner there, and she definitely did not want to try and escape. Better not to think about such complicated, negative situations. She had enough on her plate as it was.

What surprised her most about the place were the spirals. She did not know what they might represent or what their function could be, but they reminded her of enormous snakes coiled around the rock of the building. She felt that chill again, the third time she had felt the discomfort. The first one she felt when she saw the building in the distance, then when she had arrived, and now as she looked at it again more closely. There was something wrong about this place, something bad. Unfortunately, and because of her condition, she was forced to serve inside that dark place.

Two black dragons guarded the entrance. They were also young, each about forty-five feet long. They were posted on either side of the great doors of the dark-rock building. Unlike most of the doors at the academy, these were shut. The two dragons glanced at her with their black eyes and Nahia's blood froze. The black dragons seemed to her, sent by death herself to collect souls.

She stopped still in front of the door with her head down. Neither of the two dragons addressed her, so she remained waiting. She could not address a dragon, so not knowing what else to do, she decided to wait and see what happened. But waiting there between those two dark dragons made her very nervous. Her imagination ran wild and she began to think horrible things, like one of them crushing her with one of its claws against the ground while with the other it took out her soul to deliver it to death. Her heartbeat faster and harder with every passing moment.

She decided that the best she could do in her current situation was calm down, so she started to take in deep breaths, letting out long exhales. She was managing to calm down when a metallic *clack* came from the door. It began to open. As it did, Nahia became even more nervous and her efforts to stay calm unraveled.

The door finished opening. Nahia expected some terrible dragon to come out, but that was not the case. A Tergnomus came out instead. She was very surprised to see the tiny servant. She guessed there would not be any Exarbor serving there given the kind of place it was, but she might be mistaken on that too. On second thought, it did make sense that a Tergnomus would be serving in this place. They were small but tough and resilient, with a reputation for being hard workers. Besides, in this dark place they would manage well since they normally lived in caves in the underground of their country. Or at least that was her understanding.

"I'm Tarcel, Tergnomus Principal of the dungeons. What are you doing here, pupil?"

"I'm Nahia… due to some problems with my training, I've been punished with cleaning dungeons for a month…"

"Well, that's good news," the Tergnomus smiled, showing very square teeth.

"Good news?"

"Not for you, but for us it is. We're in desperate need of more cleaning hands. It is always a bonus to be sent help, even if they are inexperienced pupils, not too proficient in the cleaning world."

"Oh, I see. I'll do what I can…"

"You'll do more than that, or your leader will be informed."

"Yes, yes, I'll do everything you require of me and more," replied Nahia. The last thing she wanted was to disappoint her leader—more than anything because it was capable of biting off her head if she did.

"Well, then, let's go in, follow me."

Nahia nodded and followed Tarcel inside the prison fortress. As soon as the door shut behind her, Nahia felt like a prisoner inside this place of incarceration. There was little natural light, since the windows of the building were small and reinforced with steel bars, as corresponded to a prison. The torches that hung from the walls were what gave off some light, enough to see the inside but keeping the interior dim.

"Wait here for a moment. I must register your arrival. Don't move. In this place it is forbidden to go anywhere unless accompanied by one of us."

"I won't go anywhere."

Tarcel nodded and left, walking in that curious way of the Tergnomus that looked as if they stepped into puddles of water with each foot when they walked.

While she waited, she looked around. This fortress was also enormous inside, with wide, clear corridors along which several dragons could go through. The height of the ceilings was over a hundred and twenty-five feet; in fact, the hall she was in measured at least a hundred and twenty-five feet in every direction. It was enormous, at least for a human, and especially for the Tergnomus. For a dragon, on the other hand, it was just about right.

Tarcel returned after a moment.

"Come so we can write you down," he told her and motioned her to follow him.

They went to the next hall, and there Nahia found that there were indeed Exarbor here. She could see three sitting down at matching desks with large open tomes which they seem to be working on. Against the walls of that hall were shelves with similar tomes to the ones they had open. Nahia guessed they must be the dungeons' registration logs.

Tarcel went over to the most ancient-looking Exarbor and stopped in front of his desk.

"We have a new temporary member of the cleaning team."

The Exarbor looked up from the tome he was working on and

eyed Nahia.

"Human… first-year…" he guessed, looking at her. "Name?" he asked in the brittle voice of his species.

"I'm Nahia Aske."

"Duration… of punishment?"

"One month, afternoons and evenings," Nahia replied with a sigh.

"Registering…" he said, and with great parsimony he shut the tome he was working on, got up, and went to one of the shelves to select another tome. The other Exarbor did not even flinch and continued with their tasks.

"They keep track of anyone who enters or exits this building," Tarcel told Nahia. "Whether they are prisoners or cleaning personnel or those who perform other functions."

"Other functions?" Nahia was interested.

"Feeding is another important one. We have to provide food and drink to the prisoners daily. It's complicated with some prisoners we have in the deepest areas of the dungeons."

"Oh, I see."

The Exarbor came back to his working desk after a while and opened the tome once he had sat down in his armchair. Just the act of sitting down took him a long while. They waited until he finished writing down in the register.

"Everything is in order… she can start … permission for one month of cleaning tasks."

"Very well, come with me, I'll take you to the cleaning supervisor," Tarcel told Nahia.

The Tergnomus led her down a long, wide corridor to some stairs that went down.

"The dungeons are below," Tarcel said. "There are three underground levels. I'll assign you to the first. The lower you go, the worse things are and the more dangerous the prisoners. Never go down to the lower levels. Stay on the first."

"Understood." Nahia nodded. She did not have the slightest intention of going down to the other levels.

They went down the black-stone stairs and Nahia felt like she was descending into a dismal, dark place. Not only were the walls and floor of black rock, but down here there were no windows and the torches did not seem to give enough light. It was as if the torchlight lost intensity upon hitting the walls, illuminating very little.

They arrived at a hall on the first underground level where they found four Tergnomus busy with different tasks. The Tergnomus on duty watched Nahia and Tarcel arrive out of the corner of their eyes but said nothing and went on working.

"I'll bring the cleaning supervisor," Tarcel told her and indicated for her to stay there.

"All right," Nahia nodded, looking around her. There were large closets and several tables with chairs. From what she was able to see in the closets, there were tools and utensils of different kinds. The Tergnomus were sitting at the tables and appeared to be fixing things. One of them was sanding a bunch of thick keys. Nahia wondered whether they might be from some dungeon, or perhaps rings.

Tarcel came back with another Tergnomus who looked a little younger, although they both looked as if they had lived long lives. Nahia did not know how to guess the age of this race. They all looked quite old, although she was sure they were not as old as they looked.

"I'm Framus, and I'm in charge of the cleaning duties of the dungeons," the newly arrived introduced himself.

"I'm Nahia, first-year."

"Yes, I can tell," Framus nodded, examining Nahia from head to toe. "You are not very seasoned."

"I'll take that as a compliment."

"It's not. Newbies who don't grow up fast perish."

"Oh, I'll remember that."

"Better that you mature quickly. The dead remember little."

Nahia gave an affirmative nod.

"I will."

"I'll leave now. Do everything Framus tells you and when he tells you," Tarcel told Nahia and then went back upstairs.

"Good. Seeing that you don't have a body good for manual labor, I'll assign you to the cleaning of the south block of the first underground level, the one we're in. It's of the cleanest and less dangerous," Framus told her.

"Well, thank you."

"Don't thank me. Such an inexperienced Human can't take on larger cleaning projects. You'd be a nuisance rather than a help, and we already have enough work."

"So much?"

"And more. You can't imagine the amount of waste and filth the prisoners produce here."

"Are there so many?"

"More than enough, and they generate a lot of filth."

"What race are they?" Nahia asked to try and understand who generated so much to clean rather than out of curiosity.

"Well, let me think…" Framus looked up to the ceiling and was thoughtful. "We have prisoners from all the races, as well as dragons."

"Dragons? Prisoners?" Nahia could not believe it. She threw her head back and opened her eyes wide.

Framus nodded.

"Yes, several, of the dangerous kind."

"But they're dragons…"

"Dragons also commit crimes against other dragons. Or did you think that wasn't the case?"

"Well, the truth is I didn't think…"

"Then you must also think all dragons are bad, right?"

Nahia looked everywhere and then at the Tergnomus.

"Shouldn't you be careful talking like that? What if they hear you?" she whispered with concern.

Framus smiled.

"They don't waste their time listening to Tergnomus conversations. We could be organizing the greatest of rebellions at the top of our voices and they wouldn't pay attention to us. They believe themselves so superior and they despise us so much, especially because of our reduced size, that they don't pay us the slightest attention."

"Wow… I didn't know that."

"You're very green. There are a thousand things you don't know. With a bit of luck, you'll learn, although in your case, you're going to need great doses of luck, seeing what a small thing you are. As for the dragons, I'll tell you that they have conflicts between themselves, mostly derived from wars and quarrels between clans. But there are also those of a personal kind. Dragons that kill dragons for normal reasons such as greed, jealousy, power, avarice, and similar. They are sentenced to prison, exile, or death. Here there are several sentenced to prison."

"Why here? I mean, this is a military academy."

"Those that are here have been sentenced for crimes that happened at the academy or against the institution."

"Oh, I see."

"And just so you know, young, inexperienced Human, there are good and evil dragons."

"There are?" Nahia did not say anything else, but Framus understood that her blank look was directed at the existence of good dragons. That there were evil ones was a given.

"Yes, there are few, but there are."

"I hope to meet one someday," Nahia replied, although it sounded more like "I'll believe it when I see it."

"Who knows, you might be that lucky."

Nahia smiled, although she highly doubted that one day she would meet a good dragon. It seemed impossible to her.

"Follow me, I'll tell you where you have to clean."

"Fine, thanks."

"No need to thank me. Being here is a punishment, and you should take it as such, although I appreciate that you have good manners. When they send me Drakonids or Tauruk-Kapro, I usually have problems with their attitude."

"They probably weren't very happy cleaning dungeons."

"They believe themselves superior to us Tergnomus because they're bigger and stronger," Framus waved his hand, dismissing the point. "They don't know that the true strength isn't found in one's muscles, it's here and here," he said, pointing first at his head and then his heart.

Nahia found what the Tergnomus said very fitting.

"I believe you are very right."

"Of course I am. I know it well. They believe that because they're bigger that they're better than the rest, and that's a mistake. Not even the dragons in all their enormity would be powerful without their clever minds and warrior souls. We the Tergnomus have both in abundance, although we are small in comparison with the other races. This helps us survive. Why do you think the dragons use us for their domestic tasks and the most ungrateful work? For that same reason—because we put our soul in all the work we do. Not like the rest of the races."

Nahia was thoughtful, trying to assimilate it all.

"Your words are wise."

"Thank you, you'll do well to remember them," Framus bowed his head in acknowledgment. "Follow me, I'll take you to the others."

"The others?"

"Yes, you're not the only one they've punished to clean the dungeons. It's a popular punishment. We have pupils of first-, second-, and third-years. I consider it a small honor."

"Because the dragons consider it a punishment?"

Framus looked at Nahia in the eye.

"Exactly. What for us is work, is punishment for others. That means our work is hard and recognized as such by our masters. Although they continue to despise us all the same."

"That's what I thought."

"Because you're a smart girl. I hope your heart is also strong," Framus wished her and repeated the gesture of touching his hand to his head and to his heart.

Nahia smiled.

"I hope it is too."

Framus nodded and led her down a long, incredibly wide corridor until they arrived at a steel door he opened with a bunch of keys.

"This is where the south section begins."

"All right…"

"Don't worry. It's where they have interesting prisoners. You're not in much danger."

"Well, that's something," Nahia sighed, relieved, and then she wondered what he meant by "interesting."

"There are much worse sections in this place, believe me. The sections that house dragons are the worst by far. The amount of waste they generate is mind boggling. Besides, they have a tendency to eat the cleaners the moment they get distracted."

"Wow, that's not good at all…"

"Exactly. That's why I only send expert Tergnomus there, although sometimes I get the order to send one of you down to that section."

"The dragons' section?"

"Yes, some squad leaders have a bad temper, they really like to punish."

"Oh, then my punishment isn't so bad…"

"It's not. But if you're punished again, you might end in the north section of the third underground level, and let me tell you, you do not want to be there."

Nahia looked horrified.

"I'll remember north section of the third underground level."

Framus bit the air and then mimicked chewing. Nahia quickly realized what he meant, and her stomach turned.

Chapter 28

Framus took Nahia with the cleaning squadron to the south section of the first underground level. It was formed by three Tergnomus, a Fatum, and a Tauruk-Kapro, all boys. The last two had been sent there as punishment, just like her. She did not ask what had happened to them, although she guessed they must have failed at something.

"First, the bracelets," said Framus, and he took out a decrepit copper chest from a closet. He put it on one of the working tables, opened it, and took out three silver bracelets. They were as thick as Nahia's index finger, and there was no decoration or flourish in them. They looked more like rings than bracelets, the only difference was that they were silver and not steel.

Put your arms forward," said one of the Tergnomus with a long-twisted nose.

Nahia and the two others being punished did as they were asked.

"Very well, I'll put these bracelets on you that will identify you as part of the labor force in the dungeons," Framus told them as he proceeded to put them on. They closed with a silver clasp with several positions. The wrist of a Fatum was not the same as that of a Tauruk-Kapro, as was soon demonstrated. The Fatum used the first position of the clasp, the Tauruk the last one.

"Don't ever take them off, and don't you dare lose them," the third Tergnomus told them. His long pointy ears were very wrinkled.

"All right ..." muttered Nahia. The Fatum nodded and the Tauruk-Kapro grunted.

"Very well, I'll leave you to your tasks and get back to mine," Framus said and started to leave. "Remember: there's always a lot to do and very little time to do it."

The three Tergnomus repeated the sentence in a whisper, as if it were a dogma, which Nahia found most interesting.

"The area we have to clean is large, so we'll divide into three groups of two," said Ufrem, the Tergnomus in charge of the work crew. "The newbie will go with me, the others as usual."

They all nodded and took the material from the closets on one side: mops, cloths, barbed brushes, disinfectant, alcohol, roots, and aromatic herbs, as well as plenty of soap. They went over to the well at the entrance, filled several buckets of water, and headed to work.

"Newbie, don't leave my side," Ufrem told her and indicated for her to take a bucket with water and the rest of the cleaning supplies.

"Right away." Nahia took everything and followed Ufrem, who, with great skill, was capable of carrying a dozen things without appearing burdened or unbalanced. Nahia, on the other hand, was the opposite. She nearly tripped and fell several times but managed to recover and not drop anything.

In some sort of anteroom, Nahia saw that one crew was heading to a door on the east, another to the west, and she guessed they would go to the north door, since they had come in from the south. The doors were made of metal, and when she touched the one that led north, she noticed they were solid silver and shone with a light glow. Looking at her bracelet, she noticed it gave off the same glow. Ufrem opened the door with a large bunch of keys he carried at his waist and they went on. Nahia saw a great, clear corridor without any traces of life. It was also quite clean. This was not the area they needed to clean, that was certain.

They went on and arrived at a great metallic grill of thick bars that went from wall to wall. Nahia noticed a large gate the size of a dragon and a smaller one the size of their servants. Ufrem opened the small gate with the keys he carried. Nahia guessed that the Tergnomus had keys for all areas of the dungeons.

"From this point on, the dungeons begin. Be careful and don't go near the cells. There are all kinds of prisoners here, and it would be a pity if you had an accident."

"I'll be careful," Nahia said, swallowing. She had no idea what kind of prisoners might be here and how dangerous they might be. It was almost worse than if they had told her the area was filled with wild crocodiles.

They passed on to the area with the cells and Ufrem shut the gate behind them. Nahia looked at a huge corridor of stone slightly lit by torches. On both sides of the corridor were large silver doors. Nahia guessed they were the cells where they had the prisoners.

"Begin right here. I'll go ahead. I want it clean. I hope you know how to clean properly, or else I'll get very angry."

"I know how to clean," Nahia said.

"Good, you wouldn't be the first or last they sent me who didn't know how to do something so basic. I mean who didn't know how to do it well."

Nahia set to work. Aoma had taught her to do it properly. It was one of the tasks Nahia always did in the cabin to give some rest to her grandmother. Besides, it was a task she did not mind doing.

She cleaned the left side of the great corridor they were in without getting too close to the large doors of the cells, just in case. Ufrem was a little ahead of her cleaning the right side, and every now and then he watched her. Nahia put more verve in the scrubbing whenever he did. The surface was rugged and hard to clean.

They reached the end of the corridor that had another grill with very thick fixed bars. Nahia looked and saw another wide corridor with cells on either side going on toward the end. It was quite long, which meant they had quite a bit of work ahead of them.

"We'll go do the other corridor," Ufrem told her. "We have two more besides this one to clean today,"

"Oh, all right," Nahia looked down the corridor whose end she could not see, in part because it was very long and in part because there was little light.

Ufrem opened the gate, and they passed into the next corridor.

"I'll take the right side, you take the left," he told her and set to work.

Nahia did the same and stayed beside him. She looked up from the floor, and ahead of her she glimpsed a shadow approaching from the darkness. She was surprised. She narrowed her eyes and looked again. She glimpsed a shadow coming along the middle of the corridor. This made her nervous. Suddenly, she realized it was not a shadow. She focused on it, and once it was closer she finally realized what it was.

"A giant black viper!" she cried and dropped the mop, startled.

Ufrem turned and came over to Nahia quickly.

"Stay calm. It's a Serpetuss. They're the guardians of the dungeons."

Nahia was petrified. A huge black viper, over thirty feet long and three feet thick, was approaching her, slithering along the floor.

"It's… terrifying…"

"Stay still and it won't do anything to you."

The great viper reached them. It stopped and raised its body until its head was above them. It seemed to smell them with its long, forked tongue. It recognized Ufrem at once and stopped sniffing at him, turning all its interest to Nahia. The huge snake let out a loud hiss and showed huge, lethal fangs.

Nahia was terrified, but she stood as still as a statue. The Serpetuss seemed about to plunge its fateful fangs into her head. She thought for a moment that everything was lost, but she stayed calm somehow and did not react. The colossal snake closed its mouth and hissed loudly again. Then it lowered its head to the floor and went on its way, zigzagging. When it got to the bars it passed through them, although its body was thicker than the space between them. It went away along the corridor they had just cleaned.

"I thought I wouldn't live to tell the tale," Nahia snorted and bent over from the fear she had experienced.

"Serpetuss are unique creatures," Ufrem commented. "They watch these corridors and make sure no prisoner escapes if they manage to get out of their cells, which is already highly unlikely. They're formidable."

"I… I realize that…" Nahia could not shake the fear from her body.

"If several join forces, they're very capable of finishing off a dragon."

"They are? I thought dragons were practically invincible."

"Well, you see, the Serpetuss are distant relatives of the dragons, although more primitive and less intelligent. Yet, they share something: their magical defenses and the hardness of their scales. That makes them formidable fighters."

"But defeating a dragon… I find that hard to believe."

"It is, but it has happened, and that's why they are the guardians of this place. Four Serpetuss were able to take out the eyes of a dragon that had escaped. They blinded it and immobilized it by coiling around its wings and legs. They ended up strangling it. It died from suffocation."

"That's impressive."

"It is. The Serpetuss are a force of nature."

"How many are there?"

"About twenty. They travel the corridors of the three underground levels, day and night, watching. If anyone escapes their cell, they make sure they don't escape from the dungeons."

"It left me frozen, I swear."

"You'll get used to them. Remember, you must stay still in their presence and everything will be fine."

"How do they know I'm not a prisoner?"

Ufrem smiled.

"Because of the bracelet you're wearing."

Nahia looked down at the silver bracelet on her left wrist.

"It's not just silver, is it?"

"You're smart. That silver is enchanted with dragon magic."

"The Serpetuss detects the magic of its distant relative, and that's why it knows I'm not a prisoner," Nahia guessed, looking at the bracelet and studying it.

"That's right. So you would do well to not come down here without putting on that bracelet first."

"Has that ever happened?"

"Of course it has. The stupidity of some borders on a total incapacity to use their head."

"I understand that the Serpetuss…"

"Kills and eats them."

Nahia looked horrified.

"Eats?"

"They love meat, of any race. Of anything, I'd say. So, if you don't want to end up devoured by one of them, you'd better not be in the dungeons without that bracelet."

"I'll protect it with my life."

"You'd better. Now let's keep cleaning. There's much to do and little time."

Nahia strove to vigorously clean the area she had been assigned. As she was mopping the floor, Ufrem came over to her.

"You have to scrub with the barbed brush and soap first to get all the filth off, then mop."

"I'll do that," Nahia said and got down on her knees, putting the brush in the bucket. She started scrubbing the floor. It was going to be a tough job—she had thought so, but now she was experiencing it for real.

She had been scrubbing the floor for a while and had not even realized she had gotten close to one of the cells. She got up. She knew she should not look. That if she did she would be in trouble. That there might be a dragon inside and it might somehow tear her face off.

"Don't look inside…" she muttered under her breath, trying to persuade herself.

Unfortunately, something inside her pushed her to look. She resisted. She shook her head and went on scrubbing the floor. She must not look, she knew that, but something was urging her to do just that. She thought it was her innate curiosity but soon realized it was not that. Curiosity she could dominate—that force demanding she look into the cell was a strange force. It did not come from outside. It was not someone or something that pushed her to look and it was not curiosity either, because she could resist that. There was something else, an internal force in her that forced her to look. She tried to resist it. She realized that although it seemed to come from her, there was something else, as if the force that made her look came partly from her surroundings.

"I'm not going to look, it's dangerous."

All around her, everything was quiet. There was little light, and she could only hear Ufrem cleaning a little ahead of her. What was persuading her to look? It was one thing that she felt curious, something internal, but she also felt an external force around her which also impelled her. It was very strange.

She tried to resist, but the two forces pushed against her: the internal and the external. They were stronger than her will. She flattened up to the silver door and rose to the peephole. It had a silver pin a palm high by three wide. Nahia knew she should not slide it, but her hands did not obey her, and with a sharp movement she moved the pin. She thought it would make a lot of noise, but it made no sound, as if it were perfectly oiled.

She looked inside and checked whether there was anyone in the cell. There was one single prisoner. He was lying on the floor, half sitting. It was not a dragon, so the danger was not too great, at least in principle, although she was not too confident. She watched the prisoner. She could not see his face because he had a mask covering it, not only his face but his whole head. From his build and his hands, which she could see, Nahia guessed he was human, and that surprised her. Why would the dragons have a human locked up in here? Why had they put a mask on the prisoner that covered his whole head? She found it inhumane. They had him in the depths of a dungeon with barely any light, in solitary confinement and with a horrible mask covering his face and head.

She sighed deeply. Unless this human was an assassin or a torturer, he did not deserve this fate. She studied him. He was not very tall or strong. From what she could see of his arms and legs, which was not much, he looked wiry, like someone who had been exposed to physical work. She hesitated whether to ask him who he was. She knew that doing so was a mistake, one that might be punishable by death, but for some reason she could not understand, something within her pushed her to ask, to try and find out who this poor wretch was.

She leaned her forehead against the hole to see better. The prisoner seemed to be dozing, lying in a bed made of hay and dry grass. She studied the cell to see whether she could see anything else.

All of a sudden, the prisoner rose.

Nahia fell backward, startled.

Chapter 29

Nahia stood up quickly, and from the distance of a step away she took a glance through the peephole of the door. Her heart beat madly, and she was still frightened. The prisoner watched her through the peephole. He waited without coming close, as if he was aware that if he did, he ran the risk of being punished.

The stranger looked at her with human eyes behind a mask of old gold that represented the head of a dragon. It was not actually a real mask but more like a helmet, since it covered his whole head.

"Sorry... I didn't mean to bother..." Nahia said, showing her hand in a peace gesture from outside.

The prisoner looked at her, tilting his head. The dragon helmet made him look like a Drakonid, which gave her a feeling of deep unrest. If a Drakonid already looked threatening, this was something even stranger.

From behind the mask came a sound that Nahia identified as the prisoner's voice. He had asked a question, she guessed, since it ended in a questioning tone, but she could not understand a word.

"I don't understand you..."

Again, a sentence came out of the dragon mask. One Nahia could not understand. This was followed by another and a third one. The prisoner was speaking to her, but she could not understand a word he said.

"I'm sorry... I don't understand you. Don't you speak the unified language of Kraido?"

The prisoner pointed his finger at Nahia and then put his hand to the mouth of the mask and made as if he were speaking. Then he shrugged.

He obviously did not understand her and she did not understand him, so they were not going to be able to communicate. Nahia repeated the signs the stranger had made to indicate that she could not understand anything either.

The prisoner nodded. He crouched down and pointed his finger at his own chest and then at Nahia.

She was thoughtful. What did he want to convey? While she was trying to understand, the prisoner repeated it. Nahia thought she knew.

"You're telling me you're like me, aren't you?"

The prisoner bowed his head.

"I, like you," Nahia said and indicated herself with her finger and then pointed at the prisoner.

The stranger nodded.

Nahia was glad to have been able to communicate, even so little. She got closer to the opening to try and see him better. She assumed the stranger was a boy, at least he looked like one, but to be sure she asked him. She pointed at herself, gesturing to her long hair and chest, and then indicated the prisoner.

The stranger shook his head, which made the mask swing from one side to the other, and she could see that it looked like one single piece with a clasp at the back. She thought it had to be horrible to wear such a thing; it looked solid and heavy. Why would they have put it on? She pointed at the mask and then opened her hands and arms in a "why" gesture.

The prisoner looked at her. He understood her question, she could see it in his eyes. The problem was how to answer. He made a gesture with his hand for Nahia to wait while he thought about how to explain.

"You shouldn't talk to that prisoner," a voice said behind her back.

Nahia started. She turned and saw Ufrem mopping the floor with a wooden bucket a little ahead of her.

"You scared me!"

Ufrem stopped mopping and looked at her.

"This place would scare anyone. There are also things you shouldn't do."

"Is it forbidden to speak to the prisoners?" Nahia asked. Although she guessed the answer, she played dumb.

"It is. You can't speak to any prisoner of the dungeons."

"Fine, I'll remember that…"

"Besides, this prisoner in particular is 'special.'"

"This one? Special? Why?"

"You're here to clean, not ask questions."

"Oh, forgive me… it's just that the whole situation, and this place, it makes me a little nervous."

"I can see that. Must be a Human thing I guess."

"Yeah, and we're curious and talkative."

"The Fatum are even worse. To quell your curiosity, I'll tell you that this prisoner is dangerous."

"Him? But he's a Human, isn't he?"

Ufrem came closer, although he kept his distance and watched the prisoner.

"Yes, he's Human and a boy. Also dangerous. You must not speak to him."

"Okay, I won't."

"You'd better not. The punishment for doing so would be exemplary. Down here they don't fool around," Ufrem said and shut the peephole with a swift movement.

Nahia felt strange once the prisoner had disappeared, as if she should continue talking with him for some reason she did not know.

"I'm sorry I looked inside," she apologized.

"Curiosity killed the Felidae. Don't let that happen to you, Human."

Nahia picked up her brush and went on cleaning the part she had left. Ufrem opened the next section and they went on scrubbing. Nahia watched how he did it to try and mimic him.

In the last section, they once again crossed paths with a Serpetuss. Nahia stayed as still as a statue, showing her bracelet. The last thing she wanted to do was draw the attention of those deadly, loathsome creatures. She was sure that if it bit her she would die from poisoning in no time at all, and she was not carrying any antidote against venom on her.

They finished the cleaning shift and Ufrem accompanied her to the entrance.

"Leave the silver bracelet here. You're not allowed to take it out of the dungeons."

"Oh, okay…"

"I expect you to be here tomorrow at the same time."

"I'll be here."

Ufrem nodded and left.

Nahia left the dungeons, and after passing between the two black dragons she headed to the barracks. She looked at the moon; it was late at night. The cleaning shift had taken hours. She had not been able to go for any dinner, and on top of that, she now had very few hours of sleep to recover. She sighed. The following day she would be exhausted, which was not going to help her with classes. She could foresee that it was going to be a grueling month. That was all she needed, as she was doing so well to begin with…

"This punishment is going to be a real torment," she muttered as she walked away from the dungeons.

The following days, she went to clean after classes as she was supposed to do. The truth was that the dismal place depressed her. She was tired, and although cleaning was not so hard for her, it took away the little energy she had left after classes. One thing she realized was that in spite of being so tired, she was also intrigued. That prisoner with the dragon mask intrigued her a lot. She did not know why, and she was aware that she should not risk communicating with him because she could get into deep trouble. But even so, he intrigued her. She could not help it. He was a mystery she wanted to solve that something inside her and outside her, pushed her to crack. She decided to confide her thoughts in her squad comrades one morning as they were getting ready.

"You already have enough problems, slim, don't go looking for more," Aiden told her.

Nahia was not surprised by that. Aiden only lived to do what was right by the dragons.

"You say he's an important Human prisoner?" Taika asked in his raspy voice with a tone of intrigue.

"I think so. He must be."

"Important to the dragons, I'm assuming," said Daphne.

Nahia nodded.

"They have him in a dungeon, and they've forced him to wear a gold mask in the shape of a dragon that covers his whole head, like a helmet," Nahia told them.

"That's weird. Why do that if they already have him in a dungeon?" Ivo asked.

"That's what I keep asking myself," Nahia said, shrugging.

"He must be monstrously ugly and they don't want his face to be seen," Lily joked cheerfully.

"It's not that," Aiden said.

They all looked at him.

"You know something," Daphne said accusingly. "Spill it out."

"It's that I know something, and you don't know anything," Aiden replied. "In dragon culture, and Drakonid too, a full gold mask is used sometimes on prisoners."

"Well, what do you say!" said Daphne, making a face of disbelief that he had not mentioned it before.

"A full gold mask in the shape of a dragon head?" Nahia asked.

Aiden looked at the ceiling and said nothing.

"Speak. We know you're not telling us everything," Ivo said, and although his tone was gentle as usual, there was a certain threat in it.

The Drakonid looked at him and frowned.

"No one threatens me."

"No one is threatening you. We're asking you to share knowledge you have and we don't. It's as simple as that," Taika told him, and he looked into his eyes, narrowing his own.

"Well... if you don't know... gold masks are used to hide the face of someone important."

"We guessed as much," Daphne said ironically.

"Go on, what else?" Nahia asked.

"That the mask is of a dragon is significant. It means that whoever is wearing it is very important to the dragons, someone of great importance for them."

"So, it's a most important prisoner for our dear masters," said Lily thoughtfully.

Aiden nodded.

"That's right."

"You know why? Or could you make an educated guess?" Taika asked him.

The Drakonid shook his head.

"Power, war, victory, precious metals and jewels, one of those."

Yeah, everything they like," Daphne made a face of disgust. "We need to narrow down the reason a bit more."

"We don't need to narrow down anything. If they find out you are sniffing near that prisoner, they'll kill you," Aiden said. "I can promise you that. I don't want to be involved in it. I don't want to hear another word about the matter. Let it be. It's not your business. What our lords might want with that prisoner has nothing to do with us."

"In part, he's right," said Taika. "I don't know why we should get involved in this. We could all die. We don't know that prisoner or his importance, both to the dragons or to us, if he does have any for us."

"Taika speaks sensibly," Ivo nodded. "It's not convenient to put your hand inside a wasp's nest..."

"But if he's important to the dragons, it's possible he is also important to us," said Nahia. "I feel... that he is... I know it's only an unfounded feeling, but something tells me he's important to all of us."

"What I know is that the graveyard is filled with those who had feelings and premonitions that had to do with dragons," Daphne said. "I wouldn't want to end up like them."

"Don't take it the wrong way, Nahia, but without something more tangible, I wouldn't put my precious little nose any further in the matter," Lily advised her.

Nahia sighed deeply.

"I know... I know... it's only that..."

"Be prudent. Stay away. If you learn something more relevant, we'll evaluate the matter again," Taika said, and his gentle, intelligent tone reaffirmed her.

"Fine. For now I'll just keep alert and see what I can find out about the prisoner with the gold dragon mask."

"You'd better do it very carefully, or we'll soon have a vacancy," Aiden warned her.

"Really, what a wet blanket you are," Lily said reproachfully.

"I'm simply telling the truth. Our masters won't have mercy."

"And I'm sure you'd be thrilled," Daphne reproached him.

Aiden looked offended. His snub dragon nose rose toward his forehead.

"It's not me who's challenging our lords. I've already warned you. What you do is up to you."

"And you won't tell on us?" Daphne looked at him with a raised eyebrow.

"Yeah, can we trust that you won't go running to tell your lords?" Lily asked him.

Aiden was silent, and in his reptilian eyes Nahia saw pain. The accusations had hurt him.

"He won't say anything because he's part of our squad and his loyalty is first of all to his squad," Taika said.

"And because if he snitches, I'll break his back in two," Ivo said nonchalantly.

Aiden stood up.

"What Taika said," he stated and left the dorm.

Chapter 30

The first weeks of training flew by. Summer left before they realized it, and then autumn came. Nahia was very concerned with doing badly in classes. She had to avoid being punished by her leader for dishonoring it again at all costs, since this time it might decide to kill her. With so much tension, the days went by in the blink of an eye. The fact that she finished exhausted from classes and the punishment of having to clean the dungeons made her drop dead in her bed every night. All this made it look as if the days of her life were slipping through her fingers.

She had just finished her month of punishment and was now trying to recuperate some of the delayed sleep she had accumulated, which was a lot. She had a small grudge with herself because she had not dared to talk to the prisoner with the gold mask again. Every evening she had passed in front of his cell, stopping for a moment but not daring to open the peephole. The prisoner had spoken to her every evening, which meant he was waiting for her, but she could not understand him. She had followed her squad comrades' advice to avoid getting into trouble, but something inside her told her she had not done the right thing. In any case, she was still alive, and that for her was a triumph. She was going to try to keep on like that.

Another thing that worried her more every day, because it was very noticeable, and which she had already known since day one, was her tremendous physical weakness. Compared to her comrades, she was a lot weaker. It had become obvious in the training. That was bad, since they were only receiving basic training in magic and weapons. Just thinking about what would happen when the training got more advanced made her knees knock. This was a serious problem, and it robbed her of necessary sleep. She knew that, inevitably, her weakness was going to be a death sentence. If the dragons had made something very clear, it was that whoever was weak would not survive the Path. It was something they repeated almost every day, and they all had it engraved with fire.

That morning, before her basic magic class, she decided to share her fears with her squad. She was sure they had already realized. She also knew they had no reason to help her. Here they each had to look out for themselves and survive. Even so, if she did not ask for help she was sure she would die, and she was not going to let her pride kill her. She would rather appear weak than die for not admitting it to her comrades. Not that she was not proud—she was, as much or more than others—but it was one thing to be proud and another to be a fool and have pride blind her so that she ended up in a grave.

"If I keep going on like this… I'm not going to make it," she said at the table in the dining hall while they were having breakfast.

Her comrades stopped chewing and stared at her, puzzled by the admission.

"You say that because of your physical weakness?" Taika asked her in his raspy, gentle tone with a fox's look in his eyes.

Nahia nodded.

"We're going to start wielding weapons soon, and I'm not even capable of doing all the lists of movements unarmed without draining myself physically."

"If I can do them, so can you," Daphne said, nodding in her direction.

"You're stronger than me."

Daphne snorted.

"Only a little bit."

"I also believe that if Daphne and I can, you can too," Lily said, trying to encourage her.

"Lily, you're twice as strong as I am," Nahia said.

"Perhaps physically, but not mentally. And in magic you're a lot stronger than I am," Lily said, looking at her resolutely.

"The human is right. She won't survive this autumn if she goes on like this," Aiden predicted with the calm of an executioner passing a sentence of death.

"Don't tell her that, blockhead!" Daphne chided him.

"Don't be so ruthless!" Lily joined in.

Aiden shrugged.

"I'm only telling her the truth, and you know it too. She's always bad at all the physical exercises. And what we see our lords see."

"I feel like hitting you with a chair on that horned head of yours," Daphne told him, mimicking grabbing a chair and hitting him.

Aiden did not flinch.

"Instead of that, you might apply yourself, because she won't survive autumn, but neither will you. As for the Scarlatum, she won't survive winter. That's the simple truth. You're weak, and you won't survive the year."

Daphne and Lily stood on the table and nearly jumped at Aiden, who went on eating without a care.

"Quiet, please," Taika pleaded. "They're watching us…" he said and looked toward the dragons in the middle of the dining hall.

Daphne and Lily glanced furiously at Aiden before they sat down reluctantly.

"Our Drakonid comrade is not very gifted in the art of communication, but he's right," Ivo stated. "It's undeniable, and everyone sees that our Human has serious problems in the physical and magical areas, derived from her small body. It's also obvious our Fatum isn't far behind, and her weaknesses are more evident every day. Those of our Scarlatum will become notorious in the last part of the year."

Daphne and Lily were about to protest, but Taika intervened.

"What we ought to concentrate on is solving our problems and not arguing among ourselves. That will only lead to defeat and death. The first thing we must do is help Nahia improve. Only thus will she survive. She has to improve, and we can help her do it."

"We can?" Aiden asked, gaping at Taika with disbelief.

"I believe we can," Taika assured them.

"Do you believe it too?" Aiden asked Ivo.

The great Tauruk looked at Nahia as if evaluating her.

"I'd like to think so, although I have my doubts, I won't deny it. Her body is too fragile, like the branch of a young tree. It snaps with the strong wind of autumn."

"Aiden has the tact of a shark, but you should have a little more, Nahia is sitting right in front of you," Daphne reproached Ivo.

"In my opinion, although it hurts, the truth is always a thousand times better than a pitiful lie."

"When you get philosophical, there's nothing we can do with you," Lily told him, dismissing him with a wave.

"I don't mind listening to truths, even if they're harsh… everything that has been said here is the truth…" Nahia said with her head down.

"We're not going to let her die," said Daphne determinedly, wagging her finger.

"Why not? It's not our problem. It's hers," said Aiden.

"You're a monster!" Lily yelled at him.

"We should do it for the good of the squad, if nothing else," Taika told him.

"I don't agree. Many squads lose members along the year, it's natural. If ours does, we'll keep going just the same."

"He deserves to be killed!" Daphne was furious, and her eyes flashed rage.

"I think you're wrong about that," Taika replied, keeping calm. "A squad of six is better than one of five, even if the sixth member isn't very strong. There is always something one can bring to the group. Whoever isn't there doesn't bring anything."

Aiden weighed this, looking at Nahia.

"You might be half right, but she will also be a burden."

"A burden who can help," Taika pointed out.

"Well… you may be right."

"He is. Wolves never abandon their elders. They let them lead and adjust to their pace. The herd is more important than the individual," Ivo explained as if he were telling a fable.

Aiden shrugged.

"I guess we'll see."

"Very well, how can we help her?" Lily asked.

"We have to make her body strong," Taika said.

"And how do I strengthen my body?" Nahia asked.

"There's only one way: lots of work, suffering, and sacrifice," Taika told her.

Nahia bowed her head and nodded.

"I guessed it would be something like that."

"It's either that or die," Taika assured her. "You choose."

"I choose work, suffering, and sacrifice," said Nahia.

Taika nodded.

"That's the way to talk," Lily gave Nahia a pat on the back.

"You'll make it, and don't listen to this brick-head, or the forest philosopher here," Daphne said cheerfully.

Nahia nodded.

"This afternoon, when we finish classes, we'll go to the gym. We'll work on that body of yours," Taika said.

"I really appreciate it."

"You're welcome."

Nahia cheered up a little. There was hope: her squad was going to help her.

That evening when they finished magic training, Nahia went to the gym with Taika. She was very grateful to him for coming to the gym with her, because he did not need it. He was a strong tiger and did not need to exercise. The Felidae had an extraordinary physiognomy. From what Nahia knew, only the humans, Fatum, and Scarlatum went to the gym, since they were the weakest races physically. Ivo and Aiden did not go, and neither did Taika, until now.

They arrived at the building, which looked quite solemn. Nahia counted over fifty round columns holding up a colonnade, all in white marble with inlayed diamonds. She had to admit that the dragons had very particular tastes. The building formed a great square and was covered by a flat roof.

When they walked in, she noticed it was full of people, which surprised her a lot. She had not expected so many to use the gym. The first thing she was able to tell was that almost everyone there were Humans, Fatum, and Scarlatum. There were barely any Drakonid or Felidae. She only saw a couple of Tauruk-Kapro. The other thing that drew her attention was that there were people of all three years, not only the first-years, who obviously needed it more, but also second- and third-years. She identified them easily because they were clearly separated—the third-years near the entrance, the second-years in the middle, and the first-years at the far end of the building, which is where they headed.

As they went by the different areas, she could see there were parts where they were exercising alone, others where they fought on mats, and still others where they did exercises of strength, lifting what looked like heavy rocks carved with rectangular markings. Seeing them lifting those heavy rocks with one arm or with their legs, she was completely discouraged. She would never be able to lift such heavy things.

Taika seemed to notice her sinking spirits.

"Don't worry about those stone weights, that's not what you're going to be working on."

"I'm not? Thank goodness…" Nahia sighed in relief, looking everywhere as if she had entered a whole new world populated by people with extraordinary strength.

Taika smiled at her.

"In order to build a house, you have to start by placing a block on the ground."

"My block is more like a pebble."

"It will soon be a block of solid granite, and then you'll be able to build on it."

Nahia did not say anything, but she did not have the confidence in herself that Taika showed.

They reached the area of the first-years. Nahia recognized the two human boys in the Red Squadron: Brendan and Morgan. The two of them greeted her with respect, and this cheered her up. She returned the greeting the same way.

Although she was tired from the long training day, she felt glad to be here. She waited for Taika to tell her what she had to do, since she felt lost in this place. She looked around and saw boys and girls working on strength and flexibility in the corners against the long walls, while in the center on the different mats they were fighting in pairs. They all looked as if they knew what they were doing and were exerting themselves to the maximum. The intensity they were applying themselves with was apparent.

"I should've come here from the very first day," said Nahia, finding herself so lost and lagging in comparison with the people there.

"Don't torture yourself with the past. That can no longer be changed. Focus on the future, which is unwritten, and work to reach your goals there."

"Yes, you're right…. but, Taika, I've lost a whole season…"

"No, you haven't lost it. In your case, it wasn't possible for you to start this way. You arrived broken and weak. Just the training exhausted all your strength. And then when you were beginning to recover, you were punished."

"Huh, that's true…"

"So stop turning it over in your head. Now you can, and you're pretty whole. Let's seize the opportunity."

"You're absolutely right."

Taika smiled at her, and his intelligent eyes narrowed.

"You'll do it."

"What weight element should I start working?" Nahia asked him confidently, seeing others exercising nearby.

"One which you always carry with you," Taika told her.

"I carry it with me?" Nahia looked at herself. She was only wearing the academy clothes, which were not very heavy.

"You will perform a series of exercises using the weight of your own body in order to work and develop those muscles of yours, which are still somewhat stunted."

"And rickety."

"Well, I wouldn't say that much. You'll be surprised by how they react."

"When you say my own body weight, what do you mean?"

"I'll show you. I want you to squat with your back straight and flex your legs like this," Taika showed her how to do the exercise.

"Oh, all right," Nahia did the exercise. She did not find it at all difficult.

"Very well, repeat the movement thirty times, slowly, maintaining strength and balance."

Nahia did the thirty squats, and when she finished she massaged her thighs.

"How was it?" Taika asked her.

"At first it was easy, but the last ones were hard. And now my muscles are stiff."

"That's normal, don't worry. You've been holding the weight of your body on them."

"Oh... I see what you mean by using my body weight."

"Now I want you to get down on the floor like this," Taika got down on the floor and did a plank.

"All right," Nahia said and got down beside him in the same position.

"Back straight, and lean on the tips of your toes."

"Fine. For how long?"

"Count to thirty, slowly."

Nahia did as she was told and soon felt her arms tiring.

"Wow, it's harder than it looks," she said when she finished.

The exercises I'm going to teach you look simple and don't require lifting weight, just your own. You'll do them all in the order in which I'm telling you," Taika stood up.

"How many exercises are there?" Nahia asked as she also stood up. Already her body was complaining.

"Twenty. All very simple."

"Twenty? And how many times do I have to do each one?"

"Thirty."

"But if just doing each twice have my arms and thighs burning, how am I going to do thirty?"

"With effort and suffering, there's no other way," Taika said with a shrug.

"Are you sure these exercises will help me build up muscle?"

"Build up muscle and resistance. Believe me."

Nahia snorted.

"All right… what's next?"

"Flexed stride," Taika said and showed her how to do it by extending one leg forward and lowering his body, keeping his balance.

Nahia did the exercise, and when she finished she looked at Taika.

"Now my legs are really on fire."

"Don't worry, that's a good sign. Keep going."

Taika showed her the twenty exercises she had to do, from flexions to abdominals of different types, to jumping in place and other exercises. The last five were for flexibility.

By the time they finished the cycle, Nahia's body hurt like a nightmare.

"You're doing well. I want you to take a good rest and then do one more cycle. Rest again a long while and then do a third one. Then that'll be enough for today."

"Three cycles?" Nahia's eyes opened wide.

"Remember, work and sacrifice. There's no other way. If you can't do it all, do as much as you can."

Nahia nodded and got down to it. Taika watched her and corrected her posture in each exercise so she was doing it right. The third cycle was torture for Nahia, who clenched her teeth and fought to do all the exercises, although she could not finish several, like flexions and abdominals. Even so, she did as much as she could and fought for every repetition with all her body could give. When they got to the last five flexibility exercises, all she could do was breathe, relieved. She finished bone-weary, lying on one of the exercise mats.

"That wasn't bad at all for a first time," Taika told her, and in his raspy voice she could hear that he wanted to cheer her up.

"But I couldn't do all the exercises..." Nahia said regretfully. She was breathing with difficulty, lying on her back on the mat, exhausted from the effort.

She was sweating, more than she ever remembered having sweated with her grandmother.

"You did well," another voice Nahia recognized at once said. She tried to rise to look at him, but her abs muscles burst with pain and she dropped back on the mat. Logan's head appeared above hers. "Honestly, you did pretty well," the dark-haired boy said, looking at her with his light blue eyes like the sky in summer.

"You saw me?" she asked, trying to hide how embarrassed she was. But she could not stop her blush, and it showed abut a league away.

"Yeah, I was just coming in to exercise and I saw you."

"I didn't do well at all..."

"You made the effort, which is what counts in the end. The results will come."

"That's what I tell her," Taika intervened.

"Hello, I'm Logan, Whirlwind Squad, White Squadron," he introduced himself and bowed lightly, showing respect to Taika.

"Taika, Igneous Squad, Red Squadron," Taika bowed as well, returning the greeting.

"A pleasure," Logan said courteously.

"I think that's enough for today. I'll see you at the barracks, Nahia," Taika said, and with a parting nod he left.

"Is he training you?" Logan asked.

"Yes, he is. I need to get better. A lot better, and fast."

Logan nodded and got down on his haunches.

"You will. You have a lot of spirit."

"You think so?"

"I'm sure."

"But I can't even stand up."

"That's a good sign. It means the exercises have worked your body, which is what you have to achieve in the end."

"I feel a little ridiculous...."

Logan looked at her and bowed his head.

"Don't be. Feel proud. You're a step closer to surviving this place."

"Will we survive? Do you really believe it?"

Logan looked into her eyes.

"We will," he promised.

Chapter 31

Autumn was rough. If training with weapons was difficult, magic had become most complicated. They had to study several chapters of magic to prepare each class, and they were hard to understand and assimilate. Dragons treated magic as if it were something intrinsic to everyone, when it was not for the other races. Neither Nahia nor any of her squadmates had any knowledge of magic, its fundamentals, or how to use it.

They had already been working a couple of weeks on how to use the bond that existed between their mind and the dragon that represented their inner power. The exercises were not very difficult— they consisted of creating a small sphere of power the size of a marble on the palm of their hand while with the other they used the Learning Pearl for help. The first times they had almost all failed, but little by little they had managed to create the small sphere of pure energy. The next exercises had consisted of keeping them hovering over their hands and making them rise and fall, keeping control with their minds.

That morning, they were heading to magic class, and their nervousness showed in the group.

"Have you prepared for today's lesson?" Nahia asked her comrades as they headed to the lineup.

"Of course. We all have to have the theory part well learned before we enter the training classroom," Aiden replied.

"Well learned… has several meanings…" Lily commented.

"It has no other meanings. Well learned means exactly that: well learned," Aiden gave her a look that meant he did not understand what she was talking about.

"Nothing like a comprehensive explanation," said Daphne, and when Aiden was about to say something to her she turned her back on him.

Aiden muttered a string of things that sounded like "unbearable," "unbelievable," and "worst squad in the world."

"I tried to understand it, but these concepts are very far from spirituality, peace, and harmony," Ivo commented. "I don't fully understand them."

"We're in an academy of war, Ivo, there's little peace, spirituality, and harmony," Lily told him.

"We're here to learn to kill with weapons and magic," Daphne specified in an almost cruel tone.

"It's not anything I share or like," Ivo shrugged.

"Unfortunately, we have no choice," Taika said. "You'll have to apply yourself and learn to do it, or they'll make you pay. The dragons will see it as a weakness, and you'll be in serious trouble."

"I know… but I don't like it."

"Cheer up, big guy, you'll make it," Lily said, trying to boost his morale.

Ivo smiled at her, but his eyes were dull.

They went into class, and Mag-Zilar-Ond was waiting for them at the far end of the classroom with Mabor-Exarbor by the pedestal.

Red Squadron, welcome. Today we will begin to use that inner power you have and are starting to master. We will channel it so you will be able to attack with it as you have read can be done in the tomes of knowledge, the silver dragoness messaged them, and they all felt that it was also an important moment.

"I will get… the target… ready," Mabor said, and with his usual parsimony he headed to the west end of the classroom. Once there, he raised a pole with a solid target stuck at mid height.

Very well. Now that you know how to interact with your inner dragon of power and create a small sphere of energy, you will learn to increase it and then use it to attack. I understand that you have already studied all this, so it should not be as strange as your faces are showing right now.

Nahia hid her look of surprise. The tomes spoke of how to create the spheres of energy using the inner power of the dragon and how to send more power to make the sphere large and powerful. What the tome did not specify was the use of this energy as a weapon. Or at least she had not seen it or understood it.

Let the first pupil step forward.

"Igneous Squad … first," Mabor called.

Nahia was already expecting it. She got up and went to where Mabor was standing beside the pedestal.

Very well, Human, create the sphere, Mag-Zilar-Ond ordered.

Nahia took out the Learning Pearl from her belt, under her cloak, and held it in her left hand. She closed her eyes and sought the bright, powerful dragon in the middle of her chest. When she looked for it, she felt as if she were calling it, and it came to meet her. It was the weirdest feeling, since she was aware that all of this was taking place only in her mind. It was her mind's interpretation of her magical power, most likely so that she would not go nuts. She concentrated and opened her right hand. She joined the dragon and sought to create the small sphere in the palm of her hand. The Learning Pearl flashed a sliver-white color. Nahia knew it was helping her. The small sphere formed on the palm of her hand. She opened her eyes and looked at it. It was translucent and gave off flashes as if it were alive. She concentrated on keeping it hovering above her hand. She was not sure how she managed to do so, but it was a combination of her mind, the dragon, and the Learning Pearl.

Very well done. In your case, the power flows easily. That pleases me. Now, I want you to send more power to the sphere and make it grow until it is the same size as the Learning Pearl. Without destabilizing or destroying it, of course.

Nahia's eyes rested on the Learning Pearl. It was a lot bigger than her small sphere of energy. She was not discouraged and called on her dragon of power. From what she had read in the tomes, her mind had to send the orders to her inner dragon and the Learning Pearl simultaneously so that both forces worked together. She did this and began to send the dragon's energy to the sphere hovering above her right hand. As she did this, the Learning Pearl gave off a flash, so Nahia knew it was helping her.

The sphere began to increase in size as it received the energy that came from the middle of Nahia's chest and went into the sphere. It went on growing, and Nahia concentrated on preventing it from destabilizing and getting destroyed. What she did was strengthen the outer layer of the expanding sphere, sending extra energy so it would hold. It took her a moment, but she managed to make the sphere the same size as the pearl. She looked at both and felt very pleased: she had done it.

You have managed to form the sphere of energy. Very well done. Now is the time to learn how to use it as a weapon. There are two ways of doing this. One is by sending the sphere against the target with the force of your mind. The other one, simpler but also effective, is throwing it with your hand as if you were throwing an object. They both work and are both destructive. In your case, since you are akin to your power, I want you to use your mind.

Nahia breathed deeply. She did not know whether she could do that. Throwing an object with her mind sounded impossible. It

245

seemed like trying to move an object with her mind. That was impossible. Or was it really? At least in the earthly world it was. Up here, in the sky world of the dragons, who knew. Anything was possible.

Focus your mind on the sphere and then on the target. Do it repeatedly and faster every time until you cannot do it any faster.

The instruction was clear, albeit a little complicated to carry out, but Nahia did as the dragoness told her. She focused on the sphere and then on the target, on the sphere and then the target, and began to pass from one to the other, going faster every time. All of a sudden, the sphere left its position and headed straight to the center of the target at great speed. The sphere hit the target and there was an explosion of pure energy. Pieces of wood flew off in every direction. The target was completely destroyed.

It could not be. Nahia's jaw dropped, and her face showed absolute astonishment. She could not believe what she had just done.

Excellent work. I am very pleased. You are a star pupil, Flameborn. Now go back to your place and let us see what the rest do.

It took Nahia a moment to react and act on the order. She went back to her place while Mabor set up a new target.

"Spectacular," Daphne told her when she sat down.

"Awesome," Lily congratulated her.

"Very well done," Aiden also congratulated her, looking very pleased.

"I don't know... how it happened," Nahia was stunned.

"Next..." Mabor called.

"It's my turn, let's see what happens," Daphne jumped up determinedly.

They all watched the Fatum. It turned out that she did pretty well. She was able to increase the sphere and throw it with her mind, but she could not hit the target. For some reason, it went to the left and the sphere exploded against the wall. Mag-Zilar-Ond told her to repeat the exercise. Daphne did so and the sphere failed again, missing the target and hitting the wall a little to the right. That was enough. She would have to work on improving her focus on the destination.

Lily was next. She managed to create the sphere full of energy, then tried to throw it with her mind but failed. Mag-Zilar-Ond told her to try with her hand. Lily threw the sphere as if she threw a ball and it headed toward the target. The throw seemed to have been short, but it hit the lower part of the target and there was the explosion which destroyed it. Lily gave a cry of joy.

"Without euphoria..." Mabor chided her as he went to set up another target.

Aiden was next, fully convinced he was going to succeed. The wind quickly left his sails. He had serious trouble increasing his sphere. The first time he lost control and destroyed it. Luckily, when it was destroyed it did not explode but instead seemed to implode. The second time he managed to create the sphere, although it was quite smaller than his pearl. He did not seek to enlarge it because it became unstable.

He tried to throw it with his mind and the sphere did not budge. He had to give up after three attempts and throw it with his hand. This he did well, hitting the target in the middle, but the explosion was not very strong and only split the target in two. He returned to the group, looking very disappointed with himself.

It was Ivo's turn, and he headed to it with his calm walk. He had trouble simply creating the sphere and keeping it hovering. When he tried to send more power to make it bigger, he failed. In the end, seeing he could not, he threw his sphere at the target with his powerful arm, but the explosion was minimal and did not even damage it. He shrugged and went back to the group when Mag-Zilar-Ond terminated his exercise.

Taika headed to do the exercise with his usual calm and concentration. He also had trouble creating and maintaining the sphere. In the end, he managed to create one larger than Ivo's and smaller than Aiden's. Like them, he had to throw it with his hand. He hit the target in the center, but the explosions did not even split the target.

Once the Igneous Squad finished, it was the Ardent's turn. Its members did the exercise, and then it was the Searing Squad's turn. No one equaled Nahia's feat. It was clear that the Fatum and Scarlatum were the most apt in the use of magic. The Humans were close, but the Drakonid, Felidae, and Tauruk-Kapro were pretty poor at it.

Very well. Now that you know how to do it, I want you to all repeat the exercise against the wall, five paces away from it. Separate well so that you do not hit one another by accident. Throw the spheres with energy against the wall in front of you. Imagine an opponent wants to run you through with his sword. You will do this until you run out of inner energy. When the dragon runs out, you will have no energy left. Keep practicing until that moment.

They all stood as Mag-Zilar-Ond had told them, and they practiced the whole day. Some were faster, those who had been the most apt, and others were slower, the ones who had trouble. Nahia noticed that she was good at this, both throwing the sphere with her mind and with her hand. She even tried to overcharge the sphere to make it larger and more powerful, and she was successful. But when it exploded on the wall it made a lot of noise.

"The sphere... should not be bigger than the pearl..." Mabor corrected her. He was slow, but he missed nothing.

When they all finished, they went to the library to end the day. For once, Nahia was happy. That was not the case with Aiden, Taika, and especially Ivo, whose results had been quite poor.

As they were sitting at one of the tables at the Library of Dragon Magic, Nahia saw Ana at another table at the far end. She was so glad to see her that she stood up and ran like an arrow to speak to her without saying anything to her comrades, who watched her run off.

"Ana, I'm so glad to see you!" she said when she reached her side.

Ana looked up from the tome and realized who it was.

"Nahia!" she cried with eyes moist with joy.

They both hugged tightly, as if making sure the other person was real and flesh and blood.

Nahia sat down with her friend.

"I've tried to talk to you, but we never run into each other," she whispered, noticing that an Exarbor was watching them.

"I usually see you in the dining hall, but since we're not allowed to talk..."

"Yeah, it's the same with me. Even so, we should at least wave so the other knows we're glad to see them and that everything is going fine."

"I'd like that..."

"So, let's think of a gesture we can make," Nahia suggested.

"I can't think... wait, a wink?"

"That's going to be difficult with so many people in the hall. Besides, there's a lot of movement between those going for food and those coming back with it."

"True, but it can't be too obvious, or the watch dragons will notice, and I don't want to be punished or something worse…"

"Yeah, I heard you lost a comrade. I'm sorry…"

"It was horrible… I still can't believe it. He only protested aloud about an exercise and the black dragon killed him without warning, without mercy."

"Only for that?"

"Yes, it jumped forward like a cobra and bit his head off with its jaws. His headless body fell to the floor. Then the dragon spit out the head to one side. It was horrific."

"They're ruthless by nature."

"There was no need… he simply complained… the dragon killed him for speaking up. For not agreeing."

"I'm sorry you had to witness that."

"I have nightmares almost every night… in many it's me they kill… I live in constant anguish."

"I'm so sorry. You can relax in magic class. I don't think the silver dragoness is as evil as the black dragon. The dragoness is tough, but I don't think it has a bad heart."

"They are all horrible. They'll kill us without any consideration. Don't be fooled. I know. I see it in their reptilian eyes."

Nahia nodded.

"Yeah, you're right. Any of them could kill us at any moment. But you can't live in anguish. It's better not to think about it and concentrate on the task at hand."

"Don't think I don't try. It's like right now. I'm here studying magic, but my head can't stop thinking that if I don't do well, if I fail, they're going to kill me in a terrible way," she said and started to weep.

Nahia hugged her again to comfort her.

"Take it easy, don't worry. You have me."

"You… won't be able to save me … from them," she muttered, sobbing.

"You have to stop thinking like that. It will only depress you more. I also have bad dreams and my head tells me I could die at any moment. But I fight those feelings and concentrate on doing things well and surviving. That's what you have to do."

"I don't know whether I'll be able to… every day I feel worse… sometimes I think it's better to end this agony as soon as possible… I don't see a way out…"

"Never say that. Ever. There is a way out. We'll find it, and we'll keep going. I promise. Trust me. We'll come out of here alive."

Ana wept disconsolately, and Nahia had to cover her with her hug. They would see her weeping as a sign of weakness. There were no dragons here, but there were Exarbor, and they might report. Nahia did not know whether she could trust the Exarbor or the Tergnomus of the academy. Most likely not, even if they were also slaves like them. She thought about the Drakonid, who were also slaves and who they could not trust at all. It was probably best not to trust the two servant races at the academy.

"Thank you... for cheering and comforting me," Ana told her.

"It's nothing. Now listen to me. You can't cry. You can't let them see you crying. You give them an excuse to accuse you of weakness, and that's the worst thing you could do."

Ana nodded and wiped her nose and eyes with her sleeve.

"I'll try."

"Very well. Oh, I know what we can do."

"Tell me."

"We can do this," Nahia put her hands together, palms facing in and fingers straight and together. Then she put them in front of her face and separated them, forming a V.

"A 'V.'"

"For victory," Nahia nodded.

"I like it," Ana said, and a slight smile appeared on her face.

"And look, if you move your hands back and forth they look like a butterfly."

"It's true, it looks like one."

"We'll call it the Butterfly of Victory."

"Pretty name," Ana agreed, and she smiled, watching Nahia moving her hands and creating the effect of a butterfly.

"When we see one another, let's make this gesture. We'll remember that we have to defeat this place and the dragons."

"Yes, let's," said Ana, looking confident.

"If you see Maika or Logan, tell them. I'll do the same if I see them. That way all four of us will be able to greet one another and give one another courage."

"I will."

The two hugged again for a long moment, and Nahia wished with all her heart that Ana would not give up and would go on fighting, despite everything. She had to survive and achieve victory.

Chapter 32

That morning in martial training after half the morning was through, the instructors stopped the class. The three squads belonging to the Red Squadron had been practicing all the offensive and defensive movements in pairs for the umpteenth time.

"Line up and listen," the instructors ordered.

Mai-Beltz-Gaiz stood straight. Every time Nahia felt the dragon was going to address them, she got very nervous. If she had another seizure in that class, she was sure she would not come out alive. The rumor had spread that there were already five first-year pupils who had died during the training—two for not having been able to awake their inner dragon, another for not behaving properly toward a dragon, and two in martial training. She had been lucky, but she was sure this dragon would not spare her life again. She could not afford to have another seizure, or do badly in class, which on the other hand was a very real risk. She was the worst of the whole squadron by far.

With this last set of unarmed combat exercises, you have completed the initial basic martial training. Now you can begin weapons training, the dragon announced.

The members of the three squads of the Red Squadron looked at one another with restrained joy.

They were lined up firmly, as they were supposed to when they walked into class. No one made an excessive show of joy, since the three instructors were watching them with stoic poses and surly looks on their faces.

"I can't believe I survived," Nahia whispered in a low voice; she was in shock for having achieved this small victory.

"I knew you would, don't lose your confidence in yourself," Taika cheered her in a barely audible whisper.

"I'm also very pleased, I wasn't sure you would," Daphne said in another whisper.

"Those who put in the effort receive the fruit of the tree of life in the end," murmured Ivo.

"And bruises too," Lily complained, who had several on her arms and legs which, according to her, made her look like a little monster.

"This is only the beginning. There's nothing to be proud of yet," Aiden told them.

"This one's always so amusing," Daphne said without looking at him.

The Dragon Blood Warlocks use only three weapons and one defense element, and those are the ones you will have to master. You will begin this year with one weapon and the defense element. In the next two, you will learn the use of the other weapons so you will be able to graduate from this martial academy with honors, Mai-Beltz-Gaiz announced.

"Anyone knows what weapons they are?" Nahia asked.

"I guess one is the sword, the three instructors carry one," Taika guessed.

"Yeah, but the other two?" Lily asked.

"I bet the blockhead knows it," said Daphne.

"Of course I know."

"So?" Lily snapped.

"I prefer our dragon master and lord to announce it," Aiden replied.

"I could kill him...." Daphne muttered.

You will be wondering what those weapons are. Your instructors will show you.

The three instructors bent down. In front of each one were two large blankets. Nahia had noticed them at the beginning of class and wondered what they were going to use them for. Since it was forbidden to ask either dragons or instructors, no one had. Nahia almost preferred it, that way they did not get into trouble for asking what they should not.

The Felidae lion unfolded the blanket and took the weapon he kept in it. He stood up and showed the class.

The first weapon worthy of being wielded by a Dragon Blood Warlock is the dagger, Mai-Beltz-Gaiz said.

They all looked at it. Nahia snorted under her breath, relieved. She knew how to use knives—she had learned with her grandmother. They used them for a number of healing tasks, from cutting plants and roots to skinning hares. That dagger, longer than a knife, could not weigh much.

The dagger is a noble weapon. With it you can pierce the heart of your enemy and then tear it out.

Nahia did not like the comment at all, but she pretended that she agreed.

The Scarlatum instructor uncovered what his blanket hid and got up. He showed the weapon to all.

The second weapon worthy of being wielded by a Dragon Blood Warlock is the sword, Mai-Beltz-Gaiz said.

That weapon was made of steel and was long. That was going to be heavy. Nahia was not so happy. It was a double-edged long sword with a crosshead handle. Yes, that weapon must be heavy, and she did not see herself wielding it.

The sword is not only a noble weapon, but the most lethal in the hands of someone who has studied its use. With it you will be able to slice the neck of your opponent with a swift, sharp cut. Even the tallest and strongest of enemies will die if their throat is cut.

Once again, Nahia felt like the weapon was not for her. She had no intention of slicing the neck of anyone, whatever their race and no matter how much of an enemy the dragons told her they were.

Then it was the Drakonid instructor's turn. From his blanket, he took a weapon that was unmistakable and which even a common healer like Nahia recognized. He showed it to the class, holding it with both hands.

The third weapon worthy of being wielded by a Dragon Blood Warlock is the spear, said Mai-Beltz-Gaiz. *The spear is the safest and most efficient weapon, since you can finish off an enemy before they can even get close. With the spear, you can pierce the heart or the neck of your enemies from a distance.*

Once again, the image that formed in Nahia's mind was not appealing. Neither was the length of the weapon and the fact that it was steel, because if the sword weighed a lot, the spear would be even worse. She could use both hands to hold the spear though, and this cheered her a little. Perhaps she could manage with two hands.

And finally the defensive element, which is none other than a shield, Mai-Beltz-Gaiz announced.

The three instructors bent over, and from the other blanket they each took out a shield. They held it in their left hand while with the right one they held the weapon each had shown them.

The shield will protect you from enemy weapons and might be used as a weapon as well if necessary. One sweep, or a backhanded blow, with a shield can throw an enemy backward and even knock them out. It can also be used to crush the head of an enemy.

Nahia could not see herself crushing anyone's head with a shield.

Seeing the three instructors with the shield in one arm and the weapon in the other, her spirits dropped. How was she ever going to wield those heavy weapons, plus a shield, which had to be heavy too? It looked impossible. That was for Ivo, Aiden, and Taika, but not for her. She looked at Lily and Daphne, and by the looks on their faces they must be thinking the same thing. How were they going to fight with so much weight on?

The first weapon you will learn, and the one you will start training with is the simplest of all, but it can take a lifetime, as well as the others, if you learn to use it well. It is the dagger. This first year you will learn the use of the dagger and shield. Separately and in combination. The sword you will learn to use the second year, since the sword is a difficult weapon to use. The third year you will learn to use the spear. You will all learn to use it. Besides, the spear is the main weapon in a type of advanced combat only the best among you will be able to perform. But that will not occur until you have first mastered the other weapons.

Nahia tried to digest all that information. From what she had gathered, they would start with the dagger, which was a relief for her. Both the sword and the spear seemed too heavy in her opinion. What she did not like was that she would also have to learn to use the shield this first year. That would surely be heavy. Learning the use of the sword in her second year worried her less—perhaps by then she would have some muscle and more resistance. Leaving the spear until the third year sounded great in her opinion. By then she would be strong, or so she hoped. The advanced combat did not interest her at all. She did not know what it meant, but she was not considering being among the best with weapons, so she dismissed it from her mind. She also realized she was taking for granted that she was going to survive the academy for three years. Just thinking about it made her skin crawl. It was a lot to wish for, a heavy dose of optimism.

Now, your instructors will hand you each a dagger. Go ahead, instructors.

The Drakonid instructor approached the Igneous Squad and handed them each a long silver dagger. He did it with certain parsimony, as someone who hands over a trophy or something valuable. As he handed over each weapon, he saluted, bowing his head. Nahia and her comrades responded to the salute with a similar one. Once he had handed out the weapons, he withdrew.

Nahia took the dagger the instructor had just given her and held it in her hands. It was quite a bit longer than what she had calculated. It was almost half the length of a sword. She had always thought a dagger was similar in size to a knife. It was clear this was not the case here, these daggers were longer. Not only that, it had two edges and a very sharp tip. Nahia weighed the weapon and snorted in relief. It was heavier than she had guessed, but she did not think it would be a problem. She could handle that weapon, which comforted her some. Then she realized she had no idea how to use the dagger, beyond using it like a kitchen knife, and she got nervous again. All of a sudden, she realized she would have to kill someone with that dagger, and that filled her with terrible anxiety. She did not want to kill anyone, least of all with a weapon like that which would make anyone bleed. She found it truly barbaric.

"The dagger is used to cut with its two edges," the instructor showed them. "You can execute cutting blows with both in either direction." The instructor executed several blows in the air, slicing right and left and then backward.

This dagger you have been handed, you must look after with your life. Whoever loses it or mishandles it will be punished.

The Drakonid instructor addressed the squad.

"The dagger is carried at the waist, on the opposite side of the hand you are going to use it with," he explained. "This allows it to be drawn quickly in case of unexpected combat." He demonstrated, taking out the dagger from his belt at great speed and delivering a thrust in front with it.

They all understood at once what he meant.

"Now, we'll do exercises similar to the ones we've been doing in the unarmed combat, only using specific attacks and defenses with the dagger. Stand in a defensive stance with flexed legs and a balanced body, with the unarmed arm ahead and the arm with the dagger gathered by the body," he said and showed them how to stand.

They all stood as the instructor indicated. They knew the position well. They noticed now that the other two instructors were doing the same with the Ardent and Searing Squads.

"We'll begin with some simple moves. Do them like me, on my count. One: slice from the inside out, seeking the neck of the opponent," he ordered and attacked. "Two: maintain a defensive position and be alert of a possible counterattack," he stood in a defensive stance. "Three: we move forward and launch a thrust straight to the heart. Four: defensive stance once more."

Nahia and her comrades made the movements, following every instruction and imitating their instructor in every detail. He had them doing offensive and defensive movements all day. When he finally finished the session, he ordered them to line up and returned to the black dragon. The other two instructors did the same.

You have begun the Path of the Dagger. You must travel it and become experts in its use. What you learn here is an art, and you must see it as such. You will become masters in the use of this weapon. With it, you will be able to kill the enemy and bring glory to our realm. Now go, and remember that the path to victory is sowed with blood.

Nahia did not like those last words at all. She did not want to kill anyone or shed blood for the glory of dragons. She was glad though that at the end of the day of training, she was not as tired as she thought she would be. The dagger was not so heavy, and exercising with it would not be more tiring than their unarmed combat training, just a little more, which made her very glad.

After dinner, they withdrew to rest. Nahia sat down on her bed and took off her boots. She sat there, contemplating her silver dagger.

"If it weren't because it serves to wound and kill, it would be beautiful," she said, more to herself than to the others.

Daphne heard her and turned toward her.

"It also serves to maim for life."

Nahia was surprised by that comment.

"Yeah... I guess so..."

"Don't guess. I can swear to it. They've used it on me," she said as she took off her cloak.

"Were you maimed with a dagger like this?"

"A very similar one, yes,"

"You mean your wings, right?"

Daphne nodded.

"The dragons don't allow us to fly, and the only way to keep us from flying is to clip our wings."

Nahia nodded.

"I think it's atrocious."

"It is," Daphne said.

"Forgive me for asking... can't you use them at all?" Nahia asked, pointing at the wings folded on her back.

"It doesn't bother me that you ask, because it's you. Someone else would bother me. I can use them, or flap them, but not fly," she explained and spread her four wings. Then she flapped them.

"Wow, they're beautiful," Nahia said. "I've wanted to see them since we met, but since you always carry them folded, I didn't want to bother you."

"That's because you're a girl with good manners and a good heart. That's why I'm showing you now."

"Thank you, really."

"You're welcome. See the cuts?"

Nahia went up closer to Daphne's back and studied the wings. They were indeed beautiful—they seemed woven from translucent silk and featured designs that looked like elaborate embroidery. Then she saw the four cuts, one on each wing. They began on the inside part and went along almost the whole wing. They did not tear the wing off but rather divided the surface like the sail of a ship with a long tear.

"I see them. They stop you from flying."

"That's right, in order to fly the wings have to be whole."

"Can't you heal those cuts?"

"We could, but whoever does is sentenced to death if they're found out."

"I see. The risk is too big," Nahia felt awful for poor Daphne. Only a heartless creature like the dragons would do something like that. They had robbed the Fatum of flight and maimed them for life.

"It is."

"Did it hurt much?" Nahia was feeling one of the wings with the tips of her fingers. It was a material she had never seen before, like human silk.

"They do it to us as children so we don't fall into the temptation of flying. Then every certain number of years the cuts are done again. I still have one more cut, when I turn twenty-five. It hurts, but it pierces my soul more."

"What they do to you is atrocious."

"Yes, it is," Lily joined them, coming out of the bathroom.

Daphne turned to her and showed her wings.

"Beautiful. I love them. They give you an, I don't know, ethereal air," Lily said with a broad smile.

"I like that, ethereal."

"I have something too I'm sure you're also curious about," Lily told them and pointed at her head.

"It isn't your prodigious mind," Daphne said, joking.

Lily laughed.

"My horns," she told them and reached up to them.

"Ahhh, true," Daphne nodded.

"May I touch them?" Nahia wanted to know what they were like. They intrigued her.

"Of course, don't be silly, go ahead," Lily bowed her head.

Nahia and Daphne felt her horns, studying them.

They don't look it, but they are hard and sharp," said Daphne.

"Of course, they're a defensive weapon. You didn't think they were only to make me more irresistible, did you?" Lily laughed.

"I might have…" Nahia admitted.

"Not at all. With these little coquettish horns, I can take an eye out of anyone or make a hole in their neck if they make me very angry."

"That's why the Scarlatum have such a good reputation," Daphne said, making a face.

"Because of that and many other things of a twisted nature," Lily laughed, taking it as a compliment.

Daphne and Nahia looked at one another and shook their heads. Then they laughed with her.

At dinner that evening in the dining hall, they talked about the weapons issue. Now they all wore the Learning Pearl hanging from their belts on the right and the dagger on the left. All except Daphne, who was left-handed and wore them the other way around.

"It's a shame that we don't start weapons training on the spear," Aiden commented while he enjoyed a grilled bull steak with garlic and a side of sweet red peppers.

"Why do you say that?" Taika asked with interest.

"Because it's the most noble weapon."

"Isn't that the sword?" Taika asked again.

"Not for a Drakonid. For us, it's the spear."

"In my culture, it's the sword," Taika said.

"We are more partial to daggers," said Daphne.

"To tell the truth, I have no idea...." Nahia did not know what weapon humans preferred. She did not understand anything about weapons.

"For us it's the double-headed axe," Lily said. "But here they don't use it."

"They don't use bows either," said Daphne. "That's funny."

"Bows are for cowards," said Aiden.

"Here we go again with the absolute opinions." Daphne raised her hands.

"In the dragon culture, bows and arrows are considered lesser weapons and only used by those who are unable to master the noble weapons," Aiden explained.

"Or perhaps dragons don't like them for some reason," Daphne said.

"Because the bow is a lesser weapon," Aiden reiterated.

"Hmmm... maybe Daphne is on to something," Taika said with narrowed eyes, thoughtful. "If the dragons loath the weapon, it might be because it really is a lesser weapon, or maybe it's because it's a weapon that bothers them somehow..."

"This is becoming interesting," Lily said, looking at Taika and Aiden, first one and then the other.

"Nothing bothers a dragon. Steel can't pierce its scales. Arrows can't perforate them either," Aiden said.

"Yeah, that's true, we know..." Taika said and remained thoughtful.

"Magic doesn't affect them either. They have innate magic defenses," said Daphne.

"So if that's true, how did the races join up to fight against the dragons during the Great Insurrection?" Nahia asked, bowing her head. She could not understand. It was something she had always wondered about. "If the dragons were so formidable, how did the races unite against them and rebel? If they had no way to defeat them, it was a massive suicide."

They all looked at her in surprise.

"Don't you know what happened?" Daphne asked her.

"I don't, to tell you the truth... my grandmother hasn't told me much... only that the races joined to fight against the dragons and tried to free us from slavery."

"It's true, they did," Ivo confirmed. "The path of war is not that of wisdom, but they did so."

"But... if steel can't kill them and magic can't either, why did they try? My parents weren't suicidal, they wouldn't have tried if there wasn't a chance to defeat them," Nahia reasoned.

"Neither your parents nor the rest," Lily said, bowing her head.

"They did it because they believed there was a chance," Daphne explained.

"And they were all fooled," Aiden sentenced.

"Fooled?" Nahia asked.

"The leader of the revolt, Dramkon Udreks, a Drakonid, made all the leaders of the other races believe he had discovered the way to kill dragons," Lily explained,

"But he fooled them," Daphne added.

"And because of his lie, all those who revolted died," said Lily.

"The Great Insurrection is also known as the Great Lie," Taika said.

"But... I don't understand... why did my parents believe it? Why did the leaders of the other races?"

"Because they were naïve and gullible, and they were fooled. Nothing can kill dragons," Aiden said with his usual crudeness and certainty.

"And because what more can you expect of a Drakonid?

261

Betrayal—that he sells you to his dragon masters, nothing more or less," Daphne said.

"He didn't have the support of the majority of Drakonids to begin with, and the races deserved what happened to them."

"Take that back if you don't want me to cut off your tongue," Daphne got up and loomed over Aiden threateningly with her hand on the pommel of her dagger.

"And I'll gouge your eyes out," Lily joined her, getting up and also bending over him with her dagger half drawn.

"Take it easy, both of you, if you attack him the punishment will be severe," Taika warned them, and he gestured toward the two blue dragons watching the dining hall.

Aiden did not move. He watched them without backing down.

The two looked at the dragons and sat down a moment later, throwing daggers with their eyes at Aiden, who ignored them and went on eating.

"I refuse to believe that… there had to be another reason," Nahia could not believe that her parents were so innocent that they allowed themselves to be tricked by false promises. And not only them but the rest of the races too, because thousands had died in the revolt.

"Dramkon Udreks made the leaders of the other races believe there was a way to kill dragons," Taika explained.

"They would not take him on his word only, least of all because he was a Drakonid," Nahia said.

"True, he proved it. From what we know, Dramkon Udreks killed several dragons in front of the leaders and persuaded them," Ivo explained.

"Because of this, they joined forces and prepared the uprising. The leaders told the other races that Dramkon Udreks had the means to kill the dragons and that if they all joined together they'd bring them down," Lily said, a little calmer now.

"But when the moment of truth came, it turned out that Dramkon Udreks and his means to kill dragons were nothing but a lie. They couldn't kill them. The dragons, on the other hand, destroyed the insurrectionists, killing thousands," Daphne said with rage in her voice.

"That's how it was," Ivo nodded with great sorrow. "War and bloodshed only lead to more war and more bloodshed."

Nahia was shaking her head. Her parents, like her grandmother, were people with good heads who knew the world they lived in. How could they have let themselves be fooled like that?

"What was the lie?" she asked.

"They made the races believe that dragons could be killed when that's impossible for the slave races," Aiden said.

"Yes, but how?" Nahia wanted to know because she needed to understand.

"Who cares how? It wasn't true, and all who believed it died," Daphne replied, shaking her head, enraged.

"I need to understand," Nahia said, annoyed. She was beginning to feel sick. Heat was beginning to wash over her body.

"We all want to understand, but there's no answer we can give you. I, at least, don't know it," Lily told her.

"The leaders of the eight races were persuaded, so the evidence must have been convincing," Taika said. "Dramkon Udreks must have found a way to hurt them, but it wasn't divulged. Only the eight leaders knew about it, precisely so the dragons wouldn't know they had a weapon to use against them."

Nahia was listening and her body temperature was rising. Her heart began to beat faster and faster.

"Unfortunately, it did not work. Then the rumor spread that it had all been a lie," said Daphne.

"And that's what everyone believes as of today," added Lily.

"A great lie or a failure," Ivo commented. "In any case, it brought death to thousands."

Nahia continued shaking her head.

"I need to know... whether it was a lie... or if something happened that prevented the revolt," Nahia could barely breathe. She realized she was having a seizure.

"Are you all right?" Lily became concerned when she realized Nahia could not breathe.

"Yes... it's only that..."

"You're having one of your seizures," Daphne said, putting her hand on Nahia's forehead. "You're burning up."

Nahia nodded and took out one of Aoma's tonics, bit off the stopper, and drank it in one gulp. They all looked on, worried.

"It will... pass... soon enough."

"I don't want to reach any hasty conclusions, but it would seem that talking about certain subjects that are important to you upsets you, and that brings on the seizures," Taika reasoned.

Nahia, who was already beginning to feel better, looked at the Felidae.

"It might be… yes."

"In that case, you'd better learn to control your emotions, or you'll get yourself and your squad into trouble," Aiden told her.

"Don't listen to anything this blockhead says," Daphne told her, stroking her hand to soothe her.

"I'm… feeling better," Nahia reassured them as she felt she could breathe again and that her heartbeat was calming down.

"The truth is that no one really knows what happened. Only the eight leaders knew, and they all died. The dragons had no mercy on them," Taika said. "It might even be that the Great Lie was no such thing and that the dragons created the fake rumor so that no one ever tried anything like that again," he reasoned.

"That might be," Lily said, looking at Taika, interested.

"I bet the Drakonids spread the lie throughout the eight nations," said Daphne, glaring at Aiden.

"Maybe it was what it was: a great lie, and the truth was divulged," Aiden sentenced.

Nahia was stunned. She had not known all this. Why hadn't Aoma told her? Had it only been to protect her, or was there something else? She did not want to believe that her parents had given their lives for a great lie. She was sure they would not have let themselves be fooled like that, but what if it had been like Aiden said it was, and they had really all been fooled?

"What happened to Dramkon Udreks?" she asked.

"He was the last of the leaders to be captured. He wasn't killed by the dragons, he's somewhere unknown," Daphne said.

"Then if he didn't die or was executed, it does look like it was a lie…" Nahia's spirits dropped to ground level.

"Or that's what the dragons want us to believe," Taika casually let fall in his fox's tone.

They all turned to him.

"If they killed him, it would look like it wasn't a lie but that something went wrong," Nahia reasoned, following Taika's suggested train of thought. But if they let him live, it looks like he betrayed all the rebel leaders and everything was a lie."

"That's right," Taika nodded.

"Which leads us to consider that either thing might have happened," said Ivo. "Believing in the worst result doesn't necessarily make it the correct one. Or the best. The balance is usually the most likely result."

"You can lucubrate all you want. It was a Great Lie, and it shows that the dragons are invincible," Aiden pronounced himself. He got up from the table and left.

"I still think there's something behind all this…" Nahia said.

"We'd all like that to be the case," said Lily.

"But we also have to consider that the blockhead might be right," Daphne said.

"And I want to know the truth of what happened, one thing or the other," said Nahia determinedly.

"You're not the only one. We'd all like to know," Taika joined her.

"Most of the time, it's better not to put your head in the lion's mouth," Ivo warned.

"You're right, but I need answers," Nahia told him.

They went on eating and chatting about less transcendental, excruciating matters, and when they finished their dinner and got up to leave, Nahia looked toward Ana's table. She waited a moment until her friend noticed and looked at her. When she did, Nahia put her hands to her face and made the Butterfly of Victory. Ana saw it and smiled. An instant later, she returned the butterfly. Nahia smiled and left for the barracks.

Chapter 34

The weeks went by again as if at those heights, in the middle of the sky, they passed a hundred times faster than on the solid ground below. Or perhaps it was that the winds, which were a lot stronger, made them fly with the speed that drove the clouds away.

All the members of the Igneous Squad were devoted to their classes and studies. They knew their life depended on them. No one wanted to be left behind and fail, because it might very well mean their end. They found it hard to live with that daily pressure, but it was either get used to it or perish, and no matter how different they were, they all shared a common characteristic: they wanted to survive.

The autumn ended, and with its end it marked the conclusion of the first half of the first year at the academy. Nahia wanted to feel happy for having survived half the course, except for the fact that it also marked the day of the feared Squad Competition. Nahia was terrified. On the fated day, she woke up before the sun had even risen. She had been having nightmares all week, and the last night, they had been horrible. In them, she always ended up defeated and humiliated before everyone and punished with death for being weak and useless.

"Come on, wake up, today is the great day!" Aiden woke them up, shouting.

"It's not good for the spirit to wake up like this, least of all on important days," Ivo complained from the bed beside him.

"Today is the Squad Competition!" Aiden cried excitedly.

"We know, take it easy," said Taika, jumping out of bed.

"Victory awaits us!" he went on shouting, exhilarated.

"Shut up already, granite-head!" Daphne yelled as she got up, her temper stoked from his shouting.

"These abrupt wake-up calls affect my beauty sleep!" Lily replied.

Nahia, who was already awake and very nervous, began to dress.

"I hope it won't be a terrible day," she wished under her breath.

"Today we'll show our leader what the Igneous Squad is made of!" Aiden cried, who was already dressed and ready to go out.

"I swear that one day I'm going to strangle him with his own cloak," Daphne told Nahia and Lily.

"And I'll hold him for you," Lily smiled.

Nahia tried to smile too, but she was so anxious she barely managed the ghost of one.

They got dressed and took their daggers and Learning Pearls. They hung them from their belts, one on each side. Nahia thought they would need them today, not for class but for the competition, and she became even more nervous. Once ready and impelled by Aiden's cheers and encouragement, they came out into the great parade ground. It was still dawn. They were heading to line up like every other morning at their marked positions by the flaming banner where their leader Irakas-Gorri-Gaizt was waiting, only this morning that would not be the case. As soon as they set foot in the square, they stopped. Their leader and the flaming banner were not where they always were but in front of the great castle. The six leaders were lined up, three on either side of the gates with their backs to the building. The banners stood in front of each leader.

"Let's go with our leader!" cried Aiden, running toward the red dragon.

The others had no choice but to follow him. As they ran, Nahia saw the rest of the squads doing the same. Every squad ran to line up before their squadron leader.

Red Squadron, line up! Irakas-Gorri-Gaizt's order reached them, strong and urgent.

They lined up as they always did, the Igneous Squad on the left, the Ardent in the middle, and the Searing on the right. Aiden was upset they could not be in the center, which is where he believed they should be. The rest could care less, except Taika, who had commented that the central position was the safest because they had both flanks covered. So now, formed up like this, with Nahia as the first one on the left, she was left feeling very exposed and vulnerable to attacks.

Maintain the formation and await orders! The command reached them, together with a feeling that this was an important moment.

Nahia looked unobtrusively askance. Beside them was the Blue Squadron. She was able to see Ana, who looked terrified. It was followed by the Black Squadron, and then there was a great empty void in front of the castle gates. The White Squadron was the next, and she glimpsed Logan. He did not look afraid; he had the same hard look as usual. On his right was the Brown Squadron with Maika, although Nahia could not see her well. The last group was the Crystal Squadron. Everyone was feeling the tension—they were lined up with clipped faces and rigid bodies.

Suddenly, the gates to the majestic castle opened and Colonel Lehen-Gorri-Gogor, executive leader of the academy, appeared. Nahia watched it, trying to digest how huge and powerful that red dragon was, measuring over a hundred and fifty feet long with lavender streaks on its back. The ruby eyes in that thousand-year-old dragon head were very intimidating. Nahia took a deep breath to calm down. If she had been nervous before, now she was even more.

Escorting its Colonel was Commander Bigaen-Zuri-Indar, second in command over the academy. Nahia watched the Commander unobtrusively: it was almost as big as it was terrifying. The fact that it was white, with lavender streaks as well, did not make it less fearsome. Every step they took made the ground shake. Nahia was grateful they had made a formal entrance instead of coming down from the sky, because when they did they were even more terrifying. They stopped between the six captain dragons and the squads which were lined up a little further back.

Nahia knew what was coming now, so she got ready. Colonel Lehen-Gorri-Gogor gave a tremendous roar, announcing its presence. Commander Bigaen-Zuri-Indar also let out a tremendous roar. Some of the students were restless and shifted in their positions. That was not going to please their leaders. Luckily, the Igneous Squad stayed put.

The Colonel roared again after a moment, and they all paid attention.

Today is a special day in Drakoros, the Academy of the Dragon Bloods. As the leader of this institution of martial training, I always await this day with anticipation. Today is the half-year Squad Competition. I can promise you, it is one of my favorites. It is because we can evaluate the progress of the first-years, who although still very green, have the chance to prove that they have what it takes to become Dragon Blood Warlocks. This day, which marks the first half of the training year in this illustrious academy, is one you will not forget. That I can assure you, it messaged, along with a strong feeling of command and pride.

Commander Bigaen-Zuri-Indar roared and addressed them.

This is a test you must overcome. Whoever does not pass this test will not be apt to continue with the second part of the training year. You know the fate of those who fail. There will not be any benevolence or mercy, so I advise you to make your best effort.

Nahia was already afraid of that, so the Commander's message was no surprise. They had no idea what the test would be like, since they could not ask the second- and third-years, but they were already anticipating it would be hard. They had been discussing it for days in the dining hall and at their dorm in the barracks, and with the exception of Aiden, they were all very worried. Aiden, of course, was sure he was going to triumph.

There is no reason why you cannot pass the test, all of you. This is not the case most years, but there is always a first time. I myself will judge the test and the results. Your captains and leaders expect the best from you. You will do well not to dishonor them.

Nahia sighed and tried to calm down. Beside her, Lily looked at her and then Daphne. Nahia sent them worried glances, but theirs were looks of encouragement. Unfortunately, what they had just heard from those two dragons was not encouraging at all.

Commander, tell the pupils what the test will consist of, the red dragon ordered the white.

The Commander roared and announced, *The test will be done by squad, not by squadron, and the determination of all the members of the squad will be taken into consideration. If one or more members of the squad are not up to standard, it will affect the whole squad. The test will be divided in two parts: first a test of physical endurance, and second a combat by squads.*

Of course, the combat will come after the physical test. The combat by squads will be eliminatory. You do not want to be left in the last positions.

Nahia could not help making a horrified face.

You will start with the physical test. It is a test not only of endurance but also of speed. Each squad will have to climb four lookout towers and do it before their banner goes out. Let me tell you that the stipulated time is more than fair. It has been measured carefully. I don't think I need to emphasize that whoever does not overcome this first part will not have a good beginning. The four towers to climb are the two that form the south corner and the two that form the north corner of the academy. The test begins and ends at the sun dial, the Commander specified.

Nahia snorted in disbelief, unable to help herself. The distance they had to cover was enormous. They needed to go from the sun dial to the wall, climb the two lookout towers on each corner, and then cross the whole academy to go to the other corner and climb the two towers of the north wall and come back to the sun dial, once again crossing practically the whole academy ground. And at lightning speed. Only thinking about it made Nahia start sweating. This test was going to destroy her. Climbing a tower was terribly hard. Going up and coming down four sounded impossible. Besides, they had to do it fast. The thought of it made her feel sick. And she was not the only one—Lily and Daphne did not look well either.

Besides, to make it more interesting and as is the tradition, all the second- and third-year pupils will attend the test as spectators. Their captains too, who are already positioned on the lookout towers, the colonel messaged.

As soon as the dragon said this, the second- and third-years appeared from the barracks and lined up in front of the building on the side of the square without entering it. Nahia sighed. Not only did they have to pass the test, but they had to do it with an audience. Things were getting worse and worse,

Good. The time has come to begin the test. We will do it six squads at a time, one from each squadron. That encourages rivalry and motivation. We will let the captains choose their squads, the Colonel messaged and beat its huge red wings as if it were truly thrilled by the test.

Irakas-Gorri-Gaizt stood tall.

Igneous Squad first. March in formation to the sun dial. Take the banner. Do not dishonor me before everyone, or you will pay with your lives, it messaged.

Nahia was terrified. She looked at the flaming banner and did not dare take it. Aiden did not hesitate, however. He took it by a solid bar it had in the center and carried it off proudly. For some reason, it did not burn him. They marched in formation. The six squads lined up in front of the sun dial. Nahia looked at the other squads and saw that Maika's was beside hers. She saw her and unobtrusively made the Butterfly of Victory for her. The gesture touched Nahia's heart and she felt a little less terrified, she returned the sign unobtrusively.

At my command, raise the banner and begin the test. Now! the commander messaged the order.

Aiden stuck the flaming banner in the ground and with him, the others who were carrying theirs. The test began.

"Left tower!" Taika told them.

"Let's go, everyone!" Aiden ran off like a lunatic.

Almost naturally, three of the squads headed to the left-hand tower and three to the right-hand one, according to how they had stood in front of the sun dial. At once, competition surged between the squads. They all ran as fast as they could, and when they saw the squad they were competing with go faster they tried to overtake it. Nahia saw that Maika's Rock Squad was headed to the same tower. She was glad Maika was with her, even if it was a competition. They would climb together as they had done when they first arrived to this realm of dragons in the sky. The other squad climbing with them was the Hurricane Squad of the White Squadron.

The three squads arrived at the base of the left-hand tower almost at the same time. Since it formed the corner of the wall, it only had two inner sides they could climb up, so one of the three squads would have to stay behind for the time being. Since Aiden had run like a madman and his comrades had been forced to follow him, they had arrived second. The Hurricane Squad arrived first.

"Come on, up we go!" Aiden cried as he began to climb up the left inner side while the Hurricane Squad climbed the right side.

Nahia was going so fast, she did not have time to think. She started climbing. The tower was like all the lookout towers there, with protruding rocks and ledges and hollows that allowed climbing without ropes. They also had a similar height to the one they had climbed the first day. Nahia knew it was going to take a lot out of her to complete the climb. She trusted that all the martial training plus the extra work she had been doing at the gym would allow her to hold up much better. That was her hope, her only hope.

As they climbed, Taika took the lead. He was the most nimble of the boys and climbed easily. He was followed by Aiden, who was not as agile but was strong and relied on his strength. Ivo had started off well, but he was beginning to lose rhythm. He was very strong and could climb easily, but he was also clumsy and placing his hooves in the projections on the wall was a challenge for him. Nahia was climbing pretty well and she passed Daphne, which surprised her. Lily was a little ahead of her, and she was almost upon her.

Suddenly the members of Maika's squad started to catch up with them.

"Move over, Nahia, I'm coming through," Maika said with a smile when she caught up with her and passed her on the right.

"Be careful," Nahia warned her as she gave her a nod.

"Don't worry, see you at the next tower," Maika replied and went on climbing.

The members of the two squads mixed together, but there was no foul play or pushing, simply pure competition. Aiden did not want the Drakonid of the Brown Squad to overtake him, and they were both climbing up the wall of the tower as if possessed. But the Felidae were obviously the best climbers, and by the time they had climbed up half the tower this was made evident.

Nahia concentrated and climbed up at her own rhythm. She was surprised at how well she was doing, considering how badly she had done the first time. Three quarters up the tower, the distance between the good climbers and those who were not so good became clear. No one spoke. They were all climbing, fully concentrated and aware of the fact that they were already at a considerable height, and that if they fell, they could break their backs or get killed. Taika managed to reach the platform at the top and waited for them.

When Aiden reached him ahead of the other Drakonid, he gave him a surly look.

"Why do you stop? Keep going!"

Taika returned the look calmly.

"It's a squad test, we'll be given our points as such."

"If you arrive before the other squads, you get a positive mark."

"I'd rather wait for my comrades and help them."

Aiden shook his head.

"That's a mistake."

"We'll see at the end of the test."

"I'm not going to wait."

Taika nodded. "I guessed as much."

Aiden got onto the platform and went to the center of it.

"We have to go down with a rope," he told Taika and began to climb down.

The next one to arrive at the top was Lily, and Taika helped her get up.

"Thanks, tiger boy," she smiled.

Taika smiled and shook his head.

Nahia arrived next, very proud for having managed to climb all the way up.

"I did it!" she cheered when Taika helped her get onto the platform. She was fighting against her own strength, not so much against the test.

Daphne arrived a moment later.

"Uffff," she protested. "This is torture!"

Ivo would still take a while longer.

"Start going down, I'll stay for Ivo," Taika told them.

"Are you sure?" Nahia asked.

"It's best that I help the big guy. You get going, we'll catch up with you shortly. Take into account that your strength will run out before ours."

Nahia thought for a moment and realized what Taika had considered. At the end of the test, he and Ivo would still have ample strength left and would be able to catch up with them. Waiting for them was wasting precious time they did not have.

"All right, we'll go on."

Chapter 35

Nahia went to the opening in the middle of the tower roof. There were three ropes, so there would be no fights with the members of the other two squads.

"Ready," Lily said, about to let herself down.

"We'd better protect our hands. The rope's going to burn them. Let's use our cloaks."

"Good idea," Lily said, smiling.

"Thank goodness you have a good head," Daphne told her.

They went down the rope using their cloaks to hold it and slide their hands over it. The descent with this technique was a lot faster and easier than Nahia had calculated. They left the tower through the open door and ran off toward the other tower. They had to cover the whole width of the academy, from one side to the other, since the next tower was opposite the one they had just climbed.

As they were running, Nahia began to see clearly that this was going to be more a test of strength and endurance than speed. The distances were long and the towers high: they were going to end up worn out.

They arrived at the south tower on the right side and started climbing. The other two squads followed, more together than their own. When they were halfway up the tower, they began to overtake several members who were lagging.

"Come on, faster!" Aiden cried from above.

"You go on!" Nahia told him.

Aiden looked north.

"The tower on this side!" he indicated, pointing.

"All right!" Nahia replied.

Lily and Daphne were having a hard time climbing. Exhaustion was beginning to sink in. Nahia felt it too.

"Come on, Nahia, you can do it!" Maika cheered her from the top.

"Keep going, I'll catch up with you soon!" Nahia replied, although she doubted it.

Maika smiled and vanished.

"My hands are beginning to hurt," said Daphne.

"My feet hurt," said Lily.

"We'll make it, keep going," Nahia cheered them. In spite of everything, she was still pretty whole.

They arrived at the top when Taika and Ivo were still at the lower quarter of the tower.

"Courage! The tower on this side!" Nahia shouted.

"Thanks! Okay!" Taika replied.

Ivo was climbing, very concentrated on where to put his huge hands and hooves.

Nahia, Lily, and Daphne went down the rope with the cloak trick and overtook a couple of the other two squads. They went out and started running.

"Let's go in a straight line, hugging the wall on our left," Nahia suggested.

"You do know how far the north wall is, don't you?" Daphne said.

"Yes, unfortunately," Lily nodded.

"Don't think about it, come on, let's run!" Nahia urged them, and the three started running.

As they ran, Nahia saw Maika and another member of her squad ahead of them. The Rock Squad had a good advantage, but as long as Nahia and her friends could see them and keep up with their pace, they would be doing well. With this in mind, Nahia ran, pulling Daphne and Lily along. She was not worried yet because she knew they were stronger than her, and for now she was holding up.

They went by the sun dial and the banners. Nahia was appalled to see how fast the flames on theirs were being consumed. They were not going to finish the test before it went out. They passed the captains and the other squads who were watching the test. They also passed the Colonel and the Commander. Nahia did not even glance at them, just in case.

They went on and covered the whole length of the academy until they reached the north tower that formed the corner. When they got there, they had to stop to catch their breath.

"Come on, climb!" Aiden shouted at them, but now he was only halfway up the tower. They had gained some distance on him.

"Rock-head... isn't doing... so well in the race," Daphne said, panting.

"His… body… is too heavy… and his head… even more," Lily said, panting too.

The joke made them laugh, and Nahia started to cough.

They began climbing the third tower, and here they did notice the effort and the exhaustion. Nahia felt her hands beginning to cramp. Her arms and legs were sore, telling her they were reaching the end of what they could endure. She realized that although she had improved a lot since she had started practicing in the gym, she still had a long way to go in order to face tests like this one. Lily seemed to be holding up better than she was. Daphne was beginning to lag, which worried Nahia.

They continued climbing, and now every foot they covered was a triumph and the effort a torture.

"I'll go on to the next tower!" Aiden yelled at them, already at the top.

"Keep going, we're coming!" Nahia replied, already halfway up.

"If that rock-head can do it, so can I!" Daphne clenched her jaw and continued climbing out of self-determination.

"We're all coming!" Lily cheered.

They arrived at the top, exhausted, and dragged themselves to the opening. They rested a moment and breathed in the refreshing air at that height.

"Just a moment and then we'll go down," Daphne begged.

If they were tired, the other two squads were too—they were suffering as much as they were. Four, two from each squad, were lying on their backs on the rooftop.

"Come on, we have to go down. That's the easy part, take a good grasp," Nahia told them as she headed down first.

Her comrades followed her immediately.

Once the three were out of the tower, they looked at the last one they had to climb. The thing was, they had to cross the whole width of the academy again to get to it.

"The sooner we get there, the sooner we'll finish," said Nahia, and she started running as fast as she could, which was not much.

Running was a very different effort from climbing the tower, and now other muscles were aching intensely. Her lungs were burning with the effort. Nahia realized she was feeling very weak, the she remembered she had not had any breakfast. They had made them do the test on an empty stomach, which was not only cruel, but dangerous. Someone might faint from lack of nourishment and overexertion.

Her legs were burning, and even the soles of her feet, which did not usually give her problems, were bothering her now. Lily and Daphne endured the running better than the climb, so they held up until they reached the last tower.

"I don't know... if I'm going to be able..." Daphne admitted at the foot of the tower, looking up, panting.

"We have to," Lily told her and patted her back.

Nahia was stretching and clenching her fingers to relieve them. She knew they were going to hurt like a nightmare. She felt exhausted and weak. This last tower was a colossus, impossible to overtake.

"Marble-head isn't going so well," Daphne said, looking up.

"We'll catch him now!" Lily cheered up. "Come on, up we go," she urged them and started to climb.

Daphne snorted and followed.

Nahia followed both with a sigh. Her body soon sent her signs of pain and exhaustion. She closed her eyes and held up. She opened them, and in spite of the pain she went on climbing. The two sides of the tower were very crowded—all those who had started before them now seemed to be having the same difficulties as them. Nahia was not surprised. She saw Maika with a strained look on her face climbing the last bit of wall.

They began to catch up with other competitors and overtake them, which cheered Nahia. She was not one of the worst after all. With this additional bit of courage, she went on climbing, trying to ignore her body's tremendous pain. She was halfway up when she heard a muffled scream. One of those at the top of the tower fell. He nearly took another one with him, hitting the ground on his side. The blow was tremendous. Nahia looked in horror, hoping it was not Maika. She let out a deep sigh of relief when she saw it was not, although it still hurt her to see someone take such a terrible fall. It had been someone from the Blue Squadron. He lay on the ground, writhing in pain.

"Be very careful. Don't take any risks!" Nahia warned Lily and Daphne.

"I'm running out of strength. It's not that I'm taking risks, it's that I can't cope anymore," Daphne shook her head.

"I feel the same," Lily said a little ahead of them.

"Don't move forward unless you're sure of your grasp," Nahia advised them.

For a moment, they stopped where they were. Four Tergnomus appeared with a stretcher and took the fallen one away. The rest continued the climb. They were almost at the top when they heard another scream. This one came from the other wall, so they did not see the fall, they only heard the *thump* of the person on the ground.

"Oh no!" cried Nahia, and she grabbed the wall with all the strength she had left. Her fears were coming true. The brutal overexertion and the empty stomach were wreaking havoc on her.

"Blasted test!" Daphne cried, enraged.

"Focus, we have to finish!" Lily told them.

Suddenly, a hand appeared over the rooftop. It was Aiden.

"Take my hand, I'll help you up."

Lily grabbed it and Aiden helped her get over the edge. Then it was Daphne's turn, and finally Nahia's. The three lay on their backs on the rooftop.

"You... can't... go on, huh?" Lily said to Aiden.

"I can. But the more of us who get there, the better."

"Yeah, sure," Daphne did not buy it.

They filled their lungs with air and relaxed their muscles for a moment.

"We have to go down," Aiden urged them.

"Fine let's go."

Aiden went first, and they followed. Going down the rope, which was not exactly easy, seemed a relief compared with what they had just been through. They came out of the tower and saw the fallen one being taken away. He was from the White Squadron.

"Let's run in a diagonal to the castle and we'll border it on this side," Nahia suggested.

The others nodded.

They ran off, and soon it was clear they had no more strength left for anything. And they were not the only ones. The way to the parade ground was a river of lagging participants. The four of them were going at a sort of loping gait which was closer to walking than running because they could not even think straight. Suddenly, Daphne fell down. They stopped to help her get back to her feet.

"I'm... spent..."

"We all are," said Lily.

At that moment, Taika and Ivo caught up with them.

"I'll deal with this," said Ivo, and he lifted Daphne with his powerful arm to keep running.

The others went on. Nahia was suffering terribly. Her whole body ached and her lungs were burning horribly, but for some reason she kept on.

"When they reached the castle, it was Lily who could not go on and fell down. In front of them the White Squadron was also lying on the ground, trying to get back up.

"I'll help her," Taika offered, holding her up by the waist with his arm and helping her continue.

They reached the parade ground.

"The banner still has a flame! We haven't lost!" cried Aiden.

"Go, take it!" Nahia told him, pointing at it.

Aiden sprinted forward as if he had just begun the test. He overtook two from the Blue Squadron and a third from the White one. He was running as if a pack of hungry lions were after him. He reached the sun dial just as the banner was about to go out. He threw himself on the ground and slid along until he reached it and grabbed it in his hand. He raised it in triumph.

A moment later, the rest arrived.

You have managed to arrive at the banner in time. The test is considered passed. Since only one got here on time and five have arrived with considerable delay your total score will be penalized, but not severely, they received the mental message from their leader.

Nahia, Lily, Daphne, Taika, and Ivo stood with their hands on their thighs, doubled over with weariness, trying to recover their breath. They were so tired that they did not even realize how well or how badly the other squads had done. Maika's had done well, since it had arrived before them.

When the last participants of their group arrived, all those who had finished the test were instructed to line up. They realized that two had suffered falls and two others had finished the test late. Nahia feared the punishment they would receive. She was not sure what it would be, but their leaders were not going to like their failures.

After their group, it was the second one's turn. The results were very similar. Logan took part in this group and arrived first, raising his banner in time. Ana took part in the last group. Nahia was afraid the poor girl would not be able to finish or might have an accident.

She was lucky and finished, although quite delayed. In any case, she had finished the test, which was what mattered. In those two groups there was an injured in each.

Once they had all finished, several Tergnomus came and each pupil was given a small satchel. When they opened it, they found they had a full waterskin and some salted meat and bread.

Eat and drink. The second part of the test will begin shortly—the combat between squads, Irakas-Gorri-Gaizt messaged to them.

Chapter 36

Nahia could not believe they were being forced to complete the second test on the heels of the first. They were exhausted and could not even move. All of them. Every fiber of her body hurt terribly. She could not understand or believe it. She looked at their leader out of the corner of her eye, and then she believed it. Dragons were like that, ruthless and brutal. If any of the competitors died, they did not care, they would even find it entertaining. The hatred she felt for them grew with every day she spent at the academy.

They heard a tremendous roar they already recognized as the Colonel's.

Now that you have rested, it is time to move on to the combat test. I wish you all luck, Lehen-Gorri-Gogor messaged to them.

The white dragon roared next.

We now go on to the combat tests by squads. This test is eliminatory. Those who get the best positions will be rewarded. Those who finish last will be punished. I advise you to fight with all your heart, because your lives are at stake, Bigaen-Zuri-Indar messaged.

Nahia felt her stomach turning. Who knew what horrors they would have to go through now.

The Colonel added, *I am told that several squads do not have all their members available for this test. That is a disgrace and a dishonor to their leader. As for the competition, it will take place with the remaining members of each squad. Go ahead, Commander.*

With all the members who had fallen during the first part of the year and the casualties several squads had suffered during this test, Nahia took courage in thinking that hers was complete. That was good, very good. Not only for the test, but because it gave her some confidence in her comrades.

The combat test will be done with three squads at a time. Three will enter the elemental labyrinth, and only one will emerge victorious. Of course, the squads cannot be from the same squadron, at least not until the final. You will fight with daggers and magic. You may create spheres of energy, but not big ones. You will be given a special training pearl. The daggers you will use are also special. They do not have an edge or a tip but are charged with energy. They do not kill, but they will knock you out if applied to a vital body part. Each squad will enter with their banner, and the last fighter to come out on his feet with the three banners wins the combat, the great white dragon explained.

The more she heard, the more nervous Nahia became. They were going to have to really fight among themselves and apply themselves. Until that moment they had only been fighting in class and everything was kept under control. Here, everything would be different.

Two final notes. The combat will take place right here, on the parade ground. But to make the combat more interesting, the square will look somewhat different. I advise you not to touch the walls, other than those you are sure aren't harmful. This is also a timed test. The banner will consume itself over time. If you do not win before it is consumed, you lose.

All of a sudden, the floor of the square started to flash in the different elemental colors of the dragons: white, red, back, blue, brown, and crystal. Lines of these colors formed on the floor. Then the lines became walls fifteen feet high. A moment later, different passages and geometric shapes were formed throughout the square, creating an indecipherable labyrinth of colors. Three equidistant gates appeared in the outer wall: the squads that competed would have to go through them.

Nahia was looking at her comrades. They were all dumbstruck. That labyrinth of elemental walls that had just risen before them was surreal. The world of dragons and their magic never ceased to surprise them. Where a moment before had been the great parade ground they knew so well, there was now a battle labyrinth with walls and shapes of elemental magic.

Leaders, present your squad, the Commander ordered.

Igneous Squad. To the competition, south corner. Carry the banner. Fight with honor. Defeat the rival squads! ordered Irakas-Gorri-Gaizt.

Aiden picked up the banner which was already burning again, and it shrank to his height. He was so proud he puffed up so much he almost burst. The rest followed Aiden, who was already on his way toward the south end of the square. As they bordered the square, they took a look at the walls that surrounded it and began to worry. Some were made of fire, others of ice, and there was one made up of a troubling blackness. The walls were not whole but were made up of pieces of elemental walls on top of one another. How they remained raised or stuck to each other they could not fathom.

At the south entrance, two Tergnomus were waiting for them.

"Your daggers and Learning Pearls," one of them asked. They handed them their belongings.

"Here are the competition ones," the other one offered.

They took the daggers, and when they held them they immediately noticed a living energy surrounding the whole edge and tip, which were dull. The Learning Pearls for the test were a little smaller than the ones they normally used.

"Hoods on to protect your heads from blows," the Tergnomus who was handing them the weapons said.

They all put their hoods up, which were also covered in scales. Nahia did not like the sound of blows to the head.

Ready, Squads. Go, now! the Commander's order reached them.

They crossed the door and appeared in a rectangle of bright walls. A wall appeared behind them, shutting the entrance.

"So, what's the plan?" Daphne asked, touching one of the walls with her dagger and causing a blinding flash.

"Not touch the walls to begin with," Lily said, trying to see again.

"It's easy. We finish off the other two squads, take their banners, and win," Aiden said, looking at the banner that was beginning to consume itself.

"Oh yeah, sure, because it's going to be that simple," Nahia replied, not believing it for one second.

"Look up," said Lily.

They watched the Commander and the Colonel fly to two of the lookout towers to have a better view of the combat from above. The second- and third-years went up to the flat roof of the barracks to see the fight.

"How nice, we have an audience," Daphne muttered under her breath.

We'd better forget about them and focus on our task," Nahia suggested.

"The best thing we can do is find an advantageous position," Taika suggested.

"For an ambush?" Ivo asked.

"Yes, something like that. This is a labyrinth, there are bound to be suitable places. Surprise is always the best ally," Taika told them.

"I prefer to attack from up front and defeat them with overwhelming power," said Aiden.

"Huh, what a strategy," Daphne retorted.

"No, I don't like it," Lily was shaking her head.

"If we keep talking here, we're going to be the surprised ones," Aiden protested.

Taika nodded.

"I'll go first, follow me."

"Do we go in formation?" Nahia asked.

"Single file would be best. There's a very narrow corridor ahead," Taika told them.

"Okay, get going."

Taika moved forward and Aiden followed promptly. Ivo went after the two, then Lily, Daphne, and Nahia brought up the rear. As soon as they walked a little, they realized this was indeed a true labyrinth. There were narrow and wide corridors; rooms that varied between square, triangular, and diamond shaped; and all kinds of small lower walls they could take cover behind. There were also different shapes scattered through the rooms. Since the square was so big and wide, the labyrinth was enormous. They were going to have difficulty finding one another. They soon saw that was the case. Suddenly, the flaming banner gave off a powerful red flash that went up to the sky.

They all looked at Aiden.

"What did you do?" Daphne scolded him.

"I didn't do anything... it did it all by itself."

"Yeah, all by itself," Lily chided him.

After a moment, there was a brown flash on their left. A moment later, a blue one on their right. Each color shot up into the sky where they could be perfectly seen.

"Now we know how we're going to find one another," Ivo said.

"See how it wasn't me?" Aiden said defensively.

"Everyone, get behind this low wall," Taika said, indicating it.

"Don't touch it, it's made of the air element, and who knows what it can do," Lily warned them.

Nahia figured it would deliver a discharge of energy or a strong blast.

They crouched behind the wall. The room they were in was triangular with three entrances, one at each corner.

"Nahia, Lily, and Daphne, use spheres of energy. We'll need to surprise them. The rest of us will use the daggers."

"Yes, that's better," Ivo said with a look on his face that meant that magic was not his forte yet.

"I agree," Aiden nodded.

"Stick the banner back there," Taika indicated a horseshoe shape to one side of the room, "inside."

Aiden hastened to place it there. When the banner hit the ground, it remained upright and flaming. Aiden ran to hide behind the low wall.

Nahia sat on the floor with her back to the wall, the Learning Pearl in her hand. She called her inner dragon and with her power created a sphere of energy in the palm of her right hand. She tried to enlarge it since it was not very big, but she could not. It had to be the pearl. It controlled the power they could give to the sphere. Daphne and Lily created theirs. They were ready.

Suddenly, the Brown Squad came in by the corner more to the left of the room. They came in at a run, brandishing their daggers. They clearly intended to surprise them, and when they did not see anyone, they stopped in the middle of the room. They saw the banner and separated into two groups in order to go around the horseshoe, three around the front and three behind. The ones behind were unprotected.

"Now!" Taika gave the signal as he came out from behind the wall with his dagger in hand at lightning speed. Aiden tried to follow him, but he was much slower. Ivo was slower still. While they ran to attack, Nahia, Daphne, and Lily stood up. They came up above the wall, revealing their arms and head, and the three lunged their spheres against the three attackers at the front. Each one aimed at the one closest to them. Nahia's sphere hit a Fatum squarely in the chest. When it burst, the Fatum was thrown back and left unconscious on the floor. Daphne hit a Human in the ribs and he bent double from the explosion of energy before also falling to the ground. Lily hit the right shoulder of a Felidae lioness and the explosion unbalanced her.

Taika reached them, and with a prodigious leap he fell on the lioness before she could react. He plunged his knife into her heart. There was a discharge of energy and the Felidae was rendered unconscious. He turned like a viper and eliminated the Human with another knife stab in the stomach. Aiden arrived and finished the Fatum by plunging his knife in the Fatum's neck. The daggers did not penetrate their skin, but the discharge left them unconscious.

"Reload!" Taika told the girls.

The other members of the Brown Squad had already discovered the trap and were coming for Taika and Aiden. Ivo was so slow, he was just arriving at the fray. Taika faced a Drakonid and they started to exchange cuts and thrusts while they moved, nimbly avoiding and blocking to attack again. Ivo faced a Kapro as big as himself with ram's horns. They both opted for the dagger first, but after a couple of exchanges they managed to grab the armed arm of the other and struggled like two forces of nature. Aiden was attacking a Human who was faster and a little more agile with the dagger than he was. He was defending himself by blocking.

Nahia had her sphere ready but saw that Daphne and Lily still had not. She threw hers against the Human who had Aiden in trouble. The sphere hit the boy in the side of the head and burst. The Human fell to the floor like a felled tree. Aiden looked at Nahia and gave a signal of thanks, then he went to help Taika.

Daphne and Lily already had their spheres created.

"Help Ivo," she told them and pointed at where he was.

The two girls sent their spheres against the back of the great ram. The two explosions did not manage to knock him down, but he lost his balance and Ivo hit him in the middle of the head with the pommel of his dagger. There was a discharge of energy, but the large ram did not fall. Ivo hit him three more times in quick succession and the Kapro was left unconscious on the ground.

"We withdraw," Taika told them, and they all went back behind the wall.

Nahia, Daphne, and Lily were already calling in new spheres.

They waited for a moment, but the Blue Squadron did not appear. The banners flashed again.

"They haven't moved," Taika said, watching the flash that rose up into the sky.

"Then they must be using our same strategy," Aiden guessed.

"The Blue Squadron is quite hurt. Perhaps that squad has casualties," Nahia suggested.

"Good information," Taika told her.

"I have a friend in that squad, and today I saw another blue one fall."

"If there are fewer of them than us, it will be easy to defeat them. Let's attack," Aiden stood up.

"Get down, rock-head, or else they'll make you more handsome when they hit you in the face with a sphere."

Aiden immediately crouched again.

"Drakonids don't value physical beauty."

"That's because you have none," Lily snapped but smiled at him beguilingly.

Aiden looked very offended.

"The worst squad ever…" he muttered under his breath.

"What do we do, Taika?" asked Nahia.

"If there are less of them than us, they won't come for us," the tiger reasoned.

"Let's go then and charge. We'll pass over them," Aiden insisted. "The banner is getting consumed."

Taika looked at the banner and nodded.

"We can't wait. Let's go, but we have to study the land first."

They all nodded in confirmation, stood up, and headed through the great labyrinth to the rival position. They got to a corridor that seemed to lead directly to where the banner was. Taika signaled for them not to go that way but to go around the wall of fire and check through the other end. They did so. Taika got down on the floor and crawled forward, poking his head in very quickly. He withdrew at once. A ball of energy burst against the wall of water beside him and spattered ice-cold water all over them, making them shiver.

"Three throwers, one fighter. They have two casualties." Taika informed them.

"What's our strategy?" Ivo asked him.

"Ivo, Aiden, and myself will go in this way and charge. There is a back way. The fighter is watching it, a female Drakonid. You three, deal with her. Once you eliminate her, go in through the back and finish off the three throwers who will be dealing with us."

They all nodded.

"Get in positions, I'll give the signal to attack."

They separated, Nahia, Daphne, and Lily arriving through the back door of the room, which was round. Part of the wall was made of the air element, and the other of earth.

Taika roared like a tiger, and they had no doubt that was the signal. Lily, Daphne, and Nahia went into the room from the back. At the front, Taika was throwing himself to one side to avoid a sphere that exploded against an earth wall. Fragments of rock flew from the wall and hit the tiger hard. Aiden, who was walking toward the throwers, received a sphere in the stomach. He bent over double with pain and fell to the floor. Ivo was caught in the right shoulder. The explosion did not stop him though. Lily tried to throw a sphere at the Drakonid, but she was too slow. A knife thrust got her in the middle of her neck and she fell unconscious. Daphne threw her sphere and hit the Drakonid in the right side. When it exploded, their opponent doubled over with pain. Nahia finished her off, hitting her in the head. She fell to the floor, unconscious.

On the floor, Taika was fighting with a black panther. Aiden received a second sphere in the chest as he was recovering from a Fatum's attack, and he fell unconscious. Ivo was caught in the side by a Human and stopped to recover from the pain. Nahia and Daphne arrived at a crouch from behind. As the Fatum was turning to them, the two threw their spheres at him. They hit him in the chest and he fell unconscious. The Human turned and threw a sphere at Daphne and hit her on the leg. She lost her balance from the pain and ended up on the floor. Nahia hid behind a tall rectangular shape and created another sphere of energy. She poked out her head and saw the Human attacking Ivo, who had him almost on top. This time he caught Ivo full in the face, and the Tauruk-Kapro fell to the floor, unconscious. Nahia jumped up from her hiding place and hurled a sphere at the Human. She caught him in the neck and he fell like a log.

Taika got up. He had defeated the panther.

"Red Squadron," he called.

Nahia came out with another sphere in her hand.

"Here," she said.

"Ouch, here," Daphne moaned from the floor.

"Good. I'm going to take the three banners, there's not much time left," Taika said and ran to get them.

Nahia helped Daphne to her feet.

A moment later, Taika came back with the three banners.

Winner: Igneous Squad. In time, the Commander's message reached them.

Nahia snorted.

"We did it. I can't believe we did it."

"I can't either," said Daphne.

"We were lucky with the Blue Squadron," Taika admitted.

Suddenly, several Tergnomus appeared. They went over to those unconscious and injected something on the back of their hands. A moment later, they all began to come to.

Help them get out of the labyrinth. The next combatants are waiting, they received the Commander's message.

They came out and went to their leader.

Well done. The Red Squad is victorious, Irakas-Gorri-Gaizt messaged them.

They were all trying to recover as best they could. They were exhausted and sore, and this was not finished. Nahia sighed. They had only survived the first combat.

Chapter 37

They rested as much as they could while the next eliminatory series took place. The Ardent Squad won but the Searing Squad was eliminated, which made Irakas-Gorri-Gaizt furious.

You are a disgrace! What a dishonor to be eliminated in the first combat! You will receive a suitable punishment!

Nahia realized that after the eighteen squads had competed, there were only six winners, two of them from the Red Squadron.

The test has been quite entertaining. A lot was expected from you, and not all of you are showing the traits a Dragon Blood Warlock must have. Now begins the most interesting part. We will see who is worthy and who is not, the Colonel messaged to all of them.

Leaders, present your squads for the second round of combat, the Commander ordered.

Igneous Squad. Compete, north end. Exert yourselves! Defeat the rival squads! Irakas-Gorri-Gaizt ordered.

Aiden did not waste a moment. He grabbed the banner and walked proudly toward the entrance.

"How are you? I can barely stand," Nahia told her comrades.

"I'm dead," Daphne admitted.

"I feel like I've been given a beating by a group of Tauruk-Kapro," said Lily.

"We'll have to save our energy," Taika warned them.

"No way, we have to give our all, like our leader has ordered," said Aiden.

"Sure, you give it all and you'll learn when they hit you in your big mouth with a sphere," Daphne replied.

"No one can beat us, we're the Igneous Squad."

"Really? Please, someone hit him in the mouth so he shuts up," Lily said.

"Besides, everything hurts like crazy. I bet he loves it," said Daphne.

"All of this is a waste of positive energy. We're only attracting negativity from the universe with these meaningless squabbles," Ivo said, shaking his head.

"You know, he's quite right," Taika agreed.

"This Tauruk is wrong in the head," Aiden complained.

They arrived at the entrance, and two Tergnomus gave them the weapons to use in the combat.

"Hoods on," they reminded them.

They all put them on.

Squads, prepare. Go in, now! the Commander messaged the order to begin the test.

They went in and appeared in a rectangular room, every wall a different element. The wall behind them rose and shut the entrance.

"We'll have to be careful. The squads that remain are good competitors," said Taika, who was already crouching with his dagger ready in one hand.

"Indeed, all the less skilled squads have been eliminated," Aiden said with the dagger in one hand and the banner in the other.

"What's the plan?" Nahia asked.

"I vote for not moving. I'm dead on my feet," said Daphne.

"This entrance area has no place to hide," said Taika, indicating the wide-open space ahead of them.

"So let's look for one with protection, but not too far away, I'm also at the end of my rope," Lily said.

"Fine, follow me." Taika moved forward, and they left the entrance to enter a long corridor with walls of fire.

"This labyrinth is so charming," Lily joked.

"Yeah, a beauty," Daphne joined her.

They had to take a few turns right, and a few left, always in a southern direction, until they found a wide hall with places to protect themselves.

"Here? We've already left behind six halls at least," Daphne said.

"Yes, this one will serve. The others were too small or unprotected," Taika explained.

Suddenly, their banner gave off a flame and a red light rose in the sky.

They all watched to identify the rival squads. To the east they saw a beam of black light, and to the west one of bright crystal.

"There they are,"

"The Black Squadron and Crystal Squadron," Nahia said.

"Is it the Crystal Squadron or the White?" Aiden asked.

"It's too bright to be the White," Lily told him, "it's the Crystal one."

Nahia let out a deep breath. She did not know anyone in those two squadrons, which was a relief. She would not have to fight Maika, or Logan. Ana, unfortunately, had already fallen and been eliminated. She thought about it again and realized then that Maika and Logan would have to fight in the next eliminatory round.

"Why don't we let them fight first? That way we can rest a little," Daphne suggested.

"That's dishonorable!" Aiden was adamant.

"It's rest, and we need it," Lily corrected him.

"It's not a bad strategy," Nahia agreed, since she felt more than exhausted.

"What a lack of spirit and initiative!" Aiden was furious.

"How do we do it then?" Nahia asked Taika.

The tiger was thinking.

"For there to be a fight, there have to be two who want to fight…" he muttered.

"I want to fight!" Aiden could not believe it and was moving the banner furiously, an outraged look on his Drakonid face.

"Shut up, granite-head," Daphne scolded him.

"If they don't find us, they can't fight us," suggested Taika.

"We hide then? Lily asked.

"We do, but let's think this through first. We can't run around the whole labyrinth either. We don't have the strength to do so," the tiger explained.

"Yeah, I can't even stand on my own two feet," said Nahia.

"Aiden, you'll carry the banner. Let's move a hundred paces to the east," he told them, and they did. They arrived at another room which was pretty spacious. They waited in silence, sitting on the floor behind two square columns of water and fire. Time went by until the next flash of the banner sent a red beam to the sky. They saw the black one. It was close, and the crystal was also nearby.

"We're playing cat and mouse," Taika realized. "Let's move, a hundred paces south, in silence."

They moved on until they arrived at another hall and hid inside. They all got behind something without touching it and sat on the floor.

More time went by, and once again the banners gave off their flashes up toward the sky, marking the position they were in. Now they were all very close. Too close.

They heard shouts and combat noise on the other side of the wall of earth they had on their right.

"They're right here!" Nahia warned.

As she did, two members of the Black Squadron appeared. They were each brandishing a dagger in one hand and carrying a ball of energy in the other. They were a Fatum and a Human. They saw Aiden's banner standing out over the wall behind which he was hiding and realized they were all there hidden. They went around the half-wall behind which Ivo and Aden were and attacked. Ivo received two energy balls to the chest as he was rising, and he bent double with pain.

"Attack!" Aiden lunged at the rivals with the banner in his hand and the dagger in the other.

"Help them!" Taika was already standing.

The Fatum and the Human lunged at Ivo, who was affected. They stabbed him five times in the chest with astonishing speed and accuracy. Ivo fell unconscious.

"Ivo, no! Treacherous!" Aiden attacked, delivering blows with his dagger and banner.

The Fatum and the Human were surprised by Aiden's strange and uncontrollable attack. They avoided it and delivered two stabs to his ribs, and Aiden bent double with pain to one side.

Nahia, Daphne, and Lily jumped up to attack the assailants. Nahia caught the Fatum in the neck and she fell like a sack of potatoes. The Human received one impact in the chest and another in the stomach, and he dropped to his knees in pain. Taika arrived and finished him off with a slice to the neck. Nahia was already creating another sphere of energy when a Tauruk belonging to the Crystal Squadron appeared. She delivered a tremendous kick and Nahia flew backward. She hit the air wall and this made her fly in the opposite direction, pushed by a strong gust of wind. She was left at the other end of the hall on the floor, very sore.

Daphne and Lily fought against the Tauruk, sending two spheres at her face. She fell on her knees, and they took out their daggers and finished her off before she could recover. A tigress from the Crystal Squadron appeared behind them and cut Daphne's throat with great skill and speed. The Fatum fell unconscious. Lily turned and fought the tigress, dagger against dagger. She defended herself and blocked until Taika knocked down the tigress with a prodigious leap. They both hit the earth wall and received a tremendous shower of stones as a result. The tigress could barely move, and Taika was having trouble getting up. Lily came forward and finished off the tigress on the floor.

Aiden got up and looked toward the other room where the combat noises were coming from.

"Igneous Squad, forward!" he cried and ran to attack.

Lily looked at him in horror when she saw him charge. She ran after him to help him.

Aiden arrived in the fray when there were three from the Black Squadron fighting against three of the Crystal Squadron. Aiden charged against the two closest rivals. A huge Tauruk from the Black Squadron was fighting a Drakonid from the Crystal Squadron. They were grabbing each other's necks with one hand while with the other they were hitting their opponent's chest and stomach with powerful, dull blows. Their daggers were on the floor. Aiden reached them with eyes that flashed with the brightness of madness.

"To victory!" he cried, beside himself, and started hitting the Tauruk and the Drakonid as if madness had overcome him. He hit them with his dagger and banner over and over so frenetically that they both ended up on the floor unconscious.

Lily was behind Aiden without really knowing what to do. Suddenly, the Scarlatum of the Crystal Squadron threw a ball of energy at her. Lily reacted and lunged to one side with such bad luck that she hit the water wall. Half her body was wet and froze at once. She tried to get up but could not; one of her legs and arms had frozen stiff.

"Aiden, help!" she called. But Aiden was beside himself, he neither heard or saw anyone. He did not heed reason and was heading straight for the two combatants in front of him, intending to finish them off.

A second sphere hit Lily on the side of her head and she fainted.

Taika jumped on the Scarlatum who had finished off Lily. He caught her as she was creating another sphere of energy. He did not let her finish, stabbing her in the neck. The Scarlatum fell unconscious.

Nahia entered the hall at that moment. She was doubled down in pain and was useless for combat, but she could not stay on the floor while her friends were fighting. She saw Taika jumping on the Drakonid belonging to the Black Squadron who was trying to get up. Taika finished her off before she could manage to.

Aiden attacked the Felidae lion of the Black Squadron who was attacking the Human of the Crystal Squadron. They were both fighting with daggers, and they were very skilled. They saw Aiden coming at them, delivering blows hither and thither with his dagger and the banner, and they both turned on him to defend themselves. Aiden received two thrusts in the chest, which should have made him double with pain, but he barely seemed to notice. He continued attacking the two rivals, possessed by a strange madness.

"To victory!" he chanted over and over as he attacked.

A moment later, the lion and the Human fell under Aiden's blows.

There was no one else left standing. Aiden went over to where the Scarlatum of the Black Squadron and the Fatum of the Crystal Squadron were on the floor, apparently having neutralized one another. Aiden delivered several dagger and banner strikes anyway.

"For victory!" he shouted.

"Stop, Aiden!" Taika shouted at him.

"To the death!" Aiden said as he turned toward Taika and went to attack him.

"Taika, watch out!" Nahia warned him.

Aiden took two steps toward Taika and then suddenly fell to his knees. A moment later, he fell forward. All the wounds he had received and which he had not even noticed finally took their toll, knocking him out.

Taika snorted.

"Thank goodness."

Nahia was looking at the hall filled with fallen fighters.

"Take the three banners," she told Taika. She could not even move.

"Coming." Taika grabbed the three banners.

Winner: Igneous Squad. Within the time limit, the Commander's message reached them.

Nahia sat down on the floor, completely worn out.

They had managed to win.

The Tergnomus came in and revived everyone. They left the labyrinth as best as they could.

Well done! Glory to the Red Squadron! Irakas-Gorri-Gaizt messaged to them when they reached their leader.

They were all so tired and sore they did not even appreciate it.

You may sit down on the floor and recover your strength. You will be brought water and food, the dragon messaged next.

They dropped down on the floor and felt grateful for a chance to recover a little. While they did, the other combat took place, the one in which Maika's and Logan's squads took part. And the Ardent Squad. It must have been a close fight, because they took a long time. Finally, the winning squad was called. It was Logan's. Nahia felt bad for Maika, who must have tried with all her being, but she was glad for Logan who, knowing him, had to be an excellent fighter. The Ardent Squad came back with their heads down and had to feel their leader's anger as it called them all kinds of names.

They gave some time for Logan's Whirlwind Squad to recover before there was the final combat. They were grateful for that even more.

And we come to the great finale. The Igneous Squad against the Whirlwind Squad. I expect a good spectacle. This time it will be simpler. One squad will enter the north side and the other the south. The banners will be placed in the center of the labyrinth. You must quickly advance to them and claim them. If one team claims them before the other one, it wins, the colonel announced.

Leaders, present your squad for the final, the Commander ordered.

Igneous Squad. Compete! The glory must be ours! Irakas-Gorri-Gaizt ordered.

Chapter 38

They stood up and went on with the scarce strength they had recovered, which was truly very meager.

"Cheer up, we're nearly done with this day of agony," Daphne said as they walked.

"Why don't we just give up and that's that?" Lily suggested.

"Never! What a dishonor!" cried Aiden.

"Take it easy, you're losing your head," Lily said.

Aiden looked at her with a face that clearly showed he had no idea what she was talking about.

"What do you mean?"

"You're kidding, right?" Lily could not believe the Drakonid.

"I have no idea what you're talking about," Aiden said, walking nonchalantly.

"It appears to me that he has his seizures and then afterward remembers nothing," Nahia concluded.

"What seizures?" Aiden asked blankly.

"The ones you have, marble-head!" Lily shouted at him.

"I don't have any kind of seizures, what nonsense is that?"

"By the heavens, he's impossible!" Lily waved her arms.

"What can I say!" Daphne said, shaking her head.

"We can't give up, Irakas-Gorri-Gaizt would kill us himself," Taika said. "It would mean dishonoring the great red dragon in front of everyone, besides its superiors."

"It'd certainly kill us," Nahia nodded.

"We'll fight and we'll win, as we have so far!" Aiden raised his fist.

"Do you remember how you won the last combat?" Lily asked him.

"I fell fighting, which is what counts. The how doesn't matter."

"Yeah, that means you don't have any recollection, geez!" Lily rolled her eyes.

They got to the entrance, and there they were given their weapons.

"The banners are placed in position," the Tergnomus informed them.

Squads, go in, the combat begins! The Commander messaged.

They went in and the wall shut behind them.

"What strategy should we use this time?" Nahia asked.

"The best idea is to let Aiden loose as a total maniac and see how many he kills before he's defeated," said Lily.

"He might attack us too, like last time," Nahia replied.

"Ah, then we'd better not."

"I don't know what nonsense you're talking about, but we have to run to the center," Aiden told them.

"Run?" Daphne frowned.

"If they get there first and grab the banner, they'll have an advantage," said Taika. "We'll be forced to take it away."

"Ufff… then let's run!" said Daphne.

They ran off with Taika in the lead. It wasn't easy to cross the whole labyrinth to the center without touching the walls and all its passages and strange halls. There were a couple of moments when they seemed to get lost and had trouble finding the direction again. Luckily, the banners threw their signal into the sky and they saw it. They finally managed to reach the center of the labyrinth.

It was a large circle with an outer wall of fire. It was completely empty, with the exception of another circle in the center with walls of water within which were the banners. As soon as they arrived they saw that the Whirlwind Squad was already there. But they had not attempted to go for the banner.

As they came in, the entrance they had used became a wall of fire. There was no way out. It was a trap. They could not get to the banners or abandon the great circle of fire.

"They've played us," Daphne said furiously.

"Does that surprise you?" Lily said, raising her arms.

"The dragons want their entertainment," said Nahia. "We'll have to give it to them. That's how ruthless they are."

"Our lords know how to prepare us for the victory, this is only one step further," Aiden said, convinced.

"Let's form a line," said Taika. "Leave space so we can dodge. Knife, sphere, knife, sphere, knife, sphere," he specified.

They nodded and formed a line with Taika, Nahia, Aiden, Lily, Ivo, and Daphne.

"They're in a three-by-two squad formation," Nahia warned.

"That formation isn't favorable in this environment," Taika said thoughtfully.

"It's the one we've been taught," Aiden retorted.

"Here in the open, with throwers, ours is better. Believe me," Taika said.

Logan and his squad started to move forward to the center of the circle. Between the two squads was the square with the banners. There was no way to access them because the walls were water and anyone who touched them would be frozen stiff.

"Don't move, get your spheres ready," Taika told them.

"Us too?" Ivo asked.

"Yes, but keep the dagger in your hand."

The six took out their Learning Pearls, called on their inner dragons, and created the spheres, which appeared on the palms of their hands.

Logan and his squad also created spheres as they advanced in perfect formation. They reached the center and, in an unexpected move, they split apart.

"Do we attack?" Aiden, eager to charge, asked.

"They're still far away," Nahia told him. She had calculated the throw, and it would fall short. She was so tired that simply standing was a titanic effort. She did not know how she was going to be able to fight. Logan's squad looked a lot fresher, and Nahia began to feel an inner heat beginning to consume her.

The Whirlwind Squad passed the banners and joined to form a line like they were in. They advanced determinedly from the front without fear or hesitation.

"Get ready, they're almost within range," Taika told them.

They all prepared to throw their spheres.

The Whirlwind Squad stopped. They stared at them. The Igneous Squad stared back, without showing fear, hiding any sign of anxiety.

There was a long pause.

Logan gave the order.

"Attack!"

His squad stepped forward.

"Throw them, now!" Taika ordered.

The six Igneous members threw their spheres straight at the rival in front of them.

And the combat began.

Nahia was watching Logan, whom she had to fight since the two groups were practically identical. But Logan had swapped positions with the Scarlatum of his team. Nahia was not sure whether he had done it on purpose so he would not have to fight her; she guessed he had. Since they were friends, he must have chosen not to fight her, apart from the fact that he would definitely beat her. She focused on the Scarlatum, who looked a lot like Lily, although she was not as pretty. She threw quickly and hit her in the right shoulder, making her drop her sphere before she could throw it at her. Nahia created another sphere of energy rapidly before the Scarlatum recovered. Nahia was beginning to feel very sick, intense heat running throughout her body, and she felt her heartbeat increasing.

Lily focused on the Felidae lioness in front of her who had an impressive physical appearance. She was almost as big as Taika. Being a Felidae, she would be weaker at magic but very good with the dagger and unarmed combat, so the Scarlatum threw the sphere at the lioness before she could get too close. The lioness received the impact in the stomach and the explosion of energy made her double forward. She could not throw her sphere, which fell to the floor. Immediately, Lily created another one.

Daphne sent her sphere against the rival Fatum. At the same time, the other one threw her sphere at Daphne. The balls of energy crossed in the air and they both hit the other in the chest. When they exploded, they threw both of them backward on the floor.

Aiden faced the Drakonid of the rival squad.

"Come and perish! he cried, exalted.

"For victory!" cried his rival.

The both threw their balls of energy and hit one another. Aiden was hit in the leg and had to drop to his knee, in pain and unbalanced. His rival received the impact in the right arm, which was rendered half useless. A moment later, they drew the daggers and started fighting, one lame and the other one-armed.

Ivo was facing a Tauruk as big as he was. The rival Tauruk charged. Ivo threw a ball of energy at him and hit him in the right shoulder. The Tauruk stopped for a moment; seeing he could not throw with his right hand, he threw with the left, failing entirely. He charged again like an enraged bull. Ivo was not a charger, so he took out his dagger and prepared to receive his opponent. The Tauruk charged him and knocked him down with tremendous force. Ivo was squashed under the huge body of his rival. With great skill, he managed to stab him in the side with the dagger.

Taika saw that Logan was going to attack him, and he saluted him respectfully with a nod. Logan returned the salute. An instant later, he attacked with great speed, throwing the sphere of energy as he advanced in a zigzag. Taika threw his own and slid to one side smoothly. None of them managed to hit the other. An instant later, they both had their daggers in their hands. Logan reached Taika, and they began to fight dagger against dagger.

Nahia saw that the Scarlatum she was facing had reached for her dagger and was coming at her. She went to throw her ball of energy and felt sick and could not breathe. There was no doubt she was having one of her seizures. She managed to throw the sphere and hit the Scarlatum in the stomach as her throw went low. The Scarlatum doubled down, which stopped her advance. Nahia fell to her knees and looked for the tonic in her belt. She had to drink it, or she would lose the fight. And her life.

Lily hit the lioness in the ribs with a sphere and she doubled to one side with pain. The thing was, she already had her on top, and since the lioness was so strong she was bearing the attack of the spheres. But Lily did not lose courage: she still had time to create one last sphere and finish off the lioness if she hit her in the face or neck. Lily created another sphere, and as it was forming in her hand she saw the lioness, dagger in hand, leap onto her with all her power. Lily calculated the moment and stamped the sphere in her jaws as the lioness fell on her. At the same time, the lioness stabbed her in the heart. They both fell unconscious on the floor.

Daphne and the rival Fatum rose at the same time. They both created a sphere of energy as fast as they could and they both threw at the same time. They hit one another in the chest again and fell to the floor. This time, Daphne had serious trouble getting up. Looking as if she were really hurting, she managed to kneel, but her rival stood up. She was more whole than her. They created their spheres again, but the Fatum was faster. She threw it before Daphne finished making hers and hit her in the head. Daphne fell unconscious to one side.

Ivo rid himself of the Tauruk he had stabbed in the side until he had fallen unconscious. He stood up and saw the Fatum who had beaten Daphne. He went to her calmly, dagger in hand. The Fatum saw him and created a sphere and threw it at him. Ivo did not flinch as he crossed his arms in front of his face. The sphere hit them and he felt great pain, but he kept coming. The Fatum stopped creating and throwing spheres and hit him in the hand holding the dagger, which flew in the air. Ivo reached the Fatum, who took her dagger out and stabbed him in the side. Ivo doubled over in pain. With his unarmed fist, he hit her in the head from the top down and the Fatum fell unconscious.

"Sorry…" Ivo apologized.

Aiden received a stab in his left shoulder while he delivered another to his rival in the chest. The pain of the stab seemed to awaken something in Aiden. His eyes shone with the spark of irrationality. He suddenly began to deliver thrusts hither and thither without any consideration to technique or his own defense. He hit like a madman. His rival, surprised by the unexpected, crazy attack, withdrew, avoiding him. He delivered a couple of strikes at Aiden's stomach, which he did not even seem to feel as he continued his crazy attack against his enemy. He advanced without stopping his hits until he managed to get his opponent in the chest. The Drakonid felt it and hesitated. He received three more slices and ended up on the floor, unconscious.

Taika and Logan were launching measured attacks and precise blocks followed by counterattacks. The two of them were very good with the dagger, and their offensive and defensive movements were fast and balanced. Taika was more nimble and stronger than Logan, but the Human had a better technique with the dagger, which balanced the combat.

On her knees, Nahia was trying to get the tonic to her mouth, but she was having spasms, and if they continued she would not be able to. The Scarlatum was recovering, she was going to attack and leave her senseless with a true stab. If that happened and she had not taken her tonic, Nahia would die. Fear made her stomach turn—she had to take the tonic before she was hit by the Scarlatum. She finally managed to put it to her mouth and bite off the stopper. The Scarlatum was on top of her. She drank the tonic and fell to one side on the floor. She reached out while the spasms shook her. The Scarlatum looked at her blankly. She was standing beside her. Nahia could not get up or defend herself, not after a seizure. But at least she would not die. She had drunk the tonic. But she felt bad: she had failed her squad, she had not been able to fight like the others because of her condition. She felt ashamed, a failure. The Scarlatum crouched beside her and put the dagger to her neck.

"I'm sorry, but I have to do this," she told her.

Nahia did not answer. She was looking at the sphere the Scarlatum had dropped on the floor a few paces away. She focused on it, then she looked at the Scarlatum, and with her mind she hit the sphere and directed it from the floor at her rival's head. The sphere flew and hit the Scarlatum just as she was getting ready to press Nahia's neck with her dagger. The sphere exploded and the Scarlatum fell to the floor, unconscious.

Ivo turned around and found Aiden.

"Let's help Taika," he said, indicating the tiger.

"For the victory!" Aiden cried, who did not recognize Ivo. He did not recognize anyone. He delivered three stabs to Ivo's head in a furious attack.

"What the…." was all Ivo could say before he fainted.

Aiden turned.

"Glory to the winner!" he cried and attacked Logan, who was closer, from behind. Logan saw him coming out of the corner of his eye and avoided Aiden's furious attacks.

Taika seized the advantage and caught Logan in the side with a swift strike. Logan bent over in pain and crouched. Two of Aiden's thrusts went over his head. He countered at Aiden's stomach, who did not seem to feel the stabs, and Logan threw himself to one side to avoid another thrust from Taika. Aiden went on attacking him without any concern for being hit himself. Logan caught him three more times while he dodged his furious attacks. Taika hit Logan again in the side with a swift, precise strike. Logan moved away and delivered another stab at Aiden in the chest. Then he remained crouched with his dagger ready.

Aiden stopped suddenly. He looked straight ahead, remained like that for a moment, and the next he fell flat on his face like a felled tree.

Taika saw Logan was wounded and went to finish him off. He hit Logan's dagger to move it away and stabbed him in the heart. To his surprise, Logan had a sphere of energy in his other hand. He hit Taika in the head with it as his stab hit his heart. The energy discharged and they both fell on the floor, unconscious.

Everything was silent. No one was moving. The combat had ended.

A long moment later, the announcement came.

Combat finished. It appears there is a technical tie by elimination of all combatants. Is there anyone still conscious? the Commander messaged.

If there is anyone still conscious, let him or her stand up, the Commander ordered.

Suddenly, Nahia realized she was indeed conscious. She was lying on the ground with no strength left, but she was awake. She raised her right hand.

We have someone conscious. Get up, Human, the Commander messaged to her.

Nahia did not want to disobey, but she could not get up. She made an attempt and managed to get onto one side.

Get up and claim the glory of the victory, or remain lying down like a weak loser. Claim the triumph for your squad, or carry the shame for not having achieved it, the Colonel ordered.

Nahia clenched her jaw. She had to get up, for herself and her comrades. She had to satisfy those heartless beings. Drawing strength from her rage and hatred for those despicable creatures, she stood up and managed to keep her balance.

Winner of the final and glorious champion of the competition: the Igneous Squad! the Colonel proclaimed.

Nahia managed to stay on her feet for a moment longer, and then she fell down. The last thing she saw before losing consciousness was the Tergnomus coming in to help them.

Chapter 39

Winning the final test of the Squad Competition was incredible, something none of the six members of the Igneous Squad ever thought they would achieve. But, somehow, they had done it. There were no ceremonies or acknowledgments. According to the Commander, the glory of victory was reward enough and the minimum they could all aspire to.

Their leader did not reward them in any way either, although since they had brought glory and honor to the Red Squadron, Irakas-Gorri-Gaiz granted them an additional break of three days to recover and a pardon for the next mistake they made. Nahia found it generous, coming from their leader, and knowing they would indeed make mistakes, she was grateful.

What there was plenty of in all the squads were punishments, especially for all those who had lost in the first combat. People were sent to clean the dungeons, assist with reconstruction work on the wall with the Tergnomus, fortify the lookout towers, hammer rock, and perform double shifts of marching and formation in the mornings for a month. This last punishment was tough, because they missed the morning meal and only had the evening one. Two squads were very depleted, so they were dissolved and their members distributed among the others. There were already only sixteen squads and several had suffered casualties, so by the end of the year another two or three squads were expected to disappear. It was terrible, and Nahia suffered and became furious every time it happened. The merciless, heartless dragons killed them equally—both below in the fields and up here in the academy.

The only good thing that winning the final brought them was the recognition of the other squads. Now when they entered the dining hall, all the first-years saluted them with slight nods. It was as if everyone suddenly respected them. Aiden loved all this recognition.

"It's so nice to be respected for being victorious," he told his comrades on the first day back to normal as they were having breakfast.

"Respect isn't won in victory, it's won by being a good person,"

Ivo told him as he was already finishing his serving of roast turkey and getting ready to go and ask for a second.

"That's nonsense, of course it's won in battle."

"They don't salute you out of respect, granite-head, they do it out of fear," Daphne told him.

"They fear me? Even better!" Aiden puffed up even more.

"Because of how crazy you become," Lily told him.

"I still don't believe I have those seizures you say I get," Aiden shook his head.

"We've all told you. You can't deny the evidence, we've all witnessed it," Lily told him.

"Yes I can. I don't remember it, so it didn't happen."

"Taika, Ivo, you tell him. We've been telling him for days and he won't believe us."

"You lose your head in the fury of the fighting and don't recognize friend from foe," Taika told him.

"That can't be."

"It certainly can, because you hit me on the head three times in the final," Ivo told him.

"It must have been without meaning, by accident…"

"Three times?" Ivo shook his head. "Not accidental at all. You were in a state of frenzy and were attacking everyone. You couldn't even see straight."

"Fury blinded you. You attacked like a possessed person," Taika told him.

"You should believe them, for your own good, or you will end up hurting yourself," Nahia advised him.

"Well… but I don't remember anything…"

"Exactly. That's why you should listen to your comrades and what we're trying to tell you," Nahia told him.

"Fine… I'll think about it…"

"That's plenty," Daphne raised her hands to the sky.

"I want to take the opportunity to congratulate Taika, you were superb!" Nahia said and raised her glass of water in a toast.

"Me? I just did the best I could." Taika blushed a little, which was funny to see on a great white tiger.

"You should be the leader of the squad," Daphne said.

"Undoubtedly, you have a very good head," Lily joined in.

"Thank you, you flatter me, but I don't want to be leader. That's not my thing. I am a born survivor, guided by the law of the jungle. Be strong, smart, and survive. Not guide others, that leads to death," he said and lowered his gaze to his plate and stopped eating.

"Well, it's a pity, because you do have the guts and talent to lead," Daphne told him.

"Everyone must find their own calling and destiny in this life," Ivo intervened. "All of us are different and have different virtues and failures. Let Taika live his calling and find his destiny."

"Yes, you're right, we don't mean to pressure you, Taika, just thank you," Nahia told him.

"I accept very gladly and I return it, because you managed to triumph where the rest of us failed."

"That's true, we owe our victory to you," Daphne said.

"Perhaps you should be the leader," Taika told Nahia.

"Me? No way, I'm a walking hazard."

"Sure, one who's capable of attacking a rival with said rival's own sphere using nothing but her mind. You're a prodigy," Lily told her.

"More than a prodigy, a calamity. I had another seizure and almost left you in the lurch, besides nearly dying."

"You have a slight problem, that's all," Daphne made light of it with a wave of her hand.

"A giant problem, rather," Nahia replied.

"Life sometimes provides us with problems so we can solve them and become fulfilled," Ivo said.

"Well, I don't see how to solve this one. I also can't be the leader, I'll fail you. I'll suffer seizures again at critical moments, I just know it. You need someone more reliable."

"That's me," said Aiden confidently.

"How can it be you when you don't even remember what you've done?" Daphne said.

"You're disqualified for losing your head all the time," Lily said.

Aiden made a face but said nothing.

"Don't look at me. I'm good only for war squads. My thing is peace, love, and individuality," Ivo told them.

"That a being so built for war should say that is shocking," Daphne said.

"Well, I don't want leadership. The responsibility of making difficult decisions makes you age faster. It gives you wrinkles and white hair. As you can understand, I don't want anything to do with that," Lily said, making pretty faces and tossing her beautiful jet-black hair one way and the other.

They all looked at Daphne, the only one left.

"I love to give orders, but with my bad temper I would most likely punish you with death every other day. No, I'd better not be the leader. I'd be three times as irritable, which wouldn't be good for you."

"That's for sure," said Aiden, and before Daphne could reply he got up and left the table.

"In that case, we still have the champion team of the first-years without a leader, just everyone doing what we can as best we can," said Nahia.

They all nodded and smiled. They finished their breakfast and got up to leave. Nahia looked for Logan and saw him. He looked back at her and nodded to her respectfully. Nahia smiled at him. She saw Logan's lips curl slightly, which pleased her a lot.

Three evenings later, they were about to go to sleep when Lily left something wrapped in a piece of cloth for Nahia on her bed.

"What's this?" Nahia asked, surprised.

"A gift."

"A gift? But we don't have anything to give?"

"Don't you believe that, open it and see."

Intrigued, Nahia opened the cloth, and inside she found a leather necklace which, instead of a jewel in the middle, had a wooden container.

"Is it what I think it is?"

Lily laughed.

"Yes, it's a necklace to carry your tonics. I know you carry them in your belt, but I figured that when you have one of your seizures, the closer it is to your mouth, the easier it'll be to take it."

Nahia put the necklace on and, taking one of her tonics, put it in the container place. It fitted perfectly and stayed in place tightly with the leather strap. It functioned like a pocket. She looked at it hanging from her neck and nodded.

"It's going to work perfectly. Thank you so much, Lily!" Nahia said and got up to give her a hug.

"It's nothing," she smiled. "I enjoy doing things with my hands, and I'm good at it. I'm good at weaving, sewing, making garments, necklaces, bracelets, and every kind of handcraft. I've always been good at making things with my hands."

"Well, not me," Nahia had to admit, admiring her new necklace-container. "What I don't understand is how it never occurred to me to carry it around my neck. It's a much better option."

"That's because you don't have much up here," Daphne said. She was already in her bed, tapping her head with her finger.

Nahia looked at her, confused. Daphne did not usually mess with her much, and that comment was a little scathing. The last few days Daphne had been in a darker mood than usual.

"Hey, don't be mean," Lily chided her.

Daphne ignored her.

"Daphne, are you all right? Is anything the matter?" Nahia asked. She suspected there was something bothering the Fatum.

"Nothing's the matter. Why shouldn't I be all right?"

"Because lately you've been most obnoxious," Lily told her. "Almost worse than Aiden."

"I heard you," Aiden's voice reached them from the other side of the screen.

"So don't listen," Lily replied.

"If you spoke softer and let us sleep, we wouldn't listen," Aiden replied.

"Shut up and go snore, it's the only thing you know how to do well," Daphne said with a huff.

They heard expletives in the Drakonid language which no one understood but which they all knew were insults.

"What's the matter, Daphne?" Nahia sat down beside her on her bed without touching her.

"Yeah what is it?" Lily asked too, squatting on the other side of the bed to talk to her.

Daphne crossed her arms over the blanket that covered her.

"I'm falling behind…" she admitted in a soft voice so the boys would not hear.

"Behind? You mean in class?" Nahia asked.

"Of course. I'm not talking about the snoring competition those three have every night on the other side of the screen."

"But you're doing very well in magic," Lily told her. "You're doing better than I am."

"My, you are dense. There are days I'd rather talk to Aiden than to you. I mean the martial class," Daphne said.

"I'm the worse at weapons," Nahia told her.

"You were. Not anymore. Now it's me."

"You think?" Nahia was not sure about that.

"Before it was you, but lately you've improved a lot. I manage pretty well with the knife, but the physical part is killing me. I can't cope with it. I'm always dead beat after class. Soon something's going to happen to me and that black dragon without a heart will make me pay. And you know the rumors: soon another first-year is going to die. I don't want it to be me."

"I hadn't realized you had problems," said Nahia.

"I had," Lily admitted. "And she's right. Now she's the worst, not you," she told Nahia.

"It has to be the strength training I do with Log... Taika. It is true that I get less tired and can bear the classes better."

"Well then, Daphne, you know what you have to do," Lily told her with a look that meant it was obvious.

"Yeah... well...would you help me?" Daphne asked doubtfully and bowing her head, ashamed.

"Of course we'll help you. We're in the same squad. We're friends."

"Are we? Or are we forced comrades?" Daphne asked.

"We are friends, and friends are there to help one another," Lily reassured her. "Perhaps you haven't worked much on this concept of friendship because of that rough personality of yours, but you'll get the knack of it," she said and laughed.

"That's right. Of course we're friends, and we're going to help one another," Nahia promised. "I don't have much experience with friendships either... but I intend to learn."

"Really, what a pair of newbie friends I ended up with," Lily rolled her eyes and then laughed again.

"And them? Do we consider them fiends?" Nahia asked.

"Those three? Not even in their dreams," Lily stated.

Nahia and Daphne looked at each other, not knowing whether she was serious or not. An instant later, Lily broke into giggles. Nahia and Daphne nodded and joined in the giggling.

"Will you please stop making so much noise? We're trying to sleep here!" they heard Aiden shouting.

"You're out for being such a granite-head!" Lily shouted at him, and they laughed again.

Chapter 40

Winter had brought the cold, and although their clothes protected them from the rigors of the weather, they all walked a little faster through the open areas where the wind blew stronger. Already, living at that height meant dealing with lower temperatures, and now that the bad weather had arrived, it was even worse.

Lining up in front of Irakas-Gorri-Gaizt in the mornings was something they found harder every day. It was not because of the snow or the cold—they were warm enough in their clothes—but the red dragon made them line up and march all over the square in martial formation. It had been like this ever since the Squad Competition. The dragon had not told them the reason beyond the fact that every soldier should know how to march in formation. At first they thought it was a punishment for not having done well in the test, but they noticed that they were not the only ones. All the squadrons did military marching exercises after lining up before their leader first thing in the morning. This puzzled them. What it clearly did was rob them time from breakfast, and that was indeed punishment, especially for Ivo.

That winter morning they were on their way to weapons class after the ever-shorter breakfast under a totally clouded sky. The snowflakes started fluttering around them.

"Don't you find it strange?" Nahia asked the others.

"What? The snow, or the cold?" Daphne asked in return.

"Both things, but especially the fact that I don't know whether it's snowing above or below us."

Lily nodded and stretched her arms so that the snowflakes landed on them.

"I'd say that right now, it's snowing above us and very likely below as well."

"That I'd like to see," Ivo commented. "I mean the part where it snows below us."

"I don't think we'll be allowed to witness it," Taika said, looking toward the west wall and the two dragons watching from the two lookouts.

"True. We can't go up on the walls without our squad's leader's permission," said Aiden.

"It's not as if we could escape from here. Where would we go?" Lily asked.

"In this realm, apart from the White Pearl we arrived through, there's nothing but this academy and the mountains we see to the north, right?" Nahia asked.

"That's incorrect," Aiden told her, and they all stopped to look at him.

"What else is up here?" Daphne asked him.

"Don't they teach you anything in your countries?" The Drakonid stopped under the falling snow and waved his arms.

"Evidently not as much as yours," Lily said.

"What else is up here?" Ivo wanted to know.

Aiden heaved a deep sigh.

"I don't know everything there is, but I can tell you that the great core of power that sustains this island in the air is here."

"The great core of power?" Taika asked, interested.

"I haven't seen any, but all the dragon realms have one. It's a core of great energy whose function is to keep the whole realm in the air. It requires a lot of magical power. Or so they say in my land."

"That I'd like to see," said Ivo.

"It's not good to go near it. It's too powerful and it could kill you," Aiden warned him.

"Well, then we can look at it from afar. Do you know where it is?" asked Lily.

Aiden shook his head.

"No idea, and I don't think we're supposed to know."

"And apart from that, what else is there?" Asked Daphne.

"Do we have to talk about it under the snow?" Aiden protested.

"Yes, because once we line up with weapons we won't be able to talk," Lily told him with a face that meant she wanted to know now.

Aiden sighed while the snowflakes fell on the scaled hood of his cloak.

"This realm is known for having the Great Oracle and the Temple of Harmony. That's what makes this realm special, apart from this academy of course," the Drakonid said it as if it were a fact known to everyone.

"I've never heard of any Great Oracle or Temple of Harmony," said Daphne, crossing her arms and frowning.

"Me neither," said Lily, who stood like her, frown and all.

"It would seem that the Drakonids have more information than the other races," Taika commented, raising an eyebrow.

"Privileged information," Ivo added.

Aiden shrugged.

"We're the masters' favorites, it's natural that they share more information with us than the rest of their slave races."

"When you talk like that, I feel like asking Ivo to crush that stupid dragon face of yours!" Daphne told him.

"Violence solves nothing," Ivo said, shaking his head.

"Maybe not, but we'd love to see that regardless," Lily said, smiling.

"It's not my fault the masters don't share information or knowledge with your races," Aiden said.

"Everyone here knows why they don't do it," Daphne said, waving her hands and pretending to say something to Lily.

"What's the Great Oracle?" Nahia asked. She wanted to know and also stop the argument.

"The Great Oracle is a dragon thousands of years old that can see the future. The leaders of the five clans consult it every now and then."

"And why is it here?" Nahia wanted to know.

"I guess it's because this is a neutral realm," said Taika. "If it can really see the future and one of the five dragon leaders got hold of the Great Oracle, it would have a great advantage over the other four."

Aiden nodded.

"Taika is right. That's why the Great Oracle is here, in the neutral realm."

"And is it really an oracle? Can it predict the future?" asked Nahia.

"That's right. It's an ancestral dragon with great power," Aiden assured her.

"I'm not sure this is anything but unfounded beliefs," Ivo said, wrinkling his nose. He was not at all convinced.

"It does sound to me like children's fairy tales," Lily joined him, shaking her head from side to side.

"Among my people, there is a belief in oracles and witches with power to know the future," Taika commented.

"Among my people too," said Daphne. "There are people who predict storms, bad harvests, calamities and things like that."

"My people believe in the prophecy: one day a slave will rise against the dragons and defeat them, freeing the enslaved peoples," said Nahia.

"Every race except the Drakonid believes that, but it's a chimera. It will never happen," Aiden said, sure of himself.

"Just because you say so," Lily replied.

"You all know the prophecy?" Nahia looked at her comrades under the steady snowfall.

Daphne nodded.

"We have it."

Taika and Ivo nodded too.

"It's one of the reasons why the Great Insurrection took place. Their leader rose as the chosen by the prophecy," Daphne explained.

"That's why he managed to persuade the rest of the leaders," Lily added.

"Oh… I didn't know," Nahia said, shaking her head.

"There's a lot your grandmother hasn't told you," said Lily.

"She must have done it for a good reason, to protect her," Taika said in a pleasant tone.

Nahia nodded repeatedly.

"Yes, I'm sure of that."

"I think she did well. It's already been proven that the prophecy was a fantasy and that rising against the dragons is futile," Aiden stated.

Nahia did not want to think like Aiden, but she had to admit that he was quite right. She did not know everything that had happened during the Great Insurrection, but she found it impossible to bring down the dragons.

"And what about the temple you mentioned?" she asked, changing the subject.

"The Temple of Harmony," Aiden said. "It's a temple where the five dragon leaders gather to discuss matters of great importance. They don't do it often. Only when something very important is going to happen and they need the accord of all five clans. It also happens when they decide to consult the Great Oracle."

"Interesting," said Taika. "I understand that they come without their armies."

Aiden nodded.

"They come alone. Otherwise there'd be disputes among them. That's why it's called the Temple of Harmony, because there must be harmony, accord, and agreement among them."

"They must agree on very little," Daphne commented.

"Yeah, I was thinking that too," said Lily, taking a snowflake off the tip of her nose.

"Well, enough chatter, let's run to the weapons class, I don't want to be late," Aiden told them as he started running.

As they ran to class, Nahia was thinking about everything they had talked about. She had many questions she wanted answers for. Aoma might have some, but she might find the other answers here, somewhere in the academy or its surroundings.

When they arrived at the classroom they found that Mai-Beltz-Gaiz was not there. Instead there was another dragon, as powerful as the black one, only this one was brown. In front of it there was a Tauruk instructor, another Fatum, and a Human, all female this time, which surprised Nahia.

Welcome. As of today, you will begin a new stage of learning after passing the half-year test. I will be your instructor from now on and until the end of the year. My name is Irma-Mar-Gud. As of today, you will begin to work on a new stage of your development and pass on to the regular study of weapons, leaving behind basic instruction. The first thing you have to do is learn to work with a shield. It is a very important element, because it will not only protect you but you will be able to use it to attack. Instructors, begin the training.

Nahia and her comrades froze in place. They had not been expecting this: a new teacher and new instructors, plus a new level of learning. In this academy they encountered surprises every day. Since, whether they liked it or not, they were not allowed to say anything, they looked at one another and kept their mouths shut.

This time they had the Tauruk instructor. She was very strong and big, almost as big as Ivo. Out of a large chest by the west wall, she took a shield out for each member of the squad and handed them around.

Nahia received hers, and when she felt it and weighed it, she saw it was metal. She realized that if, with the dagger at her waist she had been lucky, this was not the case with the shield. It was heavier than she had expected. Besides, she had to carry it in her left arm since she used the dagger with her right, and that was her weaker arm.

The instructor wasted no time and began showing them how to hold it properly, as well as how to stand to stop blows efficiently.

"You, Tauruk, attack me with your dagger," she told Ivo.

Ivo looked at her, and hesitation appeared in his eyes.

"You will attack me with a thrust straight to the heart," the instructor ordered.

Ivo's mouth opened to object, but the instructor did not let him.

"Not a word. Do as I tell you."

Ivo did not seem at all happy with that, but he did as he was told. He drew his dagger with his right hand, and with the shield in the left he stood in position with his back legs a little flexed. Since his legs ended in hooves, it was a little odd.

"Deliver the attack," the Tauruk ordered him. She only carried a shield in her left hand and was waiting in a defensive stance.

Ivo heaved a deep sigh and attacked. The dagger headed to the body of the powerful Tauruk, but it didn't even graze her. With a very quick movement, she put the shield in the way of the dagger so that it hit the metal. When it did, it was deflected to one side and left Ivo in a bad position. Without a word, the instructor delivered a tremendous blow to his face with the shield. Ivo fell backward like a felled tree and was left lying unconscious.

"No one help him. He'll recover shortly," the Tauruk ordered. "As you have seen, you can defend yourself with a shield, as well as attack and knock down the most powerful of adversaries. But you must learn how and where to hit."

Nahia was frozen. Poor Ivo had been left unconscious with one blow, which seemed impossible—he was so big and tall. On the other hand, the instructor was also tall and strong, even if she was not as imposing as Ivo. It was clear her technique had a lot to do with it.

"Now, you'll get in pairs and we'll do offensive exercises with the dagger and defensive movements with shield. I want you to be able to defend yourself from any attack, from any direction. Once you master this, you'll learn to do what I just demonstrated. You will learn to attack and counterattack with your shield. Before winter ends, you'll be capable of knocking down your partners with one shield blow. I promise."

This last sentence troubled Nahia. How were they going to

practice knocking out a comrade? She had the feeling it was going to be precisely by hitting them in the face with the shield. Only thinking about it made a shiver run down her spine. She looked at Daphne, who returned the look with a frown. She was thinking the same thing.

Ivo recovered after a moment and stood up without complaint. They started to do the exercise under the guidance and careful gaze of their instructor. By the end of the class, Nahia could no longer keep her shield up. She had no strength in her left arm, as she had feared. She would have to work on her weaker arm. This made her think of the extra training at the gym and Logan. She might see him there. The thought cheered her up. As soon as they finished here, she would go to the gym, although she could not do much with that arm, it was so heavy and sore. In any case, she might see Logan and she could tell him about her troubles. That cheered her.

Chapter 41

Winter went on relentlessly, and it seemed it was always snowing. The parade ground was always covered by a white cloak, and they had to wipe off the sun dial to know the hour. Luckily, their bodies had become accustomed to the time schedule, so it was not a problem.

That morning, Irakas-Gorri-Gaizt made them march a little more than usual and they had to miss breakfast so they were not late for class. Ivo was very unhappy. Breakfast was his favorite moment of the day, and every day it was being cut shorter and shorter as his anger grew and grew.

"I don't understand why we have to march every morning. We could do it after classes," he said, waving his arms.

"After classes many of us go to the gym," Nahia told him.

"Or the library," Lily added.

"So we should have breakfast first and march then. The mind can't reason if the body doesn't have its nourishment."

"With that, I have to agree," Aiden told him.

"Wow, this is the first time you agree with what our Tauruk says," Daphne was looking at Aiden blankly.

"Our Tauruk is weird, in case you haven't realized, Fatum," Aiden clarified.

"Unique. I prefer that term," Ivo told them, not in the least bothered by the comment.

"An exceptional Tauruk," Taika told him, patting his large back.

"A hungry Tauruk," Ivo said, and they all chuckled.

They arrived at Basic Dragon Magic, and there they found something unexpected that upset them. In the class they always used there was no Mag-Zilar-Ond and Mabor-Exarbor as usual. Their places were occupied by an enormous white dragon and another Exarbor who looked even older than Mabor, which was an incredible feat.

Welcome, members of the Red Squadron. Today is a special day in the walking of the Path. You are already prepared to take an important step. You now leave behind the studies of basic magic to begin those of regular magic.

Because of this, you will also have a new teacher. From this moment until the end of the year, I will be your teacher. My name is Ande-Zuri-Koa, and the Exarbor who acts as my assistant is Borne. I am a white dragon and, as you have guessed, my main element is Air. I hope I will not have to discharge a storm on any of you. I warn you that I am not as benevolent as Mag-Zilar-Ond, so if you are not up to standard, you will pay.

The unexpected announcement about the change of teacher and their magic studies going forward left Nahia feeling restless. The fact that the new dragoness was more rigorous filled her with fear, and her stomach churned. Everything in this academy seemed to grow more complicated with every step they took.

Today we will begin the study of regular magic and we will find out your Elemental Alignment, the albino dragoness messaged them, with the feeling that this was a crucial step.

And if that change was small, there was something else different that day, something which left them puzzled. In the middle of the classroom on the floor, a long pyramid had been placed, with a silver sphere resting above it the size of Ivo's head.

"What's that?" Lily whispered as they sat down in their places.

"No idea, but I don't understand how it hovers over the top of the pyramid," Daphne murmured as she watched with a surly face.

"It can only stay that way through the power of the sphere," Taika commented.

The other two squads were also whispering about the two objects.

"Be quiet, you're going to get us into trouble," Aiden told them.

They all shut up when they saw the Exarbor watching them.

"I will prepare the process..." Borne said, and with the slowness of his people he walked over to the pyramid and the sphere on top of it.

You have already discovered your inner dragon of power. You are able to interact with it thanks to the bond of the dragon and your mind. You can use the magic within you. That is the initial part you have already passed. Today, you will begin with the most advanced part of dragon magic that is taught during your first year at the academy. For that, you must first pass a test.

The term "test" instantly made them all anxious, to a greater or lesser degree. Even Aiden, who always tried to hide that he had any feelings of fear or concern. The members of the other squads also shifted about restlessly where they sat.

The test of Elemental Alignment will mark an important milestone in your life. It will determine what type of elemental magic runs through your veins. Everyone of the dragon blood has one. It is what has been forming within you ever since you were born, and now it will reveal itself.

"Everything is ready… my lady," Borne said.

Very well. It is time to find out what type of magic you have inside you. Let the test begin.

Borne stood beside his pedestal with the great tome open on it. He flipped a page and called the first pupil.

"Nahia… of the Igneous Squad."

A deep sigh came out of Nahia's mouth as she stood up. She looked at her comrades, who looked back at her with cheering gestures. She went to where the pyramid was standing with the sphere on top, which was now rotating upon the tip with perfect balance. Nahia could not tell whether it was leaning on it or if it rotated a little above without touching it.

Very well, pupil. Stand in front of the sphere and reach toward it with your hands without touching it. Leave a distance of two handspans.

Nahia did as was told. The sphere was a little higher than her head, so she had to reach upward. She did not know what was going to happen, but she was nervous. Watching the sphere spinning, perfectly balanced, made her anxious.

Do not move until I tell you to, the dragoness messaged, closing its eyes.

A moment later, the silver sphere gave off a flash. Nahia observed how a cloak of white energy formed around the sphere. It was a mist of power the sphere itself gave off. It grew until it was a handspan thick around the sphere, covering it completely. When the sphere spun, the field of energy around it also spun but not at the same speed or in the same direction but the opposite, which caused an effect Nahia found most strange and against nature.

The sphere is ready to determine your elemental alignment. Now, first you must wake up your inner dragon and send energy to both your hands, as if you were creating a sphere of energy, immersing them in the cloak of outer energy. Go ahead. Whatever you feel, do not withdraw your hands. You must finish the process without taking your hands away from the sphere.

Nahia obeyed, but not without concern. She concentrated and searched for her inner dragon of power and found it in the middle of her chest. She sent energy to her hands using her mind. She was able to feel the energy traveling from the dragon to her hands. She put them on the mist of energy and felt a tingling in her palms, a little painful. For a moment she nearly took them away, but she managed to master her fears and tried to touch the sphere with her hands. Something odd happened. There was a flash the moment she touched the sphere with them, and it stopped. It was no longer spinning, but the cloak of energy did continue spinning. She found it most strange.

The tingling was now a lot more intense, and it hurt. She felt pain as if she had cramps all over her hands. She clenched her jaw and made a painful face.

You must bear the pain. Remember that magic always has a price. The pain is what you have to pay now.

The sphere soon began to change hues. It became an intense blue, and Nahia felt something unusual in her hands, as if water were running through them. She had to look at them to make sure she had not actually put them into a river. Both hands were on the sphere, covered by the cloak of energy. There was no water anywhere. Her hands were freezing, and the pain made her almost withdraw them. She had to concentrate in order to maintain them in place.

After a moment, the sphere changed color and turned brown. Nahia felt as if her hands were surrounded by arid earth. After a moment, she began to feel pain as if rugged rocks were rubbing against her palms. Once again, she had to make an effort to keep them in place. The next color the sphere turned was absolutely white, and immediately Nahia felt as if the wind was caressing her hands. She felt well, relieved. All of a sudden, she felt a terrible discharge that ran up both her palms as if lightning had struck them. She did not remove her hands by sheer luck. She ignored the pain as she pushed down toward the sphere, which was already changing color.

The sphere turned red, and Nahia knew what was coming. A tremendous fever went up her hands. They were burning: she felt them charring while the sphere showed deep red. It was very hard for her not to withdraw her hands and bear the pain. Luckily, the color quickly changed to one of light, very bright as if translucent, and luminous. All the pain vanished from her hands at once. She felt a tremendous relief and let out a deep breath. She was enjoying the moment when the sphere changed to a color black as night. Nahia felt her hands vanishing, as if the darkness were taking them, and an intense pain returned.

She held up as much as she could without withdrawing her hands until the sphere changed back to the initial silver. The pain decreased and was replaced, but the tingling, although somewhat painful, was a lot less.

Very well. Your alignment has been evaluated against the four primary elements of magic: Water, Earth, Air, and Fire, as well as the two secondary elements, Light and Darkness. Let us see which one you are aligned with.

The sphere flashed brightly three times and then turned completely red.

Fire is your element, Ande-Zuri-Koa messaged and made everyone feel fire in their bodies for an instant.

"Nahia ... Fire element..." Borne wrote down in his tome.

You may withdraw your hands and return to your place.

Nahia withdrew her hands and looked at them. Nothing had happened to them. She felt greatly relieved. That her element should be fire made complete sense. That was why she burned inside and out. Perhaps that was the reason for her condition. She would have to study it and see whether it had anything to do with it. It also explained why she was a Flameborn, or so she guessed. She sat down and exhaled.

"Daphne... of the Igneous Squad," Borne called.

The Fatum stood up.

"Good luck," Nahia wished in a whisper.

Daphne went up to the sphere. The process was repeated. Daphne bore the pain and did not withdraw her hands from the sphere at any moment. The sphere showed a bright, translucent light as her element.

"Daphne... Light element..." Borne wrote down in his tome.

When Daphne came back to her place, she looked at them, annoyed.

"What am I supposed to do with light?" she asked.

Nahia shrugged.

"No idea."

It was Lily's turn and she underwent the process, also bearing the pain and without withdrawing her hands. In her case, her element was Water. Lily came back to her place, very pleased.

"Blue suits me very well," she said, smiling.

Aiden was next, and he went to the test confident he would be excellent. He was aligned with the Air element, which pleased him.

"I'll be able to create storms with my magic," he told them.

"You're already a torment, so that's not news," Daphne told him.

"Storm, not torment," Aiden corrected her.

"She's pulling your leg," Lily laughed.

Ivo took the test next. They already knew he would not withdraw his hands. He was aligned with the earth element. It suited him. He sat down with a smile on his face.

Finally, Taika's turn came. He passed the test and was aligned with the element of Darkness.

"I don't know what I'll be able to do with that type of magic," Taika said with a shrug.

The others looked at one another. None were able to give him an idea because they had no clue.

When the Igneous Squad finished, it was the turn of the Searing and then the Ardent. One by one, all their members passed the test and their elemental alignment was determined.

Now you know the elemental alignment of your power. You will have realized that for most, this coincides with the color of your scales. The power was already manifesting in your body, and the scales indicate the element you have an affinity with. Now you know with certainty. There are a few whose scales' color does not coincide with the result of today's test. This might be for two reasons. One: that you are an exception, a singularity, and the color of your scales is indicative of a power even greater which will manifest later on. Second, that you have more than one affinity and that the one shown by your scales will also appear later on. In either case, you have nothing to fear. It is really a blessing, since you will be more powerful than the rest who only have one elemental affinity.

Ande-Zuri-Kao paused so they could all assimilate the information it had transmitted. Nahia realized that she had golden scales and her affinity was fire. This made her into a singular case. Although Ande-Zuri-Kao assured her she had nothing to worry about, she did worry. Her squad comrades all had scales that matched the elemental alignment they had received, and not only those of her squad but the other squads too.

"One singularity... Nahia... Golden Scales," Borne wrote down.

They all looked at her, and Nahia wished the earth would open and swallow her.

Now that you know your element, it is time to start using it. Igneous Squad, come forward.

Nahia looked at her comrades, who were as surprised as her. They stood up and stepped forward.

I want you all to create a sphere of energy like we have been doing in class. Go ahead.

The six took out their Learning Pearls and, closing their eyes, sought the bright, powerful dragon in the center of their chests. They concentrated and opened their other hand, creating the sphere of energy over their palm with the help of the Learning Pearls, which flashed in silver-white. The size of the ball of energy they were able to create now, after all the practice, was considerably large.

Very well. The spheres you have created are of pure energy, and that is not the most efficient, or the most powerful way to create them. What I want you to do is destroy them and create new ones, only this time you will use the alignment with your own element to create them. Go ahead.

One by one, they destroyed the balls of energy. They started to create them anew. Nahia called upon the dragon of power inside her and summoned a fire element ball. The Learning Pearl shone brightly, and a moment later a ball of fire was hovering above the palm of her right hand. She watched it, stunned. The ball burned and looked quite intimidating. Daphne created her ball, and it shone with a light so bright it was blinding. It looked like she had created a star in her hand. They had to look away to avoid being blinded. Lily's ball was as blue as the ocean, and inside it looked like the wavy sea itself. Aiden created a white ball which contained thunder and lightning trying to escape. Ivo created a brown ball filled with thousands of stones and pieces of rock that seemed to have a life of their own. Finally, Taika created a ball so black it appeared to devour all light around it.

Good work. Keep them stable. Borne, place the target.

"Right... away..." the Exarbor went as fast as he could.

While they were all controlling their elemental balls, Borne placed the target on the wall. Once he did so, he withdrew.

Throw your elemental ball with your hand against the target. Do it in line-up order.

Nahia was the first. She looked at the target, then at her ball of fire, and with a fluid movement she threw it, her mind and arm in perfect harmony. The ball went straight to the target. When it hit, there was an explosion of fire, which not only destroyed it but consumed everything around it in flames. Nahia threw her head back in surprise. The explosion had been a lot bigger than the energy sphere she usually practiced with. And the flames were a lot more dangerous.

As you can see, when you apply elemental magic, the effects are a lot more powerful. Next.

Borne placed a new target and signaled that it was ready. Daphne's ball was one of blinding light. Upon bursting against the target, her sphere destroyed it and created a light so powerful it momentarily blinded half the class.

The element light might not appear as powerful as fire, but I can assure you that it is. Light magic has very interesting manifestations which we will discover later on. The most important one which I can tell you about right now is that it can heal.

Nahia looked at Daphne, and she returned a glance that said she was not very pleased with the element she had aligned with.

Lily threw her ball at the target, and when it burst it froze everything around it, leaving the target encased in a block of ice. They indicated for Aiden to throw his on the frozen target. When it burst, the thunder and lightning inside were liberated and hit the block of ice, destroying it as well as the target. Aiden was very pleased.

Borne placed another target. Ivo threw his ball, and when it burst thousands of stones and rocks with sharp edges hit the target, destroying it completely. He seemed puzzled by the destructive power he had created. Then Taika was last. His ball was very dark and seemed to have a life of its own. It was frightening to see. He threw it at the target, and when it hit it something very odd happened. There was a dull explosion and the whole area around the target became black. A moment later, it vanished, and when it did the target also disappeared. Taika was taken aback. He stared with eyes wide open at what he had caused.

There you have the six main elements in action. You will learn to use them to perform more powerful attacks and develop other skills. You have a lot to learn and improve.

After the Igneous Squad had finished its demonstrations, it was the Ardent's turn. Its members did the same exercise and showed off their elemental powers. Then it was the turn of the Searing Squad. Once they finished, Ande-Zuri-Koa sent them all to the library to study how to master the use of elemental magic. For once, they were looking forward to studying. The new power they had acquired had them very intrigued. They all wanted to know how to use it and what else they could do with it. They were beginning to understand the true potential of the magic running through their veins.

That evening they were getting ready to sleep in their room in the barracks, but they were all excited with the day's new developments.

"I was frozen by what we learned today," Lily commented as she combed her long jet-black hair.

"In your case, that makes sense," Daphne joked as she was folding her cloak.

Lily looked at her and then realized what she meant.

"Oh, you mean because of my elemental power!"

Daphne smiled.

"I couldn't resist."

"Yeah, that's because you're so light," Lily replied, emphasizing the word "light."

Daphne looked at her with a raised eyebrow.

"Oh, because of light, oh yeah, very funny," she laughed.

Lily laughed too.

"You have an incredible sense of humor, it cheers my heart," Nahia said gratefully.

"If we don't laugh a little in this place, we're going to end up like the rock-head," said Daphne.

"Be quiet, he might hear you. He does have ears." Lily told her.

"I hear you perfectly well," he said from the other side of the screen, "But you're not going to ruin this day. Today my elemental power has manifested, and it's an important one. I'm very pleased."

"Yeah, with yourself. We know that," Daphne replied.

"With what I achieved today. I can encapsulate the power of a storm in a sphere and make it burst, discharging energy upon the enemy. It's awesome."

"It certainly is," Taika agreed. "What we learned today is something that leaves a lot to think about."

"Do you think it'll be dangerous?" Nahia asked. "I'm a little worried about the fire explosion and the flame that breaks out."

"It's not dangerous if you learn to control it. That's what we must do, and we'll be a force in the battlefield."

"Or we might kill ourselves in a moment of distraction," said Ivo.

"I won't make such a mistake. I'll be invincible in battle," Aiden said confidently.

"Of course, how could it be otherwise," Daphne replied.

"The thing is, it gives us power we never imagined we'd have," said Nahia, "or at least I never imagined it. It worries me a little."

"Take it easy. If your fire gets out of hand, you always have me to put it out with my water element. I'm your natural enemy," Lily laughed.

"That's true. Don't go too far away from me, just in case.

"Then I'm Taika's," said Daphne. "I'm light and he's darkness."

"That's right. We're opposing forces of nature," Taika agreed.

"So what happens with Ivo and Aiden, are they opposite forces?" Lily asked.

"You could think of it that way. Lightning can do little against rock," Taika said.

"And rock can do nothing against lightning." said Aiden.

"Seeing it that way, they are indeed neutralized," Daphne said.

"Well, now we have the elements neutralized. Now if we never separate and always form pairs, everything is taken care of," Lily said.

"Poor Ivo," Daphne took pity on him.

"He should be proud of being my opposite, I'm the most powerful," Aiden said proudly.

"Here we go again…" Daphne put her hands to her head.

"We'll learn to control our elemental powers, don't worry," said Taika. "For now, we can all feel very pleased for awakening and discovering them. Let's enjoy this moment. There aren't many joys here, and we have to enjoy the ones we have."

"Well put," Lily said. "Let's rest and dream about our new powers."

"Good night, everyone," said Nahia.

"Good night," the rest replied, almost in unison.

That night, Nahia dreamed that she was capable of throwing enormous balls of fire at the dragons and that they burned when her projectiles exploded against their bodies. She defeated all of them— no one could stop her. The dragons died as she passed by, and she went forward through the battlefield without fear. Nothing could kill her and nothing could get in the way of her goal: a free world, without dragons, with the eight races happy and living in freedom and harmony.

Chapter 42

The winter days went by with all of them making efforts to not fail and stay alive. In the whole academy, there was only one place where it was never cold. Nahia was there that evening, doing her daily routine of physical exercises at the gym. Her arms, legs, and abdominals were sore, but she was happy. She only had one more series of exercises left and then she would be finished for the day. Daphne was with her. The Fatum protested more than she exercised, but even so, she was good company.

"Keep going, I see you. The only way you'll make progress is if you give it your all," Nahia harangued Daphne.

"I haven't stopped. I'm only taking a break between sets," she replied, lying on her back and staring at the ceiling.

"The break between sets is only a moment, not an hour by the sun dial."

"It's already dark, the sun dial doesn't work at this hour," Daphne said.

"What an excuse. Go on with the next set before you get cold."

"Get cold? How am I going to get cold here? Don't you see all these people sweating around us?"

Nahia, also lying on her back, looked around and saw Logan exercising close by. This always cheered her greatly. There was nothing like going to the gym and finding him there. For some reason, her heart rejoiced by simply seeing him. Then she watched him exercise and her joy was even greater. Why? She did not know, but that was how she felt.

"They really go at it, unlike a certain Fatum I know who protests about everything and doesn't even perspire a little."

"Fatum sweat very little, for your information, and female Fatum practically not a drop. In our culture, sweating is considered vulgar and bad manners."

"Sure. In mine, if the sweat is caused by hard work, it's considered a virtue."

"All right, I'm doing the next set, but only so I don't have to listen to you," Daphne grumbled, and turning over she started doing flexions, which she was already pretty good at.

Nahia smiled before turning over and doing planks. Inside the gym, control was more lax than other places in the academy. There were two dragons watching on their lookout towers at the building's entrance and exit but not inside, which gave them some peace only equaled by what they enjoyed in the rooms each squad had at the barracks. Here they could exercise and talk at ease, which was rare at the academy.

Nahia was beginning her last series when she noticed a familiar face approaching.

"Lily! What are you doing here?"

The Scarlatum was approaching with Taika.

"I asked our clever feline to bring me over."

"I couldn't say no. She poured all her charm on me, you know what she's like," Taika said with a shrug.

"Weren't you saying you wouldn't come here, even in chains?" Daphne asked, interrupting her set to talk to her.

Lily sighed.

"I didn't want to prove the blockhead right."

Nahia and Daphne looked at one another blankly.

"The idiot said when we started out that you wouldn't hold up two seasons, and that I wouldn't last three."

"He did say that," Taika said.

"And that's why you haven't come sooner?" Nahia could not believe her.

Because of that, yes, and because I thought I didn't need it. But since we've started learning how to use the shield I'm having problems, serious ones. My body isn't holding up."

"We understand," Nahia said, nodding.

"I'm coping better already," Daphne told her. "But it's because I'm coming here and exercising."

"Well, that seems to be my fate too."

"One all three of us share," Nahia said, smiling.

"One of sweat and tears," Daphne said with a horrified face.

Lily laughed, and Nahia joined her.

"I'll leave you now, have a good time," Taika said and left.

"What torture do you recommend?" Lily asked her two friends.

"The same one we've both been through," Nahia replied.

Lily snorted.

331

"Just think, soon you'll be stronger, and then you'll be able to tell that marble-head he was wrong," said Daphne.

"Ha! That'll inspire me to put in the effort."

"Come on then, I'll explain what you have to do," Nahia offered.

Nahia watched her two comrades for a while and corrected a couple of their positions so they would do the exercises better. Then she left them practicing. She finished her set and sat down on the floor to watch Logan fighting on the mat with Markus, the Human from the Hurricane Squad, White Squadron. They were both strong and agile. They were practicing unarmed combat, and each was quite skilled. They were really going at it.

Once they finished and Markus left, Nahia greeted Logan.

"What a training session!" she said.

Logan smiled when he saw her and came over. He sat down on the floor beside Nahia.

"In order to improve, you have to find good opponents."

"And really fight."

"True." Nahia nodded.

"You're already doing the exercise set like an expert. And I see that you now have two pupils," Logan looked at Daphne and Lily, who were exercising amid grunts of pain.

"Because you've helped me and taught me. Now that I think about it, I haven't even thanked you. I am very grateful to you for your teachings and help."

"You're welcome," Logan waved it aside.

"How do you see our odds for surviving?" Nahia asked, always worried about this.

"We only have to hold up a little more and we will have survived three seasons."

Nahia nodded.

"Yeah, but there's still one, the hardest."

"Well, it'll be in spring, and that's always encouraging."

"True, spring will cheer us up. But at the end we'll have the War Test... we'll go to the front..."

Logan nodded thoughtfully.

"It'll be one mission per squadron. Don't leave your leader's side and you'll survive."

"I've heard rumors that our leader chooses the most dangerous missions…"

"Yes, the Red Dragon has that reputation. So does mine. Even so, we have to carry out their orders and not fail."

"Yeah… and if the mission is too dangerous?"

"Don't think about the danger, only about finishing it. Stay with your squad and do everything they tell you."

"Sure, because if I don't my leader is capable of leaving me on the front."

"Or killing you right there."

"You think it'd do that?" Nahia looked at him, wide eyed.

"I've heard stories, it's happened. More than once. If you dishonor them on the battlefield, they kill you."

Nahia snorted.

"That's all we needed. If the enemy doesn't kill us, our leader will."

"That's why we must complete the mission. Not give either of our leaders the opportunity."

"I hope we can…"

"We will," Logan promised, and he put both hands up to his forehead and did the Butterfly of Victory.

Nahia was touched. With misty eyes, she also made the Butterfly of Victory.

Logan got up.

"We will survive," he promised and left.

That evening, after dinner, they were already in the dorm and getting ready for sleep when Taika rapped his knuckles on the screen that separated the two groups.

"We're all decent, come in."

Taika came in and stood at the partition.

"Everything all right?" Nahia asked him. She was sitting on her bed with her legs crossed.

"Something's wrong, or he wouldn't have that look on his face or be here so late," Daphne said, who was already lying in her bed, ready to sleep.

Taika sighed and nodded.

"I'm having problems with my magic, which I believe is pretty obvious."

"Yeah, that black magic of yours is most strange, even a bit

333

grotesque," Lily said.

"I didn't choose it, believe me. I'd rather have one of yours."

"I believe you, and I pity you a little," Daphne made a horrified face.

"Well... I've tried to study and practice by myself, but I don't seem to make any progress in its dominion. And that's why, after seeing Lily reach out for help today, I thought I'd set aside my tiger pride and do the same."

"Wow, that does you credit. Good for you," Lily congratulated him.

"So, I need help and you three are good with magic..."

"Nahia and Daphne are good, I'm just average," Lily admitted.

"I'll be delighted to help with anything I can," said Nahia.

"You can certainly count on me too," Daphne said.

"Don't you dare practice magic in here," Aiden said from the other side of the screen.

"Why on earth are you listening!" Daphne shouted at him.

"Because you're not trustworthy! No magic in here! I can just imagine you creating an uncontrollable fire and all of us being burnt alive," Aiden said forebodingly.

"This time, the Drakonid is right. It's forbidden to do magic in the barracks," Ivo told them. "For reasons of risk for everyone."

"So where can we practice magic safely?" Nahia asked.

"At the library," Ivo told them. "On the top level there are special halls. If you ask one of the Exarbor for permission, they'll let you practice there."

Nahia, Daphne, and Lily looked at one another blankly.

"And how do you know that?" Daphne asked him.

"Because I use one. I'm the worst at magic in our whole group, so I asked one of the Exarbor for help and he explained all about the practice halls."

"You might have told us," Lily chided him.

"I just did."

"Go back to your meditations, we're not happy with you," Daphne said.

"Delighted," Ivo replied, who did not seem to catch the irony of the comment or else ignored it completely.

"Well, tomorrow after classes we can go practice in the library," Nahia offered.

"I really appreciate it," Taika bowed his head.

"You helped me and now it's my turn to help you, a favor must always be returned."

"If it's in good will," Ivo added.

"Weren't you meditating?" Daphne said.

"I am, but you talk too much and too loud. It's difficult to concentrate."

"We'll start tomorrow and help you with your magic," Nahia told Taika.

"Besides, with Nahia and me, you'll improve at lightning speed," Daphne promised.

"That, or you'll die blinded amid flames," Aiden said from his bed on the other side.

"Shut up, rock-head!" Daphne and Lily cried at the same time.

The following day after classes, Nahia, Daphne, and Taika went to the Library of Dragon Magic and spoke to one of the Exarbor there.

"We'd like to use a room to practice magic," said Nahia.

"You are... first-years... of regular magic?" the Exarbor asked them.

"Yes, that's it, correct," Nahia nodded.

"Names... squad... squadron."

"Daphne, Taika, and Nahia of the Igneous Squad, Red Squadron."

The Exarbor opened a tome, flipped the pages, and with his finger wrote down something in green in one of the sections.

"Very well... come with... me... you can't go without an escort..."

Daphne snorted.

"It's going to take an eternity to follow him," she whispered in Nahia's ear while the Exarbor was coming out from behind the counter.

"Patience... is the greatest of virtues..." the Exarbor told them. Somehow he had heard her comment.

"And good hearing comes in second," murmured Daphne.

The Exarbor led them to the top level, up three spiral staircases.

Once there, he took them to a silver door. He opened it, and they entered a room entirely lined with silver.

"Reinforced walls... against elemental magic," he told them. "It prevents fires and similar problems."

Nahia, Daphne, and Taika looked at one another, pleasantly surprised.

In the middle of the room, there was a large white sphere. The Exarbor went over to it and touched it with his hand. The sphere activated and began to emit pulses.

"It's a sphere... of protection... if it picks up harmful magic... it tries to cancel it."

"It tries? Doesn't it always succeed?" Daphne wanted to know.

"In the world of magic... absolutes... don't exist... you ought to know that. Study more..."

Daphne looked at the Exarbor with wide eyes. She was about to say something, but Nahia pulled on her sleeve and she remained quiet.

"We appreciate the advice," Taika said.

"When you are done... come to register... on the way out..."

"And if we forget?" Daphne asked.

"Then... you are considered dead... from a magic accident... and your leader is notified..."

"Oh, then don't worry, we won't forget," Nahia said. "Nothing will happen to us."

"Sure... they all say that..."

"Are there accidents?"

"Of course... there are accidents... you are experimenting with magic..."

"Oh, great," Daphne made a face that meant it was all wonderful.

"Good practice..." the Exarbor took his leave and walked away.

"This ancient tree head is so charming," Daphne complained.

"He explained things as they are, whether we like them or not," Taika commented.

"True," Nahia agreed.

"Good, let's get down to business," said Daphne.

"I hope we won't need that sphere," said Nahia.

"Everything'll be all right. Come, Taika. Concentrate and bring out that blackness of yours," Daphne said.

"Calmly and carefully," added Nahia.

"I'll start by creating a sphere of energy and then make it elemental."

"Take it easy. Remember that I have the elemental magic that neutralizes yours. If the darkness gets out of hand, I'll destroy it with my light."

Taika nodded.

"Let's begin."

They worked for hours until an Exarbor came to tell them they had to leave the room. There were no accidents, and Taika felt like he was making some progress with Nahia's and Daphne's help. He still had a long way to go in order to dominate the blackness he generated, but now he felt like it was possible thanks to his comrades' help.

Chapter 43

Winter ended, and spring was hard on its heels. Nahia could smell it in the air, and that cheered her up. They were on their way to practice with weapons without having had time to fully digest their breakfast because, once again, their leader had extended the practice of line-up and morning parading.

Irma-Mar-Gaud and the three instructors were waiting for the class of dagger and shield. They had been practicing for weeks, and now not only did each one have their own dagger, they also had their own shield they were responsible for.

Today, you will learn to combine your elemental power with the martial power of weapons. It is a lethal combination which only those of dragon blood have at their disposal, the great brown dragoness messaged, capturing everyone's attention at once.

The three instructors stepped forward and showed their shields and daggers to the squads.

Everyone, line up before the instructors and show them your weapons like they have shown theirs to you.

The Fatum instructor stood in front of the Igneous Squad, so Nahia and her comrades lined up before her. The Ardent Squad did the same before the Human instructor, and the Searing lined up before the Tauruk instructor.

Now, I want you all to put your shield across your back and take out your Learning Pearl. Do not put away your dagger.

This order took them by surprise. In their weapon training classes they had never used magic, so they never used their Learning Pearls. Since they all had to carry them at all times, however, they had them at their waists. They slung the shields across their backs, using a strap that crossed their chest, then took out the Learning Pearls and waited with the pearl in one hand and dagger in the other.

You must awake your inner dragon and send energy, your elemental energy, to the edge of your dagger. Each one of you must send the elemental energy you are aligned with. Do not only send pure energy, because that will not be valid for this exercise. It has to be elemental. Cover the whole edge of your weapon with it. Come on.

Nahia looked at the dagger in her right hand and then the Learning Pearl in her left. Concentrating, she awoke her inner dragon. She sent an amount of energy to the edge, enveloping it as she summoned her fire element she was aligned to. Her mind led the energy and made sure it only surrounded the edge and nothing else. All of a sudden, the Learning Pearl flashed and the edge of her dagger began to burn with an intense flame. She had to stretch out her arm to not burn herself. (I believe she is unable to actually burn however, due to her special ability) She watched her dagger, which now looked like a fiery short sword, and was amazed.

She looked at her comrades and saw they still had not succeeded. She waited, watching them out of the corner of her eye.

Once you succeed, make sure you regulate the intensity and energy you are sending to the weapon. It is not good practice to incinerate yourselves or your fellow squadmates.

Nahia regulated the power of the flame, covering her dagger, and controlled the energy she was sending to keep the fire alive. It was a little complicated, since she did not have the skill to open or close her flow of energy yet. She finally managed to create a small, constant stream.

After a moment, Daphne managed to cover the edge of her dagger with a light so powerful it was blinding.

"Regulate your light or you'll blind us all," the instructor told her, who looked much older and more weathered than Daphne. She also looked surlier.

Daphne nodded and tried to control the light her dagger emitted.

"Less intensity, control it," the Fatum told her.

With an effort clear from her frown, Daphne managed to reduce the powerful glow she had created until all that was left was an intense but tolerable glow to the eye. Lily covered the edge of her dagger with water freezing at the ends. It was a very curious effect. A layer of live water, undulating, covered the edge, and a second, wider layer of ice and frost covered the first. Nahia had no doubt that if that layer touched anything, it would instantly freeze it.

"Control the temperature, or you'll freeze the whole weapon and even your own hand," the instructor told her.

Lily clenched her jaw and struggled to do as the instructor told her. The layer of ice stopped expanding. The layer of blue ocean water looked like the undulating sea itself.

Aiden created a layer around both edges of his weapon that contained lightning that seemed to be trying to escape. If that edge touched anything, the lightning would leap from the weapon to whatever it touched. The lightning was contained in a dark cloud that looked like a mini-storm.

No matter how unbelievable the elemental effect you have created may seem to you, do not think of touching those edges. Not only because you would hurt yourselves, but because you will look stupid in front of everyone else. And stupidity is punished, in case you have forgotten.

Ivo managed to surround the edges with a layer of fine rock. Inside, pebbles and pieces of rocks with sharp edges flew at great speed. They seemed as if they wanted to break through the layer of rock containing them and fly off.

Finally, Taika created a layer with a black substance inside it, which moved like a shadow with a life of its own. It looked like death itself covering the edge. Nahia was struck dumb. She was not the only one—Taika himself watched what he had just created with eyes that looked as if they were going to pop out of their sockets.

Gradually, all the members of the three squads managed to cover their daggers with the elemental energy they were aligned to.

Now your weapons are much more powerful than before. The dagger is capable of cutting with its edge and piercing with its tip, and now, besides the physical damage, you can give it an elemental edge, which you have just added to your weapon. Instructors, show them.

The Fatum instructor stepped forward and stood in front of Nahia, presenting her shield.

"Hit it," the instructor ordered her.

Nahia obeyed and delivered a thrust to the shield. When she hit it, they heard the usual sound of steel hitting steel. But something else happened: part of the shield began to burn. It was as if they had poured spirits on it and upon contact with the flame it had caught fire. She moved toward Daphne.

"Hit my shield, but close your eyes when you do. The rest of you, watch out."

Daphne nodded and hit. When she did, there was the sound of metal against metal and a flash of powerful, explosive light. They all had to look away.

The instructor went on to Lily. Her blow froze the middle of the shield. When she moved onto Aiden, his blow caused a lightning bolt to leap from his weapon to the shield. The Fatum felt the discharge and had to shake her arm. Ivo's blow sent a stone at the shield, and it sounded as if a thousand pieces of rock were hitting it, leaving the shield with a bunch of dents. The final blow came from Taika, and his strike produced a very odd effect. When he hit the shield, the black substance surrounding his weapon moved along the shield like black tentacles wanting to entrap it. The instructor withdrew the shield quickly to get rid of them.

The rest of the pupils did the exercise, and when they had all had a go they remained still, expectant.

With each blow, the elemental power of the weapon will decrease. In order to maintain the elemental power around your weapon in all its intensity, you will have to send more energy and keep up the effect. Now you will practice the attacks with elemental weapons in pairs, working on your control over the power you must send to the weapon. It is very important to maintain your mental control while fighting. Whoever does not manage to control his or her power and allows themselves to be driven by the intensity or the feelings of the fight might end up dead or consumed by their own elemental power. In the fight, fury and rage might be your allies or your worst enemies. That is something you must learn to control.

"In pairs now," the Fatum instructor ordered them.

Nahia paired with Daphne, Lily with Aiden, and Ivo with Taika.

The instructor indicated who was to attack first and who needed to defend themselves. Those who were on the defense put away their Learning Pearls and unslung their shields.

"Begin," she ordered.

Nahia attacked and Daphne prepared her shield. When she hit it, there was a relatively large flame. When she withdrew the dagger to attack again, Nahia noticed that the flame was less intense. She sent more energy to intensify the elemental fire effect. The next attack, she sent another flame through the shield, and as she prepared to attack again she recharged the dagger with more energy so the flame would remain powerful. Nahia wondered how much energy she could send to the dagger—she did not want to overload it for fear of hurting Daphne.

Beside the two of them, she could see Lily smiling as she froze half of Aiden's shield with every blow of her dagger. Ivo, for his part, was denting Taika's shield with his earth attacks. They continued practicing for a good while. Nahia realized her inner energy was decreasing with every attack, consuming itself. If she kept hitting, she would run out of energy and her dragon would die out.

"Change roles," the Fatum instructor called.

Daphne attacked and Nahia protected herself with her shield. When she delivered a blow, her dagger gave off a dazzling flash. Nahia had to close her eyes, but it was already too late—she was blinded. If Daphne had wanted to kill her, if this had been a real fight, she would be dead.

"I can't… see anything," she said so Daphne would give her a moment.

"Stop," the instructor ordered. "You have to control the power of your elemental power. Light is a very powerful power, more than most. You can damage the eyes of your opponent if you're not careful. Control it," she told Daphne.

"Yes… I didn't know …" Daphne nodded.

Beside them, Aiden delivered a blow that made a bolt of lightning fall on Lily's shield. The shield protected her from the blow, but not from the discharge. Her shield fell to the floor while she shook her arm.

Taika hit Ivo's shield and some black tentacles spread throughout the shield. Ivo stared at it with wide eyes. The blackness covered the whole shield to the point where Ivo had to drop it before it spread up his arm.

"Don't infect me with that darkness," he told Taika, who was as dumbstruck as Ivo.

They kept practicing until the instructors told them to stop.

Now that you see the power the elements add to your physical attacks, it is time for you to also understand the advantages of that power when applied to defense. I want you to envelop your shields with the power of your element and use it to defend yourselves.

Nahia was very surprised. Using fire to attack had crossed her mind, but surrounding her shield in flames had not. Would it not consume itself? She figured it would get so hot that it would be impossible to wield. She was about to find out.

"Same pairs, use elemental shields," the instructor ordered.

Nahia concentrated and sent elemental energy to surround her whole shield. She did it so the flames only covered the outer side of the shield. She did not touch the inner side. The shield began to burn on the outside. It was very intimidating.

Daphne threw her head back and calculated how to hit so the

flames would not reach her hand. She delivered a direct thrust with her elemental dagger of light. Upon contact, there was a blinding light and at the same time a defensive flame from the shield. Nahia had to step back, dazzled. Daphne had to step back so the flame would not burn her arm.

The result was similar with their comrades. Aiden hit Lily's frozen shield and the bolt of lightning broke off part of the frozen protection. At the same time, the ice began to freeze the dagger and Aiden had to quickly withdraw. Taika struck Ivo's shield, which was covered with pure rock, and the blackness managed to break away part of the protection while some rocky rubble flew off toward Taika, who had to protect himself.

They switched from offense to defense, and now when Nahia hit with her fiery dagger she received a discharge of light with every blow on Daphne's shield, which shone with blinding intensity. She had to stop attacking because she could not see a thing. Lily attacked with her frozen dagger and Aiden's shield protected by lightning discharged upon her. After the first attack she no longer wanted to get hit by any more electrical shocks. Ivo hit Taika's black shield, and with each blow the blackness tried to swallow his dagger. The Tauruk ended up struggling with some black tentacles that wanted to devour his weapon. He managed to hold onto it, but he stopped attacking.

The other two squads were having similar struggles. They were all trying to adapt to the situation and the advantages and disadvantages of the elemental attacks and defenses. The faces and gestures of surprise were constant.

When they finished the exercises, the brown dragoness addressed them all.

Now that you know how to apply your elemental power to the dagger and shield, both in offense and defense, I want you to practice and improve your control. You must be capable of attacking and defending with your dagger and shield loaded with elemental power and send energy to support them both. It is not easy and requires a lot of practice, and you will practice until wielding your elemental weapons is second nature.

"You heard. Now practice. Change partners," the Fatum instructor ordered.

Nahia sighed. This was going to be intense. They would have to be careful, because now they could really hurt one another. They had already run the risk of cuts and stings before, but now it was all kinds of elemental attacks and defenses. She was not wrong. Before finishing the class, Draider, the Drakonid of the Ardent Squad, and Beck, the Fatum of the Searing Squad, had to be taken to the infirmary, one with burns and the other one with a frozen arm.

That evening, dinner became more entertaining thanks to the new abilities they had developed in weapons training. No one was eating the excellent roast lamb except Ivo; they were still awestruck and wanted to discuss what they had learned among themselves.

"I can't believe we were able to fight with our elemental powers like we did today," Daphne said, still dumbstruck, shaking her head.

Taika nodded repeatedly.

"It's been quite interesting and surprising."

"My elemental power is the best by far," Aiden proclaimed proudly.

"You mean for offense or defense?" Lily asked him.

"Both. I have the elemental power of air. I can create lightning storms and encapsulate them in a sphere or apply it to daggers and shields. It's awesome."

"I don't know, I prefer Nahia's fire," Daphne said. "You get distracted and she burns you whole."

"Yours isn't bad either," Nahia told her. You've blinded me four times. I didn't know what I was attacking or who I was defending myself from. I couldn't see anything. I still see big white flies. In fact, I'm looking at the plate with the lamb and can't see it."

"Then I'll help you, pass it over," Ivo said with a smile, reaching with his huge arm and beastly hand.

"Don't be such a glutton, you still have a piece of your own serving," Lily chided him.

"This won't last a moment," Ivo replied. "Besides, inner peace begins once the stomach is served."

"I don't know what philosopher guides you, but that saying doesn't sound too profound to me..." Lily said.

Ivo shrugged and went on eating.

"I'm not saying that blinding your opponent isn't a valuable power, I'm only saying that fire seems more powerful."

"I still think a bolt of lightning is more powerful than a flame," Aiden insisted, very pleased with himself.

"What would happen if I drenched him from head to toe with my water power?" Lily suggested.

"Who, granite-head?" Daphne asked.

"Yeah, when he's about to deliver his lightning."

"Well, from what I understand water is a conductor for lightning, so most likely he would receive the discharge," Taika said.

"There! He's the most powerful!" Daphne mocked him.

"I'll make sure he's drenched all day," Lily laughed mischievously.

"That's not true! Since when is water bad for discharges? Don't they go hand in hand with storms?"

Taika raised both hands.

"I'm only saying what I believe is the truth. I don't know for sure, but there are people who have died when lightning hit a river or a lake where they were bathing."

"It also rings true to me," Ivo said, and then he got up to go for a second serving.

"You're only saying that because you know I have the best elemental power and you're envious."

"Yes, of getting struck by lightning in the rain," Daphne laughed.

"Or taking a bath in the sink," Lily joined in the laughter.

Aiden got up, all discombobulated.

"You two are insufferable," he told them and left.

"Oops, we've offended the little dragon," Daphne said and made a contrite face.

"I can't believe how vain he is," Lily said.

"I think the most singular power is Taika's," said Nahia.

"It is very unique," Taika agreed. "I still don't know how to use it very well. It's as if it has a life of its own. It tends to darken everything around it."

"It kind of gives me the willies, that power of yours," Lily admitted. "Very dark."

"I don't blame you. It is dark," Taika agreed.

"What's important is that we learn how to use them so we can apply them to our weapons," Daphne said.

"Yeah. I've had to ask for another shield from the administration building. With his rocks, Ivo left mine useless," Taika commented.

"It must be the metal that isn't very strong," Ivo excused himself and went on eating nonchalantly.

"Or perhaps you're a little too brutish," Lily said, giggling.

"Nahhh, it's the metal that's poor quality," Ivo said, convinced, and went on eating.

The others smiled and went on debating the possibilities of applying their elemental powers to their daggers and shields. When they were leaving, Nahia saw Maika at her table and made the Butterfly of Victory. Maika saw it and returned the greeting with a smile. Nahia went to bed that day happy, a true novelty.

Chapter 44

As soon as the sun was out, the Red Squadron formed up before their leader as they did every morning. Nahia guessed they would have another session of lined-up parading around the grounds, as they had been doing for some time. They were not the only ones their leader had doing this exercise: the rest of squadrons also did. She hoped they would have some time for breakfast; she always liked that moment of the day, not only for the food but because she was able to greet Ana, Maika, and Logan, whom she could not see very often.

Today is a special day, Red Squadron, one in which you must behave with the utmost discipline and honor, Irakas-Gorri-Gaizt announced, and the message came with a feeling of great importance.

Nahia looked at Daphne and Lily who were beside her in the lineup, and her comrades looked back at her with uncertainty. This announcement was new, and like almost everything new that happened at the Drakoros Academy, it would not be good.

Today we will leave the academy and perform an escort mission and another of surveillance, both of the utmost importance.

The news affected the squadron: they were not expecting this. The members of the three squads were trying to hide their surprise and muffling cries of anxiety. Nahia was exchanging glances with her comrades. They were going outside of the academy. This was something they had never even considered. First because it was forbidden, and second because they had all taken for granted that once you entered the academy you never left until the war mission at the end of the year.

You will follow my orders at all times and without the least hesitation. If you dishonor me today, I swear I will bite your heads off.

Whatever it was that was going to take place, it was obvious that it was important and that Irakas-Gorri-Gaizt did not want to look bad. This was not good for them, since they still made mistakes sometimes, more so if the situation was difficult.

You will march in perfect formation all the way. That is what I have prepared you for. I do not want a single misstep or loss of balance the whole way.

We march at my signal.

Nahia was trying to stay calm, but she was finding it more difficult with every passing moment. All of a sudden, the great gates of the academy opened at the south wall. The White Squadron began to move, led by their leader. They were followed at once by the Black Squadron, also led by their leader, which was followed by the Blue Squadron. They then realized it was not only an exercise for the Red Squadron but that all the first-year squadrons were participating.

We march. Now. Follow my step. Igneous Squad, after me, with Ardent Squad in the middle and Searing Squad closing ranks. In formation! Move on! Irakas-Gorri-Gaizt ordered and started to move, following the Blue Squadron. Nahia and her comrades marched, following their leader in a parade they had been practicing for a long time without knowing why. Well, today they were going to find out the reason for so many morning martial marches. They were only hoping they were not going to war. No, Irakas-Gorri-Gaizt had said it was an escort and surveillance mission. There would be no fighting, or at least so she hoped.

They left the academy, the six squadrons forming a long retinue. As soon as they came out, a cart joined them. Nahia saw it out of the corner of her eye just before losing sight of it at the end of the line. It was a closed cart pulled by four horses and driven by two Tergnomus. She wondered what they were taking with them and why. Supplies? Weapons? Some gift? She did not know but guessed she would find out later on.

They marched south. Daphne and Lily were smiling; they seemed happy to be leaving the academy and breathing the outside air. Spring was arriving, and the truth was, that filling their lungs with the breeze of the landscape around them, made them feel very well. They moved at a martial rhythm and without stopping until they reached the Square of Neutrality. The journey reminded Nahia of how they had arrived at the academy. She felt she should thank Maika, Ana, and Logan again for carrying her practically all the way.

When they arrived at the square, instead of going south toward the Bridge of the Sky through which they had arrived, they turned left. They left the square and went on along a wide cobbled avenue. On both sides of the road were thick forests, oaks on one side and beech on the other. Nahia would have given anything right then to lose herself in that forest, looking for medicinal plants and mushrooms like she used to do at home. That world—home—seemed so far away to her now, almost alien. She was going to lose all the skills she had for healing, and that made her sad. So many years with her grandmother, learning everything that had to do with healing plants and healing, only to lose it now, to have it all supplanted by weapons and destructive magic. It was a contradiction, and it saddened her greatly. She promised herself to try and not forget everything she had learned. For that, she would need books about healing. Perhaps they had some at the library. She would have to ask and see whether they would let her consult them.

They marched on all morning at the same rhythm and formation. After noon, they glimpsed a building on their left that froze the blood in their veins. It was the upper part of an enormous sphere that stretched over forty-five feet in diameter. They could only see the upper half, and it looked as if the lower half was buried underground. They had already seen large spheres in this world, but none like this one. The left half of the sphere was silver-colored and the right half gold-colored. The sides were so bright in the noon sunlight that they all had to squint to protect their eyes from the flashes it gave off.

A wide avenue, also half silver, half gold, led to the great building.

Attention! We stop, now! Irakas-Gorri-Gaizt ordered.

The Red Squadron stopped right before the avenue that accessed the building. The Blue Squadron had stopped after the entrance avenue, so there was a space between the two squadrons.

This is the Pearl of Auspices where the Great Oracle resides. We will now wait for his eminence to join us, and then we will escort him.

This left Nahia speechless. Were *they* going to escort the Great Oracle? Why them? Where? What for? A thousand questions came to her mind. The main one being, why them. They were first-year pupils of the academy. This honor should be reserved for the third-years, should it not? Or by great Dragon Blood Warlocks, but not for them.

While she was thinking all this, a huge silver dragon, very bright, came out of the Pearl of Auspices. The building did not seem to have a door; it was somehow similar to the library at the academy, but the gigantic dragon had come from within. It was the largest dragon Nahia had seen so far. Not only that, but it was the largest and most resplendent she could imagine. It had to be over three hundred feet long, and it was silver, with golden streaks that ran down its back, sides, and wings.

As it approached, they noticed it was an ancient dragon. Nahia could not say why she had this impression, but its face, how slowly it walked and how gigantic it was, made it clear it had to be thousands of years old. Something significant she noticed as this gigantic being moved toward them was that its wings looked crumpled and dry. It did not look like it could fly.

It reached the retinue and they saw how terribly big it was. Its eyes, which they could now see better, were silver with gold irises. It was amazing. It gave off an aura of power that was almost palpable, silver with sparks of gold. It ran down its whole body, from the head to the long tail. It looked like a mythological being—it did not seem real.

Everyone, on your knees! Show respect before the Great Oracle! Irakas-Gorri-Gaizt ordered, and they all dropped to their knees without breaking formation. One thing that shocked Nahia was that they were not the only ones who bent down—their leaders did too. For a long moment, they all bowed deeply to that arcane being.

All rise and continue on our way. The destination awaits us, the message of the Great Oracle reached them, so deep, far away, and full of wisdom that it seemed like a god speaking from its distant home.

On your feet, ready to march! The order came from Irakas-Gorri-Gaizt.

The first three squadrons started to leave. The Red Dragon did not give the order to follow, so they waited. The great silver dragon began to follow the Blue Squadron, and they waited for its gigantic body to pass by. Once it had, Irakas-Gorri-Gaizt gave the order to go on.

The retinue went on along the wide avenue, and Nahia understood what their leader had meant by an escort mission. They had to escort the thousand-year-old Great Oracle some place. Nahia was beginning to suspect what the place was.

They marched on for a long while, following the avenue. The Great Oracle moved with extreme slowness, but because it was so gigantic they did not notice. They went up a shallow slope, and once they arrived at the top, they saw an enormous round temple in the distance. The avenue ended at the majestic building.

If the Pearl of Auspices had shocked them, the temple they saw now was even more impressive. It was twice as big and its shape was unique. The central part of the building formed a great ring. Around the ring were five smaller, adjacent rings. Each one of the five had a part open toward the great central ring. Surrounding it all was a great circle with five access doors. The whole structure looked like white marble.

They arrived at the temple and received the order to stop. The whole retinue did so, and the Great Oracle headed inside along a large path that led to the temple's entrance.

This is the Temple of Harmony. It is a place of great importance, Irakas-Gorri-Gaizt messaged to them all.

They all looked at the temple, in awe at how huge and majestic it was.

All of a sudden, they saw appear in the sky, a colossal red dragon over a hundred and fifty feet long. It flew over the temple and they could see it was a powerful, mature dragon that gave off a crimson aura of power. On its head it wore a silver crown with rubies.

The guests of this meeting are beginning to arrive. Listen to me carefully. The temple has five entrances. Each one of the squadrons will cover one of them, and the sixth squadron will remain here at the access path. You will cover the north entrance, the one that corresponds to the dragon you are watching flying over our heads. That is King Erre-Gor-Mau, leader of the Gondra Clan and monarch of its realm in the sky.

They all looked up at the great, powerful dragon king flying over the temple in great circles. Nahia swallowed with difficulty. That was the king of the Gondra Clan, and the Humans were its domain. It came from the realm in the sky she had seen at her home.

The dragons cannot approach the temple—it is a neutral place which only kings and the Great Oracle may set foot on, so I will not go with you. I will wait here. Do not dishonor me. Line up in front of the door and make sure no one tries to enter or spy on the meeting of the five clan kings. It is a task for a guard of honor. No one will try anything, so you will only need to line up and keep your eyes open, nothing else.

They all watched the dragon as they absorbed the orders they must follow. It was the strongest and most impressive dragon they had seen yet. The powerful red dragon came down to land on one of the adjacent circles, the one to the north.

Go and do your duty. Now, and always maintain formation.

The Red Squadron went toward the north gate without breaking formation. They stood in front of it with their backs to the gate. The great red dragon gave a roar that left them all shaking.

All the squadrons, except the Bright Squad, went to stand at the gate they had been instructed to watch. They did so quickly and efficiently.

In the sky, another enormous dragon appeared. This one was white and also wore a crown. It glided over the temple, and after checking that everything seemed in order, it descended and landed on one of the adjacent circles. Not a moment had passed before another dragon king appeared in the sky. This one was blue and also powerful and huge.

Soon, the five dragon kings arrived and occupied their places in the building. Nahia sighed. Now they only had to stay lined up until the meeting ended. She relaxed a little and looked at her comrades, who were also beginning to relax.

Suddenly, Nahia began to feel a tingling all over her body. It was a weird feeling, as if something in the air around her were pricking her. She raised her gaze and saw that above the whole outer circle of the temple a silver dome had formed. She looked up and saw that the dome shone with golden flashes—it was pure energy.

"You see that dome over the temple?" she whispered to Daphne and Lily.

"Who wouldn't see it, as big and bright as it is!" Daphne said.

"It's a silver color which makes it look as if it's been polished consistently for a month," Lily said.

"Yeah, but I'm more interested in the golden flashes," Nahia told them.

"What golden flashes?" Daphne asked blankly.

Nahia looked again at the dome behind them. It did shine silver, but over the silver flashes were others in gold, more intense.

"You don't see the golden flashes?"

Lily and Daphne stared at the dome for a moment. Then they turned to Nahia and shook their heads.

"It only flashes silver," Daphne said.

"All this marching is making you see things," Lily joked.

Then Nahia felt something even stranger. She received a message and the image of the one delivering it. It was the Great Oracle.

I have been summoned to attend this illustrious gathering as Great Oracle at the service of the five dragon kings of Kraido. I come humbly, the gigantic silver dragon messaged from the center of the inner circle where it was standing, and it bowed its head in respectful greeting to the five kings watching it.

It is your duty as Great Oracle, and you have always done so with honor, since the times before my father, and my father's father. As it is an obligation that all those present introduce ourselves so that it is so registered, I will begin with myself. I am Erre-Gor-Mau, leader of the Gondra Clan, the huge red dragon said.

The presence of the Great Oracle is always appreciated, more so when it is for a gathering of importance. As representative of the Zudrik Clan, I, King Ai-Zur-Tor, am here today, a white dragon said that also looked weathered and powerful.

Nahia looked again at the dome and realized that the golden flashes only occurred when the dragons spoke. Not only that, she was picking up the golden flashes for some reason.

Today we have a very important decision to make. It affects us all and also the future of dragons. As representative of the Urdik Clan, I, King Itx-Urd-Arr, am also present, said a blue dragon with a lethal look.

A decision which, before making it, we wish to consult the Great Oracle and listen to its wisdom. Representing the Beldrak Clan, I am King Osc-Belz-Hil, present here today, said a dragon black as night.

Nahia turned her head toward Daphne when she felt an unnatural heat on her forehead.

"Are my scales shining?"

Daphne narrowed her eyes and looked at them.

"Yeah, they are, a little."

Decisions of importance must be made with the understanding that they affect the fate of dragons, a fate that must be glorious. As representative of the Mardrok Clan, I, King Ram-Mar-Oia, am present here, the brown dragon king said.

"Now they shone once, stronger."

Of fighting, conquest, and glory—so our fate must be. All those present at the gathering have introduced themselves. Five kings. Therefore, we have quorum. Whatever we decide here today, will be, the red dragon said.

"They shone again, stronger," Daphne said.

"Yeah, I'm beginning to see a pattern."

"Pattern? You aren't having another one of your seizures, would you?"

"I hope not," Nahia said and put her hand to her neck where she kept a tonic, "although I'm having a strange day…"

"You and all of us, look where we are," Lily said with a smile.

Nahia realized that when the dragons spoke, she could hear them for some reason she could not fathom. She shut her eyes and concentrated on the messages she was receiving.

The issue we must debate here today and about which we must make a decision, is whether we begin the conquest, on a grand scale, of the continent-world of Drameia, said the red dragon.

Has a secure portal been opened to that continent-world? Has it opened from the realm of Gondra? the brown dragon king asked.

It has opened. In fact, it was not us that opened it. It was opened from Drameia to my realm. We picked up the power of the portal and went to investigate. It was not open for long, the red dragon king explained.

But it was open long enough for you to determine the world from which it originated, the blue dragon king wanted to know.

That is correct. My erudites have been able to open a reverse portal, and we can travel to Drameia. Before you ask, yes, we have tried it, and we managed to reach that continent-world.

If you have tried it, if you have sent dragons there, they might know we are coming. They might be waiting for us, the black dragon said.

It is not likely. There was only one cautious incursion, and they left no witnesses.

As it should be. The enemy must not be given the slightest option, and least of all anticipation of our arrival, said the blue dragon.

Nahia was listening to the conversation as if she were there with them. She was aware that she should not be listening. These were the five dragon kings, leaders of their respective clans, and she was a mere first-year Human on a mission as guard of honor. She told herself that she should stop listening, but she could not help it—the mental messages were reaching her, and she neither could, nor wanted to stop listening.

That continent-world, Drameia in our tongue and Tremia for its inhabitants, is one of the three primary homes of our race. It belongs to us by right, the brown dragon said.

It is, and from there we were expelled by the Golden Ones, our most hated enemies, the red dragon said.

The first thing we must do is make sure the Golden Ones no longer inhabit that world, the white dragon said.

The Golden Ones no longer inhabit it, said the red dragon.

How can you be sure? the white dragon asked.

Because we have a prisoner from that world who was interrogated when he was captured, and he said as much, the red dragon said.

The Human who arrived through the portal to your realm? the black dragon inquired.

Indeed, that Human. He is being held prisoner in Drakoros academy. As was agreed, so that none of us might benefit from his knowledge or the information he might reveal, the red dragon said.

We must maintain the fragile balance between the clans, the black dragon said in justification.

So it must be. There cannot be advantages for one above the others, said the brown dragon.

So then we have a portal that can lead us to Drameia which has been reopened to verify that we can indeed travel there, the blue dragon wanted clarification.

It has been reopened, yes, to ensure that the world is indeed Drameia-Tremia, the red dragon stated.

And has it been secured? the black dragon asked.

We have made sure that there are no Golden Ones in that world anymore, the white dragon said.

Indeed, the red dragon confirmed.

It is not that I do not trust this confirmation, but I want to check these facts for myself, the blue dragon said.

You never trust anything, but it does not matter, I will take it as a sign of respect toward the power of my clan. We can produce the prisoner for the Great Oracle and let him confirm the fact.

That seems to me a good proposal, the white dragon agreed.

Yes, let it be the Great Oracle who confirms it, the black dragon said.

The rest of the dragon kings agreed.

Has the prisoner been brought? the blue dragon asked.

He has been brought. I had guessed you would want confirmation. I asked the Colonel of the Academy to send him, the red dragon said.

In that case, bring him forward. Enter, the blue dragon said.

Chapter 45

Something Nahia was not expecting happened next. From the cart waiting on the path with the leaders of the squadrons, they brought forth the prisoner. Nahia recognized him at once, and she was struck dumb. It was the prisoner with the gold dragon mask. His feet and hands were in chains. The two Tergnomus led him to the south entrance, where they were let in. The prisoner was taken inside the building to the grand gathering.

The two Tergnomus left the prisoner before the five dragon kings and exited the temple. Nahia was speechless. The prisoner she had seen was the one the dragon kings had been talking about.

Great Oracle, go ahead, question the prisoner, the red dragon said.

The huge silver dragon looked at the prisoner with its silver-and-gold eyes.

You may remove the mask, the dragon said, and with its power it released the back clasp of the mask. The prisoner reached the clasp with his chained hands and opened the mask, taking it off and leaving it on the floor. He took a deep breath and felt his face and then his hair. He did this as if to make sure they were still there. His gestures were of someone who had not done them in a very long time.

The Great Oracle closed its eyes and created some spheres of energy around the prisoner. The energy looked like a silver gaseous substance with golden specks that floated around the prisoner. It seemed to have a life of its own and went up and down, filling the whole sphere. It started to flash. The prisoner remained calm. He looked at the Great Oracle and did not move from where he was standing.

The energy around you is to help us understand you. Not all here understand the language of your land. It will also help me know whether you are lying. I advise you to tell the truth, because I will know, and that will generate a situation of conflict which I would prefer to avoid. Lying will not get you anywhere in my presence. Tell me, what is your name?

The prisoner nodded, looked at the Great Oracle, and replied.

"My name is Egil Olafstone."

The substance that surrounded him did not change its behavior.

Are you from the world you call Tremia?

"I am."

How did you get to this continent-world?

"I came through a portal a dragon created in my world."

Nahia was listening with all her attention. She could not believe this was the prisoner with the gold mask she had met in the dungeons. She felt terrible for not having spoken to him, for not helping him. But then she thought of what the dragons would have done if they had caught her helping him and she was no longer sorry, at least not entirely.

The five kings are interested in knowing whether there are Golden Ones in your land.

"I don't know what the Golden Ones are."

They are the ones who expelled the dragons from your world five thousand years ago.

"I don't have any evidence that there are any Golden Ones left in Tremia. As far as I know, three thousand years ago they vanished without a trace."

The energy surrounding Egil which seemed to measure whether what he was saying was true or not remained constant.

Neither Dragons nor Golden Ones rule in Tremia?

"Humans rule in Tremia. There are many kingdoms and nations, of humans mostly."

The Great Oracle looked at the five kings.

He is not lying. Do you require more information, Your Majesties?

You say a dragon opened the portal from your continent to ours. How is it possible if there are no dragons left in your world? the white dragon wanted to know.

"The spirit of the dragon Dergha-Sho-Blaska remained frozen in an orb. The dragon reincarnated using the body of a fossilized dragon. With his new body, he opened the portal," Egil explained in a calm tone, summarizing what had happened.

Dergha-Sho-Blaska was a dragon from my clan, said the red dragon.

That is why he opened a portal to your realm, said the brown dragon.

Where is Dergha-Sho-Blaska now? Did he not cross over? the black dragon asked.

"I believe he died before crossing," said Egil.

The substance that surrounded them began to flash silver and gold.

That answer is not completely sincere, the Great Oracle warned him.

Egil nodded.

"The dragon died. He was unable to cross."

Who killed him? the blue dragon asked eagerly.

"We killed him, a group of humans," Egil replied.

That cannot be. Humans cannot kill a thousand-year-old dragon, said the brown dragon.

Is he telling the truth, Great Oracle? the white dragon asked.

He is.

He must have been weak from creating the portal, or sick, or his acquired body must have failed him, the red dragon reasoned.

Why did you cross if you killed him? the black dragon asked.

"It wasn't by choice. In the fight I was thrown into the portal," Egil explained.

That makes more sense, the red dragon said.

Is everything he has said true? the brown dragon wanted to make sure.

He has not lied, the Great Oracle confirmed.

That is enough for me. I already have all I need to know, the red dragon said.

The other kings also gave their consent, one after the other, nodding.

As you see, there is little to fear and much to gain. A world in which inconsequential human kings rule, with only weapons and human magic: they will not be able to stop us, the red dragon said with assurance.

I agree. We must recover our land. We will destroy those humans and their insignificant kingdoms and conquer that continent for ourselves, the blue dragon said.

The weak human beings will not be able to do anything against us and our armies. We must retake what was once ours and must be ours again, said the brown dragon.

Let me remind you we have other wars we are fighting. Entering another one might be costly in resources, the white dragon said.

Some caution is due. We must not take for granted that it will be an easy campaign and that we will destroy the humans of that continent-world, said the black dragon.

The Path of Dragons marks the way. We must conquer this world and increase the greatness of our power and global dominion. Our duty must be to raze whoever opposes us, the blue dragon said.

We must come to a definite decision. We should consult the Great Oracle. Let him give us his view of this conquest campaign, the white dragon said.

Indeed. What premonition, if any, does the Great Oracle have about this war we are about to begin? the black dragon wanted to know.

As Your Majesties wish. The Great Oracle nodded and closed its eyes. The sphere that surrounded Egil vanished. Another, larger sphere appeared, surrounding the body of the huge silver dragon. The sphere was filled with energy that emanated from the dragon's body. It was made of thousands of silver specks that glowed gently. Among them were some golden ones, although those were fewer. The sphere flashed silver three times.

Everyone was watching the Great Oracle as it threw its head back with its eyes closed and appeared to be in a trance. For a long moment, nothing happened. Then thousands of silver specks inside the sphere started to flash. A moment later, the golden specks began to flash as well. The whole space was lit up by thousands of silver and gold flashes that occurred as if the dragon were daydreaming.

The Great Oracle put its head further back so that it almost lay on its back.

The vision is coming, it warned. Now everyone was paying close attention to the huge silver dragon. The messages came to Nahia, who did not want to miss anything.

The Great Oracle said:
When the fire…
Meets the arrow…
And the five lost crowns…
It will awake an ancestral power…
Which will defeat the lords of the skies…
The prophecy will be fulfilled…
The slave will free the eight races…
And the savior of worlds be.

There were three bright, silver flashes and the Great Oracle opened its eyes. It raised its head and unmade the sphere of power surrounding it.

It cannot be that you have seen that. What does it mean? the blue dragon protested.

Again the prophecy of the slave who will free the eight races? the red dragon asked, annoyed.

Explain clearly, without mystic words, the brown dragon said.

The great oracle nodded.

If the war is started, the prophecy will be fulfilled that a slave will free all eight races. They will become the savior of worlds, the Great Oracle explained calmly.

You already made that prediction at the time of the Great Insurrection and it did not come true, the red dragon said.

We made sure it did not happen, the blue dragon said.

And it did not, said the brown dragon.

True. But perhaps it was a prelude for this premonition, the Great Oracle said.

Perhaps? The red dragon was not convinced by the Great Oracle's words.

That premonition is too ambiguous, and if you link it to the liberating slave, it becomes even more so, the blue dragon said.

How certain are you that this premonition will come true? the white dragon asked the Great Oracle.

There is no certainty at all in a premonition, since fate is whimsical and can change at any moment, the Great Oracle explained.

Then it is of no use to us, the red dragon stated.

The Great Oracle has made quite accurate predictions in the past, the white dragon said defensively.

Indeed, which is why we are here to consult the Great Oracle, said the brown dragon.

In that continent-world there are only humans and other lesser races and beasts. There is nothing that can stop us. Their magic and armies are not rivals for our own. We have the opportunity to recapture one of the three primary worlds. We must do it—it is our duty as dragons. Conquest or death, said the red dragon.

What you want us to do is accept this invasion at any cost, the white dragon said.

I have given you weighty reasons. The Path of Dragons obliges us to take that world, by conquest and because it is our right, said the red dragon.

That is true. That world belongs to us. We must take it. We must be the most powerful beings in this universe, the blue dragon joined it.

I agree. Power and glory. Nothing else matters, the brown dragon agreed.

The other two dragons were thoughtful.

We have questioned the prisoner and consulted the Great Oracle. It is time to make a decision. Who is with me in invading and conquering the world of Drameia? Let us vote, the red dragon said.

There was another moment of silence while the dragon kings each weighed their decision.

I say yes to the invasion, said the brown dragon.

I think now is not the time, least of all with the premonition the Great Oracle has just given us, the white dragon refused.

I also think it is not the best moment, the black dragon said after thinking carefully.

There was only the blue dragon left. Its vote was decisive, and they were all looking at it.

I do not like the premonition, but it is one we already know and have avoided in the past. I vote yes to the invasion.

Then it is decided! Three against two. We will invade that continent and rule over it, the red dragon sentenced.

If the five kings so decide it, so it will be, the Great Oracle cried.

Every one of the kings reiterated its position before leaving the temple one by one to return to their realms. The three kings in favor talked of conquest, glory, power, and honor. The two opposing dragons talked of caution, although they could not oppose the invasion since they were the minority. They all marched with the agreement to organize themselves to carry out a great invasion to re-conquer Drameia, one that would be epic and fill the pages of the history tomes. One in which the dragons would raze the whole continent and then rule over its ashes.

Once the kings had left, the two Tergnomus returned for the prisoner, put the gold mask back on, and led him to the cart.

The last one to leave the temple was the Great Oracle. Once it did, the retinue of honor squadrons formed again. They escorted the silver dragon back to its home and then continued back to the academy.

The whole way back, Nahia was thinking about what she had heard and trying to make sense of it all. What she could not understand was how it was possible that she had been able to hear their conversation. She was sure she should not have done it. There was also the weird phenomenon of the energies that had taken place. And yet another thought circled through her head: should she tell her comrades what had happened? She was not sure. Not only because she did not know how they would take it, and whether she could trust them entirely, but also because this knowledge might be dangerous for them. The dragons made no distinctions or exceptions. If they found out she and her friends had this private information they would kill them, without a doubt. It was military intelligence. Nothing would save them. She decided to keep the information to herself for the time being. She did not want to risk their lives.

Chapter 46

The days went by, and Nahia could not shake off what had happened at the Temple of Harmony and the poor prisoner. For some reason she kept thinking about him, and although she had not told anyone, she felt a terrible need to talk to him. It was almost stronger than her will. Her common sense told her she should stay away or she would find herself in big trouble that might even cost her life. This was a very serious matter, one where the five dragon kings were involved.

The training days moved on, and soon the year would be over. If she managed to finish, she would be sent to the battle front for the War Test, and now she knew to what front, or she suspected it. They were going to send her to the world Egil, the prisoner, came from. This knowledge, this almost certainty, made her think about him even more. Unable to resist any more, she decided she had to speak to him. In order to do so, she needed a plan. She thought one out and determined to carry it out.

The following morning, at first hour, they were running to line up before Irakas-Gorri-Gaizt. The red dragon was still making them march in formation every day, although lately this exercise did not last as long so they had time to have breakfast. As they were running to line up and were almost in front of their leader, Nahia took a bad step and her boot twisted to one side. She grunted and fell to the ground. She stayed there, three paces from the dragon, holding her right ankle and grunting.

Lily realized and went over to help her.

Go back to the lineup, Scarlatum, Irakas-Gorri-Gaizt messaged her.

When she received the message, Lily stopped and looked at Nahia. She could not disobey the order. She went back to the formation.

You have a moment to get back to your place in the lineup, Human.

Nahia was holding her ankle, lying on the ground. She acted as though she were trying to stand and dropped back on the ground with a grimace of pain.

Her squad comrades were watching her out of the corner of their eyes with great concern, fearing for her life.

You are a disgrace, Human. I do not understand how you could have been blessed with the power of a Flameborn and have such an appallingly weak body. I still do not understand how you rose to triumph at the half-year test. Since you cannot march in formation or even line up, you are punished with a month of cleaning the dungeons. I hope that cleaning excrement and ending up exhausted from doing it every day will help you strengthen that pitiful body of yours. Go to the infirmary and then to class. Your punishment begins this evening.

Nahia managed to get on her knees and nodded. She remained with her head bowed. Her comrades started the morning martial march. She got up and, limping, went to the infirmary. She explained what had happened to the Exarbor nurses, and after diagnosing the injury, two Tergnomus nurses bandaged her right ankle.

During the rest of the day, Nahia attended classes. She was sorry she had to lie to her comrades, because there was really nothing wrong with her ankle. She had faked it, but she did not tell them. She needed to see the prisoner and did not want to tell her squad so as not to get them into trouble. She also did not fully trust that Aiden would not tell Irakas-Gorri-Gaizt.

When the class ended, which was luckily magic class and not weapons, she headed to the dungeons. She knew the way and the protocol. She waited in front of the horrifying fortress-dungeon for Tercel to come out for her.

"You again?" The Tergnomus was surprised to see her and gave her the kind of look the Tergnomus put on when something did not fit. If by nature they were lacking in physical beauty, when they frowned they were really ugly. "You didn't learn the lesson the first time, did you?"

"I'm unlucky," Nahia replied defensively.

"Rather, you're clumsy," he said with a face that meant that was not good at all for her.

"That too, yes."

"Well, let's look on the bright side. I don't need to tell you how everything works," his face improved when he realized this.

"True. I remember everything perfectly."

"I'll take you to Framus, and he'll assign you to the cleaning team he sees more suitable. Come on, let's register you."

Nahia nodded and the two of them went to the Exarbor controlling the entrance to the dungeons. To Nahia's surprise, he remembered her, everything about her.

"Nahia… Aske… Red Squadron, Igneous Squad…" he wrote down in the register without asking her.

"Yes, yes, that's right," she nodded.

Tercel went with her and left her with Framus, who when he saw her, made a disapproving face, wrinkling his ugly nose and shaking her head.

"Some never learn…."

"I was unfortunate," she pointed at her bandaged ankle.

"Bad luck might be easily mistaken for weakness in this world," he warned her, wagging his finger in front of her face.

"I appreciate the advice," Nahia said. She could tell the Tergnomus was annoyed to see her there again. Well, the Tergnomus were always more or less annoyed, so it was not easy to tell whether he was more annoyed than usual.

"If I might ask a favor…"

Framus looked at her, frowning.

"We're not here to do favors or make life easier for anyone," he grumbled.

"I'd like to be assigned to the same section as last time. With Ufrem… if possible…" Nahia asked anyway.

The Tergnomus was about to say something in a temper, but then he was thoughtful.

"You seem stronger than before, you'll go to a lower level."

"Not with this ankle," Nahia leaned on her foot and made a grimace of pain. She wanted to go to the same level, not out of fear but because that was where they had the prisoner she wanted to talk to.

"When did you do that?" Framus asked her.

"This morning."

Framus sighed and shook his head angrily.

"All right. Underground level one then, with Ufrem."

"Thank you very much," Nahia said with a big smile.

"Don't forget to put on the bracelet. The Serpetuss are quite stirred up lately."

Nahia did not like this at all.

"Stirred up?"

"Yes. We don't know what the matter is with them, but they are more restless than usual. So, if you come upon one, stand as still as a statue."

"I will, don't worry."

Framus led Nahia to the section where Ufrem and his cleaning team were at the first underground level.

Ufrem saw her enter the hall with Framus and shook his head.

"I thought I wasn't going to see you again."

"Yeah, that was my intention too."

"She's lame," Framus told him, pointing at Nahia's ankle.

"Why do they send me maimed workers? As if I didn't have enough work already! This is pitiful!" Ufrem started complaining.

"Don't ask me! She came like this!" Framus replied, shouting.

The two Tergnomus began to argue and shout at one another for a long while. In the end, Framus left amid shouts and much arm waving.

"What a disappointment," Ufrem told Nahia as he put the silver bracelet on her wrist.

"Since you are already experienced, I don't have to lead you by the hand. You will pair up with Nielse. He's the Fatum over there at the end. He's only been here a week and the Serpetuss have him scared to death," Ufrem explained to her.

"All right," Nahia nodded.

"Section south, which is the closest, that way you won't punish that ankle too much."

"Thank you," Nahia bowed gratefully.

Ufrem waved it aside, his long pointy ears still red from the argument.

"Get your mops, brushes, and buckets and get on with it!" he yelled angrily.

"Right away!" Nahia replied.

Ufrem opened the door and the gates of the three areas they had to clean and then he left them, shutting the exit door behind them. Nahia and Nielse started on the first corridor. There were only a couple of torches on each side of the whole first section and the corridor was very wide, so they could not see much.

"I'm Nahia of the Igneous Squad, Red Squadron," she introduced herself to her new partner.

The Fatum turned to her; he was undoubtedly a first-year.

"I'm Nielse of the Rock Squad, Brown Squadron."

"Rock Squad, Brown Squadron?" Nahia asked, very interested.

"Yeah... why?"

"Then you know Maika."

"Yes, she's my Human comrade in the squad."

"Maika and I are friends," Nahia told him, unable to hide her excitement.

"Oh, she's a very nice girl. We get along well."

"I can imagine. She's a dear, and quite strong."

"Stronger than me," the Fatum admitted regretfully. He looked quite weak for a boy.

"If you want to improve that, I advise you to come to the gym. I've improved a lot since I've been going, and my squad's Fatum has too."

Nielse looked at her, uncertain whether she meant to help or if she was mocking him.

"If you say so..."

"Honestly, I was very weak. That's why I ended up here the first time."

"Like me now..."

"That's why I'm telling you to go to the gym."

"A little late now..."

"It's never late, I promise."

"Thanks... I'll think about it."

"Oh, and do me a favor and say 'hi' to Maika from me."

"No problem."

"But with a special greeting."

The Fatum raised an eyebrow.

Nahia showed him the greeting of the Butterfly of Victory.

Nielse looked at her as if she were crazy.

"It's a butterfly and the V is for victory," Nahia explained.

The Fatum thought for a moment.

"I think I understand... I'll greet her like that for you."

"Many thanks," Nahia smiled at him.

They started cleaning, and when Nahia went by the cell she was looking for, she recognized it. That was where they had the prisoner with the gold dragon mask. She hoped they had not switched him to another cell, or her plan to talk to him would go down the drain. Unobtrusively, she slid open the peephole and took a quick look inside. At first she could not see anything, since with it being nighttime, only the light from the stars came in through a tiny barred window, and lit up the inside of the cell. She looked closer and saw the inmate. She took note of the human feet, observing the legs and body to the head. A gold dragon head. It was him. He had not been taken to another cell.

Nahia saw Nielse cleaning ahead, concentrated on his task.

"It's Nahia, I want to speak to you," she whispered to the prisoner.

At once, he stood up and came to the door. He looked at Nahia and nodded.

Nahia pointed at him.

"You Egil."

The prisoner threw his head back, surprised that she knew his name. Then he nodded repeatedly.

"I Nahia," she said and pointed at her own chest.

"Na…hia," Egil imitated the sound.

"That's right. You Egil and I Nahia," she said, pointing at him and then again at herself.

Egil nodded.

"You Nahia," he said, and Nahia realized he was smart. He had used the same pronoun for "you" that she had just used.

"You shouldn't speak to the prisoners…" she heard Nielse say.

Nahia looked at him and saw that the Fatum was watching her. He had discovered her. She was going to say something when she saw a shadow approaching the Fatum.

"Stand still. Don't move."

"No…" the Fatum said, turning.

An enormous Serpetuss was coming toward him, upright and threatening. It opened its mouth, showing its maw and hissing loudly.

Terror overwhelmed Nielse, and he ran away.

"No! Stop!" Nahia warned him.

The poor Fatum was beside himself with terror. He ran and the Serpetuss chased after him, dragging its long body along the floor.

Nahia saw Nielse reach her level in his crazy flight, and without thinking twice she tackled him and knocked him down. They both fell to the floor.

"Don't move or speak if you want to live," Nahia said and put her hand over his mouth while she held him down with the weight of her own body.

The Serpetuss reached them and rose even higher with its mouth open and fangs revealed. It hissed, a shrill, horrible sound. The Fatum was trembling under Nahia's body, who pressed down on him so he would not move. The Serpetuss came down to the level of their heads and Nahia feared the worst. Nielse's eyes were about to pop out of their sockets. He wanted to scream, but Nahia was covering his mouth.

The reptilian beast sniffed at them, and for a moment Nahia thought it was going to plunge its fangs into the two of them with one bite. She tried to stay as still as she could and make sure that Nielse did not move either. The Serpetuss sniffed at their bracelets, and after a moment of hesitation in which Nahia thought they were dead, that watcher of the dungeon corridors continued its rounds.

Nahia and Nielse were left lying on the floor, breathing hard from fear.

"Thank you… you saved me…"

"Don't you know you shouldn't move?"

"I do… but… the terror…"

"If you run, they'll kill you."

"Yeah… I realize that…"

Nahia got to her feet, shaking her head, and offered her hand to the Fatum so he would also get up.

"Look, let's make a deal. I'll try to keep you safe from the Serpetuss and you keep your mouth shut about my conversations with that prisoner."

Nielse thought for a moment.

"It's a deal," he said and offered her his hand.

Nahia took it and they shook hands.

"Now, go on cleaning as if nothing happened."

"Fine," Nielse picked up his brush and mop which he had dropped to run away and got down to cleaning.

Nahia went up to the peephole.

"Egil," she called.

The prisoner nodded.

"I need to talk to you."

Egil shook his head and shrugged.

He did not understand her. Nahia made the sign of speaking with her hands to her mouth and then pointed at him.

Egil nodded; he had understood.

"You Egil, Tremia," Nahia said. She had memorized the name of the continent-world from which the prisoner came.

Egil nodded repeatedly.

"I, Kraido," Nahia told him.

Egil nodded. He had understood that too.

"Kraido attack Tremia," she said and mimicked a stabbing.

Egil threw his head back. He understood and nodded.

Nahia saw that the problem was how to communicate with someone who did not speak her language. But she had the feeling this prisoner was very intelligent. He picked things up right away. She decided she would make the effort to teach him a few words and see whether they managed to understand one another.

"I teach you," Nahia told him, and she made a gesture of writing something and then pointing at him.

Egil nodded and gestured at himself and then acted as if he were reading a book.

"I see you want to learn, very well. I'll teach you."

Egil did not understand that, he shook his head.

Nahia smiled and mimicked writing for him again.

"Nahia," Egil said, and then he bowed to her.

His grateful gesture surprised her.

That evening they could not communicate much, because apart from having to clean the huge, long corridors, Framus appeared a couple of times to see how they were doing and a Serpetuss came twice. Nahia realized that teaching Egil her language was going to be complicated under these circumstances. She would have to be watchful.

Chapter 47

Everyone's mood and humor improved with the arrival of spring. Finally, the cold and the snow made way for the resurgence of life. Even within the walls of the academy, it was noticeable that life was reviving. The birds especially filled the squares and gardens, and their joyful singing raised everyone's spirits.

Ande-Zuri-Koa and Borne were waiting for the Regular Dragon Magic class.

The last thing we will learn this year is mental attacks. It is the most difficult offensive magic techniques at this level, and you must learn to use it. This first year you will only learn the most basic form. In the second year, and particularly in the third, you will be taught to use this power in all its potential. This requires a lot of work and study you will undertake in the future. Borne, prepare the target.

Borne-Exarbor took a humanoid-shaped mannequin and slowly set it up in the middle of the room. It was dressed in the same clothes as them, which was a tad unsettling.

Nahia was hoping she would not be the first, which was becoming a habit, but she was not that lucky.

"Igneous Squad, first member," Borne called.

Nahia sighed deeply and stepped forward.

Human, what you must do now is call on your inner dragon and gather a considerable amount of energy. Then you must transform that energy into elemental energy, the one aligned with your power. In your case, fire. Once you have done this, it will be time to expel it. Here is where you must be very careful. The elemental fire energy must come from you in a controlled and prolonged manner. This is what we call Dragon Breath. You must channel it so it comes out through your mouth, as if it were your breath, and then you will project it. Go ahead.

Nahia was looking askance at the great white dragon, filled with doubts. How was she going to do that?

"You must look… toward the target…" Borne told her, pointing at it with his leaf-covered hand.

Nahia turned toward the mannequin, very unsettled. She watched it and tried to concentrate. She was aware the whole squadron was staring at her, which did not make the exercise any easier. She did not want to do badly before the squadron, and least of all before the white dragon. She knew how it would respond to failure.

Do not hesitate and do exactly as I have told you. Follow every step.

There was no going back, she had to do what the great dragon had ordered. She took out the Learning Pearl and held it in her left hand. She concentrated as hard as she was able to given the circumstances and awoke her inner dragon. She gathered enough energy from it to create a sphere of energy the size of her Learning Pearl, which is what they usually used to perform their attacks with elemental spheres. But, in this case, she did not have to form a sphere with the energy, but transform it into the fire element inside of her and then let it out. This seemed problematic.

I feel your power, now you must transform it. Do it.

Nahia closed her eyes and tried to create a sphere of fire inside her, transforming the energy into fire. After an instant, she was able to watch her energy become elemental fire inside her.

Well done, you already have fire inside you, I can feel it. Now, you must channel it and let it out through your breath. Open your mouth and throw it out.

"Toward the mannequin," Borne said, taking a few steps back quite fast for an Exarbor.

Naha's eyes widened to take in the target. She opened her mouth and tried to let out the fire in her breath when something weird happened. She lost control of the inner fire, and instead of coming out of her mouth it radiated out through her whole body. Her whole body burst into flame. Frightened, Nahia crouched down to her comrades cries of surprise.

Bad. Very bad. Not like that. You must control the energy at all times. You let it out without any control. That is unacceptable. You might have hurt someone, or yourself.

Nahia looked at her body. It was not burning. She touched her hair to make sure it had not been consumed by the flames. It seemed to all be there. She stood up and looked around. She had not hurt anyone. She had not reached the mannequin or Borne, and her comrades were far away, so she snorted, relieved.

Try again, and control that energy within you. You cannot allow it to explode outwardly. That would lead to an uncontrolled explosion, which could be lethal. You must manage to make the fire go forward as if it were the breath of one of us, of a dragon. Do it, and do it right this time.

The message was an imperious order. Nahia knew she should not mess up or she would end up being punished, or worse. She tried to calm down as much as possible and concentrated once again. She had no problem with the first part of the process: she gathered the energy and transformed it into elemental fire within herself. This time she did not create a sphere to encapsulate it but let it stay alive and ardent inside her. She felt as if she had to do something with that flaming energy or it would burn her inside. Her instincts told her she should put it out before it consumed her, but that would mean failing the exercise.

She opened her eyes and looked at the mannequin that reminded her of one of her comrades. It even had the hood on. She opened her mouth and directed her inner energy so it would come out as if it were her breath, but in a controlled way, not all at once but letting it flow like a river. An intense flame came out of her mouth as if it were the breath of a dragon, and she projected fire onto the mannequin. The flames reached it and enveloped it.

Very well. Maintain the flow of energy and keep it constant. Don't stop.

Nahia was struck numb. She could see the fire ejecting from her mouth toward the mannequin, which by now was burning up, entirely wrapped in flames. She let out all the elemental energy she had transformed and projected it onto the mannequin. When she was left without any more fire to throw, she shut her mouth.

That was a lot better. You must improve your control of the flow and learn to transform inner energy into elemental fire according to your needs instead of having it prepared beforehand. That is something we will practice in the next classes. Next pupil.

Nahia withdrew, spellbound, watching the mannequin burn. The frame had held at first, but little by little it had been consumed by the fire until it was all scorched just like the mannequin. Borne let the mannequin burn completely and calmly took out another one he had ready. From what they were able to see, the Exarbor had over a dozen mannequins under a canvas on one side of the classroom.

Daphne was the next, and in her case, the effect was not as destructive. Like Nahia, at first, she had trouble controlling her inner energy, and on two occasions she issued two explosions of light which almost blinded everyone. On her third attempt she managed to channel her elemental energy as breath and sent her dazzling light against the mannequin.

Lily, on the other hand, had some problems and nearly froze Borne completely when she hit him without meaning to as her freezing breath went out of control. The white dragon did not like that at all, and Lily very nearly ended up cleaning dungeons. Luckily, on her next attempt she did well and her frozen breath froze the mannequin completely.

Aiden had a very hard time controlling the storm he generated inside him. Every time he tried to make it come out as a controlled breath, he failed. The thunder and lightning came out in every direction without any control whatsoever. Ande-Zuri-Koa ordered him to stop and not continue until he managed to channel his elemental power into a direct breath aimed at the front.

Ivo had many problems turning his inner energy into elemental earth energy. The first few times he did not succeed, and when he opened his mouth and sent forth his breath, it came out as pure energy, not elemental, and although he hit the mannequin and knocked it down with his strength, it was not what he had been ordered to do. He finally had to stop because all his attempts were unsuccessful.

Taika also had problems. In his case, they were strange issues. He managed to turn his elemental energy into darkness, but when he tried to send it like a dragon's breath, what came out of his mouth were black tentacles that grabbed onto anything they found. Unfortunately, they caught Borne and nearly consumed him, so Taika destroyed them and did not try again since he had no control over the dark inner energy of his.

Once they finished, the members of the other two squads had their turn. They had similar luck. Very few did well, and Ande-Zuri-Koa ended the class by sending them all to the library to study Elemental Breath. They had to learn how to use it, since it was one of the most powerful weapons in the magical arsenal of a Dragon Blood Warlock.

At the library, Nahia was studying the skill in the initial tome when she saw someone she immediately recognized. She got up and went to speak to him.

"Logan, how good to see you."

The dark-haired boy raised his gaze and his light eyes met Nahia's.

"Nahia, how's everything? Sit down with me and tell me."

Nahia sat down beside him. One of the members of his team, the lioness who had fought her in the half-year test, looked at her and gave her a nod. She returned the greeting.

"Well, today we had a pretty tricky magic lesson."

Logan nodded.

"I find magic quite difficult."

"Have you gotten to the Dragon Breath?"

"Yes, yesterday, that's why I'm here," Logan showed her the tome he was studying, the same chapter she was.

"We seem to all be in the same place."

"You have fire breath. It must be something to see the flame you let loose."

"And your storms with your air alignment," Nahia said. She knew because they had talked about it at the gym.

"Yeah, but they're very difficult to control."

"Yeah, our Drakonid has it and he made a mess today in class…"

"I sympathize."

"Let me ask you a question… isn't it odd that you have silver scales but your element is air?"

Logan looked at her for a moment and then at her scales.

"Yours are golden and your element is fire."

"Yeah, that's why I should have red scales and you, white ones, like everyone who's aligned with fire and air."

"That's true, but you and I are different."

"That's what I think too. The thing is, why?"

Logan shrugged.

"A whim of nature?"

"Is that what you think? That it's a coincidence, chance?"

"Don't you?"

Nahia bit her lower lip.

"You see… I believe there's always a reason. I don't know what yet, but I don't think it's a coincidence. Or that you and I have met here, both having these unique scales, either."

"It's clear we're oddities. You're a Flameborn, and I am a Stormson."

"Stormson?" Nahia's mouth dropped open.

"That's what my leader called me."

"Have they tested you in any way? They tested me, and it turns out I'm immune to fire."

"I'm immune to storms, to their thunder and lightning."

"So, we're both immune to our own elemental power. This has to mean something!"

Logan looked right and left; an Exarbor was already watching them.

"Take it easy, don't get so excited or we'll be punished."

"Okay... I'm taking it easy... but this has to mean something important."

"It means that you and I are singular, odd. I don't think it means anything else."

"Well, I'm positive it does. It's too big a coincidence to not mean anything."

"I don't know..."

"We have to find the meaning."

"All right, I'll keep my ears and eyes open."

"So will I. If you discover anything, promise me you'll let me know."

"Why wouldn't I?"

"It might not be good news..."

"Oh, I see. I'll let you know, even if it isn't."

"All right, it's a deal," Nahia said and offered him her hand.

Logan looked at Nahia's hand, and then he shook it.

"It's a deal."

"One other thing..." Nahia said as she got up. "In the final part of the half-year test, did you change positions with your lioness comrade on purpose?"

Logan looked at her with his usual seriousness.

"Maybe."

"So that we wouldn't have to fight, you and I?"

"Maybe."

"I had guessed as much. Thank you."

Logan nodded and turned back to concentrate on the tome he was studying.

From that detail, Nahia knew Logan was an exceptional young man. She left, determined to find out what those scales of hers and Logan's meant. It might take her their whole three years at the academy to find out, but in the end she would. She was convinced it was not a mere coincidence. There was something important about it.

Chapter 48

One week later, they received the ill-fated news that they would be going to war the following day. The War Test, the final test of the year, was about to begin. They were all very nervous, and they went to get ready. All except Nahia, who still had a punishment to finish up. She seized the chance during her last evening cleaning dungeons to speak with Egil about it. She had continued teaching Egil her language, but they had not been able to advance as much as she would have wanted to because Framus had been rotating her from section to section. He kept her in the same underground level, but he changed her area. There were many days when she did not set foot on the south sector but was in one of the other three. Every time this happened, Nahia became very upset.

She had tried to persuade Framus to let her always clean the south area, but it did not fit in with the Tergnomus. It made no sense to do things this way. The cleaning teams must rotate between areas. She had insisted, but without any luck. She also did not want to risk arguing with Framus. If she did, he would suspect something was up. Besides, the Tergnomus had a terrible temper when they got angry; they screamed and gestured wildly.

Luckily, that evening she did have the south sector. She snorted, relieved. She greeted Ufrem and the others in charge of the sector and got to work with Nielse, who she always partnered up with. This was because Nielse begged Framus to be partners with Nahia. His fear of the Serpetuss was so obvious that the poor Fatum was always allowed to pair up with Nahia.

"Tomorrow go war," Nahia said to Egil while Nielse cleaned and watched.

"Tomorrow? War here?" Egil said, pointing his finger at the floor.

"No, not here," Nahia wagged her finger.

"Where?" Egil asked.

"Drameia, Tremia," Nahia replied.

Egil threw his head back.

"Tomorrow?"

"Yes, tomorrow."

"Great portal?"

"Yes, I guess great portal."

"Why, Nahia?"

That was a good question. How could she explain?

"Be test. Last test of year."

"Test? No understand," Egil said, shaking his head.

"Pass test to be warrior, to finish course."

Egil was thoughtful.

"Test for warrior?"

"That's right."

Egil nodded.

"I see."

"I'm not sure, but think I'm going to Tremia. Is there anything I can do for you?" Nahia tried to express through hand expressions.

Egil seemed to understand, because he nodded. He thought for a long moment.

"Seek Lasgol."

"Lasgol? Is this a person?"

"Yes. Lasgol. Seek Lasgol. Friend."

Nahia nodded. She found it farfetched that she could find a person called Lasgol in a whole continent-world, but that was what Egil wanted, and if she could she would try to find him.

"I will look for Lasgol," Naha nodded.

"Good luck," Egil said and offered her his hand.

Nahia looked right and left. Only Nielse was in the corridor.

"Thank you, I'm going to need it," she said and shook his hand through the peephole.

With the coming of dawn, the six squadrons reported to lineup. They all knew what day this was. Nahia was a bundle of nerves, and her comrades were tense. The rest of the other first-years who had made it through the academy so far were too. It was obvious in their faces and how stiff they were. The six captains, the squadron leaders, were standing in formation, three on either side of the gates of the grand castle with their backs to the east and the banners in front of them.

Red Squadron, line up! Irakas-Gorri-Gaizt's order reached them.

Nahia was trying to remain calm, but thinking about going on a real war mission had her shaking. She looked around for Ana, Maika, and Logan, and saw them with their squads. Knowing they were also there and participating made her feel a little better.

All of a sudden, they heard two terrible roars coming from above. They looked up, startled, and glimpsed Colonel Lehen-Gorri-Gogor and Commander Bigaen-Zuri-Indar flying over the castle. They glided over the parade ground and came down from the sky to land in front of the castle gates, a few paces behind the leaders waiting with their squads.

Colonel Lehen-Gorri-Gogor roared.

There are three very special days during the first year of training at Drakoros. You have already lived through the first one: the Squad Competition in the middle of the year. Today is the second: the War Test at the end of the course. I promise you will never forget it. And the third day is Graduation day. That is if you survive today, and not all of you will.

Nahia looked at her comrades with horror. Lily and Daphne looked back at her with a similar look in their eyes.

Commander Bigaen-Zuri-Indar roared.

You will accompany your squad leaders on a war mission into enemy territory. You will follow their orders to the letter. This might be the difference between living and dying, so I advise you all to follow them without hesitation and without failure. You will fulfill the mission and return. If you succeed and your performance is acceptable, you will graduate. If it is not, or you do not manage to come back, you will have failed and will not graduate from this distinguished, glorious institution.

Colonel Lehen-Gorri-Gogor roared once again.

I bid you good luck. Fulfill your duty with courage and honor. The glory be yours.

A group of Tergnomus appeared carrying backpacks, and every member of each squadron was given one to carry on their backs. The dagger and Learning Pearl they carried at their waist and the shield on their back were the regulatory equipment of the academy.

Red Squadron. We march. Follow me, Irakas-Gorri-Gaizt messaged to them.

The other six squadrons received the same order from their leader and they all set off together. Nahia did not know where they were heading, but she was sure of one thing: if they were going on a war mission, it could not be in this sky realm they were on. This meant they would have to travel to some other place. She was right. They marched south, through the Gardens of Useless Hope, the Square of Neutrality, and the Bridge of the Sky until they arrived at the Gate.

They stopped before the great Pearl, surrounded by the six lookout towers. Nahia felt a shiver run down her spine, remembering what an awful time she had experienced here. It had become engraved forever in her mind and used to give her nightmares.

Sarre-Urdin-Olto, the great blue dragon who served as the Guardian of the Gate, was waiting for them. The six leaders spread their wings, and with one leap, they took off to climb the six lookout towers. The guardian did the same and climbed onto the Pearl.

For a moment, they all waited.

"Where do you think we're going?" Lily asked in a whisper.

"Somewhere to gain honor and glory for our masters," Aiden replied in a proud whisper.

"They'll open the portal and we'll go somewhere, like we did when we first arrived here," Daphne guessed.

"It's going to be more complicated than that..." Nahia told them.

"Why more complicated?" Ivo asked. "I am strongly against complications."

"Because this pearl only communicates with nearby places of this world," Taika guessed.

"That's right, and we're going to a very distant one," Nahia told them.

They all looked at her blankly.

"You know something we don't," Lily realized. She had already guessed and was watching her with wide eyes.

Nahia blushed.

"I do know something, yes," she admitted.

"So tell us if you do," Daphne said with a frown.

"I think we're going to a world-continent called Drameia. It's very far from Kraido."

"How do you know that?" Aiden asked. "That must be a military secret."

Nahia let out a deep breath. She wanted to tell them everything, but she feared they would not understand her or that they might misinterpret her. She knew what she knew thanks to a fortuitous fact, and well, also because of Egil...

"It came to me…"

"What do you mean it 'came to you' if it's secret military information?" Aiden demanded to know.

"At the Temple of Harmony, while we were on duty, the conversations from the inside came to me…" she admitted. She did not want to keep the secret—she felt she was betraying them if she did. They were her squad and she had to trust them, more so if they were going to the battlefront.

"They came to you? We were all together and I didn't get anything," said Aiden.

"I didn't either," said Lily and Daphne at once.

"You mean you overheard their conversations?" Taika asked her.

"Yes, I don't know how or why, but I heard them."

"It's part of your power. Because you're a Flameborn," Ivo said in a convinced tone.

They all turned their heads to look at him.

"You think?" Aiden asked.

"I'm sure. She is special. You don't get it because you're not at peace and in harmony with nature and the world around us, but I am. She has a special golden aura. I can see it."

"You are a profound Tauruk," Taika said, smiling.

"I don't pick up any aura," Aiden said, examining Nahia from head to toe.

"How could you pick up anything with that stone head of yours?" Daphne told him.

"Remember that Mag-Zilar-Ond told us she was an anomaly, someone singular, and that her power was different from ours, with more opportunities to do great things?" Lily told them.

"That's what caused you to receive those conversations," Taika reasoned.

"You have to tell us everything," Lily said eagerly.

"I don't want to know. You listened in on the five kings and the Great Oracle. I'm sure that's punishable by death, I'm confident," said Aiden.

"So don't listen," Lily retorted.

"And don't snitch, because I'll gauge out your dragon eyes with my dagger while you sleep," Daphne threatened him.

"I'll hold him for you," Ivo offered.

"Aren't you the peaceful and balanced one and all that?" Aiden reproached him.

"We are sometimes forced to do what we must so balance prevails," Ivo replied and gave him a look that assured him he would do it.

Suddenly, the Pearl let off three silver flashes.

"The guardian is opening the Portal," Taika realized.

A moment later, the three silver spheres began to form one after the other. Another moment and the great portal took shape. The great sphere that seemed to have a sea of liquid silver inside was opened above the pearl.

In your backpacks you will find a silver bracelet with the symbol of the portal engraved on it. Put it on. It will prevent you from suffering the negative effects of crossing over through the portal, their leader messaged to them.

Nahia put her hand in her backpack and saw they were carrying the bracelet, a rope, and some food and water. She had thought it was a bit heavy. Since they were already carrying their shield across their backs, she was not happy with this extra burden. She put on the bracelet which reminded her of the one at the dungeons, only this one had a sphere engraved on it.

You also carry ropes. You will use them to climb the portal. Climb over one another, forming a ladder, and the last ones use the ropes. Everyone, up, now!

They obeyed and Ivo put his back to the wall of the pearl first. Then Aiden climbed onto his shoulders and put his back against the pearl. The next was Taika. Nahia went up next and reached the top of the pearl. She helped Daphne and Lily, and then the three with a rope got Taika up. Finally, Aiden and Ivo climbed up. They had to exert themselves to pull Ivo up.

While they were climbing, the other two groups belonging to the Red Squadron did so as well. The other squadrons waited their turn.

Now follow me! Irakas-Gorri-Gaizt ordered them and flew from the lookout straight into the portal. The red dragon vanished inside it. Its squadron followed.

Nahia came out of the portal and fell onto the ground in front of it. The fall was not long, and she remained hunched over. Around her, her comrades fell and the other two squads joined them. They all entered in the same way, as if they had jumped from a great height, but not a deadly one. She turned around and saw behind her a similar pearl to the one they had just used with an open portal. She also saw a dozen platform towers surrounding the pearls, and on them dragons watching. They were young dragons of medium size.

Move. Line up in front of me. The rest of the squadrons will arrive shortly.

Irakas-Gorri-Gaizt was about a hundred paces in front of the pearl between two towers. They went over to him and lined up. A moment later, the Black Squadron arrived, followed by the Blue Squadron. A short while later, the six squadrons were lined up before their leaders. Nahia was looking everywhere to try and guess where they were. She saw clouds around her and a clear sky where the land ended at about five hundred paces. Apart from that, based on the chilly air and the fact that it was hard to breathe, she knew they were on one of the dragon realms in the sky. They were not below on land, that was sure. Taika was looking around with narrowed eyes, most likely thinking the same thing.

We set out. In formation. Now. Irakas-Gorri-Gaizt and everyone else started out, following a wide avenue to the north. The six squadrons formed a line with the red one in the lead. Nahia enjoyed going first—she could see the landscape around them better. It was not very different from the one they had left behind. The avenue divided a great field of tall grass, and on either side, they could glimpse forests in the distance. They did not see any buildings.

Several dragons flew over them, and Nahia wondered whether they were watching them.

We are in the domains of Erre-Gor-Mau, leader of the Gondra Clan and king of this realm in the sky, as well as the Human race below on earth. We only have permission to pass through. And the dragons which are not of this realm cannot fly here without the king's permission, their leader told them, which answered many of the questions they were all asking themselves. Nahia felt like running to one of the cliffs and plunging down. Her home, her grandmother, and her village were down there. Unfortunately, she had no wings, and if she jumped it would be to her death.

The king's castle and the royal city are to the north of the realm. We are not going there. We are heading east.

Suddenly, they saw what looked like a great mountain in the distance. But when they approached, following the avenue, they realized it was not a mountain, although it had the size of one. It was a colossal pearl, a hundred times larger than the one they had seen.

They were all flabbergasted by the tremendous size of the object.

They reached the pearl that rose like a great spherical building and saw that there were long stairs that allowed people to climb it. Looking at the pearl and the stairs, Nahia realized they were both creations of the dragons and were not natural. She thought again and arrived at the conclusion that this pearl had been built so large to be able to open a huge portal that could reach very long distances. King Erre-Gor-Mau had built it to be able to travel from Kraido to Drameia. The distance between both continent-worlds had to be gigantic. She also clearly realized that they were doomed to make the journey. She no longer had any doubt.

The great pearl was also surrounded by a dozen lookout towers, and on top of them were dragons, only these were large and silver, which intrigued Nahia. These were no watch dragons. These dragons were old and each was silver; they were all there for some reason. Nahia still did not know what element silver dragons controlled, but since the Great Oracle being one of them, she guessed it had something to do with time, since the Great Oracle was supposed to be able to see or predict the future.

We will stop here, but maintain the formation, Irakas-Gorri-Gaizt's order reached them.

The six squadrons stopped. For a long while, they waited. Everyone was nervous. The presence of that colossal pearl was not exactly conducive to calmness. On the contrary. Even the most absent-minded had already realized what was going to happen next.

Suddenly, they heard loud roars. They all looked up at the sky. About fifteen dragons were coming from the north, flying in formation and creating a large triangle. At the head of it in the lead came an enormous red dragon. Nahia knew who it was at once. King Erre-Gor-Mau was flying toward them with a royal escort. The dragons flew over the pearl and them, making several passes and letting loose powerful roars. Nahia thought they were trying to intimidate them with their power, although she did not really know why. Seeing them come down and land a little way apart, she understood they were indicating who was master here.

Everyone, stand still. Wait, their leader messaged them as it joined the other squadron leaders who were walking slowly toward the king and the royal guard. Nahia noticed that both the king and the royal guard were all much larger than their leaders, which left her gaping.

Those were all very powerful dragons. When the leaders reached the king, they all bowed their heads until they almost touched the ground with them. She had never seen this behavior before. That a dragon should bow low seemed to them unthinkable, and their leaders least of all. And yet here they were, the six with their heads bowed, paying homage to the king of this realm in the clouds.

For a moment, King Erre-Gor-Mau seemed to be speaking to the six leaders. Then they returned to their squadrons.

We have the king's permission to use his portal. Go up the stairs, Irakas-Gorri-Gaizt ordered.

This they did, and as they went up, they saw the silver dragons flashing from the lookouts. Then the great pearl flashed as well. They were opening the portal. But unlike the portal they had just used, which had been opened by the guardian quickly, this one was much slower. The silver dragons took a long time before they managed to form the portal, and there were about a dozen of them. Nahia guessed that to open such a portal, a lot of energy was required, as well as powerful and wise dragons. Once the enormous portal was formed above the pearl, she had no doubt that was the case. She felt like an ant before the huge sphere and the silver sea that filled it.

Her comrades were not saying a word, but they all looked overwhelmed by that grandiose portal.

The time has come. Enter the portal. The mission awaits us, Irakas-Gorri-Gaizt ordered them.

Nahia took a deep breath. She did not think twice and entered the colossal portal.

Chapter 49

Nahia woke up inside what looked like a military tent. She was lying on a camping cot. She had a slight headache, but it was not too bad. Her squad comrades were sleeping beside her in the tent. She got up, puzzled. She remembered entering the great portal and then nothing else. She looked at her silver bracelet. Perhaps it was only good for short trips and not between continent-worlds. Yes, that had to be it. She saw that everyone's things were in the tent: backpacks, shields, and cloaks.

She could hear movement outside, a great deal of it. She opened the canvas flap and poked her head out to look. She was struck dumb. She was in the middle of a huge military camp. There were thousands of tents around and soldiers everywhere. Soldiers of the dragons' army. They were wearing clothes she had never seen before and that were not like the ones they wore. The armor she saw had scales but not real dragon scales, instead made of metal imitating a dragon's natural armor. They all wore metal helmets which had a dragon on the back; some had a roaring dragon with spread wings and others with folded wings. The clothes were the elemental colors of the dragons.

She shut her eyes tight several times to make sure this was not a dream. No, she was seeing reality. There were Human, Tauruk-Kapro, Scarlatum, Fatum, and Drakonid soldiers everywhere. They looked very busy, going hither and thither carrying spears, shields, crates, sacks, and all kind of supplies. She could hear shouting from those who must be the officers calling orders. Several groups of soldiers passed by in formation, and in the distance, she could see other groups practicing offense and defense with shields and spears. This was an invasion force—it could not be anything else.

What happened? Where are we?" Daphne asked, also poking her head out to see what was going on.

"What does it look like?" Nahia replied, pointing at the soldiers and the tents.

"They'd better be our own…"

"They are, aren't they?" Lily's head appeared beside theirs.

"Yes, they are," Nahia confirmed.

"Thank goodness," Daphne snorted.

"Wonderful, I already see a very handsome Scarlatum officer. It would've been a shame if I'd had to freeze him alive with my elemental breath."

A moment later, the rest awoke. They rose and came out of the tent to see where they were and what was going on. What they found was that they were facing an awesome and colossal glacier with a collapsed section. In the still-frozen part, a large door had been dug out that must lead inside.

"That glacier, doesn't it look like a fortress with a crumbled part?" Lily commented.

"Yup, it has the shape of a fortress," Daphne nodded.

"It's cold here, and there are areas still covered with frost," Taika commented, looking at an area to the east.

"We're somewhere north," said Ivo.

"That's what I think," Taika said.

"In Drameia?" Asked Aiden.

Nahia nodded.

"I believe so, I think this is the invasion force the five kings are preparing to begin conquering this world," Nahia said.

"Then the invasion has not begun yet?" Aiden asked.

Nahia shrugged.

"I don't know."

"There are no wounded, or soldiers who look like they've been fighting. Uniforms and armor are pristine—I'd say we're witnessing the preparations for the invasion," said Taika.

"Well, there are thousands of soldiers, where did they come from?" Daphne asked.

"The five kings agreed on the invasion, they've sent their armies I think," said Nahia.

"If you notice the cloaks of the soldiers and officers, in the middle of the back they have a rune, and I see at least three different ones," Taika realized.

"They must be the runes that identify each clan and king," Nahia guessed.

"That's right," Taika said, nodding.

"Do you think we'll be sent to fight with them?" asked Daphne.

"That would be an honor," said Aiden, who was looking proudly at the soldiers who went by in large formations.

"We'd be protected, so I don't think so…" Daphne said.

"No, it wouldn't be a test if we went with all of them," Lily said, shaking her head.

Nahia said nothing, but she was sure the dragons would have chosen something much more risky for their lives. She had no doubt.

A Drakonid officer approached them.

"The squadron leaders are waiting for you at the end of the camp. You must go to them," he indicated south.

"Right away," said Aiden, and he went into the tent to get his gear.

"Now we'll find out what this mission is all about," said Daphne.

They gathered their gear, got ready, and crossed the camp. As they did so, they saw the rest of the members of the squadrons leaving other nearby tents as well. They joined up together and went in formation, passing between the soldiers. Nahia saw Ana and greeted her. Ana returned the greeting with dull eyes. Then Nahia saw Logan, who looked calm but tense, as usual. Finally, she saw Maika, who smiled at her, and Nahia smiled back. They could not talk since they were each with their squad, but they gave one another encouraging looks.

As they were crossing the military camp, they realized how enormous it was. Nahia was shocked at the magnitude of that army. There were tens of thousands of soldiers here.

When they left the camp, they found themselves in an area of tundra with a few guards. They looked back and saw the camp, the glacier behind it, and a dozen dragons flying over it. Nahia realized then that the pearl they had come to, the portal on this side, was inside the glacier, hidden. That had to be the case, because there was nothing but plains in every direction and a pearl as large as this was like a mountain. It could only be inside a larger one: the glacier.

They arrived at where their leaders were. The six dragons were a league away from the camp, in the middle of a plain covered in part by frost and in part by snow.

Form up, Red Squadron, Irakas-Gorri-Gaizt's order reached them.

They formed up and awaited orders. The rest of the squadrons also lined up, each before their dragon leader.

Listen with perfect attention. What I am going to tell you is critical and secret. We are in enemy territory. We have traveled through the great portal to another continent-world. The portal you have come out of is inside the glacier. Being such a long journey, the bracelets could not keep you conscious. We are in Drameia. The locals call it Tremia. The five kings are preparing for the invasion of this world to the greater glory of our race. The army you have seen is preparing to attack soon. This world is one of the three original worlds, so it is of vital importance to recover it. When I say recover it, it is because thousands of years ago the dragons ruled this world.

A group of soldiers on patrol passed by Irakas-Gorri-Gaizt, and the dragon stopped talking and watched them pass. After a moment, it continued.

We are on a continent in the north of this world. The locals call it the Reborn Continent. Luckily, there are portals from this world's ancient times here. The first one is south of our current location, and that is where we are going. From there, we will split up to carry out the mission.

Nahia did not like the idea of separating very much. All the rest fit in with what she had guessed from what she knew. She looked at Ana, who was close by, and saw her swallow. She was very frightened.

Our mission is one of reconnaissance. We must travel to the portals in this world and make sure they are intact, operative, and reconnoiter the area where they are to evaluate the risk of using them during the invasion campaign. We will most likely encounter Humans and other local races. If so, we must eliminate them so as not to lose the invasion's surprise factor.

That did not sound good to Nahia at all. She looked at Logan and managed to meet his gaze. He gave her a nod which Nahia understood as "keep calm." She tried to, but things were going to get ugly. She looked at Maika and she looked back at her; there was no smile on her face now, only worry.

We will now go to the pearl south of this tundra. Advance at a run. Go, Irakas-Gorri-Gaizt messaged to them as it took off. The rest of the dragon leaders also took to the sky. A moment later, the six squadrons were running to the south along the tundra. Soon they arrived at a part with grass and went on further south. It took them time to reach the pearl, but they made it. It stood alone, unprotected and unwatched. Or so it seemed.

The six leaders came down from the sky and landed around the pearl. While the group recovered from the long run, they opened a portal. This pearl and the portal were similar in size to the one in Gorja. Nahia guessed that the distances they could travel with this portal and the others like it they might find there were for this world exclusively.

Each one of the squadrons will be in charge of one of the pearls in this world. It is time to begin. Wait for my order to climb into the portal.

Nahia saw that the first team to leave was the Blue Squadron and wished with all her heart that Ana would be all right. Ana gave her a goodbye look before she entered the portal, a look filled with fear and anguish. Nahia felt a shiver. She had a bad feeling which she tried to shake off. The worst thing was that they were separating, going to different places in this world they knew nothing about, with unknown people and dangers. The more she thought about it, the more she worried. The Black Squadron followed. Then Logan's White Squadron. Nahia looked at him and he looked back at her before crossing. A look of confidence, intense. Logan would come back, she was sure. Nothing was going to happen to him. Not to Logan.

I am going to select the rune of the destination pearl in the portal. Enter when I tell you.

Nahia sighed. She could not get rid of this bad feeling.

The portal flashed.

Destination pearl selected. Enter.

They climbed onto the pearl and entered the portal.

Nahia fell to the ground and hunched over to cushion the fall. Her squad fell beside her, and they all did the same. They remained hunched over and looked around. The Ardent Squad and the Searing Squad fell out on either side. A moment later, Irakas-Gorri-Gaizt flew out of the portal.

They were all looking around, alert. They were in unknown territory. Nahia studied the place. She was cold, very cold, colder than where they had entered the portal. They were in the middle of what looked like a colossal frozen valley. It was gigantic, with its walls of frozen rock rising to the sky. She touched the ground; it was frozen. Behind them was a pearl, identical to the one they had entered to get here. If the ground and the frozen walls surprised her, the sky was even more shocking. When she looked up, she could not see it very well. There was a layer of ice that did not let them appreciate it clearly. A layer of thick ice covered the entire gigantic valley. They were inside a frozen valley.

"We're inside a glacier," Ivo whispered.

"How do you know?" Aiden asked him.

"I know a lot of things, you'd be surprised."

"It has to be a glacier, or a frozen valley, whichever you prefer," said Daphne.

"It's really cold. My face is getting all wrinkled, I don't like it at all," Lily protested.

"This place is absolutely silent… it transmits a feeling of peace…" Taika commented.

"Let's not get too overconfident, there's bound to be danger," said Nahia, who did not trust the frozen serenity surrounding them.

Irakas-Gorri-Gaizt flew over them inside the valley.

I am going to secure this area. Do not move, I am detecting a lot of magical power here.

"As I was saying…" Nahia said, looking around, worried.

They all remained crouching in front of the pearl, whose portal faded away until it vanished. Nahia realized they could not get out of this valley if Irakas-Gorri-Gaizt did not open another portal. She looked around and saw several caves and grottoes at different heights on the walls of rock and ice. She had the impression that they were the huge lairs of dangerous beings. Or perhaps it was only her imagination fed by the fear she felt. They waited in tension until the red dragon returned and landed on the pearl, folding its wings. It addressed them.

This place is quite unique. There are creatures here with power resting, ancient and powerful beings. I pick up a lot of power. We must not awake them. We are going to secure the surroundings. We are in the north of this world in a place known as the Frozen Continent by the locals. There will be cold and ice out there. Also, possibly, natives of the ice. Everyone, be alert. Follow me.

Irakas-Gorri-Gaizt took off to the north of the valley. The three squads followed at a trot, looking at the frozen valley with apprehension as they went through it. Those caves and the profound quiet gave Nahia a bad premonition. They arrived at the north wall and a great cavern tunnel appeared before them. Their leader could not fly out from there, so it landed and walked toward the cave.

Suddenly, a giant albino spider came down the wall. Irakas-Gorri-Gaizt sent a tremendous flame with its fire breath and the spider withdrew to the heights with several legs and part of its body horribly charred. Irakas-Gorri-Gaizt went into the cave and they followed. They went along a large, long tunnel and another impressive creature appeared before them. It was a snow-white snake of enormous size. Irakas-Gorri-Gaizt stared at it and opened its mouth as if it were going to use its fiery breath. The snake hissed, showing its fangs. They all waited with shield and dagger in hand. Suddenly, the snake withdrew and let them pass.

They are guardians of this place. Now we have free passage, Irakas-Gorri-Gaizt informed them.

They went along the tunnel without any other setbacks and came out to a freezing, icy world that left them dumbstruck. Wherever they looked, everything was frozen. A layer of ice and frost covered everything as far as the eye could see. The wind blew in icy gusts, and it was fiercely cold. In the distance they could see great glaciers like the one they had just come out of.

For a moment, they all just watched the landscape that was at the same time so shocking and so desolate. It did not look like a place where anyone might survive for long.

We must reconnoiter the whole area and secure it. I will do that from the air. I will give a few long passes flying away from here. I will reconnoiter the land. Ardent Squad, secure the area west of the glacier. Searing Squad, the east. Igneous Squad, the north and then the south. Remember there might be ice natives here. If you find a group, do not leave witnesses of our presence here. Await my orders once you have secured each area, the red dragon ordered, and with a leap it spread its wings, beat them hard, and took off.

The three squads looked at one another uncertainly. A moment later, they all started moving.

"To the north, cautiously," Nahia told her comrades, unable to shake off the bad feeling she had experienced ever since they had arrived in this world.

The three squads soon lost sight of one another. The Igneous Squad went in formation, stepping on the ice and frost-covered ground. They went north for a good while.

"This icy wind is destroying my beautiful skin," Lily protested.

"Cover as much as you can with your hood," Daphne advised her.

"How are you adapting to this cold?" Ivo asked.

"Very badly," Daphne replied.

"The same, and I'm not speaking so my lips don't chap," Lily told them.

"I'm doing well, it's quite cold in my land," Aiden said.

"Me too, but of course I come from the north of my country where it's cold and I have fur to protect myself," Taika said.

"I prefer this cold to the heat spells I get," Nahia looked on the bright side. "With a bit of luck, I won't get them here with such low temperatures."

"Let's hope so," Ivo said, smiling at her.

They went on north until they reached a small glacier with a cave entrance.

"Should we go in?" Daphne asked like someone considering a bad idea.

"We have to reconnoiter the area. I don't see any suspicious activity," Taika said.

"Or footprints," Ivo added.

"This looks like a frozen desert. I don't think there's anyone here," Nahia commented.

"That cave might have hostiles inside ready for an ambush. We must secure it." Aiden said.

"Here goes granite-head with his Drakonid ideas," Daphne protested.

Lily said nothing but shook her head.

"I'm going to secure this cave, it's our duty. You can do whatever you please," Aiden said and moved to the entrance.

"I hope a thousand-year-old creature comes out and gobbles him up," said Daphne.

"It would throw him up at once," said Lily and immediately put her hands to her lips.

"We can't let him go in alone..." Nahia said, watching him advance.

"It's inhumane and contrary to the principles of nature and harmonic balance," said Ivo.

"Let's go before he gets into trouble," Taika said.

They all followed Aiden reluctantly and grumbling.

When they were a few paces from the cave, Aiden stopped where he was.

The rest of the group reached him.

"What is it?" Taika asked him.

"I saw something moving…"

"Could you be more imprecise!" said Daphne.

At that moment, six natives of the ice came out, so big and muscular that beside them Ivo looked like a youngling, which on the other hand he really was.

Nahia stared at them with her mouth open. They had blue skin and their hair and beards were whitish. Like ice. They seemed to have been frozen. They carried large double-headed axes in their hands. What impressed them most was their fierce, brutal look.

"These don't look friendly," Daphne pointed out.

"Get into formation, quickly!" Taika said.

They formed with Nahia, Daphne, and Lily in the first line and Aiden, Ivo, and Taika behind them.

The six wild-looking natives moved toward them, brandishing their large war axes with blue blades. They came in one line without apparent concern, like someone who knows their rivals are mere ants they can squash.

"What shall we do?" Nahia asked.

"They don't seem to be coming with any intention of chatting," said Daphne.

"My goodness aren't they ugly and brutish," Lily said, making a face.

"If they're looking for trouble, trouble they'll find," Aiden said, very sure of himself.

"They're a head taller and look like your older cousins," Daphne told him.

"That's because I'm young. In five years, I'll be like them."

"Yeah, and I'll be bigger, but the moment is now, not the future," Ivo told him.

"These look like weathered native warriors. We are young and inexperienced, it would be better to avoid a confrontation," said Taika.

"Our leader said no witnesses. We have to kill them," said Aiden.

"I swear I'm going to blind him so they shred him to pieces for being a granite-head!" Daphne grumbled.

"First line, switch to magic. Maybe that will scare them," said Taika.

"Fine, although I doubt these savages would be scared even by a thousand-year-old dragon," said Lily.

The three put their shields and dagger away and took out their Learning Pearls. They concentrated and created three elemental balls in their hands, which hovered above them.

The six blue wild ones stopped in front of them. They pointed and one of them, the strongest, started shouting at them in a language they did not understand.

"We don't understand you," Nahia said.

The wild one began to gesture, pointing at them as he shouted.

"He doesn't seem to like us," said Daphne.

Suddenly, he gave a war cry and the six lunged in to attack.

"Throw at them!" Taika shouted.

Nahia looked at her elemental ball of fire. She sent more energy from her inner dragon and made it bigger. Then she looked at one of the wild ones. She used her mind and sent the ball against his powerful blue chest. The ball hit him and exploded in flames. They consumed him where he was in a moment, enveloping him in intense flames. Daphne sent hers, throwing it with her hand. She hit one of the wild ones, and there was an explosion of light that blinded him. He stopped running and cried to high heaven while rubbing his eyes. Lily threw her ball of ice, and when it hit the wild one's feet as he was approaching her, they froze. He could not keep running.

"Cover yourselves!" Taika told them, and the three ran to get behind the three boys who, with their shields and daggers ready, prepared to withstand the clash of the wild ones.

The wild leader went straight for Ivo as if he were the leader of the group, since he was the largest. Ivo defended himself with his shield. He received a tremendous axe blow, which he bore by a hair's breadth. Aiden, on the left, was fighting against a wild one with his usual self-confidence, only his rival was stronger and more weathered. With a crossed blow with the axe, the native sent him flying to one side. He was left lying on the ground. The wild one raised his great axe to split him in two before he could get back up. Nahia threw a ball of fire at the attacker and burned him up. He died at once without being able to kill Aiden. Taika dodged his opponent's great axe instead of blocking it with his shield and plunged the dagger into his side. The wild one roared with pain and rage. He delivered a side blow with his weapon and Taika stepped back, letting the blade pass in front of his stomach. Then he gave a powerful leap and plunged his dagger into the other's neck up to the pommel.

There was only the leader left, and he was fighting Ivo. The wild one had torn away his shield with an axe blow, and now Ivo was holding the wild one's weapon with his two large hands as they both exerted all the strength they were capable of. It was a fight between two colossuses. The wild one delivered a kick to Ivo's stomach and the Tauruk doubled over, letting go of the axe. The wild one raised it to hit him but Daphne's ball of light burst in his face, blinding him. He took a step back, surprised. He tried to come forward, blinded, but Lily's ball of ice froze his feet. Even so, he tried to come, but Nahia's ball of fire hit him in the head and he burnt in a raging bonfire, dying right away.

"Well fought!" Taika congratulated them all.

"There's the blinded one and the frozen one," said Aiden, who was getting up with his arm sore. "We have to finish them off."

"We're not going to finish off anyone," Ivo told him. "That would be very bad for our karma. We'd break the natural balance."

"Our leader has ordered as much," Aiden retorted.

"I'm going to freeze them alive. Since they're from here and have those blue furs, I think they'll survive my cold. That way we do our duty and don't have bad karma," Lily said.

"That's not..." Aiden started to protest, and Daphne threw a piece of ice at his head.

"Shut up, ice-head." Lily froze them completely with three elemental balls of ice thrown at each one. Once frozen, Taika knocked them down on the ground.

"That's settled. There's no one left standing."

"What do we do now?" Daphne asked, looking around,

"I think we've explored this area north of the glacier well enough. There are large, aggressive wild ones here. That's what we have to report," Lily said.

"Correct. Let's go south and fulfill our orders," said Taika.

"Very well. To the south," Ivo indicated.

"Let's see what we find..." Nahia said, worried.

"Whatever it is, it will surely break the harmonic balance..." Daphne said with a glance at Ivo. The Tauruk smiled and said nothing.

Chapter 50

They went on toward the south, which led them back to the great glacier in the frozen valley and the pearl. Since they had already been inside the valley, they decided to go around it by the west side. Halfway to the great glacier, they saw the Ardent Squad not too far away.

"Lazy bums! They haven't advanced almost at all," Daphne said, pointing at them.

"It's not that they haven't advanced, they're being attacked!" Nahia realized.

Farther to the west, beyond the Ardent Squad, they identified about twenty natives with spears.

"Let's go help them! For the glory of dragons!" Aiden was already running toward them.

Daphne looked at Ivo, and he shrugged. He smiled at her and ran off after Aiden.

"Karma," he said.

They all followed. Running through the frozen tundra was no easy feat, and they had to be careful not to slip and fall. Besides, the strong and cutting wind of that place pushed them around haphazardly.

They arrived where their squadron comrades were defending themselves from a superior number of attackers. These were different from those they had just fought against. They were thinner, not as strong, and brutal, although tall and athletic. Their skin was crystal white and it shone, reflecting the sunlight as if it were made of crystallized snowflakes. Their snow-white hair shone equally intensely, and looked like frozen snow. No doubt they were also natives of the ice. They were armed with javelins they carried on their backs and long knives at their waists. They were throwing their javelins at the Ardent Squad.

As they arrived, they stood behind their comrades.

"Igneous Squad to the rescue!" Aiden warned.

"Native enemies with throwing spears!" Brendan warned them, the blond Human who was behind Draider, the Drakonid who was holding his shield and dagger in a defensive stance. They were at the left end of the formation.

Cordelius, the huge Kapro, was also in the middle with his shield and dagger. Evelyn, the Fatum, was behind him. She was bleeding from a nasty wound in her right hand. It appeared that a javelin had pierced it.

On the right side, in front, Lara the black panther was holding her shield and dagger. Right behind her, Elsa, the Scarlatum, was hiding. She had a javelin in her thigh and was crouching.

Suddenly, several javelins flew over the Ardent Squad and fell on the Igneous Squad.

"Shields!" Taika warned.

They all raised them and managed to protect themselves. The javelins bounced off.

"We can't fight back here," said Aiden.

"He's right. We should stand like them on the left," Taika ordered, "Change formation!"

The boys stood in front and the girls behind. They maneuvered and stood beside the other squad. Now they made two rows of six. The enemy was on top of a small frozen hillock. There were more of them and they had the height advantage.

"What do you suggest?" Brendan asked.

"Let's all move in close formation with the shields on top until we reach them," Taika told him.

"We have two wounded," Brendan replied.

"If we don't finish off the enemy, we can't tend to them," Aiden told him.

"He's right," Taika said. "They'll cut down our numbers with their javelins."

Brendan thought about it.

"All as one! We move, shields to the front!" Brendan gave the order.

They advanced in perfect formation as they had practiced so often, every morning before their leader.

The natives threw their javelins, but the shields they all carried up front or over their heads deflected them. They reached the foot of the hillock, and the natives changed tactics when they saw them so close. They ran down with their javelins and knives in their hands and lunged at them. The first line withstood the crash. Aiden, Ivo, Taika,

Draider, Cordelius, and Lara rejected the attackers with their shields, maintaining the formation.

"Second line, elemental attacks!" Brendan ordered.

Nahia, Daphne, Lily, and Brendan created elemental balls. Evelyn could not throw. She was covering Elsa with her shield, since the Scarlatum had collapsed on the ground. They threw the balls over their comrades' heads, straight at the attackers. When they exploded among the attackers as they ran down like a horde they were hit with fire, ice, blinding light, and more fire. They heard screams of pain, and several fell, wounded or dead. The shields saved those in the first line from some explosions which fell too close to them.

Elemental weapons!" Nahia cried to Brendan.

The other Human nodded.

Nahia and Brendan concentrated and began to apply a layer of fire to their comrades' shields. A moment later, the six shields were burning on the outside. The attackers were surprised to see this, but they went on attacking with javelin and knife. Ivo and Cordelius had no trouble since they were stronger than the natives, but the rest were fighting for their lives.

"More elemental weapons!" Nahia told Brendan, and they began to set fire to the blades of their daggers. This would help their comrades.

When the enemies saw the fiery weapons and shields and that they could not break the first line of formation, they stopped. They decided to attack the flanks. They went around the formation, on the right and left.

"Cover the flanks!" Taika called.

Nahia saw an enemy appear on her left and did not think twice. She called her inner dragon and, gathering energy, called her Dragon Breath. From her mouth there issued a tremendous flame, which caught the native fully as he was coming to plunge a knife in her heart. He died, incinerated in an instant. On the right side, Brendan was protecting the two wounded, and he did the same, using his own Dragon Breath. Lily went to help him and used her icy Dragon Breath on another attacker. Daphne stayed with Nahia and helped her, blinding the next attacker. The battle lasted a little longer as the last attackers fell scorched or frozen in their attempts to break the defensive formation, which they did not manage to do.

"Enemy defeated!" cried Brendan.

"A glorious victory!" Aiden cried, excited.

Cordelius, Ivo, go up the hillock and tell us if you see more enemies," Taika told them.

Nahia went over to the two wounded.

"We have to make a tourniquet," she said, and leaving her backpack on the ground, she opened it and took out a small sachet with some medicine they had been given in case they were wounded. It was not much: a needle and suture thread, disinfectant ointment, another for scarring, and herbs against fevers. Nahia got to work.

"There are no enemies in sight!" they heard Cordelius confirm, which eased them.

"I thought steel couldn't pierce through our dragon scales," Daphne said, watching Nahia treat the wound.

"The edge entered between two scales... there's quite enough space between each scale... and it's cloth," Elsa said, bearing the pain.

Daphne looked at her breeches and realized Elsa was right.

"And we don't use gloves in order to have better control on our magic," said Evelyn, whose hand was bleeding profusely. Nahia healed them, making use of her knowledge as a healer. They were all very impressed, and she had to explain about her old profession.

"I'm very glad to have a healer in the squad," Taika told her.

"And I'm happy there's one in the squadron," said Brendan, smiling at her.

"I'm happy to be able to help. I would have rather been a healer than a Dragon Blood Witch, but this is how the cookie crumbled."

"The life that awaits us is mysterious in its complexities," Ivo commented, returning from the hillock.

They all stared at him with blank looks, but he did not mind.

"What are you going to do?" Nahia asked Brendan once she finished curing the two wounded.

"We'll wait for the leader here. We can't move her," Brenda said, indicating Elsa.

You could take them to the pearl," Nahia suggested.

Brendan made a face showing he disliked the idea.

"It might be interpreted as weakness... we'll wait for the leader before retreating. Those are the orders."

Nahia sighed. She understood why, but she did not like it.

"All right, we'll go on south," said Taika.

They took their leave, and the Igneous Squad went on to the south of the great glacier. It took them quite a while to go around it, and at last reach the area they had to investigate. They went over it in silence, alert. They arrived at another glacier—smaller, completely blue, and very beautiful—and stopped at a prudent distance. They had already had two unpleasant encounters in this continent of ice and frost, and they did not want a third one. Not even Aiden made any attempt to go and explore it.

Unfortunately, their wishes were not granted. A group of a dozen natives came out from inside the glacier, which they could not see into. That area was filled with natives in every direction it seemed.

"In formation!" called Taika, and they all did so quickly.

"These are different... stranger..." Daphne commented as the dozen natives approached.

"Yeah... I don't like this..." said Nahia, who noticed they had a very strange look. They had blue skin with areas like their necks and arms a crystalline white, as if snow had crystallized over their skin. Their faces were very similar to a human's, with eyes of very intense blue. They wore their heads shaved, and on them they could see white tattoos with strange runes. They wore seal skins and bone necklaces. In their hands they carried staves, and they did not see any other weapons. They were neither tall nor strong, and yet they emanated power, one of ice.

Suddenly, at about a hundred paces, they stopped. They watched them in detail, studying them. One of them stepped forward and spoke in his language, but they did not understand him. He pointed at them and at the glacier behind them.

"I think he's asking us if we've come from the glacier," Nahia guessed.

"What should we say?" Lily looked at her comrades to see what they thought.

"We should confuse the enemy, so say no," Aiden said.

"Isn't it better to tell the truth and avoid another conflict?" Daphne suggested.

"The truth is always the best way," said Ivo.

"Both answers might work well, or not," Taika shrugged.

"Fine, I'll say yes and see if we're lucky," Nahia looked at the leader of the natives of the ice and nodded repeatedly.

The native leader retreated to the others, and suddenly they began to move their staves and intone some kind of prayer in their language.

"What are they doing?" Nahia was confused.

"They're singing us a song, how nice," said Lily.

"That's not a song, that's magic," said Ivo.

They all looked at the Tauruk.

"Magic?" Nahia looked at the natives and began to feel her skin crawl. "It certainly is magic," she nodded.

"Good or bad?" Aiden asked, drawing his dagger.

"We'll find out in a moment," said Taika.

Around them, a low mist began to form. It seemed to come out of the frozen ground. It was a pretty light-blue color. The mist got thicker and soon covered the whole area around them.

"What's this?" Nahia began to have a feeling of danger.

"It doesn't seem to do anything, does it?" Aiden said.

"It's not natural, I don't like it," said Ivo.

Suddenly, Lily's eyes became the same color as the mist. Without saying a word, she drew her dagger and approached Taika, who was looking at her blankly, and delivered a thrust to his stomach. Taika reacted and deflected the dagger with his forearm in an almost instinctive defensive move.

"What the?" Aiden reacted and grabbed Lily's dagger arm. She turned toward Aiden and opened her mouth.

"Watch out, Aiden, icy Dragon Breath!" Nahia warned him.

Aiden opened his eyes and threw himself to one side. Lily threw her frozen breath and missed him by a hair's breadth.

"Ivo, we have to knock her out!" Nahia told her.

The Tauruk moved forward, and before Lily attacked him, he hit her on the head. She fell to the ground, unconscious.

"It's the mist, we have to get out of it!" Nahia said.

"Do we attack?" Aiden asked.

Daphne let out her light breath and blinded Aiden. Nahia looked at her and saw that Daphne also had blue eyes.

"Ivo, quick!"

It was not necessary. Taika hit Daphne on the back of the neck and she fell unconscious too.

Get out of the spell's area of effect. Those are magi. Never get closer than two hundred paces when dealing with a mage. Go back to the pearl. I will deal with them, the message of their leader reached them as it came flying over them.

"Let's get out of here!" Nahia shouted.

Ivo slung Lily over his shoulder. Taika did the same with Daphne, and Nahia grabbed Aiden's hand to guide him, since he was still blinded.

They ran toward the glacier while their leader sent a terrible flame over the dozen ice magi. Nahia looked back and figured it must have incinerated them all. She was wrong—they were still standing. They had withstood the dragon's fiery breath. How was that possible? She saw them withdraw at a run toward their glacier. Irakas-Gorri-Gaizt gave another pass and attacked them again with its fiery breath. Two fell dead, but the rest bore the elemental attack. That left Nahia speechless.

Chapter 51

When they reached the glacier, they did not stop and went on inside. There was a similar entrance to the one at the north side. They went in and continued running. They saw the huge albino spider, one of the watchers of that place, but it let them through. Nahia guessed that Irakas-Gorri-Gaizt had permission to go in, and that permission extended to them because they were with the great red dragon.

They arrived at the pearl and saw no one there. They left Lily and Daphne on the ground.

Nahia examined them. They were fine, but they had fainted. She took the waterskin out of her backpack and wet their faces. The two came to at once, and their eyes were no longer blue. Nahia sighed with relief.

"What happened?" asked Lily, who had a terrible headache.

"Did anyone hit me in the back of my neck?" Daphne asked, massaging it.

"I had no choice…," Ivo apologized.

"You were going to kill us," said Taika.

"I'm still blinded," Aiden told them.

"I can do nothing about that, but it'll go away in a short while," Nahia told him, looking at Daphne and asking her with a nod.

Daphne shrugged.

"It'd better, or else Daphne is going to get what for."

Daphne looked at Nahia and made a gesture of "was that me?" Nahia nodded. Daphne grinned and shrugged.

Suddenly, they saw a native mage in the distance arriving with others. The pearl was covering them, and they had not been seen yet.

"More magi!" Nahia said, looking around.

"What do we do?" Ivo asked.

"Better not confront them," said Taika. "Their reach is much farther than ours."

"Then we'd better hide. There are hundreds of caves here," Lily said.

"Good idea," Daphne nodded.

"Come!" Nahia ran off with the pearl behind her hiding their presence, and she grabbed Aiden.

She passed a cave which she did not like for some reason. Then she got to the next and this, for some unknown reason, she did like. She went in, dragging Aiden, and the rest followed her.

The cave was dark and enormous. Nahia went in a little further to get away from the entrance, although she doubted they could be seen from outside in that darkness. Then she thought better and went even further in, feeling the wall until they were where they could not see the entrance.

"This is better, they won't see us from outside," she told her comrades.

They remained hunched in silence. Outside, they heard footsteps. They were different than theirs, the being seemed to drag their feet over the frozen ground. They all stayed silent.

Nahia reached for her dagger and remained quiet. Suddenly, a pair of cat's eyes appeared in the middle of the reigning darkness and they heard a growl.

"A panther," Taika whispered, recognizing the eyes and the growl.

A new set of eyes appeared beside the first and a threatening growl followed.

"Wolf, big," Taika recognized.

The two beasts did not move from where they were, but they heard another growl and a roar, and the eyes were threatening.

"They're inviting us to leave..." Taika whispered. "This is their cave, their territory."

"We can't go outside," Nahia told him.

A third pair of eyes appeared above the other two pairs. These were reptilian and large, which surprised everyone.

"Dragon?" asked Ivo.

"No, but from the same family..." Taika guessed.

"This is getting ugly," Lily said.

Suddenly, Nahia felt a frozen blade at her throat.

"Shhhh," someone whispered in her ear.

Nahia was silent and stayed as still as a statue.

Suddenly, in front of them appeared a small white light that illuminated them all.

They saw a snow panther which watched them, ready to attack. Beside her was a giant wolf, both with thick furs of the frozen lands. Behind them was a creature they had never seen before. It was a mixture between a dragon and a gecko, with bluish scales. It was watching them with great bulging reptilian eyes.

They all stared at the creatures in front of them and did not notice the fourth occupant, who had his knife on Nahia's neck.

Taika realized.

"Human," he warned and turned toward Nahia.

They all did and saw a Human with a white cloak and hood pressing a knife to Nahia's neck.

"Don't kill her!" Lily pleaded.

"Take it easy …" Ivo told him, raising one hand.

Nahia dropped her dagger and raised her hands in front so her attacker would see them.

With his other hand, the attacker indicated for the others to drop their weapons.

"Do what he says," Taika indicated, and they all left their daggers on the ground in front of them.

I Camu, Higher Drakonian. This be my cave. You leave, they received a mental message to all with a feeling of great sleepiness and weariness, as if this being had just awoken from a deep sleep.

The snow panther growled and the great wolf roared, showing its fangs.

"We don't want to hurt you," said Taika.

"You have nothing to fear from us," Ivo said, gesturing with his large hands.

Nahia did not dare speak with the knife at her throat. She was looking at the Higher Drakonian and sensed he was a creature with power. A lot of power radiated from him.

Lasgol, and I not understand your language, Go. Now, he messaged, and the creature's feeling of weariness reached them with it.

Once again, the snow panther and wolf threatened them with growls, showing their maws. They were going to leap onto them if they did not leave.

All of a sudden, Nahia realized she recognized the name Lasgol. She remembered that Lasgol was the name Egil had given her; the fear she felt had kept her from making the connection earlier. Was this a coincidence? Or was it fate guiding them? She did not know, but she had to make sure.

"Egil," she said.

The Higher Drakonian fixed his eyes on her. The blade of the knife pressed less on her throat.

"Lasgol, Egil," said Nahia.

Her comrades did not understand what she was doing and were staring at her with puzzled expressions.

"Egil?" a male voice asked in her ear.

"Egil Olafstone," said Nahia, who had memorized the prisoner's last name.

"The pressure of the knife vanished from her throat. The attacker turned her toward him, and she could see his face. He had white skin, blue eyes, and blond hair, and was the same age as Egil. He carried a bow with arrows on his back and was dressed entirely in white with a hooded cloak, as if to camouflage with the snow.

"Lasgol," he said, pointing at himself with the knife.

Nahia nodded.

"Nahia," she said.

"Egil?" he asked her.

"Egil with Nahia," she replied and indicated herself.

She saw the being and the Human look at one another, and she had the feeling they were communicating. Could this Human send messages like the dragons?

Where be Egil? Be well? the Higher Drakonian asked, and she received a feeling of great worry.

Nahia nodded several times, then she put her hands together with her wrists upward.

Prisoner?

Nahia nodded.

Where?

"In Kraido, at the Drakoros Academy. Dungeons."

Once again, the Human and the Drakonian looked at one another. They were exchanging messages.

Kraido world dragons. You come from there?

Nahia nodded.

Great portal open in Reborn Continent?

Nahia nodded again.

Much bad, the Drakonian messaged, along with a feeling of great sorrow.

406

All of a sudden, they heard footsteps running outside. Many. They were boots. The Ardent and Searing Squads were coming back.

Nahia looked at Lasgol.

"Egil, you," she said and pointed first outside and then at herself and then at Lasgol, trying to make him understand that Egil had sent her to get him.

Lasgol smiled and nodded. Then he looked at the creature and they seemed to talk.

You say Egil we rescue.

Nahia opened her eyes wide and made gestures that it was very dangerous, shaking her head repeatedly.

Lasgol took out one of the arrows in his quiver. He broke it and put the tip in Nahia's hand, then closed her fingers around it.

"Egil," he said.

Nahia understood. She nodded.

A terrible roar sounded outside. Irakas-Gorri-Gaizt had arrived.

Nahia pointed outside urgently.

Powerful dragon. I feel. You go, the creature named Camu messaged to them.

Lasgol made a gesture for them to leave.

Nahia left, and with her, the others. They came out of the cave and found the two other squads waiting. The Searing Squad also had two wounded. Irakas-Gorri-Gaizt was coming back after taking another pass. Nahia guessed the dragon had killed the native magi, or perhaps they had gone into hiding like them.

We are leaving. This area is filled with aggressive natives. Some have magic. It is a dangerous area, we must report this, their leader messaged to them and descended onto the pearl. A moment later, the portal opened.

Get inside. We are going back.

The three squads climbed onto the pearl, helping the wounded, and went in.

They came out at the pearl of the Reborn Continent. The three squads fell, hunched down, and got up at once. The Black and Crystal Squadrons were already there with their leaders. They also had a couple of wounded

Line up with me, Irakas-Gorri-Gaizt ordered, and they moved away from the pearl. Nahia wanted to tell their leader they had to take Elsa to the war camp so she would be looked after, but she could not address the dragon. She was sure the dragon was well aware they had two wounded who needed attention, but it simply did not care.

The White Squadron arrived and Nahia looked at Logan. He appeared unscathed. He moved, and she could not see any wounds on him. She sighed, relieved. Logan saw her and looked at her for a moment as if also making sure she was all right. She greeted him with a nod, then ran to line up before her leader.

The squads continued arriving. The Blue Squadron arrived without any wounded, and Nahia was glad from the bottom of her heart that Ana was all right. She smiled at Nahia and greeted her with a nod, and Nahia exhaled, relieved.

Finally, the Brown Squadron, Maika's, arrived. At once, Nahia saw that something was not right. Two people were lying on the ground and two others could not stand because of their wounds. Nahia's heart skipped a beat—one of the two who could not stand was Maika. Her squad comrades dragged her to their leader. Nahia saw Nielse keeling beside Maika. He was trying to reanimate her heart while another filled her lungs with air through her mouth.

"Maika, no!" Nahia cried and ran to her side.

Stay at your post. Maintain the formation! Irakas-Gorri-Gaizt's mental message reached her.

Nahia ignored it and got to Maika. She was purple.

"What happened to her?" she asked with her heart in her mouth.

"Jungle natives, with blowpipes and poisoned darts," Nielse told her.

Nahia saw Maika's right hand very swollen, and she held it and turned it around. She had two clear punctures—two darts had hit her. She took out her dagger and made two cross cuts on the wounds. She put Maika's hand to her mouth and began to suck to extract the poison. It was the only thing that could be done. The situation was similar to a poisonous snake bite. When she thought of that, she became more anxious still: poisons were deadly most of the time. She sucked and spit it out.

"Antidote! Bring me an antidote!" she cried, looking at everyone.

Ana and Logan were beside her.

"Who has an antidote?" Logan asked.

"An antidote please!" Ana pleaded.

But there was no one there but them. There was no healer, no one with an antidote. Logan checked his backpack and searched through the small sachet of medicines in case there was one, but there was not.

Maika opened her eyes suddenly.

"Maika, hold on," Nahia told her.

Maika looked at her and coughed up blood.

"Fight… for freedom…" Maika said.

"We'll do it together, hold on," Nahia told her as she went on trying to get all the poison out.

Maika started to convulse. A moment later, she was dead.

"Noooooo! Maika! Noooooo!" Nahia cried.

"She's gone," Nielse said with his head bowed.

Ana was sobbing without control, and Logan was on his knees and shaking his head with moist eyes.

Nahia looked at the swollen, purple face of her friend and rage filled her heart. She pointed at their leader.

"It was you! You killed her! I curse you!"

Watch what you say, human, or your fate will be the same as hers, was the reply.

Nahia, beside herself, was about to tell the dragon what she thought of them with all the rage of her being, but Logan covered her mouth with his hand.

Nahia resisted and tried to free herself to cry "murderer" with all her might at those blasted dragons without heart or scruples.

She felt Logan do something to her neck and everything went black. She fainted.

Chapter 52

Three days later, Nahia lined up with her squadron in front of the castle. It was Graduation day. Her heart was broken from Maika's death, which had not been the only casualty of the end-of-the-year War Test. Two more had died, and several had been wounded. For three days Nahia had wept with sorrow and rage, cursing the dragons and their dark and twisted hearts. But, lining up here on this day, she realized something that gave her strength: she had survived the first year of training. She was graduating and was still alive. She had achieved what they had set out to do when they had first arrived.

She looked at Logan, who was lined up with his squad, and waited for him to look at her, knowing he would eventually. And she was right: Logan looked at her briefly and she gave him a nod. He returned the nod. Then she looked at Ana, who smiled. Another positive thought came to her mind. Nahia had not only survived, she had learned to fight, to use her elemental magic, and she was in excellent physical shape, something totally unthinkable when she lived with her grandmother. The dragons would pay for having taught her all this, for turning her into a Dragon Blood Witch. They would pay dearly. Now she saw her goal clearly. She had to become a powerful Dragon Blood Witch, the most powerful ever, not to fight for the dragons in distant worlds, but to fight against them and defeat them. One day they would regret training her, taking a poor healer and turning her into a powerful Dragon Blood Witch.

"They will pay," she muttered under her breath.

Daphne and Lily eyed her with concern. She smiled at them. She was fine—better than fine. She had a clear purpose: fight for freedom, as Maika had asked her to with her last breath. And she would fight until she had avenged Maika's death.

Colonel Lehen-Gorri-Gogor roared, standing in front of the castle gates with Commander Bigaen-Zuri-Indar beside it.

Today is a glorious day. Today the first-years who have finished the course alive will graduate. Graduation day, a day of glory and honor. Those who line up before me have completed the training of the first year and are graduating. You should feel proud and honored, since others have not made it. Not only that, many more do not even have the chance because they do not have dragon blood like you do. Today is a day of celebration and honor, Colonel Lehen-Gorri-Gogor messaged to them.

Honor the first-years, Commander Bigaen-Zuri-Indar ordered.

The second- and third-year pupils who were lined up behind them with their squadron leaders cheered to the sky.

"Blood and Glory!"

"Conquest and Power!"

Let us proceed with the award of the badges, Commander Bigaen-Zuri-Indar announced.

And when Nahia thought that nothing else in the world of dragons could surprise her, she saw something that made her rub her eyes to make sure she saw correctly. Six powerful dragons came down from the sky, one of each elemental color. But that was not what struck her dumb, but the fact that they carried a rider. She looked at them dumbfounded and realized they were ridden by a Human, Tauruk, Fatum, Drakonid, Scarlatum, and Felidae. Dressed in heavy armor, they carried a large shield in one hand and long spear in the other. They landed in the middle of the great square. They leapt from the dragons with great agility and headed to the six leaders. They were each carrying a silver chest. They stood under the banner of each squadron, facing the group with their backs to the leader.

One day, the best among you will perhaps get to be like them. They are Dragon Riders, an honor like no other, only reserved for the best of the best, Colonel Lehen-Gorri-Gogor messaged to them.

Nahia was left wondering why the dragons would allow themselves to be ridden. It made no sense to her. They were powerful, ruthless creatures who hated them for being weak. Why were there a few among the slaves who could ride them? What was the reason behind this? She did not know what it might be, but it had to be important. She would make a point to find out.

We proceed with the award of graduation badges, announced Commander Bigaen-Zuri-Indar.

The leaders called every member of the squadron, one by one, and the rider gave each one a silver badge with an engraved dragon and the number 1 on it. Nahia took hers without even glancing askance at Irakas-Gorri-Gaizt—she did not want to get angry and risk being killed right there and then. She knew the red dragon wanted to do it because she had disobeyed its order in front of the other leaders of the mission. She returned to her position and kept her head bowed.

Once the riders finished handing out the badges, they shut the chests. They went back to where their dragons were waiting and mounted once more. A moment later, they took off. No one could believe what they were seeing.

Congratulations to all of you who have graduated. In the second year, most interesting things await you. You will learn to use the sword, find out your Talent Mark and a new martial affinity, learn mind magic, discover new mental attacks, and we will have more competitions between squadrons and more surprises which I will not reveal now. It will be a year to remember. Now, go and enjoy a week of rest, Colonel Lehen-Gorri-Gogor messaged to them.

The second- and third-years cheered again, honoring them.

"Blood and Glory!"

"Conquest and Power!"

Amid these cheers, they broke formation and headed to the barracks.

Nahia was heading to the dungeons to fulfill her punishment. Irakas-Gorri-Gaizt had punished her again for what had happened when Maika died, and she was beginning this evening. As she was walking toward the dungeons, she met up with Logan.

"Dungeons?" he asked.

"Re-building the north wall?" she asked.

Logan nodded and looked resigned, and Nahia smiled.

"Ana is on her way to the kitchens for cleaning tasks."

"The three of us have been punished. It was logical," Logan shrugged.

"I wanted to thank you for... saving me." Nahia was truly grateful.

"I really think I saved the leader," Logan said, smiling, which was rare for him.

"Yeah, from a load of insults I was going to deliver."

"Which might have become elemental breath."

Nahia smiled.

"Thank you, really."

"You're welcome," he said, bowing his head.

"I don't know how you did it. You'll have to teach me the neck thing,"

"No problem, I can at the gym," he said and looked up. There was a dragon on watch duty on one of the lookout towers watching them.

"We'd better head to our respective punishments," Nahia said.

"Yes, we'd better,"

They started to walk away.

"Logan,"

He turned to her.

"We survived,"

"I told you we would."

Nahia nodded.

"Will we survive the second year?"

"We will," Logan said with assurance. Then he put his hands together and did the Butterfly of Victory.

"The gesture touched Nahia's heart. She returned the greeting, and they went their separate ways.

Already late evening, Nahia slid open the peephole of Egil's cell in the dungeons.

"Egil," she called.

The prisoner rose and came to the door.

"I only have a moment, Framus hasn't assigned me to this section."

Egil nodded.

"I Tremia," she said.

"Well?" Egil asked.

"Very well, I found Lasgol."

"Lasgol? Yes?"

Nahia put her hand through the peephole and gave the arrow tip to Egil, who took it and studied it.

"Ranger arrow. Yes, Lasgol," he said, moved.

"Also Camu."

"Camu? Well?" Egil asked, very emotional. Nahia could not see it because of the mask, but she could feel it in his tone.

"Yes, well. Both well," she assured him, nodding.

Egil sighed so hard she heard it through the mask and the door. "Thank you. Thank you."

"You and I fight," Nahia told him.

"Fight?"

"For freedom."

Egil nodded.

"Fight. For freedom."

Nahia put her hand through the peephole and Egil clasped it. The pact was sealed, and the destiny of worlds with it.

The adventure continues in the next book:

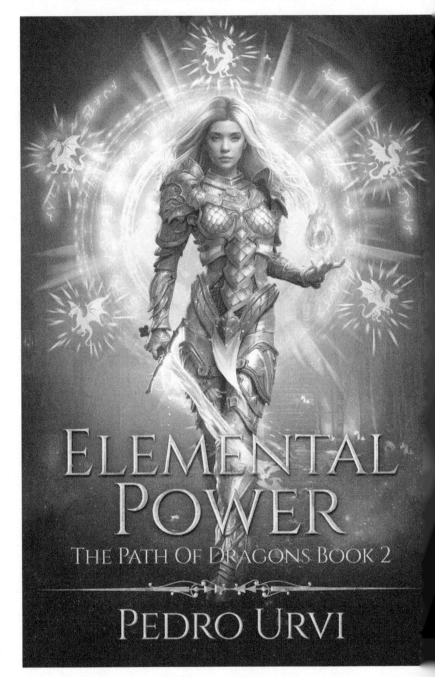

Acknowledgements

I'm lucky enough to have very good friends and a wonderful family, and it's thanks to them that this book is now a reality. I can't express the incredible help they have given me during this epic journey.

I wish to thank my great friend Guiller C. for all his support, tireless encouragement and invaluable advice. This saga, not just this book, would never have come to exist without him.

Mon, master-strategist and exceptional plot-twister. Apart from acting as editor and always having a whip ready for deadlines to be met. A million thanks.

To Luis R. for helping me with the re-writes and for all the hours we spent talking about the books and how to make them more enjoyable for the readers.

Roser M., for all the readings, comments, criticisms, for what she has taught me and all her help in a thousand and one ways. And in addition, for being delightful.

The Bro, who as he always does, has supported me and helped me in his very own way.

Guiller B, for all your great advice, ideas, help and, above all, support.

My parents, who are the best in the world and have helped and supported me unbelievably in this, as in all my projects.

Olaya Martínez, for being an exceptional editor, a tireless worker, a great professional and above all for her encouragement and hope. And for everything she has taught me along the way.

Sarima, for being an artist with exquisite taste, and for drawing like an angel.

Special thanks to my wonderful collaborators: Christy Cox, Mallory Bingham and Peter Gauld for caring so much about my books and for always going above and beyond. Thank you so very much.

To my latest collaborator James Bryan, thank you for your splendid work on the books and your excellent input.

And finally: thank you very much, reader, for supporting this author. I hope you've enjoyed it; if so I'd appreciate it if you could write a comment and recommend it to your family and friends.

Thank you very much, and with warmest regards.
Pedro

Note from the author:
I really hope you enjoyed my book. If you did, I would appreciate it if you could write a quick review. It helps me tremendously as it is one of the main factors readers consider when buying a book. As an Indie author I really need of your support.
Just go to Amazon end enter a review.
Thank you so very much.
Pedro.

Other Series by Pedro Urvi

THE SECRET OF THE GOLDEN GODS

This series takes place three thousand years before the Path of the Ranger Series.
Different protagonists, same world, one destiny.

THE ILENIAN ENIGMA

This series takes place after the Path of the Ranger Series. It has different protagonists. Lasgol joins the adventure in the second book of the series. He is a secondary character in this one, but he plays an important role, and he is alone…

READING ORDER

Chronological order of the series

Top to bottom

Author

Pedro Urvi

I would love to hear from you.
You can find me at:
Mail: pedrourvi@hotmail.com
Twitter: https://twitter.com/PedroUrvi
Facebook: https://www.facebook.com/PedroUrviAuthor/
My Website: https://pedrourvi.com

Join my mailing list to receive the latest news about my books:

Mailing List:
http://pedrourvi.com/mailing-list/

Thank you for reading my books!

See you in:

Elemental Power (The Path of Dragons, Book 2)

Made in the USA
Las Vegas, NV
25 November 2024

12601779R00246